COLD HEAT

COLD JUSTICE® - MOST WANTED

TONI ANDERSON®

COLD HEAT

Copyright © 2025 Toni Anderson

Publisher: Toni Anderson. Toni Anderson Inc. C/O Fillmore Riley LLP, 1700-360 Main Street, Winnipeg, MB, Canada. R3C3Z3. Telephone: (204) 808-3112.

Contact email: info@toniandersonauthor.com

Cover design by Regina Wamba of ReginaWamba.com

Digital ISBN-13: 978-1-998554-52-2

Print ISBN-13: 978-1-998554-51-5

NO AI TRAINING: Without in any way limiting the author's [and publisher's] exclusive rights under copyright, any use of this publication to "train" generative artificial intelligence (AI) technologies to generate text is expressly prohibited. The author reserves all rights to license uses of this work for generative AI training and development of machine learning language models.

The characters and events portrayed in this book are purely fictitious. Any similarity to real persons, living or dead, is coincidental and not intended by the author. Any real organizations mentioned in this book are used in a completely fictitious manner and this story in no way reflects upon the reputation or actions of those entities.

All rights reserved.

No part of this book may be reproduced, scanned or distributed in any printed or electronic form without permission. Please do not participate in encouraging piracy of copyrighted materials in violation of the author's rights. Purchase only authorized editions.

For more information on Toni Anderson's books, sign up for her newsletter or check out her website (www.toniandersonauthor.com) or author store (toniandersonshop.com).

ALSO BY TONI ANDERSON®

COLD JUSTICE® SERIES
A Cold Dark Place (Book #1)
Cold Pursuit (Book #2)
Cold Light of Day (Book #3)
Cold Fear (Book #4)
Cold in The Shadows (Book #5)
Cold Hearted (Book #6)
Cold Secrets (Book #7)
Cold Malice (Book #8)
A Cold Dark Promise (Book #9~A Wedding Novella)
Cold Blooded (Book #10)

COLD JUSTICE® – THE NEGOTIATORS
Cold & Deadly (Book #1)
Colder Than Sin (Book #2)
Cold Wicked Lies (Book #3)
Cold Cruel Kiss (Book #4)
Cold as Ice (Book #5)

COLD JUSTICE® – MOST WANTED
Cold Silence (Book #1)
Cold Deceit (Book #2)
Cold Snap (Book #3)
Cold Fury (Book #4)
Cold Spite (Book #5)
Cold Truth (Book #6)

Cold Heat (Book #7)

Cold Rage (Book #8) - Coming soon

"HER" ROMANTIC SUSPENSE SERIES

Her Sanctuary (Book #1)

Her Last Chance (Book #2)

Her Risk to Take (Novella ~ Book #3)

THE BARKLEY SOUND SERIES

Dangerous Waters (Book #1)

Dark Waters (Book #2)

SINGLE TITLES

The Killing Game

Edge of Survival

Storm Warning

Sea of Suspicion

For My Amazing Family.

COLD HEAT
Cold Justice® – Most Wanted (Book #7)

Every operator has a weakness.
She just became his.

FBI HRT operator Jordan Krychek has built his life around discipline and duty, hiding scars that run bone-deep. The night his family was murdered, the man responsible vanished into the wind. Now that ghost has reappeared—and a woman Jordan has sworn to protect is caught in the crossfire.

Daisy Montana doesn't need a bodyguard, least of all her father's dangerously intense teammate. But when a terrorist targets her area of research, and a killer from Jordan's past resurfaces, she becomes a pawn in a deadly game of vengeance.

Forced into hiding—and into each other's arms—the line between duty and desire combusts. From Mexico to Virginia, a relentless enemy draws them into a web of deception and betrayal. As the stakes rise and the body count climbs, Jordan and Daisy must untangle the mystery of what the next target might be, before it's too late.

This time, Jordan's mission is personal. And protecting Daisy might cost him everything—including his heart.

COLD HEAT delivers explosive action, heart-stopping suspense, and the kind of forbidden love that will bring even the most hardened operator to his knees.

Cold Heat is the seventh book in the Cold Justice® – Most Wanted series, featuring agents from FBI's Hostage Rescue Team.

All books standalone.

Sign up for Toni Anderson's newsletter to receive new release alerts, bonus Cold Justice® stories, and a free copy of The Killing Game: Toni's Newsletter (www.toniandersonauthor.com/newsletter-signup)

PROLOGUE
TEN YEARS EARLIER

Jordan Krychek shoved his chapped hands deep into the pockets of his battered leather jacket and blew out a cloud of frost. Jesus Christ, Chicago was *cold* in the winter.

He'd forgotten.

The past few years in Texas and other desert regions had made him soft. First chance he got, he was headed somewhere the winter wind didn't flay flesh off the bone.

With a nod, Krychek ducked behind the bouncer, out of the frigid temps, and into the Bare Naked Ladies strip joint in West Town, not far from where he'd grown up. Jordan ran a hand through hair that he'd let grow since leaving the Army a year ago, then sent a wink to Ana who hung upside-down on the main stage pole, doing the splits, while wearing only a G-string and glittery silver pasties.

Impressive.

Ana credited her athletic ability to her mom dragging her to gymnastics lessons for years when she'd been a kid. It had certainly paid off, judging from the hundred-dollar bills tucked into the strings on her hips and her strength and flexibility, which she'd demonstrated to him up-close and personal on one memorable occasion.

He didn't make a habit out of "touching the merchandise," as Konrad Bocharov liked to call the women who worked for him. Jordan had been ordered to drive her and a bunch of other women home after a Christmas party. Last to be dropped off, Ana had insisted on bringing him inside to give him a "tip." He'd told her there was no need, but it had gotten to an awkward point where refusing made him look weird. He didn't have a girlfriend or a wife. He'd worried it had been a test, to make sure he wasn't a homosexual—as if a gay man had never fucked a woman for show.

Being gay was probably worse than being an undercover FBI agent as far as the Russian mafia was concerned. Their overbearing version of masculinity simply couldn't handle it. A man in Jordan's perilous position couldn't afford even the whisper of suspicion, so he and Ana had shared some hopefully fun, mindless sex—the one and only time he'd been lucky enough to have sex since he graduated from the academy at Quantico—and they'd never spoken of it since.

She blew him a kiss as he walked through the crowd, and his cheeks bloomed. What that woman could do with her mouth.

Konrad was in his usual booth at the back. Normally, the illegal arms dealer was surrounded by a plethora of goons. Tonight, only Micky and Dmitri stood nearby, watching Jordan in their usual distrustful fashion. He'd gone to school with Micky, less than five blocks from here in a place where half the kids spoke Ukrainian and the other half spoke Russian—all with thick Chicago accents.

Micky's nose was out of joint because Konrad liked Jordan better than he liked Micky, even though Micky was the one who'd introduced them and brought Jordan into Konrad's fold. Micky had expected to be bossing Jordan around, but the pecking order hadn't worked out quite the way Micky had hoped.

Os' také zhyt-tya.

Such is life, *motherfucker*.

Jordan grinned at the guy and watched Micky's eyes narrow into thin slits of hate as he stared back.

"Ah. Here's my favorite soldier," Bocharov boomed loudly, banging his fist on the table.

Bocharov got a kick out of the fact Jordan was former Army. Jordan had enlisted to get his degree, but he'd loved the structure, the discipline of military life. Despite that, he'd always known what he really wanted to be—a Special Agent, a G-man, oozing Fidelity, Bravery, and Integrity out of every pore.

He'd needed the bachelor's degree to apply. And, now, here he was, a fully fledged Special Agent, working undercover for one of the most evil men in America, operating in his old backyard, less than a mile from where he'd grown up and where his family still lived.

Bocharov's lips curved, no humor in his shark-like blue eyes as he poured two small glasses of *Stolichnaya*.

"Drink."

Jordan picked up one of the shots. "*Budmo!*" He spoke the Ukrainian toast, and they clinked glasses before swallowing the drink in one throat-searing gulp.

His eyes watered.

He fucking hated vodka.

Which was probably worse than being gay in the Russians' eyes, so he drank it with gusto and held out his glass for another.

Konrad poured two more shots, and Jordan wondered if this was going to be one of those nights where he staggered home in the small hours, barely able to walk. Getting a hangover was the last thing he wanted when the Chicago Police Department and FBI were about to close the noose around this fat bastard's neck and lock up his ass for about a thousand years.

Although, getting Konrad hammered might make the arrests go more smoothly.

Jordan could not fuck this up. Too much depended on not letting anyone in this organization suspect something was about to go down and making sure no one fell through the cracks.

"Are we celebrating?"

"*Da.*" Konrad wiped a meaty fist over wet lips. "I made a sale today." He leaned closer. "A *big* sale. I need you to make the delivery."

Jordan's pulse skipped up a couple of notches. He hadn't anticipated that. "Where to?"

He'd been working for Bocharov for six months—seven months for the Bureau. He'd been recruited for this mission before he'd even graduated the academy. Officially, he still had First Office Agent status, but in reality, he'd never even set foot inside the FBI's Chicago Field Office. He was more intimate with this strip bar than his own apartment two blocks away. He'd lived and breathed Bocharov's world since moving back to the city.

Getting anyone inside Bocharov's organization had proven impossible in the past.

Bocharov swept for bugs more often than the Russian Embassy. He did not trust strangers. Barely trusted his own goons. Micky had gotten Jordan a job as a bouncer. After breaking up a fight—staged in a way Russian psyops would have been proud of—Bocharov had brought him on as a driver and then as a delivery man. They'd shared a few drunken nights as Bocharov appeared to have taken a shine to him. Krychek wasn't sure whether to be flattered or insulted.

He refused to wear a wire or a hidden camera as there was no telling when he might be searched. Micky took particular joy in frisking him at random moments.

But Jordan's cell phone recorded everything even when it appeared to be turned off.

Bocharov knew the FBI were watching him—the FBI *and* Russia's Foreign Intelligence Service, the SVR. He was always careful to speak in code and never have the goods on his property. He rented a warehouse under a shell company and seemed naïve or arrogant enough to believe no one else knew about it. The FBI had it under surveillance, also his apartment, his mistress's apartment, and this strip joint—as much as was possible anyhow. In this tight-knit community, strangers stood out as vividly as a streaker running through the Nave during Mass.

The most damning information had come from key loggers Jordan had planted, accessing Bocharov's computers, cloning his cell phones. The information attained had enabled CPD and the FBI to connect the dots of this world-wide illegal arms trade and build a rock-solid case with RICO implications.

It had worked on the mob. About time it worked on the Russian Mafia too.

"Arlington Heights." Bocharov shoved a piece of paper with an address written on it across the sticky varnished wood.

Jordan checked his watch. "What time?"

"Ten sharp. Buyer will be driving a green Ford pickup. Don't be late." He placed a set of car keys in front of Jordan.

Jordan memorized the address and then put the paper in his pocket. The more evidence the better. It was a forty-five-minute drive. Plenty of time. "Whadda you sell 'em?"

He held his breath, hoping against hope the man would incriminate himself.

"Bagels." The grin was malicious. "Lots of bagels. All you need to do is drive up there. Unload the bagels and get my money. Vehicle is out back. They don't get the merchandise without payment upfront. Forty." Bocharov leaned closer, and Jordan smelled sour onion on his breath. "And don't get stopped by the motherfucking pigs. If you do, ice the fuckers, *da*?"

Bocharov held his gaze menacingly. Jordan nodded. It was the first time the Russian had ever told him to outright kill anyone.

The fact that it was a cop...

Coincidence?

Had to be.

If Bocharov had the slightest notion Jordan was FBI, he'd have bundled him out back and put a bullet in his skull. He certainly wouldn't be hanging around waiting to be arrested.

"You know where to drop the money afterwards."

"Sure thing, boss. Shouldn't take more than a couple of hours. Need me for anything else later?"

He needed to meet with his handler, Special Agent Jenna Stork and an old buddy from his school days, Detective Tobias Granger, to go over the finer details of tomorrow's takedown. They couldn't afford to tip anyone off, so they usually met in a grocery store miles away from either of their usual stomping grounds.

"Not tonight." Bocharov wet his pudgy lips. "Just don't be late."

Ana walked past them having finished her set. Bocharov grabbed her by the wrist and jerked her onto his lap. Licked his fleshy tongue up the side of Ana's sparkly cheek. He held Jordan's gaze as he did it. "How did you like the Christmas present I gave you?"

Jordan kept his gaze steady on Bocharov's eyes and ignored the tension in Ana's thin body. "What's not to like, boss?"

"You want more of this?" Bocharov's hand slipped down Ana's naked body.

Was Konrad pissed because he'd discovered Jordan and Ana had had sex?

Or was this some test of Jordan's manhood or loyalty in order to climb the rungs in the Bocharov organization? Bocharov had done similar things in the past. Including making him play a round of Russian Roulette, while blindfolded, with an old Colt .45 that was supposed to have belonged to Clyde Barrow. Jordan knew enough about weaponry to believe the gun was unloaded but pulling that trigger had almost made him piss his pants. Another guy had chickened out—Jordan had never seen that guy again, and the Feds had put him on a missing person database.

Bocharov was a master of manipulation and torture.

Jordan wasn't about to fail now.

"Up to you, boss. More is great." *If Ana wanted more.* "Less is fine." *None is better.*

Ana's cheeks paled as Bocharov's hand went under the table. Her eyes met Jordan's and for a moment he saw a flicker of panicked fear before she blinked it away and shifted positions, twisting so she straddled Bocharov's lap. She gyrated over the gangster. "Is this what you want, baby?"

Jordan swallowed. He'd seen her fear, and yet he could do nothing about it that wouldn't either get them both killed or jeopardize the case. Plus, witnesses would say she was into it. Hell, Ana would swear an oath on a Bible in a court of law to say she was into it too.

No one went up against the *bratva*, not in this part of town. Not if you wanted to live. And Jordan had family nearby. Family CPD were moving to a secure location in the early morning, just before they started rolling up Bocharov's entire organization.

Konrad bent his head to one side but didn't stop the woman giving him a very thorough lap dance.

Jordan stood before the Russian forced Ana to do anything else.

Konrad had a mistress and always said he didn't like to share. The man disappeared sometimes for days at a time, and there was a rumor of a wife and child secreted away somewhere, but no one knew for sure, and even after months of looking, the FBI had never tracked them down.

So why was Konrad looking as if he were about to have sex with Ana in this very public space? Was he simply demonstrating his power and superiority in case Jordan was getting cocky and thinking about maybe skimming the profits or cutting Bocharov out all together? Or was the bastard simply jealous and horny, and Ana was handy?

She *was* a beautiful woman.

Jordan suppressed his anger and the desire to arrest the motherfucker.

They didn't want Bocharov for "penny-ante shit"—as if assaulting women wasn't a felony—but, as the guy was selling black-market weapons to criminals and suspected terrorists, the DA wanted to make sure that when he went down, he stayed down.

"Call me when you get there." Bocharov twisted around to watch Jordan walk out. Ana's gaze met Jordan's as she kissed Bocharov and silently told him to get the hell out of there.

He was making it worse.

He turned away and walked down the narrow corridor, past old movie posters of old Hitchcock classics, past the changing rooms the strippers used, past Bocharov's office, the rudimentary kitchen. Jordan hated leaving her. He was an FBI Special Agent, and the FBI was supposed to help people, not turn away.

But as much as he wanted the law to make sense, it didn't always. Tomorrow, he'd make sure Ana, and the other women, were treated as victims, not accomplices.

The back of Jordan's scalp prickled as Micky and Dmitri followed him out and watched him with expressions that told him nothing.

Shit.

Was he about to get a bullet in the back of the head?

He climbed into a red mustang he'd never seen before—probably boosted—and slid the keys into the ignition, wondering if this was going to be his last act. According to their intel, Bocharov had a penchant for car bombs. But the car didn't explode, and Jordan crawled down the poorly lit back alley and out onto the street.

He headed north toward I-90 and O'Hare, the roads glistening with a fresh fall of snow that melted the moment it touched the asphalt. He probably wouldn't take the toll road if he was really selling arms for the Russian Mafia, but he wanted this delivery done quick, so he could meet up with Stork and Granger, and figure out what his part, if any, should be in tomorrow's arrests.

He inserted a special FBI designed wireless earbud into one ear and called Stork's cell via a proxy number that FBI had backstopped in case the Russians were listening in.

He had no idea if this car was bugged or not, but he had to assume it was.

"Hey, babe."

"Where are you?" she sounded agitated.

"Have to do a little errand for my boss, but I was hoping to meet up later. Maybe I could come over to your place, you know. Have a little drink?"

"Everything okay?"

He'd left a woman being assaulted by a vicious gangster, and he was on his way to drop off $40K-worth of guns with God knew who. If Jordan failed to deliver, he'd either be dead by morning, or he'd have blown a seven-month-long undercover operation to smithereens.

"Come on, babe. Don't be *pissy* and *weird*."

Stork was smart enough to read his simple code.

"We've been watching him all day. No reason to believe he knows anything. He hasn't been anywhere or met anyone unusual. Chicago PD have people watching the front of the club from a nearby apartment and another unmarked unit on the girlfriend's apartment. That's all the manpower the police commissioner would spare tonight, but"—he heard the frown in her voice—"we assumed you'd be with him all evening. Takedown is planned for five a.m. tomorrow morning." Considering Bocharov's crew rarely went to bed before 3 a.m., that should catch everyone asleep. "We'll have units on all of them and at the bakery by then. You didn't warn them, did you?"

She meant his family.

"Of course not." Months ago, he *had* told his family that they needed to be ready for any eventuality and to put together go-bags, which they should keep in the storage closet by the back door. They knew what he was doing was dangerous, but they were willing to do anything that helped keep him safe. They'd faked an estrangement, but Jordan had figured out a way to sneak into his childhood home without anyone else knowing. His grandparents, mother, and sister were the only people in the city who knew he was an FBI undercover agent, except for Special Agent Stork and a couple of CPD detectives and the brass.

When he'd agreed to this operation, it had been on the condition that the safety of his family, and their home and business, would be everyone's top priority.

"I have you on the tracker. Might wanna slow down there a little, Krychek."

"Slow down?"

"I'd hate to have to bring Highway Patrol into the fold at this late stage in the game."

He checked the speedometer and saw he was going more than a hundred mph. Even though he wanted to press his foot harder to the accelerator and get this over with, he forced himself to ease off the gas. He'd have time to scope out the place before the arranged time anyway.

"Baby, I've been told I'm a fast mover in the past and never had any complaints." He was trying to get her to laugh, but she was a serious woman, wound up and tense.

"Get as much info on these buyers as you can. I'll see if the SAC will spare some manpower to pick them up in the morning. Last thing we need is more illegal arms on the streets."

They'd amassed quite the list of bad guys over the months, and Jordan hoped every one of the fuckers shat themselves when they heard Bocharov had been snatched up in an undercover op. Let them sweat. Let them scatter. Bocharov certainly wouldn't show any loyalty to them.

"Okay. Can I see you tonight anyway, just to talk? Pretty please?"

Stork gave him an address of a late-night diner in Englewood. "Ding me if you have any problems."

"Can't wait." Jordan wouldn't have minded backup on this, but the time crunch meant he couldn't wait. He deepened his voice. "Hey, so, what are you wearing?"

He grinned as she hung up on him.

Thirty minutes later he turned south onto North Arlington Heights Road and then west on East Higgins Road. He checked the map and realized it was a nature reserve. Quiet. Remote.

He didn't like it.

Not even a little bit.

He pulled to a stop in the shadows of the parking lot and got out. Looked around but there was no one here. It was 9:55 p.m.

The cold wind whistled through the trees and made his ears sting.

He walked to the trunk and opened it, checked the large duffel bag full of automatic weapons and stolen munitions. Didn't look like 40-thousand dollars' worth but hopefully the buyer would disagree.

He closed the trunk. Walked the perimeter of the parking lot. Took a piss. Checked his watch again as a creeping sensation that something was *wrong* started to hit him.

He was about to call Stork when he realized there was no cell service.

Fuck.

He didn't like this.

Not at all.

He bounced on the balls of his feet to try to restore circulation. It wasn't uncommon for people in these situations to turn up late. Buyers often suspected a trap and wanted to get the lay of the land before they moved in. The last thing an illegal arms dealer liked to do was dick around in some parking lot waiting for a skittish buyer. They didn't want the shit? Plenty of others would. Hanging around invited trouble from the cops, and no bad guy wanted that.

But if Jordan left, he risked Bocharov getting pissed with him, or worse, with the buyer. Leaving too soon risked Bocharov starting a war with whoever failed to show up, and that might disrupt Bocharov's usual routine and put tomorrow's arrest timetable in jeopardy.

By 10:35 p.m., Jordan couldn't wait any longer. The buyer was showing discourtesy to Bocharov that no self-respecting *bratva* would stand for. Jordan drove out the front entrance and took a left back toward town.

He tried to call Stork but still no signal. Finally, he hit the tollway, and his phone lit up like it was his birthday. He answered her call, "Hey."

"Are you okay?"

His heart sped up a little at her urgent tone. "Sure. Why?"

"Bocharov is in the wind."

"What do you mean?"

"He's onto us."

"Not possible."

"The team across the street from the club was found dead. The cops in the unmarked unit. Shot. Point-blank range. Mistress is alone. He's gone. Warehouse is on fire."

Jordan shook his head as if trying to clear his ears. "That doesn't make any sense."

"He knew, Krychek. The son of a bitch knew."

"Then why am I still alive?" he yelled.

Perhaps Bocharov was planning to blow up this car with some radio signal, a phone taped to some C4 under the gas tank. Perhaps in saying those words he'd just signed his own death warrant.

"I think he knew before he sent you out of the city." Stork's voice trembled.

Trepidation pounded his consciousness. "Why would he send me out of the city? Why not put a bullet in me?"

But he knew why. He *knew*.

"He wanted you out of the way." A sob tore out of her throat. This experienced FBI agent was crying.

"No." Jordan punched it. He hung up so he could concentrate on the drive. Concentrated on the leather steering wheel beneath his fingers and the slick conditions under the tires. He didn't allow himself to think of anything until an eternity later when he pulled up on North Oakley Boulevard.

Flames poured out of the windows of the three-story building. He pushed past patrol officers who held back crowds of onlookers. Four firetrucks were fighting the blaze, but it wasn't enough. The building was gone.

It didn't mean his family were gone.

He clung to hope.

They were smart and always took precautions.

He looked around. Where the hell were they?

"Krychek!" Stork grabbed his arm.

"Where are they?" He pulled away from her.

Detective Tobias Granger, his childhood friend, whose idea this whole operation had been, approached him with tears streaking the black soot on his face.

"They're gone, Jordan." Tobias tried to grab him, but Jordan stepped back.

"What do you mean, *'they're gone'*?" He stared at the building and then started heading that way, past firefighters wielding heavy hoses.

"You can't go in there!" Stork was screaming at him, but what the fuck did she know?

He put his head down and tried to shield his face with his arm as he approached the inferno of his childhood home. Black smoke billowed toward him in choking waves.

Someone grabbed his arm, and he decked them. Another person clamped him around the waist and lifted him clean off his feet. Jordan struggled as three firefighters pinned him down to the ground.

"Let me go! Let me go!" he screamed. "My family is in there!"

"It's too active. We can't get inside until we can get the flames under control," one of the firefighters told him. "I'm sorry, but it's too dangerous."

"You can't save them, Jordan." Granger sobbed. "It's too late. I'm so sorry."

The firefighters let him go and Jordan lurched to his feet. He took another run, but Granger tackled him to the ground. Cuffed his hands behind his back.

"For your own good."

Jordan headbutted the guy.

"Stop it. Stop it!" Stork screamed, dragging him to a stop. He tried to shake her off again, but she didn't let go. "They're dead, Jordan. They're already dead!"

He stared at the flames and knew in his heart nothing could survive that inferno. As much as he wanted to be with them, first he wanted to find the man responsible and make that evil sonofabitch pay.

"What happened at the meet?" Stork demanded, pulling him out of his dark fantasies of blood and death.

"*Nothing* happened at the meet. Nothing fucking happened. It was a distraction to get me out of the city so he could do this under your fucking noses. You were supposed to *protect* them." He yelled so loudly his throat hurt. "You promised me they'd be safe."

Stork wouldn't meet his gaze.

Granger closed his eyes. "I'm sorry. I'm sorry."

"Sorry isn't good enough. It will never be good enough." He turned to Stork. "You need to shut down all the airports and train stations. Issue an International Red Notice for this motherfucker."

"It's been done, but he's in the wind."

"You try his jet?"

"Of course! We searched and confiscated his jet," she snapped. "We're not amateurs, Special Agent Krychek."

His snarled. "You could have fooled me."

Glass shattered, and firefighters battled to contain the blaze so it didn't spread, but it had already reduced everything he gave a damn about to ash. Jordan closed his eyes as the realization hit him. His beloved family were gone, and it was his fault. All his fault. The grief wanted to blast out of him, but he didn't let it. "Get these cuffs off me."

"Are you going to behave?" Granger demanded.

"I am not planning to kill myself or harm any firefighters, but I make no promises about you."

Granger pulled in a ragged breath and then removed the cuffs.

Rage, anger, and grief fought inside Jordan as he stared at

flames destroying his family and the home they'd built since leaving Ukraine more than a century ago.

Jordan stared at the detective, the man he'd grown up with, and at the line of cops nearby. "Someone on your team let it slip. You're the reason they're probably dead."

And the fact he still hung on to a kernel of hope showed him he was a fool.

"Could have been from your side."

Jordan ignored the tears dripping down his cheeks and held out his arm. "Special Agent Stork, did you tell Konrad Bocharov I was working undercover for the FBI?"

Eyes massive, she frantically shook her head.

He tried to catch Granger's stare, but the man wouldn't meet his gaze. "What about you, Granger? Did you tell anyone?"

Granger wiped his hands over his dirty cheeks. "I can't believe you'd ask me that."

"That's not a fucking denial!"

"No! I didn't do it. I would never have done that. You know me. You know me, Jordan. I would never hurt your family."

Jordan looked away. His throat hurt. His eyes hurt. His heart hurt. "I don't know anything anymore."

An Asian man jogged over to Stork. "We've found two bodies in the strip joint. Man and a woman." He showed his cell to the other agent.

Jordan hadn't thought he could hurt any more than he did. "It'll be Micky and Ana."

Stork's eyes widened with suspicion. "How did you know that?"

His lip curled. "Because I thought it was weird earlier why only Dmitri and Micky were with Bocharov at the club. The others were obviously carrying out Konrad's orders. When Ana finished her set, he pulled her into his lap even though she didn't want it. Because we'd had sex once and he found out, and because Micky brought me into the fold. That's why they were killed. Micky was too stupid to have even seen it coming."

Jordan was stupid too. He hadn't trusted his instincts, hadn't realized the gig was up, hadn't called his family to tell them to run. To hide.

Stork strode away talking on the phone.

Granger stood, face in his hands.

Jordan closed his eyes and then opened them to look up at the smoky sky as he made a silent vow. He was going to find Konrad Bocharov, and he was going to make the sonofabitch pay. It wouldn't be by the rules. It wouldn't be pretty. And he'd show Konrad the same mercy the man had shown to his family.

He'd avenge them, and then he'd deal with the fallout.

1

VERACRUZ, MEXICO.

Daisy Montana sipped sangria at a round table surrounded by her colleagues and was so grateful her life had returned to normal. Her brain was about to explode after being jammed full of cutting-edge research and new ideas. Inspired and re-energized, this had been exactly what she needed after the distraction and sky-high stress levels of the past couple of months.

Her advisor, Professor Wilson Williams, sat opposite and raised his glass. "A toast to a successful symposium."

They all raised their glasses, even Amed Hussein, who was sticking to water because of his faith.

This had been a *fantastic* conference, and her poster on the initial experiments she planned to conduct on the new fuel rod technology Wilson had designed had been well received. She was excited to test the theory that these fuel rods would produce more energy for longer while still being highly controllable. Her work followed closely on Amed's research, and she found him to be a patient and generous researcher with both his time and his knowledge.

"And I hope you all used the opportunity to connect with others in our field."

"Daisy definitely did." This snark came from Emilia Osbourne, a first-year master's student who'd started the program at the same time Daisy had started her PhD. She was dark-haired and pretty but also casually catty and default mean.

But she was right. Daisy had networked her ass off—a little too successfully, in some cases.

Professor François Tremblay, an influential French scientist who worked in Paris, was proving a little...*over* attentive. The guy was handsome, slick, and generally full of himself. He was also very, very smart and she was genuinely fascinated by his lab's area of research. She didn't need to be a nuclear physicist to know he was interested in more than her brain. She wasn't interested in a relationship, not even a short-term, physical one. Especially not with someone so high profile in the relatively small world of nuclear engineering.

"So did Roger." Daisy nodded to the Yorkshireman who was at the next table chatting to another post-doc who just happened to be the prettiest woman in the room.

She held Emilia's gaze until the other woman looked away with a petulant shrug. The last thing she needed was her reputation being called into question. Women always had to put up with that shit, and she was over it.

And, even though François was handsome, she wasn't attracted to him.

The face of another man flashed into her brain, and she forced it away.

Thoughts of Jordan Krychek elicited everything from nuclear-fission rage to throat-choking gratitude, to...something else entirely. Part of her wanted to kiss him until neither of them could breathe, while the other part wanted to hold him underwater until he couldn't.

Mira Jahood raised her glass in another toast. "To Mexico. A beautiful and welcoming country with a warm and generous people."

Daisy smiled gratefully. "To Mexico."

At least being here, submerging herself in the science, had been a well-needed distraction from all the events of the year so far.

Not that her attendance here had gone down well with her dad, but thankfully he was stuck in England, and she hadn't told him about the conference until just before it began.

She'd been careful. Despite her natural inclination to explore the local area, she hadn't left the hotel grounds except to attend the conference tour of Laguna Verde Nuclear Power Station with its two boiling water reactors on the Gulf of Mexico yesterday. She didn't take foolish risks.

He needed to learn to trust her.

It wasn't as if he'd been around much when she was growing up. And with her mom busy working, she'd gotten away with murder.

And yet *now* they were both pulling the concerned parent cards?

Emotions hit hard when she thought about how much the teenage version of herself could have done with that level of care and attention. She loved them, but she was a smart, independent woman who could take care of herself—and they both needed to deal with that reality.

"Well, I don't know about anyone else, but I'm getting some dessert." Wilson patted his stomach with a smile.

Fighting emotions that she was usually better at suppressing, she stood and crossed over to the dessert table and debated between the cheesecake and the chocolate mousse.

Emilia stood next to her with a look of distaste on her features as if the offerings offended her.

"Nothing you like?"

"It all looks like it was made last week."

It looked fine to Daisy, but she wasn't that fussy. Screw it. She'd take a slice of both.

She turned and almost collided with Professor François Tremblay, who stood behind them in the food queue.

Emilia smirked and headed off to talk to someone.

Daisy moved away with an apologetic smile and a wave at her full plate. "I'm starving."

Tremblay's dark eyes flashed. "I've always liked a woman with an appetite." Thankfully, he said it quietly enough no one else could overhear him and gossip about it.

"Right. Nice to have met you, Professor Tremblay."

"Call me François."

She shook her head on a laugh. The man was persistent if nothing else. "Nice to have met you, François."

And she went back to her table, being sure to sit in the spare seat between her boss and Mira so she could eat her dessert in peace.

Hostage Rescue Team Operator Jordan Krychek would rather be running twelve miles with a sixty-pound pack on his back or jumping out of an airplane at ten thousand feet, parachute optional, than working this particular op.

He'd positioned himself at a bar with a view of the wide open, double doors that led into the ballroom. He used the mirror behind the bar to monitor anyone going in and out of the final event of this nuclear engineering conference while keeping his face largely averted.

A woman with jet-black hair and eyes to match slid onto the stool beside him. She wore a dress that showed off tanned, mile-long legs and toned shoulders. Her feet were tipped in strappy stilettos that could kill if applied with the right pressure to the right body part.

She ordered a margarita and tapped her finger rhythmically on the bar.

Not part of the delegation, but maybe she was a wife or a girlfriend tagging along or joining for a post-conference break. Maybe she was a tourist staying at the hotel. Hell, maybe she owned the joint.

Not his business.

Not his mission.

He lazily scanned the bar and lobby, looking for anyone paying him undue attention. A middle-aged couple sat intimately, hip-to-hip, sharing a drink. Two older male conference attendees sat at a table and talked in earnest about the merits of Muon-Catalyzed Fusion. Two younger men—in their twenties—both sat alone at scattered tables, one reading a newspaper, the other scrolling on his phone. Two women giggled drunkenly over cocktails. A mix of conference goers and hotel guests, enjoying the laidback atmosphere of this beautiful, beachside hotel resort in Veracruz.

This part of the country had seen an increase in violent crime and gang activity in the past few years, and though the vast majority of the Mexican people were honest, hardworking, law-abiding citizens, Jordan couldn't afford to let his guard down. Not when the FBI's Hostage Rescue Team had gone head-to-head with one of the Mexican cartels at the start of the year.

It was the reason his boss and friend, Kurt Montana, had asked him to do this personal favor. Having recently been kidnapped himself, Kurt couldn't bear the idea of the same thing happening to his daughter. It was a fear Kurt was going to have to deal with because life wasn't safe, and Jordan couldn't see Daisy Montana approving a 24/7 bodyguard even if she could afford one.

Not his problem.

Except, right now it was very much his problem.

He exhaled his frustration.

Jordan had agreed to use some vacation time to alleviate his friend's concerns. Let him enjoy his impromptu honeymoon, helping his new wife settle her affairs in England and get moving on the documentation she needed to join Kurt in Virginia.

And perhaps he'd agreed because he felt guilty for the terrible things he'd said and done to Daisy before he'd figured out her identity. He closed his eyes as shame rushed through him, then opened them again to keep watch.

He was on assignment, not vacation.

Through the open doorway he spotted his target safely eating dessert and drinking coffee.

Jordan took a swallow of the single malt he was nursing.

"Are you here on vacation?" The woman on the next stool asked suddenly.

The small talk startled him.

She was an American, probably West Coast, with the faintest hint of something European.

"Yeah." He raised a brow. "You?"

She choked out a wet laugh, the sound more like a sob. "First time I've vacationed alone in a very long time. I don't think I'm very good at it."

A sadness hit her expression as she stared at her left hand with its bare ring finger.

Jordan steeled himself against the feelings of empathy. He wasn't here for damsels in distress, and he certainly wasn't interested in hooking up. Since his most recent sexual partner had tried to kill him, he was abstaining from sex until he got his shit together. He had a job to do and couldn't afford to let himself be distracted. But part of that job was blending into the background and not standing out like some grumpy asshole who didn't know how to hold a conversation.

"Nasty divorce?"

She bit her lip and tears flashed, bright and glittery in huge brown eyes. "No."

He knew what loss felt like, and empathy gave him a jab in the chest whether he wanted it to or not. "Sorry."

"People keep telling me I should move on." She laughed self-consciously then cleared her throat. "It's not that easy." Her lips trembled as she held his gaze.

Was she hitting on him?

Or did she recognize another bruised and battered soul?

She was beautiful, but he wasn't interested—his last liaison had scarred him for life. But that wasn't the real reason. The real reason was something he only acknowledged in the deep, dark, secret recesses of his dreams.

"Looks like you're in a good place to figure it out." He raised his glass and indicated the nearby banquet room. "Apparently, it's the last night of some engineering conference. I'm sure there are scores of guys in there who'd be interested in helping you…enjoy your vacation, if that's what you wanted."

Her brown eyes widened at the less than subtle brushoff, and he wasn't proud of the flash of hurt that flickered in her gaze.

He was doing a lot of that lately. Hurting women.

Through the thick fronds of a large potted fern, he spotted the blonde flyaway curls of the petite scientist he was supposed to be guarding. Daisy exited the ballroom and headed around the corner toward the restrooms.

She wore a simple halter dress of cream satin which showed off her toned back and arms. She'd spent time in the sun over the past five days, and it showed in the warm glow of her skin.

His mouth went dry as he remembered what she looked like naked and wet. And pissed. Volcanically pissed.

If looks could kill, he'd already be laid out in a coffin.

"Are you here with someone?" The woman caught him staring after Daisy.

He turned to assess her again. Why was she so interested? Normal curiosity or something more? Or was he so cynical now he viewed everyone as a potential threat?

Everyone *was* a potential threat.

And he'd earned every cynical bone in his body.

"No." His less-than-friendly tone didn't invite further conversation.

He debated following Daisy. The problem was, aside from the restrooms and an outside exit, there was nowhere to hide in that corridor, and she'd easily spot him. No way did he want her to catch him. She'd likely punch him in the face and report him as a stalker.

He wouldn't blame her.

Chances were, she'd be back in a couple of minutes.

He could pull up the hotel security cameras on his cell, but he didn't want anyone in the bar catching sight of what he was looking at.

Working alone had its drawbacks. He hated the unknowns—the unmanaged variables, uncovered exits, lack of intel, backup, and support—but he had no reason to believe Daisy was actually in danger.

Except from this guy...

He ground his teeth as the professor who'd been chatting up Daisy at every opportunity headed out of the banquet hall, carrying a bottle of wine and two glasses. François Tremblay walked in the same direction as Daisy had taken.

Jordan narrowed his gaze.

Was he following Daisy? Had they arranged a rendezvous? Or was François simply hopeful his classic good looks might get him a little extra mileage in the networking department?

A bolt of something hot and ugly shot through Jordan. It shocked him. It definitely wasn't jealousy, more protectiveness. For his best friend's daughter. The way any decent human being would feel protective over someone who was being taken advantage of.

As the professor slipped around the corner Jordan hesitated. He wasn't here to police Daisy's love life. Only to protect her from harm.

His jaw fused.

Goddamn it.

Did he give her space or make certain she was safe?

No one could exist in a bubble, he knew that better than most. He had no desire to spy on her, especially if she hooked up with this guy.

His stomach churned.

He didn't want to think about her hooking up with anyone.

He was still trying to get that stupid innocent kiss out of his brain. Not to mention the knowledge of what she looked like naked.

He silently cursed.

What if François Tremblay was a predator? What if he planned to get Daisy drunk and take advantage of her? He was in a position of power compared to a lowly grad student.

Jordan couldn't sit here like a numb nut until he ascertained exactly what the situation was. Her father would never forgive him if something happened to her. He'd never forgive himself.

If she saw him, God help him, she'd go ape-shit. Rightfully so.

Jordan tossed back his drink, threw some cash on the bar, and climbed to his feet. He had the horrible feeling whatever he decided to do in the next five minutes would be the wrong choice, but, as profound regret formed the backdrop of every thought, every movement, what difference would one more mistake make?

He paused beside the woman. "It takes bravery to go on after losing someone you love. I hope you find what you're looking for."

Her eyes crinkled as her mouth turned into a strained smile. "You, too."

He held back a grim laugh. He wasn't looking for anything except to be allowed to get on with his job. At least he got to fly home tomorrow. He forced a smile and pulled on a black baseball cap he'd bought in the airport, headed off, hoping like hell he didn't walk straight into the one woman he desperately needed to avoid.

2

Daisy used the restroom and then washed her hands, before grabbing a fistful of paper towels from the dispenser to dry them. One look at her pale features in the mirror had her digging her lipstick from her tiny purse.

Jordan Krychek's disproving visage popped into her mind and pissed her off. Why him? Why not Roger with his warm laugh and sexy British accent? Why not Tremblay with his French charm and urbane sophistication?

As a physicist, she understood attraction at the subatomic level, but she didn't understand sexual attraction, not one little bit. Why would one guy give her goosebumps and someone else, just as objectively handsome, leave her cold?

Why couldn't she stop thinking about him?

She didn't want a relationship. The emotions that went along with relationships made you vulnerable, and she had no intention of being vulnerable with a man ever again. Her boyfriend in college had turned her into a walking talking cliché when he'd ditched her for her best friend last year. As if she'd needed another reminder the world was full of liars and cheats.

But maybe she should give herself a break. She was feeling exposed right now. Her defenses low. Ground shaky beneath planted feet. The grief she'd experienced after being told of her dad's death, followed by the euphoria at discovering his miraculous survival, had been a rollercoaster that had almost destroyed her. It had stormed all her usual defensive walls and left them in ruins. She needed time, and a little breathing space, to rebuild those fortifications.

She put her lipstick away. She'd stalled for long enough. It was time to head back to the banquet.

Suddenly, the thought of talking shop with even the most brilliant minds in the industry wasn't enough to stop the tiredness from dragging at her. She yawned widely and decided to head to bed. She texted the lab group chat to say she'd see them in the morning. She was mostly packed. It might be nice to sit on her balcony for a half hour with a glass of wine from the bottle she'd lifted from dinner yesterday.

She headed out into the corridor and bumped straight into François Tremblay.

"Sorry." She started to head around him, but François held up a bottle of red wine and two glasses. "Ms. Montana." The light in his dark eyes was decidedly flirtatious. "Would you like to join me for a walk on the beach? I fly back to Paris tomorrow, and I am afraid our weather is a lot less temperate at this time of year. I want to dip my feet in the ocean one last time and was hoping someone would join me. The others are all busy."

She gazed wistfully outside.

The idea of a walk on the beach was tempting. The resort had security who patrolled the grounds, and the beach area was well lit. Tremblay was unlikely to try anything unless she was a willing participant, and she was more than able to take care of herself. Her dad had insisted she learn a martial art, and she had a three dan black belt in taekwondo to prove it.

Was François the sort of man who held a grudge if a woman rejected his advances?

She didn't think so, but she'd been wrong before.

"I'll join you for a glass of wine and walk on the beach, but just so we're clear," she held his pretty, dark-eyed gaze, "I'm not interested in *anything* else, Professor."

His eyes sparkled. "What more could a man ask for than a fine night, a decent glass of wine, and the company of a beautiful woman?"

Okay.

She wasn't sure if France had caught up in terms of what did and did not constitute sexual harassment these days, but she'd been upfront and honest. If Tremblay stepped out of line, she'd let him know about it.

They headed outside and the breeze was cool on her skin. She shivered.

"Wait." François placed the wine on a nearby table and shrugged out of his suit jacket. "Here, let me." He slipped it over her shoulders, the material still warm from his body. It smelled good too. "I insist."

He smiled at her, and she couldn't help but smile back. "Thanks."

He picked up the wine and the glasses and carried on along the path. When the path ran out, she slipped off her sandals, the sand shockingly cold against her feet. The cool breeze off the ocean was a vivid reminder it was February not June. They headed for the calm waters lapping the shore.

"Do you think you would ever work outside of the US?" François placed the bottle of wine and the glasses on the sand as he sat, then removed his shoes and socks. Rolled his pants up over his knees. He looked slightly ridiculous but kind of cute too.

The silk lining of his jacket caressed her skin as she hugged herself. Traveling the world with her career was definitely something she was interested in doing. "I need to finish my PhD first."

"Maybe you could come work with me in France? A post-doc perhaps." He sounded thoughtful as if searching through his mind for possible funding opportunities.

Her lips twitched. "In which case this situation is highly suspect."

"Not really. We are talking shop, are we not?" The man laughed as he climbed to his feet. "But perhaps maybe it is better if I don't suggest it, yet. I wanted to spend a little more time with you as a person rather than as a scientist. I find you fascinating." He reached out a finger to move her hair off her forehead and looked as if he wanted to kiss her.

"Sure." She stepped away. "*Fascinating.*"

He sighed and reached down to pour two glasses of red. She watched him carefully, to make sure he didn't spike it with anything.

What a world they lived in where a woman had to be cautious about what she drank because losers liked to drug women.

He offered her both glasses as if reading her mind.

She took the one on the right. "How old are you, if you don't mind me asking?"

He sent her a glance through his lashes. "Why? Are you worried about the age difference? I am not *that* old."

The age difference didn't bother her. It was the power imbalance that was the real issue.

"You seem young to be so high up in the field."

"Ah, yes, well, that, I'll take as a compliment."

Vain as well as smart.

Figured.

He took his glass and her free hand and drew her forward until they stood up to their ankles in the water. It felt surprisingly warm for the time of year.

She let go of his hand and took a sip of wine staring up at the clouds that drifted across the night sky. The wine was rich and full-bodied, not the same as they'd been served at dinner. "Nice."

"Bordeaux." He looked down his nose in disdain. "It was the best they had."

She laughed softly. "Watch out, your *French* is showing."

"I'm very proud of my '*French*.'" He cocked a brow and took a healthy swallow of wine. "Having standards should not be a character flaw."

She sipped her wine and said nothing.

He sent her a sideways glance. He obviously knew how pretty he was—and how that angle made him appear boyish.

"Can I ask you a question?" she asked.

"No, I'm not married or in a serious relationship." He sighed as if he was asked the question a lot, which was telling.

"I was thinking more about your career path. What are your ambitions? Where do you want to be in five years' time?"

His eyes widened. "Ah, that seems like the sort of question I should be asking you."

She sent him an amused smile. "Don't tell me you are one of those rare creatures, a man who doesn't like to talk about himself?"

"Now I'm caught in a trap. If I talk about myself, I'm a typical man, which I most certainly am not. If I don't, I'm evasive and secretive." He tipped his glass toward her and tapped his nose. "I've been here before. You tell me about where you want to be in five years first."

She swished her foot through the tranquil water. "Mine is easy and obvious. I want to finish my PhD, publish a bunch of research papers, and be offered a full-time job in my field."

"All very do-able—in more than one country. How's your French?"

"Terrible."

"I could teach you." The guy oozed charm.

She should be tempted.

She wished she were.

"And, for myself? Perhaps head of the International Atomic Energy Agency?"

Her brows shot up. "Aiming high."

He pulled a face. "Perhaps. Perhaps not. I just want to help the world power itself with smarter and safer technology."

"Saving the world."

He gave the quintessential gallic shrug. "It's the only one we have, after all. Why are you interested in this field?"

She imitated his shrug. "Saving the world, of course."

Her interest had been spurred by the tsunami that had damaged the Fukushima nuclear reactor in Japan. The far-reaching impact and understandable fear that had arisen in the aftermath, the obvious need for ever-safer nuclear technology and facilities. She'd found herself wondering why she shouldn't help achieve something better, something resilient and long lasting.

No one had ever accused her of being humble or not reaching for the stars when it came to her ambitions.

It was personal relationships that she failed at.

Water lapped at her ankles. François took a step closer, and she thought about having sex with him. Presumably, he'd be good at it. Perhaps choosing a partner based on the lack of a spark and minus the messy emotional baggage would actually be the smart choice?

He stared down at her, a half hopeful expression on his face.

She glanced at the wine. "What did you put in it?"

His mouth opened in horrified denial.

She smiled. "Whatever it is has me reconsidering what I said earlier."

Shock passed over his features and morphed into a rakish grin. He took another step closer, slid his hand under the jacket she wore and caressed the bare skin of her lower back.

Her mouth went dry but not with desire. It felt a lot more like dread. Her mood changed. She stepped away and his hand dropped to his side.

"Sorry." She hugged herself. "I don't mean to be a tease."

He didn't appear angry. "Bad experience?"

The man who flashed inside her brain wasn't the ex who'd broken her heart a year ago. She swallowed the wine and licked her lips. Found François watching her with avid interest in his dark gaze.

"I can help you forget, you know." His voice was low, seductive.

"I am sure you can." She was tempted to try. But she didn't

want to throw away her professional reputation for a quick fling that meant nothing to her and that could prove awkward in the future. "I don't think it would be the smartest career move on my part."

"It's no one's business." He waved his hand. Frowned. "Except they all gossip like little girls." He pulled his lips to one side, considering. "No one has to know." He rifled in his back pocket and pulled out a room key. "Room 514. I have another keycard," he tapped the breast pocket of the suit jacket she wore, his finger dangerously close to her nipple, "in there."

She quivered in response.

He handed her the first keycard and then lifted the jacket off her shoulders. The cool breeze rushed over her flesh and made her shiver.

"I'll walk through the lobby, alone. You can follow later." He sounded eager.

She shook her head. "I don't think so…"

He tilted his head to the side. "No one would ever know—just you and I. Our little secret."

She bit her lip. He made it sound so easy, but sex was messy and complicated.

But, perhaps, it didn't need to be.

As she hesitated, he backed away, carrying his wine, eyes sparkling. "Come on, Daisy Montana. Live a little. What harm can it do?"

Jordan watched the Frenchman hand Daisy his room key and walk away with a quick stride as if in a hurry to get somewhere.

That smug sonofabitch.

Daisy stood in her backless dress staring after the asshole as he strode toward the front entrance.

Jordan wished he had a weapon on him.

What would he do if she went to Tremblay's room?

According to the data he'd unearthed, Professor François Tremblay was a respected academic in Nuclear Physics who taught at the Sorbonne. He had an ex-wife but lived alone in an apartment in Montparnasse. No criminal complaints, but the guy was an obvious player.

Motherfucker.

Jordan didn't know what the hell to do. This was not the kind of situation he trained for.

Daisy stood for another moment, staring out to sea. Then she finished the wine and turned toward where he was watching from deep in the shadows. For a second she stared, and he froze, wondering if he'd misjudged the lighting.

His mouth dried.

A noise from the left had her looking away, and then she seemed to become aware of how exposed she was, standing alone on that beach. He used the moment to sink deeper into the darkness.

She hurried toward the side door of the hotel, and his heart began to pound.

3

François whistled as he strode through the lobby with a spring in his step. He was hopeful there was going to be a knock on his door shortly. Little Miss America was definitely thinking about taking him up on his offer and he'd make sure she enjoyed herself. He was not a selfish lover. He'd open her eyes to the advantages of an experienced man. One who understood what a woman's body needed and secretly craved.

He spotted an attractive brunette as he passed the bar and his step slowed. Older, for sure, but she obviously looked after herself.

Perhaps, if there wasn't a knock on his door in the next thirty minutes, he'd come back down for a nightcap. The night was young, after all.

He grinned and saluted several acquaintances as he walked across the room. Mimed going to sleep as he stepped into the elevator. He didn't want to ruin Daisy's reputation, although as far as he was concerned *reputations* were stupid things when it came to anything except your mind and how competent you were at your job.

Who people made love to was their own business.

If sex was good, life was good. And why shouldn't life be good?

And if Daisy Montana didn't come to his bed this time, well, there would be other conferences, other opportunities. Yes, she was young but not *that* young. She was a PhD student, not in high school.

He didn't seduce students at home, but here? Away from the norm? Away from his colleagues? Away from the vindictive and judgmental eyes of the administrators who were too old and ugly to gain his attention? Here it was safe to pursue whomever he wanted to pursue and, on this occasion, that was a pretty blonde wearing half a dress.

He was, after all, French.

The human body should be shown off when it looked as good as that. She was a beautiful woman and spending a few hours naked together would be an excellent way to end a conference that had been a little on the dull side.

All work.

No play.

However, he was an optimist.

He whistled as he strode to his room. He reached his door just as the one opposite opened. He slapped his card on the reader as a tall, bulky man with a shiny bald head exited the other room. François looked over his shoulder and caught the startled expression of one of the conference delegates inside the other room.

François smirked then turned away.

Perhaps he wasn't the only one taking advantage of being away from home. Well, they all had their little secrets.

He pressed down on the door handle and stepped inside, thoughts of a certain young blonde replacing those of whatever may have been going on across the hall. Something brushed against his back and then wrapped around his neck. A beefy arm trapped him against a solid chest as someone forced their way into his room.

François threw an elbow over his shoulder, connected with a solid jaw. His attacker grunted but didn't loosen his hold. François dropped the wine glass but remembered the bottle he held. Swung it around like a club and caught the man's head.

The assailant let him go.

François brandished the bottle, not caring that good red wine was running down his arm and drenching the pale carpet like blood.

"Get out. Get out now!" he spluttered angrily, pointing to the door.

The man wiped the blood that was beginning to drip down the side of his face on the black leather jacket he wore. A slow and terrible grin unfurled over is lips. "I'm afraid I can't do that."

His accent was Russian or some Slavic country.

"I won't say anything. *I* don't care what you get up to."

"I'm afraid I can't take your word for it."

A sliver of fear moved through François at the cool intensity of the man's eyes. "I don't have any money. There's nothing here to steal." He thought about the contents of his laptop.

"It wouldn't matter if you did."

The man took a step forward and François swung the bottle, missed, and tried to dodge him.

"*Aidez-nous ! Je suis attaqué !*"

The big man grabbed him by the shirt and shoved him so forcefully into the wall that it winded François.

"*Au secours !*"

Again, and his head hit the wall hard enough to daze him. He dropped the wine bottle and tried to wrench the powerful hands away. The next moment he was whirled toward the balcony door that he'd left open for the cool ocean breeze. He gripped onto the doorframe and found his voice to scream, only to have his jaw clamped shut, as well as his nose.

His heart pounded like a drum as his fingertips clung to the wood. He couldn't breathe. Sweat drenched his body. This man was trying to kill him.

He kicked out and had the satisfaction of hearing the other man grunt as he connected with his shin.

Then he found himself ripped away from the doorframe and launched as if by a catapult, flying through the darkness, knowing with horror that these few seconds were going to be his last. He was going to die. He didn't want to die.

4

Jordan followed Daisy soundlessly up the hotel stairwell, unreasonably relieved when she carried on past level five, where Tremblay's room was located, and instead exited the stairs at level seven.

Why did she always take the stairs?

It kept him fit, that and the regular runs he put in in the hotel gym while watching the security cams to make sure Daisy was where she was supposed to be.

He stood outside the fire door leading to the guest hallway. God help him if she came back and caught him standing there like a fool.

For logistical reasons his room was also on this floor. He pulled the hotel's live security feeds up on his cell's screen. Frowned when he realized the cameras were all down.

Dammit.

He put his hand on the door handle about to risk a quick peek to check that the corridor was indeed empty. A stairwell door opened with a squeal a couple of floors below.

Fuck.

What if it was François headed this way?

If it was, someone was going to pull the fire alarm in approximately two minutes.

Jordan peeked over the edge of the banister. Instead of Tremblay, a bald man wearing a black leather jacket trotted down the stairs. The sight jolted him like an electric prod. Instantly, Jordan flashbacked to another man, another place, but that was impossible.

Konrad Bocharov was dead.

He'd died in a fiery explosion only weeks after he'd arrived back in Mother Russia, only weeks after annihilating Jordan's entire family. Enough DNA had been pulled from the ashes to confirm it matched the sample Jordan had provided the FBI.

Jordan's thirst for revenge had had to be satisfied with that. He'd managed to slowly move on from his grief and his pain. Maybe not move past it, but move on.

This wasn't Bocharov.

It couldn't be.

Blood poured from a cut on the man's head which he covered now by pulling on a ball cap. Jordan watched as the man got out a cell phone and then spoke softly in Russian.

His breath jammed in his throat. Memories surged and threatened to swamp him.

The voice was the same.

The accent was the same.

Jordan remained frozen in place.

His eyes were telling him one thing, but the facts another. He was being paranoid. He was wrong.

He had to be wrong.

Didn't matter. Jordan *needed* to see this man's face.

He hesitated as he thought about Daisy.

She should be safely in her room by now.

Compelled to know for certain that this wasn't the man who'd murdered his family, Jordan moved swiftly and silently down the stairs. He needed to know if he was imagining things, if his mind was playing tricks on him.

He didn't want to spook the guy—who could be an innocent vacationer who just happened to resemble his old nemesis—so he resisted full-out running. He gained but was still a floor behind when the Russian exited the stairwell into the main lobby.

Jordan legged it then, clearing a flight in one leap, heart drilling, not with exertion, but with dread.

It couldn't be.

He burst into the lobby, surprised to see a crowd of people, some sobbing into their cupped hands. Something had happened. Something bad.

He scanned the crowd and caught sight of the Russian heading around the corner to leave by the back door on the other side of the hotel.

As Jordan pushed his way through the crowd in pursuit, a man from the conference stumbled into him, looking pale and shaken.

"He fell off his balcony. François Tremblay. I've known him for twenty years. His brilliant brain is splattered all over the patio."

Something hit the pit of Jordan's stomach and bounced back up with the same force.

He pushed through a gap and sprinted after the Russian.

Throwing people out of windows was a favorite pastime of Russia's SVR, and this seemed like too big a coincidence when Konrad Bocharov had been an agent for that same organization before he'd moved on to trafficking weapons of war.

Jordan saw the door closing and pushed outside as the Russian climbed into the back of a black limo with dark tinted windows, pulling off his black cap and tossing it on the seat as he did so.

"Konrad!" Jordan called out.

The man glanced up, and surprise widened his pale, blue eyes. Then his lips pulled back into a grin. But it wasn't Konrad Bocharov's face. The cheekbones were sharper, the jaw less hammer-like. This man was a lot more handsome than the man Jordan had known.

Despite that, recognition flared in those cold depths as he held Jordan's gaze for a split second before slamming the door, and the car sped off. Jordan dashed forward to get a plate number, but it was too dark, and the car moved too quickly.

His blood rushed through his ears in a deafening cacophony.

The face was wrong, and yet everything else pointed to that person being his old nemesis, Konrad Bocharov.

And faces could be changed.

If it were true that Konrad wasn't dead the way the FBI had been led to believe, the way *he'd* been led to believe, then the man who'd murdered his sister, his mother, his grandfather, and grandmother was alive and well. With a new face, but the same dead eyes, the same brutal psychopathy.

As if nothing had ever happened...

And if Jordan had suspected that even for a moment, he'd have hunted him down and killed him years ago. Rage, an all-consuming conflagration, rose up inside him.

He wanted to race after the limo and pull the man from the vehicle and demand answers. Demand blood.

But he needed to think this through. He had no weapon, no jurisdiction.

And what if he was wrong?

What if he was imagining a connection where there was none? Triggered by an accent and a common build?

Flashing lights began to strobe the beach side of the resort and pulled his attention back to the present.

Jordan stood in the middle of the road and stared.

Tremblay was dead.

Jordan had no doubt who'd killed him—that Russian—who instinct screamed at him was Konrad Bocharov reincarnated.

Why?

His hands clenched into fists.

Daisy.

No. She was okay. But he started to move now. He knew she

was okay. She'd hit the seventh floor only seconds before the Russian had exited the fifth.

How close had she come to death? And that's what Konrad Bocharov was, pure death, risen from the grave.

Jordan wanted to punch himself. Daisy could have been in danger, and he'd hung back like some second-rate rent-a-cop because he was worried she'd see him. Another thought struck him. How many people had seen François on the beach with Daisy?

Dammit.

She'd be a suspect in Tremblay's death.

She'd be detained and questioned by the Mexican authorities —*unless she had an alibi.*

Jordan slipped back inside, keeping his cap pulled low while checking the security feeds on his cell as he jogged up the seven floors to his and Daisy's rooms.

Feeds were still down, but at least now he knew why.

He needed access to Daisy's room because he doubted she'd let him in if he knocked on the door, and he didn't have the right tools to pick the lock. He called Florence Cisco back in Quantico. She worked for the FBI's TacOps Division and was a genius with electronics. She was the one who'd hacked the feeds for him.

She didn't answer.

He headed to his own room, careful to hide his face from the cameras as a precaution. As he got inside, the security feed came back online. Now he couldn't risk using the corridor to enter Daisy's room. Because as far as the authorities needed to be concerned, he was already *in* Daisy's room.

He threw his cap on the bed and went straight to his window and opened it. He reckoned he had twenty minutes tops before the authorities decided to question her.

He stripped off his T-shirt and quickly changed into a black button-up shirt. He stuffed his cell in his pocket and climbed onto the balcony, swung over the rail before jumping to the adjacent room. He worked his way quickly around the side of the hotel, grateful Daisy was on the opposite side as Tremblay because everyone and his dog would be scrutinizing that façade.

A few windows were open, and he had to be careful not to be spotted. He calculated the number of windows to Daisy's room and didn't look down. The distance between balconies was only six feet. The drop was much farther, as Tremblay had undoubtedly discovered.

He went to jump, saw a shadow, and faltered—enough that he miscalculated. Suddenly he was dangling one-handed, seventy feet above that same concrete patio.

Thoughts of Tremblay's fate flashed through his brain as he took a breath. He didn't have time to die. He heard someone come onto the balcony above, and he changed tactics, dropping to the one below. He heard laughter and then the kind of murmurs that led to sexy times.

"Get a room," he muttered under his breath.

It took a minute he didn't have before the couple disappeared inside, and he set off again, hoping this time he didn't fall.

Daisy tossed her heels onto a chair and went into the bathroom to wash the sand off her feet. Gave up and decided instead to strip and shower. She let out a soft sigh. Going to François's room would have been a colossal mistake, and she was glad it wasn't one she'd made.

As her dress fell to the floor and she stepped under the warm spray, emotions welled up inside her, making her feel wrung out and exhausted. Feelings were near to the surface tonight and she wasn't sure why. She was probably still processing everything that had happened with her dad.

She shampooed her hair and then worked in conditioner. She washed the sand and ocean from her skin and grabbed the cleanser to remove what was left of her makeup. She was keen to get home now. To get to work. Dad and Rowena were due back from England in a few days, but they'd been delayed waiting on a visa for Row. Daisy hadn't made the impromptu civil ceremony in Shropshire, but the two of them were planning another ceremony in Virginia soon. A big one. She'd see Jordan Krychek there as he was going to stand up as best man for her dad.

Row wanted her to be Maid of Honor along with her two cousins from Zimbabwe. Her uncle was giving her away.

It was going to be fun—except having to pretend to be nice to Krychek.

She wished she hadn't kissed him. *Gah*. It had only been a simple peck, but the fact *she'd* pecked *him* was maddening.

She'd flirt with some of the other guys instead. And if the numbskulls from Blue Team had the nerve to show their faces... Well, then she'd humiliate them as often as she could get away with without starting a riot.

At least *they* hadn't seen her naked.

She pushed thoughts of Jordan *freaking* Krychek from her mind. Perhaps she should go to François's room and work the FBI operator out of her system. She doubted the Frenchman would object.

But while Daisy had no qualms with Row and her father's relationship, the twenty-plus-year age gap between her and François was a little much for her. As was their relative positions in the nuclear physics community. Or maybe it was simply that she wasn't interested in François and everything else was irrelevant.

Row seemed perfect for her dad.

Daisy hoped they could be friends.

Her mom had been scathing about the whole thing, her bitterness showing. Said, *like father, like son*, whatever that meant as no one ever spoke about her paternal grandfather.

The kernel of resentment in her mother's snide comments had surprised Daisy. She hadn't expected that from the woman she thought she'd known so well. It spoke of jealousy even. Probably because, for the first time since her mother had left him, her dad was finally moving on. Daisy rinsed the conditioner out of her hair and hoped it worked on memories too.

At least since the fiasco with Krychek, she hadn't been wallowing in sadness about her ex and former best friend.

Obviously, she had lousy taste in men.

It was time to concentrate on more important things in life than men or sex, like thermo-dynamics and nuclear fission. Time to think about clean energy saving the world.

Maybe she had more in common with François than she thought.

5

Jordan slipped through Daisy's drapes, grateful she'd left the balcony doors open, but also irritated she'd left her balcony doors open. She should know better—even seven flights up.

But he wasn't about to say anything stupid to annoy her. *Uh-huh*. He was ready to placate her and beg forgiveness and explain he wasn't some attacker. He wasn't there to hurt her.

He had a plan.

Unfortunately, she was nowhere to be seen.

Damn.

Had she left? Gone down to Tremblay's room while Jordan was busy chasing some Russian ghost?

Then Jordan registered water running in the shower and closed his eyes.

She was naked.

Again.

She was going to kill him this time.

And he was going to deserve it.

Again.

He tossed his cell on the bedside table and toed off his shoes and socks. Draped his shirt over the back of a chair.

He pulled the bedsheets back and then jumped on the bed for good measure, tossing a pillow onto the floor.

The knock on the door had him cursing. They'd arrived much faster than he'd anticipated.

He scrabbled his hand through his hair and slapped his cheeks and wet his lips. Undid the top button of his pants as if he'd just pulled them on to answer the door.

Hope struck him. Perhaps they could do this without Daisy even knowing he was here?

He checked the peephole and sure enough, there was the hotel manager in a gray linen suit, alongside a man in the state police uniform.

He blew out a breath and got ready to act his ass off. Daisy's protection was a great motivator. He'd do whatever it took to keep his promise to Kurt and keep his daughter safe. The manager went to knock again as the shower turned off.

Jordan quickly opened the door wide and braced his hand against the jamb, blocking entry.

"What's up?" He gave them a chin lift and a curious, but unconcerned, frown.

"The police want to question Ms. Montana."

Jordan straightened. He could hear noises behind the bathroom door. He deepened his voice but kept it low. "Why?"

"Who are you?" The policeman tried to muscle the manager aside.

The noises in the bathroom stopped. No way she'd missed that strident demand.

"Jordan Krychek. I'm with the FBI." He made himself bigger and spoke loudly enough for Daisy to hear. He hoped she'd figure out something serious had happened. "Ms. Montana's boyfriend." Both men's eyes widened. "What's this about?"

Boyfriend?

Yep. She was gonna kill him for sure.

The manager's round cheeks puffed out in outrage. "She's listed as a single occupant of this room."

"Relax. I have my own room at the end of the corridor. I just haven't slept in it much." He gave them both a shit-eating grin. "Now what's this about? Because I don't know about you, but *we* have plans." He let himself sound impatient.

For more sex.

With Daisy.

God help him.

The bathroom door opened, and the woman in question stood wrapped in a towel, outrage burning her navy eyes and rounding those pretty lips. He silently begged her to go along with him. To make an impossible intuitive leap. She inhaled, clearly about to lay into him.

Not good.

He moved into her and wrapped one arm around her waist and captured the back of her damp head with the other, pulled her flush against him and up off her feet. She felt tiny this close, and, also, incredible. A pity she hated his guts.

She opened her mouth, but he couldn't risk it.

He crushed his lips to hers and felt her freeze. Then she must have figured out something serious was going on as she melted into him and put her arms around his neck and kissed him back like she was chasing her last breath.

Every nerve in his body electrified. Every cell in his body crackled back to life. Kissing her almost made him forget why he was here. It felt better than any other thing had in a long, long time.

A cough in the doorway had him pulling his lips away and staring into her deep navy eyes which held so many questions.

The manager cleared his throat again.

Her towel had loosened, so he didn't let her go straight away even though holding her close was a particular kind of torture. She turned to face the men at her door—and the cop's eyes roamed up and down her body like he could see through that damp towel.

She turned back to meet Jordan's gaze as she grabbed onto the top of the towel and held it tightly in place. Her cheeks went bright pink. "What's going on?"

"That's what I was asking these guys while you were in the shower, but they wanna talk to you. Shall I order that champagne in the meantime?"

She nodded vaguely, and her eyebrows pressed together in a frown. "Can I get dressed?"

"This won't take long." The policeman stepped inside the room, and Daisy stepped back. Her face was naked of makeup now, and those eyes were dark with worry set against pale skin.

Jordan lifted the phone and connected to room service. "Can I order a bottle of champagne and two glasses. Room 735."

"Why are you here?" asked Daisy.

"I'm afraid there's been a terrible incident," the hotel manager began.

Her catch of breath broke his heart. "My dad?"

"No, your family is fine as far as I know."

"Thank God. Next time lead with that."

Jordan found a bathrobe inside the wardrobe and draped it around Daisy's shoulders. It swamped her, but at least it stopped the police officer leering.

She shrugged into it and cinched the belt tight around her waist. "What incident?"

"Mr. Tremblay? You know him?" The policeman watched her expression carefully.

"Professor Tremblay? Yeah, of course, I know him. So does everyone at this conference. He's the leading expert on the miniaturization of nuclear power facilities."

"Some people, they say you and he walked on the beach tonight together." The cop flicked a glance at Jordan. "Looking as if you were having an intimate moment."

Daisy's confusion was written all over her face along with something else—anger. "I *spoke* with François earlier—"

"She's been with me since she left the banquet." Jordan put his arm possessively around her shoulders. "What's going on?"

The hotel manager wrung his hands together. "I'm afraid Mr. Tremblay took a fall."

Lines pinched Daisy's forehead. "Is he hurt? Does he need—"

"A fall out of his window." The cop pointed to the balcony. "He's dead."

Daisy's mouth went slack with shock. "That's impossible."

"His brains are splattered across the pavement proving otherwise." The cop's English was excellent, and he was obviously an experienced investigator trying to get a reaction out of Daisy. He succeeded.

Fine tremors moved through her frame as she started to tremble. "What? Are you *sure* it's him?"

The police officer nodded.

She put her hand to her mouth. "Oh my God. That's awful."

"Did you see anything?"

She shook her head frantically.

"We have several witnesses who say they saw you on the beach with Tremblay."

"Tremblay the guy who gave us the wine?" Jordan asked Daisy, whose brows crinkled with confusion.

She nodded.

"She met me on the beach. A guy in a suit waded in the surf nearby. He offered us a glass of wine, which we accepted, but he didn't stay long, and neither did we." Jordan held the cop's brown-eyed gaze and let an annoying smirk rest on his lips. "We had plans. You can check hotel security and verify."

"You confirm that is what happened?" The cop addressed Daisy who held his gaze as she crossed her arms over her chest. Jordan kept his expression impassive but mentally begged her to go along with his story.

"Yes." Her voice was a hollow whisper. "We saw François on the beach before we came inside."

The cop's gaze wandered over the crumpled bed covers and Jordan's bare chest. Daisy's jaw clamped so tight Jordan could see the muscles playing in her cheeks.

"You have ID?" The cop pressed Jordan.

Jordan reached into his back pocket. Pulled out his creds and flashed them. "I'm not here in an official capacity. I'm on vacation."

The cop made a note on his phone. "I'll need to talk to your superior."

"You go waking up my boss over some guy I barely met taking a dive off a balcony, is not going to win me any favors."

A sneer formed. "You think I care?"

"You'll care when my boss wakes your boss at midnight to complain."

The policeman harrumphed. "A man is dead. I have a job to do." But he looked more subdued now. Less like he wanted to start an argument that might have personal repercussions.

Daisy turned away and sat on the end of the messy bed. Tears filled her eyes but didn't fall.

Shit. Maybe she'd had genuine feelings for the Frenchman. Or maybe she was simply a decent human being who cared about others.

"I think you should go now. Daisy needs some time to process what's happened. You'll have her contact information on file," Jordan said to the manager. He pulled out his own business card. "Do me a favor. Cancel that champagne, will you? I don't think Daisy will feel much like celebrating now." He turned away from the officials and put his hand on her shoulder. Then he sat down beside her and took one of her hands in his.

The policeman seemed reluctant to leave. *Because Daisy was a genuine suspect or because he liked the view?*

Jordan ignored him. "Are you okay?"

"No." She sniffed and shook her head. "It's so terrible. We were talking earlier about our careers and what we each wanted in the future. He had big ambitions. I had no idea he might end his own life. If I had, I would have tried to get him some help."

"This is not on you, sweetheart." He pulled her head to rest against his shoulder. Held the cop's gaze.

François hadn't ended his own life. The cop knew it. Jordan knew it. And the Russian he'd seen earlier also knew it. Jordan would bet his life savings that same Russian had actively assisted Tremblay with his deadly descent.

Jordan didn't believe in coincidence.

It was murder. And he intended to figure out why.

As soon as the door shut on the two men, Daisy sprang to her feet and cradled her face in her hands.

What just happened?

François couldn't be dead. He couldn't be.

Was it her fault?

If she'd known he was experiencing suicidal ideation, she'd have stayed with him. They could have sat on the sand and watched the moon rise over the ocean. Perhaps they could have connected enough to distract him from his dark thoughts. Hell, she'd have had sex with him if that would have helped.

Had he been drunk?

He'd seemed fine but she had no idea how much alcohol he'd consumed earlier. Had he accidentally fallen to his death? She flinched away from the thought of him plummeting to the earth.

She grabbed a bottled water and took a sip.

She stared at Jordan who now sat shirtless on her rumpled bed, looking ridiculously handsome with six-pack abs and ropey muscled arms like some guy on a modeling assignment.

What was he doing here?

He stared at her. Waited patiently for her to speak, which perversely pissed her off.

"My *boyfriend*?" she sneered, screwing the cap back on the water. "*Really*?"

"Seemed like the most expedient choice."

Expedient? That was so Krychek.

She scrubbed the back of her hand over her mouth, trying to

remove the lingering pressure of his lips. That kiss had scorched her down to her bones, but she had no intention of letting him know that. Another terrible thought struck her.

"Oh my God. Did you kill François?"

"Don't be ridiculous. And keep your voice down. I don't want to get arrested for the murder of some guy you hooked up with."

"I didn't *hook up* with anyone." She spat the words in a savage whisper. "And, even if I did, it's none of your business."

He grunted. "It is now."

She reared back. "Did my father send you?" She tried to read his expressionless features. "Or have you turned into my own personal stalker?"

Not likely considering most days he could barely tolerate her.

"If I was going to stalk you, you wouldn't know about it until it was too late."

She held his stare, unimpressed by his argument.

"Hey, I just lied to an officer of the law to keep your ass out of a Mexican jail. A little gratitude wouldn't go amiss."

"Gratitude?" She put the bottle down and crossed her arms. "Gratitude for breaking into my hotel room and getting me tangled up in a web of lies about a death that I had nothing to do with." She planted her hands on her hips. Leaned forward, keeping her voice low. "Maybe you killed François in a jealous rage—and this way you have an alibi too. And I'm supposed to feel beholden to you for *saving* me and then maybe show you a little *gratitude*." She let her eyes drift down his chest. All the way down.

His eyes narrowed, and his jaw worked, but he swallowed whatever his first reaction had been. "You've seen through my dastardly plan. You're right, of course."

She blinked in surprise.

He raised his hands impatiently. "Not about me killing anyone in a jealous rage, but that is how a deranged stalker might think. You can relax. I'm not here because I have some secret crush or care about who you sleep with." His expression said exactly how little he thought of her in that department. It made the effect of his kiss all the more galling.

He climbed to his feet and pulled a black shirt off the back of the chair and slipped it on. Started buttoning it up.

She dragged her eyes away from his body. "Of course, you don't care."

He was so freaking annoying.

She began to shiver, the damp towel under the robe cold against her skin. She turned around and loosened the belt, dropping the towel before pulling the robe back around herself.

She caught Krychek's gaze in the mirror—the heat in his eyes definitely not indifferent, but then he was a guy, and guys were easy. She'd forgotten about the mirror, and he was the type to pay attention to every detail.

Her cheeks burned.

"Nothing you haven't seen before," she muttered bitterly, reminding them both that he'd once yanked her out of a bathtub and tied her naked to a bed.

And if she could have reached one of her father's weapons that day, she would have put a bullet in him.

She was relieved she hadn't because, it turned out, he wasn't some sadistic attacker but instead one of her father's closest colleagues, searching for answers about what had happened to him. Regardless, she owed him payback for what he'd done to her. Serious payback. Payback that would make him regret thinking he could do whatever the hell he wanted to another human being without consequences.

Not that she wanted to physically hurt him—not permanently anyway. Just *impact* him in the same way he'd impacted her. Dent that stoney demeanor. Prick that rhino hide.

There were a multitude of other sins she held against him more than seeing her naked—like the way he'd deliberately scared her outside that bar, and the fact he'd casually handed her off to be detained by some of his fellow HRT operators who'd openly discussed *sedating* her to keep her quiet.

But it was the way her body reacted to the heat she saw in his eyes that angered her most—the knowledge she found him attractive made her seethe with resentment. Him figuring that out would be the final humiliation. She'd die before she admitted it.

She turned away.

"Daisy. Look, I'm sorry." He sighed.

He sounded completely defeated and that got to her more than anger would have.

"For everything I did to you. I was an asshole." She watched him in the mirror as he rubbed the back of his neck. "I screwed up, big time. I was wrong. I apologize for all of it."

The fire went out of her.

He'd apologized before, but it was different this time. Her father was safe now. She didn't have that incessant worry nagging at her, making her willing to forgive anybody anything so long as someone brought him back to her alive.

She wasn't sure she was ready to let go of all the things Jordan had done to her—not yet. "I'm still mad."

"Oh," he slipped on his socks and shoes. "Trust me, I know. You wanna get dressed?"

Dressed?

She was going to bed. Why would she get dressed?

Then something clicked into place inside her brain. "What happened to François wasn't an accident, was it?" She tried not to watch as he tucked the shirt into his pants and folded those sleeves over ridiculously sexy forearms.

How could arms be sexy? It didn't make sense.

He met her gaze. "I don't believe it was an accident, and I don't believe he took his own life."

Her mouth went dry in panicked realization. "Murder?"

That was why Krychek had broken in here and put on that crazy charade. But who would murder a man who was generally well-liked and respected in their arena, despite his womanizing ways?

Panic grabbed her as another thought struck. "They'll see on the security footage that you arrived after I did. They'll know we lied—"

"The hotel security feeds were down, and I didn't use your door."

She glanced at the window as her stomach pitched. Had he climbed down from the roof? She hated heights the same way she hated enclosed spaces. The idea scared the heck out of her, but she refused to give him the satisfaction of asking for more details. Or of being impressed.

Then she registered what he'd said about the cameras. "How do you know that the cameras were down?" She crossed her arms tight over her chest again as a terrible feeling swept over her. "Is this some sort of op?"

Did he kill François? Is he working with someone?

"No." He came toward her and curled his fingers around her upper arms. She found herself staring up into earnest pale blue eyes that were gray-green around the iris. Maybe that's why he always looked haunted—the ghostly color of his eyes. "At least, if it is an op, it's not one that I have any knowledge of, and I don't believe the US is involved."

She gripped his arms, felt the steel in him. Found herself believing him because despite all their fiery confrontations, she trusted him. "Tell me everything that you do know."

"I will, but we need to get out of here first."

Daisy let go as he stepped back. "My flight isn't until morning."

"We can't risk staying here. Get dressed while I pack. We'll figure out a plan. Please."

It was the "please" that did it. She grabbed a pair of jeans and a black T-shirt covered in white graphic physics equations, along with underwear. Headed into the bathroom.

"Talk while I dress." She left the door slightly ajar.

He grunted.

She could hear him opening and closing drawers. It felt really weird he was in her room, handling her things. "Start with why you're here."

If this was her dad—

"If you want to hold this against anyone, hold it against me. I wanted to set your father's mind at ease so he could be with Rowena without any stress after what he's been through. So I volunteered. And I figured I could use the time when you were in sessions to kick back and relax. Catch up on my holiday reading."

She stilled. "You've been watching me all week?"

"Not every step. More like broad strokes, making sure you weren't kidnapped by some pissed-off cartel member."

She hadn't known he'd been there. She considered herself pretty savvy and paid attention to her instincts the way her dad had taught her, but she hadn't spotted him once. That was sobering.

"You followed me enough to see me talking to François on the beach earlier."

"That guy wanted to do a lot more than talk," he growled.

"I know. I considered doing it with him." That got her the stoney silence she expected. "How do you have access to hotel security feeds?"

She heard the zipper on her suitcase opening as she stepped into her jeans.

"I asked a friend to help me access them." The words came out reluctantly. "That way I knew when you left your room in the mornings. The last thing I wanted was to bump into you and for you to discover I was here. It was a great plan. Worked like a charm." The wryness in his tone slayed her.

She wasn't about to show weakness. "So you were stalking me."

"Protecting you."

"You say to*may*to, I say tom*ah*to." She raised her brows. "You disabled the feeds after you heard about François?"

"I never messed with any feeds. I simply watched them. Someone else disabled them."

Everything stilled inside her at that. "That same someone killed François?"

He seemed surprised she'd reached that conclusion even though it was the only one that made sense if François had, indeed, been murdered.

"That would be my guess."

She pulled on the bra and T-shirt. "How do I really know it wasn't you who cut the feed and who killed François and is now using me as an alibi? Maybe he was the op all along, and I'm the patsy."

"Why would I come to your room? I could have gotten in and out exactly as you said. You'd never know I'd been here." His voice came deep and frustrated from the other side of the door jamb.

That was true.

"And the only reason I'd have to hurt him is if he laid hands on you—and he didn't."

She jerked open the door. "Who lays hands on me isn't your business."

Something flared in his eyes, but he ignored her statement. "Finished?"

Without waiting for her to answer, he slipped inside the cramped bathroom and swept all her makeup and skin care products into her travel bags. He even snatched up her dress and underwear from earlier, plus the keycard François had given her. He gave her a look that obviously judged her morals, which revived her fury.

The physical reminder of François made the idea of his death seem all the more surreal.

If she'd gone with him maybe he wouldn't be dead—or maybe she'd be dead too…

That was a sobering thought.

She watched enough crime shows to know the keycard was evidence that could be used to point blame in her direction. Access. Her fingers bunched into fists. They needed to get rid of it.

"If you didn't kill him, do you know who did?"

He hesitated. "No."

"But you have suspicions?" She ran her fingers through her damp hair as she followed him out of the bathroom.

He grunted again. Obviously, he wasn't planning to tell her anything. It reminded her of conversations she'd had with her father over the years, and it irritated the crap out of her all over again. She wasn't after State secrets, just a little reciprocal honesty. If she lied, it was all *felony offense*, when they did it, it was *national-freaking-security*.

"Where are we going?"

He stuffed her toiletries bag into her case and zipped it up. She checked the room for anything he'd missed, including the safe where she'd locked up her passport, but he'd been thorough and proven hotel safes weren't exactly secure.

She put on her socks and sneakers, stood, and held out her hand. "Passport and wallet, please." She had no intention of being dependent on him.

He thrust her purse into her hand. "Check it on the way out of here."

He opened the door and strode down the corridor. He rubbed François's keycard against his pants then slipped it into a bag of garbage on a maid service cart. His room was at the far end of the hallway, the other side of a fire door. He opened it, and she stepped inside. It wasn't as tidy as she'd imagined, but he packed in less than thirty seconds, then shouldered his backpack, took her case handle in one hand and her fingers in his other.

Together, they headed for the stairs.

6

"Wait." Daisy pulled back suddenly. "I need to talk to my boss."

"Why?"

"Because we were all supposed to go to the airport together in the morning."

"Text him tomorrow."

Jordan felt her resistance building. Knew she was about to start fighting with him again.

Inside, he sighed.

Life would be so much easier if people simply obeyed orders. Unfortunately, Daisy wasn't in the Army or the FBI. She was a smart, independent woman, and he needed to remember that and not treat her like a suspect, or the enemy, or an underling. When he'd believed she was someone sent to seduce information out of him or kill him, he hadn't listened to her, assuming the words coming out of her mouth were lies.

He hadn't respected her.

He needed to respect her now.

Even if she never changed her opinion of him, he needed to do better. Dragging her around and forcing her to do what he said wasn't going to work this time.

He stopped and turned so abruptly she bumped into him, and he had to catch her against him so she didn't fall down the stairs. He hated how much he enjoyed the contact. He had no right.

They were almost eye-to-eye.

He leaned forward and kept his voice low so only she could hear him. "I want to get us out of here to somewhere safer, somewhere that no-one else knows about. We have to play this as if people are watching us constantly because they could be." He ran a gentle hand through her damp, silky hair. Hooked a strand behind her ear. "And we have to sell the fantasy, however difficult this might be for you, that we are completely into one another. That we are in love or lust or whatever you want it to be. To the point there's no way you'd be flirting on the beach with another guy because you have me and I'm more than enough for any woman."

Her mouth opened on a silent gasp.

"We cannot have them suspecting that what happened earlier in your room was theater." He pressed his finger to her bottom lip as she started to tremble. Leaned in and pressed a chaste kiss on her lips, resisted the urge to take it deeper, to hold her closer.

There were limits to this charade.

"They might not see us leaving here tonight, but if they do, if they try to follow us, if they separate us or try to question us, we need to act as if we're in love and stick to the story. No deviations. No variation. Once we get out of the country, then we can try to figure out what went down with Tremblay."

He stared into her eyes and watched her pale lashes sweep over the velvety blue, cloaking her thoughts and her feelings.

"They're not going to want to cause an international incident by detaining a senior FBI agent with zero cause or evidence. Sure, they might speculate I was involved, but they've got nothing on me because I never even spoke to the man. You, however…"

Her eyes met his, pupils widening as the implications finally sank in.

She was the one at risk.

She was the one with everything to lose. She was the one they'd put in a jail cell without worrying about how it might look to the US government. Because as far as almost anyone else was concerned, except him and the actual killer, she was the last person to see Tremblay alive.

She *could* have met the Frenchman in his room. She could have pushed him over the railing.

She nodded then and surprised the hell out of him by leaning forward, gripping the sides of his face, and kissing him. Not a chaste kiss either, but one that had hunger rising and lust churning in his blood.

She pulled back, smiled as she murmured, "I'm still not forgiving you, but I understand better now. I am grateful for the assist. Thank you."

His heart gave a wild stumble. "Let's go."

They went down a level from the lobby to the parking garage. The white Toyota he'd rented from the airport was parked nearby. He pulled her closer to whisper in her ear. "Stay here for a moment. Let me check the vehicle before we get in."

Her brow furrowed, but she waited with the baggage near the door. He slid all the way under the chassis, the concrete floor scraping his back. He ran his cell phone light over the engine and exhaust system—making sure Konrad Bocharov, merchant of death, hadn't already known Jordan was at this hotel and planned a surprise.

Nothing appeared out of place. No explosives or wires were visible. He wriggled out and checked the wheel wells and fenders for trackers. He popped the trunk, went over and helped Daisy with the luggage, which he stowed.

They both climbed in.

She went to lower the window.

"Leave it up." He softened his tone. "Windows are tinted."

He felt her intent gaze on his face as he drove out of the garage and onto the highway.

She turned in her seat to face him. "What's the plan?"

"Drive around a little and look for a tail. We need to get to somewhere we won't be followed."

"A bit tricky as we are driving a rental car with a beacon in it." Her tone was upbeat, but her eyes were worried.

He called Cisco, and this time the FBI geek answered. "How do I disable the GPS system in my rental car?"

Cisco groaned. "What did you do now?"

"Nothing."

"If that were true, you wouldn't need to disable the tracker. Do you have that signal blocker that Regan gave you?"

"Yeah." It was in his pocket. "That'll work?"

"As long as it's on, sure, but you won't be able to use your cell at the same time. Can I go back to sleep now?"

"No. I need you to download the hotel security feed going back to the beginning of the week. Actually, make it a full seven days. As soon as possible." *Before anyone deletes it.*

More moaning. "Which camera?"

He flicked a glance at Daisy. "All of them."

Cisco's voice grew sharper. "Did something happen? Is Daisy okay?"

"Is that Florence from TacOps?"

Of course, the woman could hear both sides of the conversation and recognized the agent she'd recently met at Quantico.

"She's fine," he told Cisco. But Daisy's skin was pale and eyes wider than normal. "A little shook."

Daisy hugged herself. "A lot shook."

"What happened?" Cisco asked.

"I'm hoping you can fill in a few blanks and help me figure it out. Pay particular attention to any bald men you see in the footage."

"Bald men?" She snorted.

"Yeah. It's important. I need to call Ackers."

"Uh-oh."

Jordan wasn't looking forward to it either. He checked his mirrors for anyone following. Changed lanes. "Just get that footage downloaded, can you? I know it's late, but someone turned off the cameras for a portion of the evening during which a French guy fell out of a window."

"Fell?"

"I'm guessing he had help."

"From a bald guy?"

"Yeah."

"Shit."

"Yeah. Shit. We're going to find somewhere to spend the night and get flights out in the morning without authorities detaining Daisy."

"Why would they?"

"He was chatting her up earlier before they both headed to their rooms. Someone might suggest she went to his room first and with no footage…" The potential to get caught in his own lies kept nagging at him. "Once you've downloaded the footage"—hopefully without the Mexican cops knowing—"take a look at the feeds for the south stairwell and the fifth floor. Between nine and ten local time." He shot Daisy a look. "And the corridor on the south side of the main banquet room. And the bar. And anything that covers outside that corridor heading to the beach. I'm officially Daisy's alibi for the time of Tremblay's death." He explained the situation. "I need to make sure the cops don't find evidence that contradicts our story that we were together."

He needed to know why the man he believed was Konrad Bocharov had been at that hotel and why he'd killed the professor. What secrets did the Frenchman have?

Could François have been selling nuclear material or plans to the arms dealer?

Possible.

But his attempted seduction of Daisy hadn't seemed staged, and why would he do that if he'd already agreed to meet with the arms dealer?

Jordan took a turn off the highway and headed down to the old part of the city—founded by the Spanish in 1519.

"Okay, okay," Cisco said. "I'm looking now, and the hotel cameras all go dark at 9:07 p.m. Found you just prior to that—chatting up a hot brunette at the bar."

"Hey, she was chatting me up."

Daisy rolled her eyes in his peripheral vision.

"You should be in the clear."

Then why was he freaking out?

He was overreacting. There was no reason to think the authorities would suspect Daisy when she had a solid alibi. But inside he knew he wasn't overreacting. Not if he'd actually seen a Russian arms dealer responsible for countless atrocities, not least the murder of Jordan's entire family.

But had he?

Or had his imagination shown him things he wanted to see? Because as much as he wanted Bocharov dead, he wanted to kill him more.

"Can you run the footage through facial recognition software?"

"All of it?"

"Yeah. All of it."

"Jeez, Krychek, Regan's gonna have words to say about this."

"Regan always has words, but I'd rather we keep this between you and me to start with. It's important."

"Okay, okay."

"I owe you one."

"Considering I'm about to have a sleepless night, you owe me many."

"Appreciate it." He hung up then fished his personal keys out of his pocket and switched on the jammer on the fob.

Daisy crossed her arms. "You know she has a crush on you, right?"

"What, Cisco? No way." The idea was ridiculous. He was pretty sure she was gay. "You're imagining things."

"Yeah, sex on the brain. That's me." The fire that flashed

through her eyes was multifaceted. Regret, embarrassment, sadness, anger, and…something else.

"It wasn't your fault."

Tears suddenly glittered in her eyes. "If I'd done something differently—"

"Like gone to his room?"

"He offered."

"I bet he did." Heat poured off Jordan's skin as he ground his teeth together.

"I wasn't attracted to him. Otherwise, I might have said yes."

"And then you'd probably be dead too."

The words were sharp, but the fact she'd come so close to such evil when he was supposed to be protecting her was humbling and terrifying. How would he ever have faced Kurt again?

Yeah, *that's* why his jaws were fused together and white-hot anger seared his brain. Because of Kurt.

Images flashed through his brain of Daisy bloody and naked on white sheets. Nausea rolled through him.

Maybe he should visit the department shrink the way his boss kept insisting. He was used to dealing with danger and high stress situations, but this felt different. Maybe it was the ever-present guilt for how he treated Daisy in the past. Maybe it was the reality that he knew what Konrad was capable of.

He looked in the rearview mirror and saw the same shit-brown Buick tailing them as had followed him back on the highway. He took a left down a side street, then another. Pulling a surveillance detection move past graffiti-scrawled one-and-two story homes and businesses, over cracked and broken pavement. The Buick followed.

"We have company."

Daisy twisted around in her seat. "The cops? Does that mean they genuinely believe I had a hand in Francois's death?"

"I don't think it's the cops."

Daisy's face twisted in fear. "Who then?"

Respecting her meant telling her the truth when he could. "Maybe the same people who killed Tremblay."

"Who do you think it was?"

The fear in her eyes pissed him off. He hated that Tremblay had involved her in this. He hated that he hadn't kept her safe even though that was the whole reason he was in Mexico. He hated Konrad Bocharov with every cell in his body.

His fingers clenched around the steering wheel. "I can't tell you who I think it was because I don't know for sure, and if I am correct, it would be a matter of National Security."

"Oh, for fuck's sake."

Daisy's irreverent response made him want to laugh for the first time since he'd seen her on the beach earlier.

The shit-brown car followed, and Jordan spotted another vehicle behind the first. But this didn't look like the slick operation the Russian usually led. This looked like local trouble.

Fucking Konrad.

He'd known Jordan would split from the hotel, and he'd probably contacted a few local gang members or friendly cartel contacts about the fact there was an active-duty FBI agent likely roaming the city, unarmed.

Hopefully, Konrad didn't know about Daisy. The Russian could never know she was with him.

"Get down where they can't see your face."

Bullets from an automatic weapon shattered the relative peace of the night but thankfully missed their vehicle.

Daisy put her hands over her head and hugged her knees with her face.

Jordan took another turn, aiming back for the highway. He needed to lose these motherfuckers, switch vehicles, and get the hell out of the city.

It cemented in his mind that the Russian must be Konrad Bocharov. Otherwise, how would they have identified Jordan as the man who'd followed him leaving the hotel after the Frenchman's death? Konrad may have changed his face, but the arms dealer hadn't changed his ways.

Jordan pressed his foot to the accelerator and sped away. A car appeared at the end of a long road, and a man poked a sub machine gun out the window. Jordan jerked left, down a narrow side road before the assailant could open fire. Maybe they'd get lucky and he'd kill his buddies instead.

"I'm scared."

Because she wasn't stupid, and this wasn't some Hollywood movie.

"Keep your head down." They were out of sight now, and he took another turn. He spotted a small, dilapidated hotel up ahead with underground parking. He whipped inside. No obvious surveillance camera.

"Out. Quickly."

She scrambled out of the seat, and he grabbed their luggage. He had items he didn't want to end up in the hands of potential enemies. He jogged between a bunch of parked vehicles and tried doors along the way. He found an unlocked, dented burgundy Toyota Avalon that had seen better days. He popped the trunk then locked the doors. Thankfully, the trunk was empty except for an old, dirty blanket.

He pulled it out. "Get in."

Daisy's eyes went huge, but she didn't argue. She scrambled inside and pressed herself tight against the back of the seats.

He slotted the luggage in first and then maneuvered himself over it and next to Daisy. There wasn't a lot of room. He spread the dirty blanket over their feet and twisted and pulled the trunk lid shut, locking them into darkness.

Just before the lock clicked, he heard the low vibration of an engine.

They were out of time.

7

Daisy was shaking so hard she couldn't breathe and couldn't see. Her teeth began to chatter. "Did I mention I hate enclosed spaces?"

"That's why you don't take the elevator?"

"Yes." The old blanket smelled ever so slightly of grease and clogged her mouth and nostrils.

Jordan had wedged himself into the cramped space, his back pressed tightly against her front. Her leg was bent in an uncomfortable fashion, and her knee was beginning to ache.

"I'm sorry. Close your eyes, and whatever you do, don't move or make a sound," he murmured. "They're here."

Oh, God.

The blackness pressed down on her, along with a sense of overwhelming fear. Going from drinking wine on the beach with one of the top professors in her field, to him being brutally murdered, and now, her cowering in the trunk of a stranger's car along with Jordan Krychek of all people, made her head spin.

Thankfully, she wasn't fully phobic. She wasn't. She squeezed her eyes shut. It was just dislike. An intense and visceral dislike. Mastering her fear could be the difference between life and death —and she really wanted to live.

Gradually, she got a hold of her breathing.

She followed the news. Knew the sort of criminals her father and Jordan pursued. She had a good idea what the cartel could do to them if they were caught. She'd seen articles about mass graves in Veracruz and dead bodies dumped on the side of the road. The violence had calmed down in recent times and rarely affected tourists—as long as they kept to the resorts. And, yet, François was dead.

Had the cartel killed him?

She heard their pursuers then. Shouts and curses in Spanish. Men sounding frantic and angry.

Her heart pounded as she gripped the back of Jordan's shirt so tight her fingers hurt.

Oh, God.

Footsteps echoed around the garage, and the entire car shook as someone tried to open the trunk. Fear filled her throat and mouth. Every muscle in her body wept as she held back a whimper. The shouts and voices moved away.

Had they gone? Were they safe now?

She was about to say something when Jordan reached back and squeezed her thigh as if in warning.

She clamped down on her words.

After another full minute passed, there was a shout from a few feet away, and terror ping-ponged inside her like neutrons in a reactor. To think she'd almost said something that could have given away their location...

The sound of a police siren cut through the night air, and she could hear swearing and footsteps as the men hunting them ran away.

After another anxious minute, when all seemed quiet, Jordan shuffled around to face her. Not that she could see more than dense shadows.

"How are you holding up?" His voice was a soft whisper of breath.

She was shaking, sweat making her skin clammy. "Sick, scared, may have peed my pants. How about you?"

"Same."

That got a quiet chuckle out of her because, despite the situation, he wasn't even sweating.

"What would you have done if they'd opened the trunk?"

"Blitz attack the guy and grab his gun, kill the others, get back into the rental, and head for the airport."

He made it sound so easy and matter of fact, when she knew it was anything but.

"What are we gonna do now?" She stretched her leg to ease the kink in her knee. "Can we get out?"

He folded the blanket behind their heads to form a kind of pillow and shifted slightly so he was lying diagonally on his back with his feet over his backpack. "Smartest scenario would be to hold position."

"Here?" she squeaked.

He stroked her hair away from her face. "They'll probably keep eyes on the area for the next hour or so. I figure we stay here for a few hours and try to get some sleep, then drive away when the cockroaches have crawled back under their rocks. Here, use me as a pillow. I've got you."

She found herself drawn against the hardness of his body and inhaled sharply as he pulled her knee across his thighs. Her reaction had nothing to do with not liking enclosed spaces.

He froze and removed his hand. "Sorry, I was trying to help you get comfortable, but—"

"It's fine." She forced herself to relax, then flexed her lower leg a few times until her knee cracked. She sighed with relief.

Jordan swallowed audibly, and she realized she was moving against him in such a way…

She gripped his shirt. "Sorry," she whispered. "My knee was stiff."

He muttered, "I can sympathize."

She laughed because it was that or cry, but as he drew her head against his chest, her pulse started to settle.

"Try to get some sleep."

"I hate being in a tin can." She gritted her teeth.

"It's not a tin can. Just the extended back seat of a car."

She huffed out a laugh.

"There is air all around us."

Her mouth went dry again, and she sucked in a breath.

He stroked her arm, and she concentrated on the touch of his fingers and the way they felt on her bare skin. Soothing. Electric. Nice.

Gradually, her breathing slowed, and the rhythm of her heart eased.

"Do you think we'll have any issues at the airport tomorrow?"

"It's hard to say. But I doubt anyone will trouble you."

She frowned. "What about you?"

"I'm gonna see if I can get on standby on an earlier flight."

She raised her head a little. "You're worried someone might target you specifically?"

She felt him nod.

"This person who you think might have killed François Tremblay, do you know him?"

Poor François, she hadn't had the chance to really take in that the man had died tonight, only minutes after she'd turned down his offer of no-strings sex.

"I'm not sure. But if it is who I suspect, then yes, I know him. Which means, there can be no link between you and me."

"What about the police report or being seen on the hotel cameras? You said they had access."

"Fuck. Good point. As soon as we're clear of any involvement in the Frenchman's murder, you and I are going to have a public, extremely vitriolic breakup."

Unexpectedly, the idea didn't bring her any joy. It was probably a reaction to the night as a whole. It had been horrible. She shivered, and he gathered her closer.

Cold Heat

The temperature, thankfully, wasn't stifling. In fact, it was a little chilly, so she was grateful for Jordan's body heat. She closed her eyes and let herself relax as she breathed in his scent. She let her imagination play with happy thoughts rather than the reality they found themselves trapped in. It was nighttime. She was safe.

She snuggled against his chest and found a position where she was comfortable, in the circle of his arms. Slowly the terror faded into exhaustion as she finally drifted off.

8

She awoke slowly to the light of a cell phone. Despite the rigid confines of the bed, her human cushion worked surprisingly well. Not that she was comfortable or happy being in a box, but the knowledge the wall at her back was actually a car seat helped. Maybe she should be embarrassed to be climbing all over this guy, but they hadn't exactly had a choice.

Not that he seemed to mind.

The thought gave her pause.

Was he attracted to her despite his protestations?

Did she *want* him to be attracted to her?

As much as she wanted to pretend otherwise, she could admit to herself that the spark missing between her and François was alive and kicking with Jordan Krychek.

His attitude toward François had been scathing at best, but that wasn't necessarily jealousy. The age difference, the power imbalance, the fact Jordan had no idea whether or not she was being coerced…and simply the fact she was making the job he'd signed up for—without her permission, so she felt no guilt—more difficult, could all contribute to his pissy attitude toward the Frenchman.

She knew Jordan's type.

Assertive. Controlling. *Alpha.*

She'd been dealing with it her whole life.

Jordan loved her father, probably as much as she did. All of Gold Team appeared to care deeply for Kurt Montana. They'd die for him. They'd certainly see protecting his daughter as a matter of duty.

But did that explain the heat she'd seen flare briefly in Jordan's eyes last night? So very different to the cold callous nature of his stare the night he'd dragged her naked out of the bathtub.

Had she grown on him?

She inwardly laughed at the idea.

But she wasn't the enemy anymore. She was no longer a potential threat. So maybe the heat in his eyes wasn't attraction so much as the basic biological lust of a straight guy for a naked woman.

Attraction made more sense if she thought about it in terms of biology and animal reproduction. Her inner animal wanted the best male specimen to fertilize her eggs and take care of her and any potential babies. His inner animal wanted receptive wombs to spread his progeny far and wide.

Which sounded gross and demeaning.

It certainly didn't sound very romantic when she thought about it in those terms. But what did romance matter?

Romance was a malignant force. Romance was mirrors and deception. Pain and heartbreak.

As far as she was concerned, romance was dead—*and she wasn't wrong.*

She didn't want any messy entanglements or false promises and didn't intend to make any. She could look after herself and didn't need a man to take care of her or any babies she possibly chose to have. She had a full scholarship and was pursuing a career in the growing field of clean energy.

But while she had no intention of getting emotionally involved with anyone, she still deserved a sex life. One where she got to make the decisions and have some fun.

Jordan only really seemed to care about her in terms of keeping his promises to her father and his team—except for that small flare of heat.

And wasn't that the perfect setup? Especially if she got to tweak his guilt, in exchange for all the humiliation he'd put her through? Sex with Krychek would not only be *interesting*, it would be the best revenge on him and her dad. Serve them right for interfering in her life without consulting her.

She was still mad at them for pulling this stunt, but considering François was dead, she was grateful for the support. The idea of ending up in a Mexican prison and inadvertently starting a war—because her dad would rescue her or die trying—made sleeping in the trunk of a stranger's car on top of a man she vacillated between hating and lusting after worth it.

She wouldn't lose her father again.

She wouldn't destroy his Happily Ever After.

But he needed to learn he wasn't responsible for her anymore. He'd had his opportunity when she'd been a kid, and he'd blown it. Both her parents had blown it, although they'd done their best. She was an adult now. They needed to respect that.

Jordan was texting with someone. She could make out the outline of his sharp features when she tilted her head up to look at him.

"You awake?" He cleared the screen.

She nodded and tried to stretch out her limbs in the cramped confines. Failed. "What time is it?"

"Almost five a.m."

She grunted. She'd slept longer than she'd anticipated. "That means it's actually four something. Did you sleep?"

"I got an hour."

She wasn't sure she believed him.

"Ready to get moving?" he asked.

Considering her dislike of enclosed spaces and the fact she needed the bathroom... "More than happy to get out of here."

Although, it hadn't been as terrible as it could have been, and that was mainly because of him.

He reached over above his head and found a T-shaped pull on the side panel. Tugged it and the trunk popped open.

Daisy braced herself, but there was no one around. No lingering bad guys or shocked locals. No one to wonder why they were in the trunk of a parked car.

Jordan pulled himself up and climbed to the ground, then hoisted out their two bags. Then he held out his hand, palm up, and she stared at it, realizing it felt different between them now.

After a night cramped together like a couple of kidnap victims, they'd gone from adversaries to…something else.

She took his hand, enjoyed the heat of his skin in a way that was both new and familiar. He put his hands around her ribs to lift her out.

He didn't meet her gaze.

Did he feel it too?

Was it simply the suspension of hostilities? A peaceful interlude during a war? Or was it a transition from enemies to…

She couldn't finish the thought.

His gaze moved to his white SUV. "Let me just—"

"Yeah, yeah." She waved him away. "Check the vehicle. I know. I know." She knuckled sleep out of her eyes as he jogged over to the rental car. She folded the old blanket and placed it back into the cargo space. Who'd have thought she'd have *ever* voluntarily spent the night in a metal box—or be grateful they'd had the option.

Jordan found a small black box—obviously a tracker—in the wheel arch. He placed it on the vehicle next to theirs. He waved her over and she quietly closed the trunk, then grabbed the luggage and hurried across the stained concrete. Jordan placed her case and his rucksack onto the back seat.

She climbed into the passenger side with her purse and flipped down the mirror to check out the damage. Her hair was a frizzy mess, her skin as lifeless as a wraith, marred by dirty smudges under tired eyes.

All her seductive fantasies died an instant death at the sight of herself. Who'd want her looking like this? Certainly not a guy like Krychek. She'd seen the type he went for—tall, stacked, perfect blondes.

Just as well she hadn't embarrassed herself by doing anything impulsive. She was such an idiot. "Have you heard anything from the authorities?"

"No." He reversed out of the parking spot. Aside from his formerly crisp, black shirt looking a little crumpled, and the darkening of his jaw from a day's growth of beard, he looked the same he always looked. Serious. Capable. Stupidly handsome.

Haunted…

She wanted to know what that was about.

It didn't matter and was none of her business, but her curiosity was piqued, and she really wanted to know his story.

Unrequited love? Family tragedy?

He reached between the seats and dug into his backpack. Tossed a black ball cap onto her lap.

She tried it on, reduced the band size, then twisted her hair into a knot at the back and tucked it up under the cap, smoothing as much as she could under the edges.

She looked over to see Jordan watching her with a strange expression on his face. "Everything okay?"

"Yeah." He cleared his throat. "Fine. Keep your gaze down to avoid any surveillance cameras."

She pulled the peak low over her eyes. "Aye-aye, Captain." Who exactly did he think was chasing them? The Mexican equivalent to the CIA? "I'd kill for a coffee."

"Yeah, but I'd rather not die for one," he replied drolly. "We'll get something on the plane."

It was still dark as they hit the main road and Jordan navigated without the need for a map through pitted streets lined with poor-looking houses and struggling small businesses. Dogs roamed the street, and she watched a cat switch its tail as it stared down at a mutt that was jumping up the wall beneath it.

There was no chance the dog was going to be able to reach the cat, but it kept on trying. The cat sat there, licking its paw, and silently taunting the dog.

She turned to watch the tableau until she couldn't see them anymore. "Are you a cat person or a dog person?"

His brow hiked. "I like both, but I'm out of town too often and too unpredictably to have either. Why?"

"No reason." She'd never had pets because her mom had always said she had enough things to deal with being a single mom and refused to even consider anything except the sad interchangeable goldfish who'd lived on the kitchen counter. Like Jordan, her father didn't have a pet because he was always being deployed to dangerous situations without warning.

Maybe that would change now. Rowena struck her as a dog person.

Part of Daisy wanted a houseful of rescue pets, but she wasn't sure she was strong enough to deal with the heartbreak when they died. Easier to stay alone, she decided. It hurt less in the long run.

Jordan hit the highway, but they were going in the opposite direction of the main airport.

A diversion? Or were they looking for another tail? The idea that someone was still chasing them sent fear surging through her once more. Was this what her dad and Row had felt for weeks on end? She hadn't fully appreciated how awful that must have been for them. No wonder her dad had come home a changed man.

She had to gather moisture for her tongue before she could ask, "Where are we going?"

"Slight change of plans. I spoke with the friend of a friend, and he arranged alternative transportation as a precaution."

She relaxed a little at that.

He took an exit, and she saw a sign for a small municipal

airport up ahead. A small, fancy jet sat in the distance outside a hangar.

"Who the heck owns that?"

He flicked the headlights off, so they were suddenly driving blind. He seemed to be able to see the road so her heartbeat slowed back down to only slightly panicked.

"As of a month ago, the US Government owns it. The jet formerly belonged to a cartel leader who died during a confrontation—which he started and we finished. It's been swept from top to bottom and is clean."

"Okay. I need to text my boss and tell him I'm getting a different flight. I don't want him or the others in my lab to worry about me." She had to work with them when she got back home.

Jordan shook his head. "We want everyone expecting you to be on that original flight—especially the authorities. By the time they figure you're a no-show, we'll be over US soil. You can text him then."

She bit her lip. Wilson and the others were going to be pissed she'd disappeared without a word last night. She didn't want to upset her advisor at the start of her project. He'd been super supportive of the situation with her dad. She felt like she was becoming a liability to his research program.

Jordan pulled up in the shadow of the hangar. Scanned the surroundings. Her eyes had adjusted to the darkness, and she could see surprisingly clearly.

She gnawed her lip. "Any news about François?"

"The French government is sending their own investigative team, as is the International Atomic Energy Agency." He glanced at her. "The Mexican police have that witness who says you were on the beach with François not long before he died and now everyone wants to know why you disappeared, and what you have to say."

"They don't believe our story?"

"Our story will hold as long as we do. Eyewitness testimony is notoriously unreliable, and it was dark. As for why we disappeared, tell them I didn't feel safe in that environment, so we left. Tell them I'm a horny, paranoid, control freak."

He shot her a grin that made her blink in surprise. She wasn't used to seeing him smile.

"Tell them we slept in the back of the car, no need to specify the trunk. You don't know the location exactly but somewhere quiet, near the ocean. Then I arranged this flight because I was concerned about possible information leaks that might mean I was identified and a potential target for the cartel, which might, in turn, have put others in jeopardy."

Her eyes grew wide at the reminder of all the people who'd died on the flight her father was supposed to catch in January. Sacrificed to keep ugly secrets and prevent billionaires being held accountable for their actions. That threat was locked up now, neutralized. The technology controlled by the US Department of Defense and its allies, who she had to hope were the good guys. But what if others used similar tactics to stop her and Jordan leaving the country? The thought was terrifying.

"When we get interviewed, *that's* the story. No matter who's asking the questions. The eyewitness was mistaken about it being just you and François on the beach. I was there too. And I came to your room via the balcony every night because I'm a macho asshole and you're a romantic fool—or, more likely, you were ashamed of me and didn't want anyone to know I was at the conference with you, but the sex was great." He shot her a forced grin. "Unfortunately, we can't talk about this onboard the jet. We need to get our stories straight beforehand. We have to assume the plane is bugged. I can't use my jammer inside as I'm not sure whether or not it might interfere with the flight instruments."

"*That* would be bad." She frowned. "What do you mean, 'no matter who's asking the questions'?"

A muscle worked in his jaw. "Apparently, the FBI Director wants to know what the hell I was doing in Veracruz at a conference for nuclear engineers, and she is suspicious about Ackers running some sort of off-the-books operation. Don't worry. I'll tell her the truth about why I was there, just not the rest of it. Your alibi needs to be rock solid."

"Don't tell her."

He glanced at her sharply. "What do you mean?"

"I mean, if I have to lie to my boss, then why can't you? I don't want my dad to be in trouble with the FBI leadership. He doesn't deserve to get shit from anyone except me. Tell everyone you and I formed an attachment when you kidnapped and held me hostage in—what did Ackers call it? Oh, yeah, *protective custody*."

His lips compressed but those haunted eyes stayed fixed on hers.

"We hooked up afterward but kept our relationship secret because you were concerned about my dad knowing, which I think is patriarchal bullshit. When I told you I was headed to this conference, you lost your mind because you're a macho asshole and you insisted on taking vacation time and coming with me."

He sighed. "What if she decides to polygraph me?"

"The polygraph isn't foolproof, and you know it. Especially if we blur the edges of the truth rather than outright lie." She slid her hand up his thigh and felt him tense. "Surely you can fake a little biological attraction to me?"

He gripped her hand. "You're my best friend's daughter—"

"So what?" Disgusted, she snatched her hand away. "My dad is not in charge of my sex life."

Jordan huffed. "I'm trying really hard not to think about who you have sex with."

"If this is going to work, you're gonna have to get over that because *you* are the person I'm having sex with. Lots of it. I'm not a virgin," she snapped impatiently, "and neither are you. The patriarchy wants me to be 'pure' because it suits their agenda. Fuck the patriarchy. Fuck their agenda. It's okay for men to 'sow their wild oats' and be a stud, but a woman lives by the same rules, she's a slut?"

"Your father—"

"Fuck my father!" She exploded. "My dad wasn't around

enough to police what I got up to when I was a teen when maybe it mattered. My mother was too busy being a martyr to notice me sneaking in and out of the house." Her bitterness was leaking, and she refused to let her insecurities show more than they already had. "You'd be an idiot to ignore the perfect plan that gets us both off the hook. And you can tell my dad privately that you never touched his precious princess's vagina or any other orifice for that matter." She shook her head at his shocked expression. "Why are we sitting here, rather than getting on the jet?"

"Waiting on a signal that all is well." He turned toward her with eyes that glittered in the gloom. "That was quite the speech."

She bumped a shoulder. "Whatever."

"I'll lie to my boss about why I was in Veracruz, but I can't lie to her about my security concerns."

"No one asked you to."

He was staring at her. "Daisy, those concerns put you in very real danger if you are in any way associated with me. If the person I believe killed Tremblay finds out you and I are involved —even pretend involved—he would hurt you to get to me." His eyes were alive with feelings right now.

"Who on earth do you think killed François Tremblay?" When he didn't reply she decided it didn't matter. "Look, we talked about this. You know as well as I do that the fact you're my alibi for Francois's murder will leak. We can't say we lied about that because then I don't have an alibi, and it looks even worse than before, because…well, we lied."

Jordan swore as he rested both hands across his brows and pressed his thumbs into his temples. "Okay, so we pretend we're really together for long enough to convince the FBI director and whatever authorities she decides to involve, that we're a genuine item and this wasn't some goddamned op. But the potential threat is serious enough that you will need protection."

"I'm not going into protective custody." She crossed her arms. "No way."

"You can stay with me. Work on base like you did last time."

He eyed her almost nervously and continued, "I wouldn't ask if I didn't know he was dangerous."

"Well, you think he threw François off a balcony, so I have a pretty good idea."

"You have no idea." The gravel in his voice jolted her. He grimaced. "After a week you are going to dump my ass so convincingly that anyone with a brain would believe you hate my guts and vice versa. Maybe I can persuade Meghan Donnelly to pretend to have an affair with me and you can slap me in the face or something."

"Kick you in the balls more like." She looked away, reminded of her ex and former BFF. Apparently, she was easy to cheat on, even in fake relationships.

The engine ticked quietly as it cooled. The pre-dawn silence should have felt peaceful, but until they were safely out of the country, she didn't think she'd be able to relax.

He was patiently waiting for her agreement to his plan, which beat the hell out of the last time when he'd strong-armed her in the name of "her own good."

"I can stay with you for a few days and work remotely, but then I have to help my boss with an experiment that I'm using as the basis for my entire thesis at the facility on Lake Moses next week."

Lights flashed in the cockpit, and Jordan immediately climbed out of the car and grabbed their luggage.

"Can you delay the experiment?"

She shook her head. "The timing depends on the nuclear power plant where we're conducting the research. They are switching out old spent fuel rods, and we plan to insert in a new type of rod that's only been tested in an Advanced Test Reactor so far. It's what he gave his talk on at the conference."

"He's running experiments in a nuclear reactor?"

"They've done all the preliminary work. Now they have to test it on a commercial scale. The company funds a lot of our research along with the feds." She sniffed at his judgy expression. "Professor Williams is one of the smartest people I know. Scientists have been running these experiments since the Manhattan Project. Why do you think safety has improved so much over the past sixty years?"

He grunted and took her hand as they started across the tarmac toward the airplane steps. "Considering someone targeted a member of your community, we're going to be running background checks on everyone who was at that conference and in that hotel."

"You think one of the attendees had something to do with Francois's death?" The people she worked with were dedicated professionals. None of them seemed the type to push someone off a balcony.

"I honestly don't know yet because I haven't had time or the opportunity to even discuss it with my colleagues."

"Except for *Florence*." She winced because that sounded a lot like jealousy in her tone.

"I needed someone I trusted to gather that surveillance data in case someone decided to wipe it, and she'd already helped with the cameras—let me just suggest she keep this all to herself for now." He paused and sent a quick text, presumably to Florence. Then he scanned the gray dawn as they hurried toward the jet. "A few days should be enough time to allow me to figure out some details, and then the FBI can determine the threat level to you. You can decide how you want to handle it."

He caught her gaze, and she saw those ghosts once again haunting the depths of his eyes. He was trying not to be a neanderthal and think about how this affected her, which she appreciated.

"I'd rather lose my job than endanger you," he said earnestly.

Her heart melted.

"Or any other innocent civilian."

She mentally rolled her eyes at herself.

She was such a loser.

Well, she wasn't going to be that loser anymore. She was doing things her way this time. On her terms.

"Okay. I agree. For now." She turned on the bottom step. Touched his face. Caught him by surprise. "But you better hurry up and figure it out, because I have a life to live that doesn't include *protective custody* no matter how sexy the FBI agents doing the guard duty." She ran her palm over the scrape of his beard. "Although, you never know, I might be persuaded to wear handcuffs under the right circumstances." She leaned closer and watched his eyes fix on her lips. "Get ready to act your ass off for the next few days, Operator Krychek, because I am going to be madly in love with you, and you better not leave me hanging. And then I'll happily dump your ass in a public display of female empowerment, and you will have to live with that humiliation and regret for the rest of your life. In the meantime, why don't we enjoy the ride? No strings. No expectations. No messy emotional baggage. Until we can get this thing figured out."

She tapped his cheek and then sauntered up the stairs with a little extra bounce in her step.

Her terms.

And they felt glorious.

9

Enjoy the ride? No strings? No expectations? No messy emotional baggage?

What the hell did that mean?

She had to be fucking with him.

Jordan shook his head as he followed Ms. Daisy Montana up the steps.

What was she up to?

Did she actually just call him "sexy"?

Him?

Sure, he was sexy if you liked grim and haggard. He needed a shave, a haircut and seven hours of solid sleep to even pass for human.

He paused. Or was she talking about someone else on Gold Team?

He scowled.

Did she have a crush on someone?

She better not be planning to seduce one of the guys. Her dad would go ballistic. Jordan wouldn't be far behind, but it wasn't because of any paternal feelings. He knew himself well enough to recognize straight-up jealousy.

Not that it mattered. She might dismiss his loyalty to her dad as patriarchal bullshit, but you didn't mess with your best friend's daughter, especially when he was also your boss and could kill you in a thousand different ways. And Jordan would have to stand there and let him, because he'd have broken the code.

The co-pilot greeted them and quickly secured the door behind them. The man put their luggage into a low compartment. "No flight attendants, so help yourself to bathroom, bedroom facilities and tea, coffee, water, and snacks in the kitchenette. Flight time of just under four hours. Wear your seatbelts when you can, we're expecting a smooth flight, but you never know when we might hit some turbulence."

That was for damned sure. "You're going over the gulf, right?"

"That's the plan." The co-pilot nodded and watched Daisy as she removed the ball cap and shook out her hair. Interest lit the man's eyes.

She looked feminine, genteel and fragile—she was anything but the latter. She also looked exhausted.

"If you want to grab sleep or a shower after take-off, help yourself."

Jordan did not like how the co-pilot's gaze traveled over her. He shifted so he stood in front of her and held out his hand to the other man, who took it.

"Thanks for picking us up at such short notice."

The guy squeezed his hand firmly. "That's the job, and you're welcome. Buckle up." He headed into the cockpit and closed the door behind him.

Daisy dropped into a comfy-looking, cream, leather chair that looked as soft as a cloud.

He grabbed two bottles of water from the back and then took his seat opposite. "I'll make you that coffee as soon as we take off."

The plane began to taxi to the runway.

She twisted the cap off the bottle and took a long drink. Licked the moisture off her lips while holding his gaze. "Coffee can wait until after I've showered, *babe*."

Something about the calculating glint in her eye told him he was going to have to step very carefully over the next few days. The woman was smart and determined and quite capable of manipulating him to get what she wanted. Although he couldn't actually figure out what she might want, aside from the whole not-getting-arrested thing.

He inhaled deeply as he figured it out.

She'd told him what she was doing. She was *acting*, doofus. Role-playing, so that when they got to DC they'd be in sync and look like a couple rather than two prickly, almost-strangers, pretending not to hate each other.

Not that he hated her.

Not even close.

The plane hit the runway and immediately gained speed. Daisy stared out of the window with a strange look in her eyes. Sadness. Regret.

The last ten hours had been harrowing for her. He hated to admit he'd actually enjoyed being stuck in that trunk last night.

The sun was beginning to crown over the horizon, and the pink light of dawn saturated her profile. He found himself staring at her sometimes just to see the way her lips formed words.

He needed to remember none of this was real. She was *enjoying the ride*. Having fun. Enjoying making him squirm. He had to remember that, and no matter how tempted, he wasn't going to sacrifice his principles or break his promises—he'd already let too many people down.

He didn't need to pretend to be attracted to her. Ever since he'd discovered she wasn't some undercover operative sent to seduce and kill him, he'd been employing all his considerable acting skills to hide the fact that he found her…captivating. Pretending he didn't feel a desire that itched at his skin from the inside out whenever he thought about kissing that smart mouth was something he excelled at.

Weirdly, even though he knew it was wrong, he felt alive again in a way he hadn't in years. The horrors of his past hadn't left him, but he'd learned how to live with his ghosts.

But if Konrad Bocharov was alive that changed everything...

He frowned.

What if he were mistaken?

What if the guy had recognized him for some other reason?

The accent had been the same, the voice, the way the fucker moved. Everything was the same, except the face.

As soon as Jordan got back to Quantico, he'd be contacting people to see how it was possible that the FBI had made such an enormous error as to believe Bocharov was dead.

They reached cruising altitude, and Daisy unclipped her seat belt and stood. Went over to where their luggage was stored and pulled out a few clothes. She put the case back in the cupboard.

"I'm going for a quick shower." She batted her eyelashes at him and gave him a sly smile. "Feel free to join me, *babe*."

He sat frozen to the seat as he watched her hips sway until she disappeared inside the small suite. He blew out a sigh. Damn, she pushed all his buttons.

And he had no intention of acting on any of it.

Even ignoring the fact Kurt was her father, she was younger than he was, and she deserved a hell of a lot better than a guy like him. But he needed to get into character because the FBI Director, the Mexicans, the French, the IAEA all needed to be convinced he and Daisy were *together*.

So he made her coffee—milk, no sugar—and walked into the bedroom suite. He tapped on the bathroom door and opened it a crack to place the mug on the washstand.

He caught a hazy glimpse of her outline in the steamed-up mirror, his memory and imagination filling out the rest.

He looked at the floor. "I'm going to get some sleep, *babe*."

Jeez.

He'd never called a woman "babe" in his life before, and he was going to Hell because he wanted it to be real. He kicked off his boots and peeled off his shirt. Shut the window blinds and closed his eyes. For the first time in thirty-six hours, he finally slept.

———

Daisy managed to keep her hair dry beneath a towel and some judicious pointing of the nozzle. She toweled off and pulled on fresh underwear, a clean T-shirt, and the same jeans as she'd worn last night. She grabbed the coffee off the sink and took a long gulp. It tasted perfect, exactly the way she liked it.

Her mood buoyed. Because she was safe, she realized. Whatever Jordan's concerns, she doubted anyone would attack the plane or her when she was back in the States. Not when she hadn't seen anything and this fictional relationship with Krychek would be over in a few days.

Whoever killed François had no reason to hurt her. She was a student. A nobody. Unless it was some jealous ex, but even so, she hadn't done anything. She had a handgun and license to carry concealed. She could take care of herself.

She tossed the towels into a hamper and eased out of the bathroom. It was dark in the bedroom, and she saw Jordan flat on his back, asleep on the bed.

She knew she was playing with fire as she lay down beside him. She reached out to blow on the embers, but he looked so peaceful for once, she couldn't bring herself to disturb him.

He hadn't slept last night. He'd been busy setting up this jet and listening for danger. In a few hours, they'd be grilled by people with the power to arrest them if they discovered they were lying.

Tiredness filled her.

She was sad about François, but she didn't know who'd killed him—or why. She snuggled closer to Jordan's warmth and rested her hand on his stomach. At least now they'd be able to say, with complete honesty, that they'd slept together on multiple occasions.

10

Jordan was dreaming.

The *best* sort of dream. One he dreamed regularly.

About her.

She was pressed up against him. Her scent engulfed him, and her warmth felt like the sweetest gift to his cold, cold heart.

He moaned as he found himself growing hard. Wrapped his hand around himself and stroked. Unable to resist, he slipped his hand under her T-shirt and found her nipple beneath the cup of her bra, pinching and rolling the sensitive tip. She pushed her breast eagerly into his palm. She kissed him, and he took her lush lips and dove in deep, tasting her unique flavor.

God, everything about her was perfect, especially the fact that she loved what he was doing.

He slipped his broad palm slowly down the smooth skin of her stomach, under the waistband of her jeans and into her panties. She parted her thighs as he slid a finger through slick folds and sank it deep inside her. She was wet and arched against him, capturing his mouth with hers and pressing her hand over his, urging him deeper inside her. He forced in a second finger and felt her muscles quiver around them.

He burned for her. "Daisy."

In his dreams, she burned for him too.

Small, deft fingers snapped open his jeans and lowered the zipper carefully over his swollen flesh, wrapping around him, strong, demanding.

"Daisy…" He wanted to whimper. *God, yes, like that. Just like that.* He wanted to sink his cock into her velvet heat, but even in his dreams he never crossed that line.

But this, driving her up, her thighs spreading wider for him, her breath gasping his name. This was safe. Safe because it was secret. It was his and his alone. His favorite dream.

He rubbed her clit with the heel of his hand every time he rocked into her. Her body tightened, and he growled, knowing she was close. "Come on, Daisy. Come for me, baby."

In dreams, unlike in real life, she always did as she was told, and she did it again, now, giving a sharp cry as her whole body shook with orgasm. But she didn't release her grip on his throbbing dick, and he knew it was too late for him.

He'd wanted her to take him into her mouth.

Delighted in the idea. Knowing even subconsciously that the dream could never come close to the reality, he imagined how good it would feel with her lips closing around him.

Someone started tugging his waistband lower and jarred him out of sleep.

His eyes sprang wide, and he found himself staring into Daisy's ocean-blue gaze. Her mouth formed a pretty bow as she stared at him. His fingers were still buried deep inside her slick heat.

Her hand stroked him, and he was toast.

"Oh fuck." He closed his eyes and strained back against the mattress as he came in a rush all over his own stomach.

Christ.

He closed his eyes as horror and humiliation crawled over him.

This wasn't a dream. This was a nightmare.

He couldn't believe what he'd done. He quickly withdrew his

fingers, covered his face with his hands, tried desperately not to smell her all over his skin.

His throat went dry. After his last disastrous sexual liaison, he'd begun to worry he was a sex addict. This proved it.

She gave a low satisfied hum. "Do you always wake up horny?" Her tone was light.

He stared at her in shock.

Her eyes sparkled as if this was no big deal. "I don't know whether to be insulted or grateful. I haven't gotten off like that in forever, so I'll go with grateful—although, I was hoping for a little more…"

Her gaze moved over his body, obvious appreciation lighting her features. His dick twitched optimistically, and he grabbed his shirt from the floor beside the bed to cover and clean himself.

"I don't know what to say." His voice was hoarse. "I'm so sorry. I was asleep, dreaming. I basically assaulted you—"

She snorted. "If I hadn't wanted to have sex with you, you'd be bloody and crying on the floor."

"We didn't have sex."

She hiked a condescending brow. "Fingering isn't sex? Or the handjob? Coming all over each other isn't sex?"

It was definitely a type of sex. He swallowed with difficulty. "I didn't get your consent. For all I know, you were asleep too."

Her expression sobered. "I gave you all the access you needed, Jordan. I'm the one who touched you even though you apparently were asleep." Her teeth caught her bottom lip. "I thought you were pretending so you didn't have to deal with the guilt about the whole thing. Sorry."

She went to climb off of him, but he held her in place.

"None of this was your fault." His intensity startled them both. "How were you to know I'm some sort of sex freak? I'm genuinely sorry."

"Don't be." Her upbeat tone sounded forced. "If that's not enjoying the journey, I don't know what is."

"I—"

"Shush, Jordan." She traced a finger over his lips, and he couldn't move. "You're not a freak. It's just sex. Chill." She smiled. "There are few enough upsides to hanging around alpha males. Let me at least enjoy some of the perks."

Alpha males? He frowned. "Perks?"

"I told you what I wanted. No strings. No expectations."

Apprehension filled him because she *had* been talking about having sex with him. "This can't happen again."

Ignoring him, she took his shirt out of his hand and finished cleaning him up. "Do you often have sex dreams?"

He gave up, covered his face with his forearm. Nodded. "Yeah." *Lately.*

The last thing he needed was for her to figure out she was the only one who affected him this way. No one else. "This is the first time I've had sex while asleep, although…"

"Although, what?"

He held her gaze as he zipped up his pants. Forced frost into his tone. "I never usually sleep with anyone, so how the hell would I know?"

Her eyes twinkled. "FYI, I'm giving you advanced consent for any future shenanigans. If I change my mind, I'll be sure to let you know."

His hands started to shake. "No. Daisy, this can never happen again." He sounded desperate even to his own ears. "I don't consent."

She climbed off him, picked up her shoes, and went to the door. "So, I'll have to make sure you're awake first." She pouted. "Which is a shame because I could think of several *very* satisfying ways to wake you up, but if I don't have permission…"

The visions her words sparked…

"It's not a joke, Daisy," he snapped. "It's serious. I'm not interested in you that way." He made himself say words that would convince her even though he knew they'd hurt. "It was situational —you happened to be here. This can never happen again."

"Hmm." Amusement danced in her eyes, and a smile twitched

the edge of her mouth as she canted her head to one side and tapped her pointer finger against reddened lips.

Not the reaction he was expecting.

"You know, I might actually believe you except for one small detail, Mr. Sleeping Beauty. And now I have to wonder what else you've been lying to me about."

His heart contracted in dread. "What are you talking about?"

"Did you know you talk in your sleep?"

His eyes bugged, sweat formed on his brow. What the hell had he said?

"Coffee?" she asked jauntily.

When she closed the door, he sat up and cradled his face in his hands. What the hell had he done this time?

―――

Disappointment that Jordan had apparently slept through their sexual encounter was tempered by the fact that, unless there was another woman in his acquaintance called Daisy, he'd definitely called out *her* name in the throes. And what was more, he knew it.

Ironic that she had better sex with Krychek when he'd been asleep than she'd had the whole time she'd dated her ex. That little hint of dominance had been such a turn on. It had tipped her hard and fast over the edge. Possibly the only upside to being with a domineering man—a type she'd actively avoided dating in the past because she was intimately acquainted with their flaws.

She grinned with satisfaction as she made coffee. Tormenting Jordan would serve him and her dad both right for interfering in her life without permission and hopefully make them hesitate to treat her like a child again in the future. Didn't matter that their paranoid hearts were in the right place. The rest of the world had to get on living their lives without highly trained bodyguards watching their backs. Not to mention, the danger in her field was generally invisible and no amount of weapons or muscle could neutralize radiation poisoning.

Science, safety measures, rigorous accountability, and common sense, that was what would keep her safe on a day-to-day basis.

How did her dad think this was going to play out long term anyway? Was she supposed to get permission to travel? Curtail certain opportunities presented to her throughout her career because it might be too dangerous when he'd always done whatever the hell he pleased?

It was infuriating even though she understood his reasoning.

He had to let go.

Her new goal was to get Jordan to admit that, despite his almost desperate denials, this attraction was entirely mutual. That was all. No hearts. No flowers. No mad declarations of undying love.

And, knowing Jordan was so uptight about having sex with her because of who her father was, getting him into bed would be revenge enough for the things he'd done to her in the past. They'd be even. A few more excellent orgasms, and she could get him out of her system and go back to concentrating on her thesis.

If he felt he had to somehow "deal" with his relationship with her father because of it, that was his problem. She had no such hangups.

She heard the shower turn on and grabbed his mug and took it in to him. Placed it nonchalantly on the sink as he'd done for her. "Coffee, *babe*."

She heard his strangled groan but left without taking a peek. She already knew what he looked like—almost—naked. Which made them *almost* even.

She grabbed her coffee and went to sit back in the comfy chair, first putting her dirty laundry into her case and pulling out her phone charger.

She thought about getting a clean shirt for Jordan and decided that going through his stuff was too much of an invasion of privacy, though she doubted he'd hesitate to search through her things if he deemed it part of the mission—in fact, he already had, back at the hotel.

She clenched her jaws.

She so totally understood the breed.

Her cell was completely dead. She plugged it in and left it on the table to charge. She heard the door open behind her and waited for the man of the moment to pad into view. He shot her a look as he bent, bare chested, to retrieve his backpack. She watched the muscles play in his six-pack abs as he rooted out and then pulled on a T-shirt that molded his chest like a coat of paint.

She raised her eyes to his angry ones. Tried not to smile. *Ah.* They truly were balancing the scales.

"Can I text my boss now, *oh majesty*?"

He dragged his hand through his damp hair and checked his cell. "Sure. Don't give him any details. Just say you're making your own way home and will be talking to the FBI ASAP. Tell him you'll be,"—he swallowed audibly—"staying with me for a few days until it's all sorted out."

A smile spread over her lips, despite her best efforts to contain it. "Yes, sir."

His gaze narrowed, and her smile widened. But he stayed quiet. Withdrawing and reevaluating. That was fine with her. She knew how to wear people down. She'd grown up being fed battle plans and strategy for breakfast, right alongside feminism and female empowerment for dinner. She was good at both.

"Daisy…"

"Yes, Jordan?" she asked brightly.

He stared at her, unspeaking, for five whole seconds. "Never mind." He shook his head and stalked back to the cabin with his belongings.

11

Though it shamed him to admit it, Jordan hid in the bedroom for as long as possible. He might be an elite operative, but he wasn't capable of dealing with Daisy right now. Not after what had happened.

The sound of voices drew him out with about thirty-five minutes before landing.

The co-pilot sat opposite Daisy, elbows on knees, leaning forward, hanging on her every word.

Her laugh tinkled, free and easy—a laugh he didn't think he'd ever heard before.

Jealousy reared its ugly head, and he forced it back down into its box.

What did he care who she flirted with?

Except, he was pretty sure she was doing it deliberately to annoy him, and for the next few days, she was supposed to be his. It wasn't in his nature to share.

He pushed his bag back into the luggage compartment and sat next to Daisy, reaching for her hand.

He didn't miss the subtle flattening of the other man's too-white smile.

"Where are we landing?"

The co-pilot named a small municipal airport south of Quantico.

"I know it." Cas Demarco and Delilah Quinn had gone up against a cartel member there last month, and the bastard had murdered a couple of innocents and burned down one of the hangars. "Any issues?"

The co-pilot shook his head. "Smooth flight so far."

"It's a nice jet." Jordan turned to smile at Daisy. "Especially the bedroom."

Daisy's cheeks stained pink.

So Ms. "Advanced Consent" could actually blush? That was news. "Need any help landing this thing?"

The co-pilot's cool gaze met his. Pilots were generally possessive about their aircraft. Jordan was feeling pretty damned possessive himself right now.

"We've got it." That smooth smile again. "I was telling Ms. Montana if she ever needs a tour guide in DC to let me know. I know my way around pretty well. I'd be happy to show her the sights."

I bet you would.

"That's kind of you." Was he a plant? Sent undercover to determine the true nature of Jordan and Daisy's relationship? "Pretty sure I can handle any services Daisy requires."

He brought her fingers to his lips while holding the other man's gaze. He was staking his claim, however short the duration of this fake relationship. She was his, and this guy should know better than to sniff around like a horn dog.

A smile tweaked the man's lips as he climbed to his feet. "Just being friendly."

"Well, you never know, Carl." Daisy watched the man from under her lashes. "If Krychek is ever too busy to *entertain* me, then I may take you up on that kind offer."

Over my dead body.

Carl grinned at her and shot Jordan a victorious look before swaggering into the cockpit.

Jordan leaned close to her ear and tried to ignore that scent of hers that always sent his brain into a tailspin. "What part of 'madly in love with me' flirts with the goddamned copilot?"

She put her mouth to his ear in turn, her breath warm on his skin. "It was an innocent conversation."

Nothing about Daisy was innocent. "He was salivating like a dog with a bone."

"I'm not responsible for the effect I have on men."

Was she referring to what had happened in the bedroom earlier?

Maybe.

He leaned back and stared at her, perplexed. She was right. She couldn't help the sweetheart good looks that made people underestimate her and *want* her—including him. She tied him in knots. Or maybe it was the gravity of their situation that was getting to him. He hadn't spelled it out clearly because he hadn't wanted to freak her out—yet.

He cleared his throat. "Listen up. Apparently, there's quite the furor been stirred up in the media over this."

He suspected Russian bots were out there amplifying conspiracy theories to take the pressure off Bocharov and put it onto the FBI instead. And on Daisy.

Her brow furrowed. "What sort of *furor*?"

"Conspiracy theories abound that the US had a part in the Frenchman's death. Your face is all over the internet." So was his, which seriously pissed him off. "You need to be prepared when we land. I'd lock down your social media accounts if I were you as soon as you get the opportunity. FBI Director is on the warpath."

Her chest rose as she sucked in a deep breath. "Do I need an attorney?"

They spoke in quiet whispers, faces close together.

"That would be the wisest course of action."

"Are *you* getting an attorney?"

He shook his head. "Not unless I figure they're trying to frame us for something. It'll look too suspicious if that's my start position. But you're not in the Bureau, and lying to an FBI agent is a federal offense."

"So my father reminded me whenever he thought I was up to something." She pressed her lips together. "I'll let them interview me without one to start—I know they'll want to talk to me without you being present. If I feel like I'm being railroaded, I'll call for an attorney."

He was hopeful the Bureau would believe a man who'd dedicated the last decade of his life—not to mention everyone he loved—to its service. And that they'd give Daisy, Kurt's daughter, the benefit of the doubt.

"Remember what we talked about. No one's going to pin Tremblay's death on you. I won't let them."

Her eyes were wide and dark now, somber with the understanding that playtime was over. This was serious.

About damned time.

The seat belt sign beeped, and he belatedly let go of her hand, then closed his eyes as they descended.

He could do this. Keep Daisy safe from anyone suggesting she was involved in Tremblay's death, sound the alarm about his suspicions that Konrad Bocharov was still alive, and at the same time, protect her from that monster.

He wished there was some way for him to contact Kurt and tell him the truth. Except for the fact he'd had his hand down Daisy's pants. He wasn't planning on telling him *that*. He wasn't sure how he was ever going to face his old friend again. The man had asked him to protect Daisy, not finger fuck her.

He couldn't even think about it without shame and desire churning inside him in a tangled mess. The sight of her was a bright, shiny temptation to a man who had a weakness for sex, even though his code of honor refused to give in—at least not while he was conscious.

He was such an asshole.

And none of that mattered.

All that mattered was protecting Daisy and proving Bocharov was alive, then finding him before the bastard hurt anyone else. Plus, exacting revenge for the murder of his family, of Ana, of Micky, of the four cops who'd been slaughtered while on stakeout duty that night.

The FBI needed to investigate his old task force buddies to discover how the arms dealer could have faked his own death and where he'd been in the intervening decade. Bocharov couldn't have managed this disappearing act alone.

Had the Kremlin been involved? Or had Bocharov used the explosion to get away from his Russian masters and start over somewhere else with a clean slate?

Jordan didn't know, but he planned to do everything in his power to find out.

12

When they were safely on the ground and taxiing, Jordan climbed to his feet and pulled out their luggage, shouldering his backpack and dragging Daisy's case to the entrance.

The plane came to a standstill, and he rapped his knuckles on the door of the cockpit. "Thanks for the assist."

The co-pilot opened the door and shook his hand. "No problem."

Jordan ignored the fact the guy slipped Daisy his business card. Who could blame him for trying?

Maybe Carl was Daisy's type.

Scowling, Jordan released the outside door mechanism. The stairs descended to reveal that the plane had come to a stop beside a small hangar. He moved onto the top step and scanned the small waiting crowd.

Shit. Ackers was here. So was the new FBI Director, Ursula Rhodes.

This couldn't be good.

He held out his hand to draw Daisy forward, and she took it without hesitation.

"Showtime," he muttered into her fine blonde hair. Now they were back on US soil, he was more worried about the potential danger from Bocharov than the Mexican authorities—except the new director was an unknown entity, as were the political agendas at play. "I promise I won't let anything bad happen to you."

She placed her hand on his chest and her fingers burned through the fabric of his T-shirt, but her gaze was cynical. "Until they send you away on a new mission."

"I have a few more days of leave. Hoping we can figure it out by then." He pressed a kiss to her forehead before they started down the steps. "I would, respectfully, suggest you don't travel to Mexico for the foreseeable future, but we've got this, Daze. As long as you do what I say."

She indicated he come closer and then he jerked back in surprise when she nipped his earlobe. *Ouch.*

"I'm not a dog," she muttered. "I won't be ordered around like one."

He rubbed his ear. "Understood."

He helped her off the bottom step.

"I'm hungry." She pouted, but he knew her better now and the expression was an act, a distraction from something more important. She was feeling vulnerable but didn't want it to show.

"I could eat too. We'll see if the FBI Director will let us stop for burgers and fries on the way to our interrogation."

Her grip tightened on his hand, but he had no intention of letting go, not until he had to.

He walked over to his boss, Daniel Ackers. "Quite the welcome home committee, sir."

Ackers indicated the FBI Director. "Director Rhodes meet Operator Jordan Krychek and Daisy Montana, Kurt Montana's daughter."

"Ma'am." Jordan drew Daisy forward and wrapped an arm around her shoulders, ignoring the look of surprise that flickered in Ackers' eyes.

Ursula Rhodes' handshake was an iron grip. "Operator Krychek. You caused quite the international incident."

"No, ma'am." She looked shocked he disagreed with her. "I did what we're trained to do. Get off the X. Get out of danger."

"You avoided the local authorities."

"Again, with respect, that's not true. We both gave verbal statements regarding François Tremblay's death last night. They never said we couldn't leave, and we were both on record as flying out this morning. They have our names and contact details." He took a breath. "I believe I have important information about who might have had a hand in Tremblay's death that you would—"

"You didn't think the Mexican police might want to know that as he was killed in their country?" Rhodes' tone was scathing.

"Absolutely. But I believed I needed to discuss it with my superiors first." He scanned the surrounding area. A good parabolic mic would easily pick up their conversation. "We need to go somewhere more secure to discuss it, ma'am."

The director's sharp features tightened.

"It's not like we went on the run, Director Rhodes." He let his own impatience show. "We made contact with US officials and arranged through them to get back into the country ASAP. And here we are."

"It looked as if you were fleeing the scene."

"I was doing what I'm trained to do. Keeping American citizens safe."

"We'll discuss it in the car." She indicated he climb into her official vehicle, so he urged Daisy toward the door. Something about being out in the open like this made him nervous. That's what happened when you knew what a sniper bullet could do to the human skull.

One of Rhodes' bodyguards, a guy Jordan had helped train, held out a hand to block Daisy's way.

The director spoke up. "The invitation doesn't include Ms. Montana, I'm afraid."

Jordan ground his teeth. "I'm not leaving her."

"If you want to keep your job you don't have much choice." The director's tone was ice.

Daisy put a hand on his arm. "It's fine. I know I need to give a statement about François. You don't—"

The director cut her off with a dismissive wave of her hand. "These agents will escort you where you need to go and question you about the events of yesterday."

Two black-suited men approached.

Daisy eyed the new agents with obvious dislike. "Er, sure."

"Where exactly are you taking her?" demanded Jordan.

"To be questioned by all the various authorities who want to talk to her."

"Where?" he repeated, not budging.

The director tilted her head back to eye him. "A secure location."

Ackers stepped forward. "Don't worry. I'll stay with her. We'll be on base."

Director Rhodes gave Ackers a plastic smile. "Now if you could possibly follow orders, Operator Krychek? I thought you people were supposed to be good at that sort of thing."

Jordan pulled Daisy close and kissed her, long and hard, in front of everyone—selling the story and going to Hell because he enjoyed it regardless of circumstances.

"Don't leave the base." He leaned his forehead against hers. "I'll see you as soon as I can."

She nodded, then climbed into the back of another ubiquitous government vehicle. Ackers' mustache twitched before he nodded and then climbed into the car with her. They drove off, and Jordan didn't bother to hide his dark mood from the director.

"Why the theatrics?"

"You and Ms. Montana have caused an international incident, and I have POTUS blowing up my phone every ten minutes demanding answers about one of *my* men."

He bristled, he belonged to the FBI and the American people, not to one person. "So tell him the truth."

"I would." Her cool blue eyes lasered into him. "But I don't know the truth, Operator Krychek, now do I? Get in the damned car, and we'll talk about it."

He handed over their luggage—he was given zero choice. He went to climb in the back of the limo, but the bodyguard demanded Jordan raise his hands while he frisked him for a weapon.

Jordan was kind of proud the guy followed procedure and insulted down to his core that he believed it was necessary on a fellow senior agent.

Jordan climbed into the back of the limo and sat opposite Director Rhodes.

The bodyguard sat beside her.

"What were you doing in Mexico, Operator Krychek? And don't give me any bullshit about dating that child."

He stared at Ursula Rhodes, his boss's boss. "I can tell from that statement that you have no idea who you are talking about."

"Oh no? The daughter of your immediate superior, a student who you yourself placed into the protective custody of another HRT team only last month."

"I believed I had valid reasons to do so at the time, but that was a mistake," he admitted.

"So was carrying out an unsanctioned operation south of the border last night. Why did you assassinate François Tremblay? On whose orders?"

He shook his head. "With respect, ma'am, that's crazy talk. There was no mission. I never touched that guy."

She snorted. "Don't treat me like an idiot."

"I wouldn't if you weren't acting like one."

The bodyguard's gaze widened while the director's narrowed into slits.

Jordan decided not to give her the chance to reprimand him. "Daisy Montana is not a child. She's an intelligent woman pursuing a career in nuclear engineering, and you are prejudiced against her due to her age and hair color, which means the joke is on you. Her IQ leaves both Einstein and Hawking in the dust, and she easily outwitted Blue Team and escaped protective custody, which I remind them of every opportunity I get. She's the daughter of my best friend, and I haven't figured out how to tell him I'm involved with her, yet—*with respect*." He didn't hide the snide tone because she was insulting him and Daniel Ackers to suggest they'd do anything illegal. "After I found out she had this conference in Mexico, I figured I'd tag along. It would give us time alone when she wasn't attending presentations."

Kurt was smart enough to know Jordan might have had to improvise and that he wouldn't blurt out the truth if questioned.

"You had separate rooms."

"I spent the nights in her room, but I didn't want her associated with me should the cartel target me as a federal agent. Her safety was—*is*—my priority."

No lie there.

"Then why is there no evidence of you entering her room via the hotel security system?" Her smile suggested she'd caught him in a lie.

They'd already searched the security tapes. Then she'd know the footage from the time of Tremblay's death was missing.

"I didn't use the door." Jordan crossed his arms over his chest.

"Then how did you get into her room?" She snapped impatiently.

He flicked a glance at the bodyguard. "It was a very scalable hotel."

"You were seven floors up."

"So?"

The director obviously didn't know whether to be pissed or impressed. She went with pissed. "Tremblay—what do you know about him?"

"A professor from Paris."

"His relationship with Daisy Montana?"

"They didn't have one, outside of being colleagues who were both interested in nuclear energy."

"From all accounts, he was quite the womanizer."

Jordan shrugged. "Like I said, I didn't know him."

"Many suggested they believed he was interested in Ms. Montana in more than a professional manner."

Many?

"Daisy is an attractive woman."

"Did he attack her in his hotel room?"

Jordan frowned. "She was never in his hotel room."

"Did you attack him in a fit of jealousy? I've heard she's quite the handful."

Daisy was beyond a handful.

"I never went to his hotel room either, ma'am."

"Maybe he didn't fall from his room. Maybe he fell from hers, and you helped cover it up."

He'd forgotten the new director was a former prosecutor.

"Then he must have had a hell of a wingspan as he landed fifty-feet away on the other side of the building. Surely the hotel security feed told you he was never in her room?"

Her lip curled. "In an amazing feat of coincidence, the camera feed from the time of Tremblay's death is missing."

Did he admit to knowing this? That would pull Cisco in, and he had no desire to get her into trouble, and she might blab about the real reason he'd been in Mexico.

"I might know who interfered with the security footage, but it wasn't part of any clandestine mission that I am aware of."

Rhodes looked unconvinced.

His patience ran out. "Would you like me to tell you what happened, or shall we keep on playing Twenty Questions and hope we get there in the end?"

The director looked as if steam was about to blow out of her ears. "Fine. Tell me what happened."

He talked her through it, only rather than watching Daisy on the beach with François, he was sitting beside her in the sand. And, as the conference was over and they were leaving the next day, rather than following Daisy up the stairwell to her room, they walked there together as a couple.

"Why on earth would you voluntarily climb *seven* flights of stairs?"

"She's claustrophobic. Not to a crippling degree. She *can* take an elevator if she has to. But she avoids them when possible." He shrugged. "Plus, it's good exercise."

That seemed to piss the director off all over again, probably because her office was on the seventh floor, and he bet she never used the stairs.

"This next bit is what I didn't tell the locals."

She leaned infinitesimally forward. "Go on."

"We reached our floor, but when I heard someone come out on to the stairwell below, I glanced down—habit, I guess—and saw a man heading downward, moving fast. He had a cut on his head which was bleeding. There was something familiar about him that made me pause, so I told Daisy to head to her room and that I'd join her there shortly.

"I followed him, and when I reached the lobby, I saw a large crowd of people, and everyone is walking around in shock. One man tells me François Tremblay fell from his fifth-floor hotel balcony and his brains are all over the patio. I catch a glimpse of the bald guy exiting the hotel, so I cut through the crowd to follow him."

Her sharp brown eyes judged him. "Who was it?"

This was where she fired him on the spot or put him on leave for psychological evaluation. "He looked like a Russian arms dealer I'd worked undercover to put away back in Chicago when I first joined the Bureau. But that's impossible. Konrad Bocharov was supposed to be dead. So I called out his name as he was climbing into the back of a car. I swear he recognized me."

He swallowed hard, knowing it sounded crazy. "The face was wrong, but the eyes, body shape, height, the gait, the accent, the voice, the language—shit, even the shape of his ears and skull was right. Everything matched, except for the face."

And faces could be changed.

Jordan felt all the eyes in the vehicle watching him, judging his sanity.

A crinkle formed between the director's brows. "Bocharov was reported blown up by one of his own grenades shortly after he arrived back in Moscow after fleeing Chicago," the director stated.

He leaned back in his seat. "That's the story."

"You think someone was lying?"

"Yes," Jordan said shortly. "I was told they shoveled what was left of that sack of shit into a bag and DNA comparisons confirmed it was Bocharov. That's the only reason I didn't go to Russia to find him and get payback."

"Taking the law into your own hands, Operator Krychek?"

He flicked her a contemptuous glance. "Talk to me after someone locks everyone you love into a house and deliberately burns it to the ground."

Her gaze wavered under his.

"It took time, but I was able to get past it with counseling." Hell, he'd even convinced himself of that lie, enough to pass the polygraph before he returned to duty. "But the fact I saw Bocharov—or any Russian bleeding from a head wound—entering the stairwell off Tremblay's floor seconds after the Frenchman apparently took a nosedive out of a window? That's too big of a coincidence to ignore. That's why I left the hotel with Daisy ASAP. I'd made a tactical error letting the other man know I'd seen him." The realization annoyed him, but how else could he have looked the man in the eye?

"I headed back to the room and a few minutes later the Mexican police were knocking on the door."

"Witnesses say they saw Daisy and Tremblay on the beach in what looked like a romantic assignation."

"You know how reliable eyewitnesses can be. I was there too but wearing dark clothes and I prefer not to stand in the spotlight." He jerked his shoulders. "Gossips like to see what they want to see. You said the Frenchman had a reputation."

"Enough for you to throw him off a balcony and make up some story about seeing a dead Russian arms dealer if he hit on your girl."

"Firstly, she's not a *girl*. She's a grown woman. Second, we're having some fun, not planning a wedding. Thirdly, Daisy chooses who she spends time with. Fourth"—He held Ursula Rhodes' gaze and let her see the trained killer hiding within—"if I'd decided to take François Tremblay out, trust me, no one would have found the body. Finally, why make up a story guaranteed to make me look either paranoid or insane?"

Her mouth pinched but she looked thoughtful now. "You think it was a Russian hit? Why?"

"I don't know, but the FBI needs to investigate the hell out of it. That was a nuclear engineering conference not a fucking makeup convention."

"I am well aware. How long have you been sleeping with Daisy Montana?"

He pulled a face. "Really?"

"She's a convenient cover to be at that conference should someone want to get rid of a certain French professor."

"There is nothing convenient about Daisy, and I don't know enough about the professor to warrant killing him. Plus, I don't work off-book missions." *Aside from acting as an unofficial bodyguard.* "We have the CIA for that shit."

She blew out a frustrated breath. "I need proof this isn't an act, that you and she are actually involved…"

"You want to watch next time?" He shook his head and then relented. "Look, we've been keeping it low key for reasons which have nothing to do with national security."

"Her father." The director's gaze pieced him. "Prove to me it's real."

"How?" He frowned. "By telling you I get tied in knots when I speak to her? Or that she smells like lemons and she looks feminine and sweet but is also incredibly resilient and resourceful?" Not to mention cunning and determined.

"Tattoos?"

"No tattoos. No birthmarks. Today's panties are green, and yesterday's were cream to match her dress if that's any help."

The director was texting. "What else?"

Jesus. He forced himself to remember her naked body which he'd tried so hard to forget. "She has a mole on her right hipbone and another darker one beside her right nipple." And she comes like a rocket being launched into outer space. He scrubbed his face as he tried to get the memory of that out of his brain.

The director texted, and he realized she was giving the info to whoever was with Daisy.

"Are you going to strip search her?" His stomach hit his toes. "You better make damned sure you get a female agent or medical professional and her permission to verify." She was going to go ballistic. Her father would go ape-shit. "I'd rather face whatever bullshit punishment you decide on than subject her to any more of this. She doesn't deserve to be treated like a common criminal."

Rhodes shot him a look. "I could just ask her father."

Jordan gave her a dead-eyed stare. "Then why don't you?"

Her lips pursed as he called her bluff. "What do you think he'll say when he finds out about the two of you sleeping together?"

"What do you think he'll say when he finds out the organization he dedicated his life to treated her like shit?" But Jordan's mouth went dry. Kurt was probably going to throat punch him and cut off his dick. "Look, Daisy is a grown-ass adult, and so am I." He looked out of the window as they passed through Quantico. "Are we done now?"

Her phone dinged, and her eyebrows rose. She cocked her head. "Well, I guess that saves us time." She pointed her screen at Jordan, and he saw a photo of a familiar chest, bra cup covering her nipple but mole on full display as Daisy mugged for the camera. Then a second one of the mole on her hip and the top of her green panties.

Blood heated his skin. Anger made his heart beat harder. He reminded himself this was all for her protection. "The asshole who took those better delete them. They don't need to be entered into some bullshit evidence file. My word should have been enough on this."

Rhodes smiled slowly. "If nothing else, I believe you've seen each other naked and you're jealous as hell, but give me one good reason to believe you about Bocharov?"

This was the heart of it. Not Daisy's privacy. Not his promise to Kurt. The crux was Konrad Bocharov, where he was and what evil he planned to do.

"You don't have to believe me about Bocharov, ma'am." He leaned forward. "The FBI doesn't have to act on this information. Maybe I'm wrong. Maybe I imagined it because of unresolved anger issues and grief triggered by someone who sounded similar to that evil sonofabitch. But what if I'm not wrong? What if I'm right?"

She didn't interrupt so he carried on. "This might be our CIA/FBI pre-9/11 moment where information either isn't shared or isn't acted upon. The biggest terrorist attack in history was about to take place, but they were all so busy protecting their own territory they didn't see it coming. They didn't stop it."

He sat back. "We're meant to be better than that now. So when I observe a man I believe to be a supposedly dead arms dealer at a conference full of nuclear power experts, I have to report it even if it makes me look like a goddamned freak. Just like I have to report that we were chased through the streets of Veracruz, shot at, a radio-tracker attached to my rental vehicle, afterwards." The implications of what Bocharov might be planning made his stomach clench. "You don't have to believe me. You don't have to act. But that doesn't mean I'm wrong. In fact, I know I'm right. Bocharov is alive, and he was at that conference meeting someone, planning something, and it wasn't regarding clean energy. You need to bring in the CIA."

Rhodes smoothed back her long, straight hair, looking less certain now.

"Do you want me to tell the Mexicans, the French, and the

people from IAEA about my suspicions regarding Bocharov? This is what I wanted to check before I spoke with them again."

"Of course not." Her lips pinched. "If you're wrong, I'll look like a fool, and the president will be furious because I'll have made him look like a fool too. He might want to share the Bocharov theory with the Mexican president though."

"Who will tell his advisors. We don't know if we can trust them. We risk spooking Bocharov and letting him and whoever is paying him know that we're onto them." Then he said the thing that scared him most. "If they have plans for a terror attack, it might make them accelerate their schedule before we have time to stop them."

"You already said that Bocharov, if it was Bocharov, recognized you and knows you're onto him." She eyed him shrewdly.

"True."

"What do you think we should do?"

"I think you should publicly reprimand me for leaving Mexico so quickly. Maybe suspend me."

"Trust me, I'm considering it."

He ignored her comment. "Then set up a secret task force based out of Quantico with me on it."

She crossed her long legs. "I'm not sure that would be a good idea."

"No one knows him better than I do. I'm the best resource you have, and we need to figure out what he's planning, fast."

Her foot tapped in the air. "It's been ten years."

"That old adage about leopards not changing their spots is true for a reason. No one can know about it, aside from whoever is in this car and who you decide to put on the task force."

She looked intrigued now. "Why not?"

"Because if Bocharov did fake his own death, we need to figure out how he did it."

"You really believe he had help from inside the FBI?"

"The DNA sample taken from the bomb site was attributed to Bocharov. Either the person who took it was a liar, or it was swapped out after it entered the chain of evidence, or whatever DNA we have in the databases for Bocharov was substituted for whoever was blown to hell in Russia. I don't think he could do that from outside the system. So, yeah, I think it's possible he had help, and we need to figure that out."

She stared at him, intelligent eyes weighing him shrewdly. "Why didn't he kill you? Why only attack your family? You were the one he was angry with. You were the one who betrayed him."

Emotion burned, but he'd learned to control his grief rather than letting his grief control him. "I got close enough that he trusted me, confided in me, and the whole time I was an undercover FBI agent. Worse, a rookie.

"I humiliated him, made him look weak and foolish, and essentially helped destroy his US operation." He still didn't know how Konrad had figured out he was undercover. "He sent a message. You mess with me, I'll kill everyone you love. Killing me would have been too easy. Konrad prefers his victims to suffer." He thought of his mother, grandparents, sister dying in those flames. "The fucker got what he wanted."

Understanding finally began to filter through the director's features. "Why would Konrad Bocharov kill this François Tremblay?"

"I have no clue. We need to dig into every aspect of the Frenchman's life, research, and background, looking for potential links to terrorism." He leaned forward again and watched the bodyguard tense up, as if he couldn't kill the woman in front of him with his bare hands before the bodyguard could reach his service weapon. "One immediate problem, with all this media attention, some of which I suspect is bot-driven, means he'll know Daisy and I are an item. I need to make sure she's safe."

"Yes, you wouldn't want to lose another girlfriend the way you lost the last one."

He flinched at the callousness of her words. Blinked slowly. "Everything that happened to Ellen Mires was a self-inflicted wound. Daisy is an innocent. She's a part of the FBI family by way of Kurt Montana and by way of me—and if you truly understood what it means to be part of the FBI, you'd understand that."

She glared at him.

"As much as I want to be on this task force—as much as that task force *needs* me—Daisy's safety is my priority. Otherwise, I'm done. I'll walk away."

She looked skeptical. She didn't know him. "She needs to answer questions. We can't be seen to be hiding anything."

He nodded. "Agreed."

"Did you tell her of your suspicions regarding Bocharov?"

He shook his head.

The director drew her lips into a tight line, clearly unsure whether or not to believe him.

He pressed his case. "Her expertise is in a similar research area to Tremblay's. I think you should consider, at least temporarily, including her on the task force in an advisory capacity. That way I can be on the task force and at the same time protect her. Assigning her HRT bodyguards to accompany her when she leaves the base in the short term might work in our favor too. It protects her, but also there's a chance it will lead us to Bocharov if he decides to go after her." The thought of using her for bait made him want to vomit, but if she refused any other form of protection, it made tactical sense. "I can persuade Ackers that we could use this as a training exercise because she can't know they're there or she won't cooperate."

Director Rhodes stared at him, considering his arguments.

"If all goes to plan, we'll catch this sonofabitch before he can hurt Daisy or anyone else. Before he can carry out some plan that involves nuclear terrorism. The ball is in your court, Director. What do you want to do?"

13

Daisy tucked her panties back below the waistband of her jeans and then ignored the red-faced Special Agent Crabtree, who'd taken the photos of the side of her breast and her favorite emerald underwear.

Ackers had averted his eyes and stared fixedly out the window. Heaven forbid he see some skin.

"Have you heard anything from my dad? Does he know about any of this?"

Crabtree paled a little at the reminder her father was a senior agent, a hero, who'd recently been held hostage and who'd helped take down a corrupt billionaire and his global empire—a man who was about to replace Ackers as top dog at HRT.

Ackers hesitated. "I texted him to say Jordan had you safe in his custody and not to worry."

She resisted the urge to roll her eyes.

The man watched her with a troubled gaze. "You and Jordan…?"

"Well, he's hard to resist." She gave him her patented sunny smile.

No matter how good his intentions, she hadn't forgiven him for how he'd treated her at certain points last month either.

However, Jordan was the only person she wanted to sleep with as part of her payback strategy—and that was purely personal. An itch she wanted scratched and done. No messy emotions getting in the way, so they could part ways and both carry on doing what they loved.

He certainly wouldn't want more than a short fling. He was even resisting that.

She yawned and stretched out her stiff limbs, a reminder that she'd been trapped in the trunk of a car last night—and how Jordan had calmed her, made her feel safe.

"Any chance of some food? I haven't eaten since last night."

Thirty minutes later, Daisy sat at a table, bit into her slightly cold burger, and decided life could be a lot worse.

Agent Crabtree sat opposite with a stern expression on his narrow face. The other agent had been called away, but the whole setup felt very much like an interrogation. She dipped a salted fry into ketchup and eyed the agent as he surreptitiously watched her eat.

People often underestimated her because of her looks and her stature. Over the years, she'd learned to use that to her advantage. But her grad program was all about the nuts and bolts of nuclear reactors, and her appearance was irrelevant. She'd forgotten how refreshing it was not to be judged on her looks alone.

"Miss Montana—"

"Call me Daisy."

He cleared his throat. "Daisy. I need to ask you some questions about François Tremblay."

"Do investigators from France, Mexico, and IAEA intend to question me too?" She licked the salt off her fingers.

"They do, yes, but the director wants us to question you about what happened first."

She sighed. "I'd rather get it over with in one go if that's okay. I'm tired, and I need a nap."

"I'm not sure that's advisable. I don't mean the nap," he

assured her rapidly. "If you need to lie down somewhere, I'm sure we could arrange it."

"Like, in a cell?" Distaste soured her stomach.

He rubbed the back of his neck as she ate another fry. "That's not what I meant, but I'm unsure of what the facilities here actually entail."

"Where are you usually based?"

He gave her a modest smile. "The J. Edgar Hoover Building. Headquarters. DC."

Headquarters. So he was ambitious. Probably wanted his own field office someday. She could tell that just by looking at his perfectly pressed shirt and sedate blue tie.

"Why can't I get interviewed by everyone at once? Beats getting asked the same questions over and over again. It's not like I have anything to hide." She picked up her burger again and took another big bite.

A knock on the door had Agent Crabtree climbing to his feet and talking with someone. When he came back, he was carrying a printout from a security camera.

She tilted her head and squinted at the zoomed-in image of a man who stared down at the ground about to get in the back of a black car. Not much of his face was visible.

"Who's that?"

"I was hoping you could tell me. Did you ever see this man before? Was he part of the conference delegation?"

She took a bite of spicy pickle. Slowly shook her head. "Not a great photo, but I don't remember ever seeing him. I don't believe he was a delegate, but not everyone attended all the seminars or events." She ran her tongue over her teeth. "Still, he's not familiar."

Who was he? The guy Jordan thought killed Tremblay?

"And what's your relationship with Jordan Krychek for the record?"

Hadn't they already covered this in the vehicle?

"Purely sexual." She wiped the corner of her mouth with a napkin, smirked. "Or, perhaps more accurately, *im*purely sexual."

Those serious eyes held hers. "How does your father feel about the relationship?'

"Are you kidding me?"

"I'm afraid not."

"I'd like to see you ask him that question." She took a long pull on her soda to give her temper time to cool. "Are you a virgin, Agent Crabtree?"

His shoulders went back. "I fail to see how that matters."

"Join the club. I'm trying to create a comparable scenario so you might understand. Did you get permission from your partner's father before you slept with her or him?"

He sighed. "Of course not."

"Did you ever consult your parents before you did the dirty with anyone?"

His cheeks began to redden. "No."

"So why would I? Why are you asking me these asinine questions that have nothing to do with François Tremblay's death?" She popped another fry into her mouth.

"Because there is an eye-witness that places you on the beach sharing a romantic moment with François Tremblay shortly before he was found dead, which is at odds with your claim to be in a relationship with Jordan Krychek."

"Romantic moment. *Jeez*." So much for trying to protect her reputation. Everyone would know her name now for all the wrong reasons. Everyone would believe she'd been having an affair with Tremblay—or worse, that she'd killed him. She had to hope news of her secret, hot, FBI *boyfriend* would be enough to stop people speculating—except it wouldn't, not until they figured out how and why François died.

"I told you already, I did see Professor Tremblay on the beach when I met up with Jordan after the banquet. And, despite what the gossips might allude to, we weren't arranging a threesome in François's room. I'm not *that* adventurous and I doubt Jordan is either, although I've never asked him about multiples."

Her sarcasm seemed to be lost on the agent. "I'm not saying the professor wouldn't have been into it, but Jordan and I had our own plans. We chatted briefly with François. I accepted a glass of wine from him. He's a leader in my field, so I couldn't very well ignore him. Then we went our separate ways."

She thought about the suave, sophisticated man she'd spoken with on the beach. A player, sure, but he hadn't tried to force her—a low bar, but one most women could appreciate. She pressed her lips together. She'd liked the professor more than she'd expected even though he'd tried to proposition her.

"I'm sorry he's dead. I enjoyed his company." She watched Crabtree carefully. "When he left, he seemed fine, happy even." Her voice hitched. "There was no indication he was thinking about taking his own life, even though I know suicidal ideation can be a lot more complex than what people reveal on the outside. But I really don't think that's what happened with Tremblay. He was talking about wanting to be head of the International Atomic Energy Agency one day. It's too big an emotional shift in too short a time for me to believe he took his own life."

Agent Crabtree refused to meet her gaze. "You definitely don't know this man?" He tapped the printout again.

"I have never seen him before." She had a good memory for faces. "Who is he?"

"I'm not at liberty—"

"Oh, for God's sake." She slapped her hand onto the printout before he could remove it, committed those vague features to memory. "Did this man murder Tremblay?"

Crabtree snatched back the printout. "I can't say."

"Can't or won't?" She finished her burger, wiped her mouth. "Can we maybe invite the others inside and get this over with, all in one go? I really don't have anything to hide, and I want to talk to my boss and friends, reassure them I'm okay. My dad, too."

"Well, if you're genuinely okay with that—"

"I am—as long as they are not all delving into my sex life constantly. That's my business. I don't mind telling them I have a partner who's an FBI agent and we were together when Tremblay was killed. But if they start probing for details about Jordan, you shut that shit down, or I'll be calling in a lawyer, and they can go through proper legal channels. I may be open about my sex life, but that doesn't mean I want it on the front pages of some newspaper—nor the fact I was wearing green panties listed in twenty-five different police reports in three different languages with photographic evidence."

He ran a hand under his collar. "I'll verify with them that you're in a relationship with an FBI agent and the two of you were together at Time of Death. That should be good enough to satisfy them."

"As long as they don't decide Jordan and I killed the professor together." She swallowed her last fry with no small amount of regret.

Agent Crabtree mistook her expression. "Just tell the truth, and everything will be fine. But please, don't mention this man." He tapped the photo and then slid it into a file folder that sat in front of him.

"Why would I? I never saw him, and I don't know who he is."

"Excellent. Ready?"

She nodded and prepared to lie her ass off.

14

Jordan sat in a building on the grounds of Quantico known only as Building 64 and stared at the photograph of the man he believed was Konrad Bocharov. A sketch artist sat beside him as they tried to create a fuller image of the Russian's face.

The image had been captured from the adjacent hotel's security feed just before the Russian had climbed into his car. It was pixelated and grainy, but at least it supported that part of Jordan's story—especially as he was also on camera in the background of another image as he chased down the Russian. Despite the terrible angle, the Bureau was running the image through every facial recognition software program they had access to.

No hits so far.

He glanced at his watch. They'd refused to allow him to observe Daisy's interviews, but at least she was nearby—a short walk away in the main Academy building. He figured the more he hovered in a secure space, the more others would suspect they did, indeed, have something to hide. So he forced himself to trust that she could handle herself, and trust Ackers to look out for her best interests.

Director Rhodes had reluctantly agreed to organize a task force to track down Bocharov—or at least determine if the fucker was still alive.

Jordan had zero doubts.

Would Rhodes let him be involved?

She'd be foolish not to, but the potential conflict of interest might make her take the high road. Balancing that against a possible attack with nuclear weapons should be a no-brainer.

What he'd do, if and when he caught up with the Russian, was something he couldn't afford to think about. The desire to hurt the other man was like a physical ache. He wasn't sure he'd be able to resist. They had to catch the sonofabitch first and ascertain the terrorist threat. Neutralize it. Then he could weigh the benefits of revenge versus carrying on in the career he loved.

His insides twisted. The idea of not beating Bocharov to a bloody pulp or not covering him in gasoline and lighting him up felt like a betrayal of the people he'd loved.

Didn't matter. Nothing mattered except finding the bastard.

Analysts were trying to track down the vehicle he'd seen the Russian climbing into before being driven away, in the hopes of collecting fingerprint or DNA evidence.

Nothing yet.

"How's this?" the sketch artist asked.

"Jawline is tighter. Chin not as heavy." He refused to look at the old photo of Bocharov. He didn't want to taint the memory of what he'd seen last night. "Nostrils were broader than you have there, and the cheekbones a little more pronounced."

Assuming this was Bocharov, the guy had undergone major facial reconstruction that would have taken months if not years to complete and recover from.

Had he been blown up by those explosives? But rather than dying he'd miraculously survived? If anyone could, it would be a cockroach like Bocharov. Was that the reason for the extensive surgery? Or was it simply a ruse to avoid detection?

Jordan would bet the farm on the latter.

Had the bastard been in Russia this whole time? Why had he been in Mexico? The timing of the conference on nuclear engineering couldn't be a coincidence. Bocharov never did anything without a reason.

"Any way we can compare Bocharov's ears to this new guy's?" The shape of ears was as unique as a fingerprint.

The sketch artist glanced at the surveillance image. "Not from that angle."

Jordan compressed his lips. "Could he have changed them too, do you think?"

The tech shrugged. "Wouldn't be easy, but then none of this would be easy. Only thing he can't alter to any large degree is his height and his cellular DNA, but ears, yeah, it's possible."

Jordan's phone buzzed. He glanced at the text. Director Rhodes. They'd found the black limo in the mountains, burned out on the side of the road.

Jordan swore.

The registered owner of the company ran a fleet of similar cars. The Bureau was applying for a warrant to covertly access the company's records.

"Everything all right?" The sketch artist was in her mid-fifties, and he'd seen her around the campus, but he'd never worked with her before. Not much call to when he worked Hostage Rescue. She was extremely talented.

"Another dead end." Except it proved the Russian who took off in that vehicle wasn't some innocent tourist. You didn't torch a car and set the cartel on someone, unless you had a big fat reason.

"How's this?" She held up the drawing that looked so alive he wouldn't be surprised if it started breathing on its own.

Jordan scanned the picture and compared it to his memories from last night, that brief glance, then nodded. "That's him."

"I'll load it to the system and see if it gives us any hits."

She gathered her things and left, just as Ackers walked in the room with Daisy in tow.

The relief was instantaneous. Jordan strode over and took her by the shoulders. "You okay?"

She nodded quickly, although she was pale, her lips almost the same shade as her milky cheeks. She crossed her hands over her chest, her expression mutinous.

His stomach twisted. "What did they do?"

"I don't like being treated like a murderer or a slut just because I spoke to some guy on the beach who was known for *his* philandering ways."

Anger snaked through him. "You told them I was there too, right?"

"They made it clear they didn't see having a boyfriend as an obstacle for a woman like me when it came to advancing my career. I felt like I'd traveled back in time sixty years, and then I remembered not that much has actually changed—not when there are people today who believe women shouldn't have a vote. Like we're subhuman."

Anger glittered like shrapnel in her eyes.

It wasn't fair, but he knew investigators often wanted to throw their suspects off by pissing them off or scaring them a little.

"I'm sorry."

"Not your fault—unless you're of a similar opinion, in which case we can skip straight to the goodbyes."

"Believe it or not, I'm not a complete asshole."

She looked unconvinced, which made him feel like a peach.

Ackers watched them together, and Jordan quickly dropped his hands away from her shoulders so that they both stood awkwardly. Then his boss's mustache twitched before he broke out into a full-on smile.

Shit.

So much for being convincing.

Jordan opened his mouth to try to save the situation, but Ackers held up his hand.

"Whatever it is, I don't want to hear it. I still have to report to the director for the next four weeks until Kurt gets back from leave and is ready to take over."

"Do you know who's in charge of this task force?"

Ackers shook his head. "Only that they'll be arriving soon. Director Rhodes isn't confiding in me." He shifted his feet. "I've no idea what made her believe I was running some sort of black-ops mission south of the border, but hopefully she knows better now." He looked from him to Daisy and back. "And I think I have a pretty good idea what's going on. Be careful, is all. The knives are out." His cell buzzed, and he checked it and then put it back in his pocket. "That was admin. We're between New Agent intakes, so the members of the task force will be bunking at the academy for the next week or so."

"Any idea if I'm going to be on it?"

Daisy shot him a frown but didn't speak.

Ackers shook his head.

Jordan turned to Daisy. "I suggested you could be a consultant on the case if you have time, but Rhodes hasn't decided yet. I'll get you set up with somewhere to work, regardless."

"Okay."

"Are you all right?" He touched her arm with concern.

She shrugged. "It's not just being questioned by assholes. I checked social media, and there are thousands of vile comments, death threats, and rape fantasies on my account, plus emails from just about everyone I've ever met wanting to know if I was involved in Tremblay's death."

He swore. "Give me your phone."

She shook her head. "I locked down my accounts. It doesn't matter. It'll blow over. Eventually." She hunched her shoulders.

"We take death threats seriously, Daisy."

"That's not true." Her lips pinched. "I see women in online spaces threatened with rape and murder all the time." The tendons in her hands stood out with strain as she hugged herself. "Nothing ever happens to the assholes."

Shit.

The sheer volume of vitriol made online hate hard to combat. Most offenders never acted on their threats. They hid behind their keyboards and wielded their fake bravado and then pissed themselves when a cop came to the door.

"Let me at least pass the information on to our analysts. See if we can track the source and vet them for threat levels."

"Okay." She nodded, reluctantly.

Jordan sent a text to an analyst he knew in HQ who worked in SIOC and probably saw this sort of thing on a daily basis.

"You look exhausted." As if she might shatter if he touched her. But pissed too. Incredibly pissed.

"I've had better days." Gooseflesh pebbled her skin.

He wanted to wrap his arms around her and warm her up. Something about her expression told him not to touch her.

Which was good.

Touching her led him into all sorts of trouble.

Her cell phone rang, and she looked at the screen. "I have to take this. It's my supervisor. Assuming he hasn't decided to throw me out of the program because he's scared to be in the same room with me now."

She walked away to speak in private and stood staring out of the window.

He hated to see her down, but the past 24 hours—hell, the past two months—had been a lot for anyone.

"You think Bocharov will come after you?" asked Ackers.

Jordan nodded. "I have no doubt of it."

"Isn't having Daisy close by a risk to her safety?"

"Yes, but she's in danger wherever she goes now and, as we know, she isn't a fan of protective custody." Jordan closed his eyes for a brief second and thought of beautiful Ana, who'd had her throat slit for having had sex with him once. He wished more than anything he'd never accepted Kurt's request.

She was in more danger than ever thanks to him, and he didn't think breaking up with her would change that in Bocharov's eyes. She was marked for death.

"Anyone close to me, that includes Daisy and everyone I work with, will be in danger until we neutralize this sonofabitch." He cleared his throat. "You need to warn everyone at HRT, including support staff."

Ackers nodded. "I can do that. I can arrange a room for you both at the academy for tonight also."

"That would be great, short term." Jordan nodded his thanks. "Can you arrange for my place to be swept, including getting a bomb dog in there? And how about we reactivate those cameras TacOps installed around my place a couple of weeks ago?" He remembered something else. "My closest neighbors gave me a key to their place as they're off for six months in Australia and New Zealand. Told me I could use it for emergencies. We could set up surveillance and some sort of quick reaction force there."

Ackers frowned. "Good idea. I'm fine with forming a covert protection detail. Gold Team have been twiddling their thumbs since they got back from the Caribbean."

Hardly.

"However," he lowered his voice. "That request to TacOps might come better from you than me. Jon Regan hates my guts."

The two didn't get along.

"I'll call him." *And Cisco.*

Jordan straightened as six people he recognized walked into the room, including Jon Regan and Florence Cisco, who sent him a warning look, and one of the agents who'd interrogated Daisy earlier.

At least, he now knew who was running the task force—ASAC Steve McKenzie, a hard-nosed, but competent supervisor from HQ, who'd worked with HRT while Jordan had traveled across the African continent with Kurt. With him were Alex Parker, a civilian cybersecurity expert who regularly consulted for the FBI. And Detective Tobias Granger, a man who'd once been Jordan's best friend and whom he hadn't spoken to since the night his family were murdered.

His mouth went dry.

Daisy came to his side, and he was surprised but grateful when she slipped her hand into his. Not because he deserved the comfort. But because they still had a relationship to sell and he'd completely forgotten about everything except the memories of that awful night a decade ago.

15

Introductions were made and Daisy watched Chicago PD Detective Tobias Granger send Jordan a wary look as he held out his hand. She felt strangely protective of the big, tough Hostage Rescue operator, and she wasn't sure why.

Agent Crabtree watched them avidly. Had the director sent him to spy on them?

"It's been a long time, Jordan. How've you been?" Granger asked.

"You two know each other?" She was surprised, maybe because she knew so little about Jordan that didn't relate to HRT.

"From all the way back in high school."

High school? She'd never thought about Jordan being a child.

"Tobias joined the Chicago PD same time I went into the Army." Jordan shifted his weight as he quickly withdrew his hand from the other man's grasp.

"And we both somehow ended up in law enforcement." The detective shot her a strained smile.

"When Tobias heard I'd joined the FBI, he put in a request to the Chicago Field Office that they set me up with a fake background and kick me straight undercover in my hometown."

She cocked her head. "I thought undercover agents avoided working where they were known?"

"Yeah, to protect their homes and their families." Jordan's voice was flat, devoid of emotion.

Foreboding crawled over her skin.

"It was my call. My poor judgment," Tobias admitted with a tight swallow. "We'd been chasing Bocharov for years. CPD tapped me when I was a beat cop because people me and Jordan both knew from school were working for the Russian Mafia in West Town. We needed someone on the inside, but the asshole wouldn't accept anyone unless they were personally vouched for by one of his contacts."

"If they got it wrong, they died."

Granger's Adam's apple bobbed in his throat.

"Bocharov?" Daisy hadn't heard that name before.

A slight sneer twisted Jordan's lips.

The detective winced.

So Bocharov was the name of the man in the photo. The man Jordan believed killed François. The man Jordan thought might want to harm her.

Steve McKenzie—Mac—who was apparently the boss of this group sent the detective a quelling look.

"Ms. Montana, you can temporarily consider yourself a civilian consultant assigned to this task force, but you can't talk about anything you hear outside of these confines, understood?"

Daisy eyed the tall man. "Understood." She wasn't stupid. "But I don't have much time to spare you. I have work to carry out for my thesis next week, so you'll have to do without my *expertise* then. And, no, I can't put it off." She gave a humorless smile. "Nuclear reactors wait for no woman."

She was more interested in why Jordan had gone rigid like a piece of hardwood when Detective Granger had walked in. There was something going on there. Something important from their shared history, and she wanted to know what it was. "You persuaded the FBI to allow Jordan to come work undercover in Chicago?"

"Yeah." The detective was a good-looking guy with thick, black hair and thick brows, but something nameless and heavy rode his features. "A lot of our friends from school ended up on the wrong side of the law. Dealers. Thieves. Fixers. Enforcers. It was well known I'd joined the force, so I wasn't a good fit for undercover work, but not many people knew what happened to Jordan after he left, except that he'd enlisted. I happened by his family's bakery to buy bread for my wife who was pregnant with our first child at the time."

Bakery?

She shot Jordan a look, but he wouldn't meet her gaze.

"No one baked bread like Jordan's *baba*." He sucked in his upper lip as if suppressing emotion. "She, er, knew we'd been tight back in school. We were both on the basketball team and competed in track. Hung out. Knew I was a cop. Took me aside and told me Jordan was at the academy. She wouldn't have told just anyone. The family is told to keep it a secret, and being associated with the FBI wasn't something she'd have talked about in that neighborhood, no matter how proud she was of him."

Jordan flinched.

"FBI agreed with the request as it was believed Bocharov was moving military-grade weapons across state and international borders and had links to major money laundering outfits and probably the Kremlin. They rewrote Jordan's background from after he left the Army. Put him in fictional lockup for a while. Kept it down south where the records can be spotty and depend on the local sheriff as much as anything else. Spoke to the right people with the right things so the backstory was thoroughly backstopped. He came back to Chicago and accidentally-on-purpose bumped into a guy we'd both gone to high school with at a local bar. Asked him if he knew of any jobs going. Micky introduced Jordan to Bocharov."

"Apparently, I was a very convincing bad guy and worked for

Bocharov for six excruciating months before the DA finally decided we had enough evidence for RICO charges to stick. Plan was to move my family into protective custody"—he shot her a grim smile because he knew how much she hated forced confinement—"and put the bakery under police guard while we served warrants and swept up Bocharov and all of his cronies and put them in prison where they belonged. Other gangs in the city wouldn't cry any tears. He supplied them with weapons, so they tolerated him, but there was no love lost."

Daisy gripped Jordan's hand like she was hanging off a cliff. She had a terrible feeling she knew where this was going.

Jordan's expression hardened. "The police department fucked up."

Tobias hunched his shoulders, shook his head but not with denial. "We don't know how, but somehow Bocharov discovered that Jordan was undercover FBI."

"What happened?" Looking around at all the faces, she realized they all knew. Everyone except her. Even Agent Crabtree knew.

Tobias opened his mouth to answer, but Jordan dropped her hand and took a step forward, fists clenched. "Enough. You don't get to talk about my family. Hell, you don't even get to utter their names."

She knew then.

They'd died.

Because of this Bocharov monster.

The ghosts in Jordan's eyes were his lost family.

She tried to take his hand again, but he pulled away. Then he paced in a tight circle with his hands clasped behind his head, clearly distressed.

"You going to be able to handle this, Operator Krychek?" McKenzie asked quietly. "There's no shame if the answer is 'no.'"

Crabtree's eyes darted, gathering information, presumably to report back to Ursula Rhodes.

Jordan took a moment to compose himself. "I can handle it. I just don't think what happened to my family needs to be openly discussed. It's in the files. Read it if you need to remind yourself what's at stake and whom to trust." He pointed straight at the cop. "But he doesn't get to talk about them as if CPD didn't sign their death warrants."

The knife-edge tension in the room made Daisy's heart squeeze in sympathy.

"Well, if introductions are finished, let's get started, shall we?" Mac announced. "I'm going to speak to Ms. Montana about how the type of work François Tremblay did could be weaponized. Regan and Cisco will be setting up equipment to examine all the footage from the hotel and the surrounding area in Mexico in the days prior to Tremblay's death, while simultaneously running the facial recs on the image we have, plus the sketch from the sketch artist, and then any other images we find. They'll be cross-checking with legal points of entry just in case we get lucky. Alex Parker has kindly offered some of his own time to see if we can track Bocharov's activity on the Dark Web. Jordan, you're with him, giving any breadcrumbs you can think of. Parker also plans to trace whoever shut down the camera system during that vital time period at the hotel."

Daisy intercepted the look Florence Cisco sent Jordan. Jon Regan crossed his arms and stared pointedly at his feet.

Daisy didn't know what to make of that exchange.

"Detective Granger is going to work with Agent Crabtree and start runs on the conference delegates and anyone else staying at the hotel. Looking for possible connections to Bocharov. I have a couple more agents joining us later this afternoon, and they can help with that. Plus, we've recruited a former CIA officer with Russian expertise to come onboard as a consultant."

Alex Parker narrowed his gaze.

Daniel Ackers cleared his throat. "HRT would like to be involved as long as we don't get a call out. We plan to check Operator Krychek's house for explosives, etc."

Jordan addressed Regan and Cisco. "Hoping TacOps could reactivate all the bells and whistles you guys set up last month."

Regan shrugged. "Sure. Cisco can handle that. You aren't idiot enough to actually plan to stay there, are you?"

"Why wouldn't he?" Daisy asked.

"Well, because if Bocharov knows the location, what's to stop him hitting it with a drone strike?"

Her eyes popped wide.

Jordan rubbed his brow as he swore. "We need to draw this sonofabitch out, but I won't place others in danger." He sent her a look of apology. "If he thinks I'm alone and unprotected, he won't send a drone. He'll try for me himself."

"And, what?" she snapped. "You'll just fight him?"

Agent Crabtree leaned forward.

Jordan's mouth tightened. "Arrest him."

"What's to stop him sending a mini army?"

"We'll have HRT positioned nearby."

Daisy took a step back. "You'd endanger yourself in order to confront him? Endanger your teammates?"

"To put this guy out of commission?" His expression turned mean. "Hell, yes. And my teammates are not civilians, and neither am I. This is what we do. You know that. But don't worry, we'll keep you somewhere safe."

Keep you somewhere safe?

Fury rushed through her. Her suitcase was just outside the door in the hallway, and she marched out of the room without another word and grabbed it.

Jordan scrambled to follow. "Daisy."

She hurried outside and across the grass, dragging the stupid case with her. Why had she packed so much stuff?

"Daisy."

Words could barely squeeze past the anger closing her throat. "I'm leaving."

He grabbed her arm. "You can't—"

She turned the move into a flip that had him flat on his back.

No one put hands on her. Not like that. She leaned down and drilled her finger into his chest, where he lay on the ground.

"Do *not* tell me what I can and can't do. I am sick of you people thinking you can order me around. Am I under arrest?"

He cocked his head as he stared up at her, a matching anger spiking in his eyes. "You know you're not."

She turned away frustrated. Why had she expected better from him? Because despite all her tough self-talk, it turned out she had a weakness for men like this, and if anyone ever accused her of having daddy issues, she'd break both their fucking arms.

She grabbed her case and marched on. Decided she should be able to arrange a cab from the main office at the Academy building so headed in that direction. With her luck she'd bump into one of her interrogators from earlier and they'd arrest her for being…a woman or something.

"Daisy…" Jordan implored, following her.

She whirled. "It took you ten minutes to go straight back to being a controlling jackass." Her heart thumped erratically, and a lot of that was hurt. "You acted all reasonable in Mexico, and then as soon as you're back here, it's *Daisy do this. It's for your own good, but you're doing it regardless.*" She sucked in a breath. "I don't need anyone telling me what to do, even if it's for my own damned good!"

The fact she was yelling at the top of her lungs gained attention from everyone within hearing distance. Several people turned toward them.

Great.

Now she was going to get arrested for being loud.

Jordan caught her fingers, but gently. Her limbs were shaking.

She lowered her voice. "You don't get to put me in a box when I'm not convenient to you anymore, Jordan. You don't get to decide for me what is safe and what is dangerous. I am not your *responsibility*." She spat out the words between clenched teeth.

"I'm sorry. I'm genuinely sorry." His eyes went shiny with what looked suspiciously like tears, and she froze. "The thought of Bocharov doing to you what he did to my sister, my mother, my grandparents made me lose it for a moment." He dragged his hand through his hair. "If I fail to protect you the way I failed to protect them," the words were honest and raw, "it would destroy me this time."

Her heart pounded, and her throat ached.

"What did he do to them?" Her voice was a thin whisper.

His eyes raised to the sky, and she watched his throat constrict as he swallowed. "He burned them alive."

Horror washed through her. That was so much worse than she'd imagined, and yet, she'd instinctively known they'd suffered terribly. She put her hand on his arm. "You don't have to tell me anything else. That's enough."

He shook his head. "No, you have a right to know what we're dealing with. I'm asking you to trust me. I'm making promises to keep you safe that I may not be able to keep. You deserve to know the truth about who I am and who he is." He inhaled deeply. "He will kill you to get to me. If nothing else, you need to believe that."

His ghostly blue-green eyes held hers.

"The night before we were supposed to arrest him, Bocharov sent me on some bullshit mission across town. He was in a pissy mood at the club, but he was often in a pissy mood, so I didn't suspect I was blown." He laughed, a small bitter sound that rattled along with the branches on the trees. "If I was blown, I figured I'd get a bullet in the brain and an unmarked grave somewhere in Cook County. But he liked me—my family was originally from Ukraine and so was his grandmother, so we both spoke a little of the language." His expression twisted with remembered antipathy. "I went to deliver the arms as instructed. I never suspected..." He shook his head, the haunted expression firmly back in place. "You don't argue with the boss. Not in the *bratva*. He sent me to do a job, and if I wanted to keep everything smooth until he was picked up by CPD, then I had to do what he told me."

"*Bratva?*"

"Russian Mafia."

She squeezed his arm.

"I knew something wasn't right, but there was no cell service at the meeting place. I waited half an hour after the buyers were supposed to show, longer than I normally would, so that Konrad wouldn't start a war and inadvertently jeopardize our arrest plans. Called my FBI handler on the way back. She told me something had happened at the bakery, and I knew. I just fucking knew. I drove like a lunatic, but I didn't get there in time. The firefighters held me back. They couldn't get inside either. The fire was too fierce. It had taken time for the fire engines to get close enough to get to work. The roads had been blocked with cars and a dumpster."

Daisy made a sound of distress, but Jordan wasn't seeing her right now.

"Bocharov or one of his goons started a fire on the ground floor beneath where my family lived, and then they barricaded the doors so when they tried to escape they couldn't." He clenched his fists. "My sister broke an upstairs window to climb out but they shot her, drove her back inside. My *baba* couldn't have climbed to safety anyway, nor my Pop. My mother wouldn't have left any of them."

She watched him force back the emotions that were surely ripping him apart.

The tears shone, but they didn't fall. "When the firefighters found them the next day, they were all together, all holding one another even though they'd died in agony. They never let go. They died because of me."

"No."

"Yes." He swiped his forearm over his eyes. "They died because Bocharov wanted to punish me. He also slit the throat of a stripper I had sex with once and the man who vouched for me, even though that guy was completely loyal to Bocharov and hated my guts. He also killed four police officers who were on surveillance duty that night." He opened his eyes, and his feelings were laid bare in their depths. "I couldn't bear if the same thing happened to you, Daisy. *That's* why I'm controlling. Not because I'm an asshole, or not *just* because, but because he would kill you as easily as most people order a coffee. He'd kill you and enjoy doing it, and it would be my fault. I can only kill him once, but he can kill me in a thousand different ways."

She trembled with a mix of anger and heartbreak. "I'm sorry. I'm so sorry."

They stared at one another for a long moment, but she couldn't move. All his truths were alive in his eyes, and some of those truths were the way he felt about her. Not because she was Kurt Montana's daughter, but because she was her. And that scared her.

"I know I fucked up, Daze. It's the easiest thing in the world for me to give orders and expect them to be obeyed."

Her breath shuddered.

"But you're not in the FBI. You're not a criminal. You're you. Smart. Independent. Unpredictable." His smile wobbled. "Beautiful, especially when you're angry."

It sucked the air right out of her lungs to see a man like this so openly emotional, but she wasn't backing down. "You don't get to put me in a box. Not without my permission."

"Definitely no boxes. I know how you feel about boxes." He took a cautious step toward her. "I should have consulted you. Gotten your opinion. In the heat of the moment, I reverted to trying to impose what I thought was best on you. I should know better by now."

She nodded. "You should. Despite what you think, I'm not stupid, and I'm not reckless. At least, no more than you are."

He took another tentative step until he was almost touching her. "Let's go back inside and see what ideas we can come up with as a group to draw Bocharov out while keeping you—*us*," he corrected quickly, "safe."

"There's no such thing as a hundred-percent safe, Jordan."

"I know. But we can make it as difficult as possible for the sonofabitch." He pushed her hair back behind her ears even though the wind ruffled it again.

She swallowed and leaned against him, raised her face to his. They had an audience at the window. "You know you're going to have to kiss me now, right?"

"Yeah. And not just any kiss. A make-up kiss." He sounded resigned. He put his hands around her waist and lifted her up until she was looking down at him.

"Do your best not to enjoy it." Her lips twitched into a grudging smile.

"No promises." He moved in to take her lips in the sort of kiss that they wrote romance novels about. It hit her like a lightning bolt that electrified her bones and sparked across every nerve with heated pleasure. She tingled, everywhere. Moaned as she wrapped her arms tight around his neck and kissed him even deeper.

He slowly pulled back and let her slide down his body, allowing her to feel every solid inch of him.

She wanted to be with him tonight. For comfort. Not because she had feelings for the guy except, of course, she did. She liked him. Enjoyed him. Admired him. When he wasn't being a dick. It didn't mean she was emotionally involved. She knew this wouldn't lead anywhere, didn't want it to, but, damn, the man was hot when he let his guard down.

Thankfully, he ruined her witless mooning by opening his mouth.

"Trust me. I won't let anything bad happen to you."

She cupped his cheek then tapped it, sharply. "You can't make those kind of promises, Jordan. You can't control everything."

"I can damned well try."

"Then control this. Get me a weapon. Dad has a safe full of them back at his place, and he trained me well. I have a license to carry concealed. If this guy comes for me and you aren't around, I want to have at least a chance of defending myself."

Jordan stared down at her for one long moment, and she thought he was going to argue, probably about him always being around, but that wasn't going to happen, and they both knew it.

"Not possible on FBI grounds, but I'll see what I can do for when you're not."

She rose up on tiptoes and kissed him again. Watched his nostrils flare and his eyes darken as she sank back down. "I'll even promise not to shoot you when you say stupid things."

One side of his mouth curved up in a grin, and he clicked his tongue against his cheek. "I think you're going to regret making that promise."

"Me too, babe. Me too."

16

Jordan entered the classroom in Building 64, still thinking about the practicalities of arming Daisy when Jon Regan hooked an arm around his neck and pulled him close enough to whisper in his ear.

"If you get one of my agents into shit with the director, I will personally end you."

Jordan caught the worried look Cisco sent them both and refrained from violently shoving Regan aside.

"I have no intention of implicating her in anything."

"Yeah," Regan let him go with a playful shove, "but you're not the one digging into it, are you?"

They both glanced at Alex Parker who was working with one of his analysts, picking through the dubious offerings of the Dark Web.

No point arguing Cisco hadn't disabled the feeds during Tremblay's murder. Accessing security feeds without a warrant, especially in a foreign country, could be grounds for dismissal or even criminal charges.

"Dammit, Regan." Jordan dragged his hand through his hair and kept his voice low enough that the director's snoop couldn't overhear. "If I'd had any idea what was going to happen, I'd never have asked her to help me access those feeds."

"Yeah," Regan stared at the floor, hands on hips. "But if you hadn't been there maybe we'd be having to help Kurt figure out how to conduct a Mexican jailbreak, so I guess there's that. I'll talk to Parker, but if you want something in the future, you come to me. Understood?"

Jordan inhaled and nodded gratefully. He didn't care what happened to him. But he hated the idea Cisco would be punished or lose her job for doing what was supposed to be a harmless favor.

A woman with short blonde hair knocked on the door. Jordan recognized the crisis negotiator behind her as he'd worked with the guy many times. Max Hawthorne.

"Lucy Aston." Jon Regan whistled. "I thought you retired."

She gave him a dazzling smile as she came inside and received a warm hug from the usually acerbic man. "I definitely retired from that *which-shall-not-be-named*, but I'm taking a little time figuring things out before I start my next job." She smiled up at Hawthorne, and Jordan realized there was more than professional appreciation in that exchange. "Patrick Killion contacted me about consulting on a case. Said there was some possible Russian involvement?"

Steve McKenzie and Alex Parker both stood and introduced themselves.

Jordan nodded to Max. "You being assigned to this task force too?"

Max pulled a face. "I'm just showing Lucy where you're at."

"Pity."

"You think you'll need a negotiator?" Max sounded hopeful.

Jordan looked at Daisy, enthusiastically shaking Lucy's hand. "Only in my personal life. Lucy's a Russian expert?"

Max's expression grew somber. "Unfortunately."

"She any good?"

"The best."

That was reassuring to hear. Hawthorne clapped him on the back and took his leave as Lucy grabbed a seat.

"So, Konrad Bocharov was before my time," Lucy began, "but I read up on the case when I was doing my training, and I'm familiar with the work you guys did." She looked first at Tobias Granger and then at him. Jordan flinched away from the pity in her pretty hazel eyes. "And the revenge he took on your family. I'm afraid you've become a cautionary tale at the Agency."

He hardened himself against the resentment. He *was* a cautionary tale. "Have there been any rumors at the Agency of Bocharov still being alive?"

"Not that I am aware of." She steepled her fingers in front of her. "The thing is, I was thinking—Russia has suffered quite a few defeats in the past couple of years. The Russian Ambassador being shot to death in DC along with his personal assistant." She swallowed tightly. "They lost a couple of their long-term assets during that fiasco too."

Regan shook his head. "Scarlett Stone sure kicked the hornets' nest with that party trick."

"Do you blame her?" Parker asked.

Regan scratched the side of his neck. "Not even a little bit. But I sure as hell wish we hadn't fallen for their bullshit in the first place."

"No argument from me," Parker agreed.

Lucy continued. "Then Vladimir Ranich was picked up on terrorism charges last summer along with a whole host of other arms dealers who tried to buy weaponized anthrax in the French Riviera."

Regan swore. "It's like playing goddamned whack-a-mole."

Parker took a drink from a bottle of water in front of him. "You think Bocharov is responding to a gap in the market?" The idea seemed to bother him.

Lucy's lips formed a canted line. "I don't think that type of person ever stops looking for opportunities." She glanced around their group. "I wonder—and this is pure speculation—but I wonder if Bocharov may have been part of Ranich's operation and, with his boss's imprisonment, is now able to exert his influence more. Climb the ladder, so to speak."

Granger spoke. "He probably had some groveling to do when he crawled back to Moscow with his tail between his legs. Probably one of the reasons he was so violent when he discovered he'd been compromised."

Jordan crossed his arms and tried not to react to the word "violent" in relation to his beloved family. "You don't think Bocharov perhaps planned to escape his Russian masters as well as us?"

"I guess that depends on whether or not the man you saw is truly Bocharov. If it is, then no, because throwing a nuclear scientist out of a window is a sure-fire way to catch the attention of his former masters back in the Kremlin, and I don't think he'd risk it."

"It's definitely Bocharov."

"We're still waiting on the Mexican authorities to analyze blood samples found in Tremblay's room to confirm," McKenzie interrupted.

"It's him," Jordan insisted. And from Lucy's deduction, that meant Moscow was still running the bastard.

Lucy wore a sparkly diamond on her ring finger which she kept glancing at. He hadn't realized Max was serious about anyone. Romance seemed to be contagious as half the confirmed bachelors he knew seemed to be getting hitched lately.

He glanced at Daisy who was glued to Lucy's every word.

Looked away, unsettled.

"We also had that situation up in Maine where the FBI killed one of their scientists and detained an old KGB operative who the CIA secreted away somewhere unknown. That would have been a major blow to their egos." Lucy looked at Daisy when she spoke. Most of the others were already briefed on these older cases. She cleared her throat. "And, over Christmas, I was part of a group that broke up a sophisticated Russian spy ring in Argentina, and we arrested one of the Kremlin's pet oligarchs, Boris Yahontov."

Jordan's eyes widened. He'd heard about that. Operation

Soapbox. Hard not to, even on a road trip across sub-Saharan Africa.

"Yahontov was found dead in his cell two days ago, a supposed suicide—the day before he was due to be extradited to the US on money laundering charges." Lucy's face was expressionless, but everyone was thinking the same thing.

Assassinated before he could talk.

Shit.

"They ever catch Anatoly Agapov?" asked Parker.

"A Russian spymaster who thought he'd turned me into a double agent, who disappeared with a bunch of cash in December," Lucy explained. "No, they never caught him, but I have no doubt he'd have headed back to the Motherland with his tail between his legs, begging for forgiveness with some wild plan to extract revenge."

That didn't sound good.

Jordan leaned back in his chair. "The Russians are pissed. What's new?"

A flutter of uncertainty crossed her features. "Well, this isn't based on any rigorous analysis. It's based on my interactions with them over the years and how they think. The US has dealt them a series of devastating blows over the past eighteen months, and they haven't reciprocated. Worse, the last blow was dealt to them by a woman they thought they owned. They'd hate that more than anything."

She was right.

From his personal experience and deep Ukrainian roots, he knew exactly where she was going with this. "They're looking for a win."

"That's what I'm afraid of, yes. A big win." Lucy met his gaze. "When Killion asked me to be part of this task force, initially I said no. I'm out of the game and probably heading to the State Department for a cushy translator job. However, when he mentioned the nuclear aspect, I couldn't refuse. They might crave revenge, but they'll want plausible deniability to stop the US from retaliating by dropping a bomb on the Kremlin."

Jordan stared hard at the blonde woman. "They'll muddy the waters."

"Always." She pointed at Jordan. "So, first we need to identify the man you saw in Mexico. Then we need to figure out if he killed François Tremblay—who had no known connections to Russians or arms dealers in general. Then figure out why. At the same time, we need to discern what the potential threats might be and see if we can get eyes and ears on their operation. Homeland, NSA, and CIA should all be updated and asked to weigh in with any pertinent information, as should Counterintelligence in WFO."

"You want to lead this task force?" Mac joked. "Because you're doing a hell of a job."

She went bright red. "No, sorry I—"

"I'm kidding, except for the part where you're doing a great job. Appreciate you coming out of retirement as my experience has largely focused on domestic terrorism. I'd appreciate you working with Detective Granger on vetting the other attendees and people seen at the hotel. Agent Crabtree—track down the contact details of all the Russian specialists in all the departments Lucy named. Okay, people, let's get to work."

Jordan watched the group scatter to their assigned tasks, a well-oiled machine gearing up to hunt a ghost. *His* ghost. His personal nightmare.

Lucy might be brilliant at what she did, but she was wrong about one thing. The Russians didn't just want a win.

They wanted blood.

And Bocharov had already proven whose blood he preferred to spill.

Jordan's gaze drifted to Daisy.

How was he going to keep her safe from this new and terrible threat? He'd promised Kurt he'd protect her, but instead he'd painted a giant bullseye on her back. And Bocharov wouldn't stop until she was dead.

17

Mac leaned over the table as Daisy showed him some basic schematics for small modular reactors—SMRs— on her laptop, which had been François Tremblay's area of expertise.

"It's a mini nuclear reactor, which has the advantage of being able to be set up in more locations. They could be advantageous for remote communities and space exploration. Tremblay's lab has been working on increasing the fuel efficiency of the current designs because they're not as good as the more common, large light-water reactors and use more raw uranium."

"Safety-wise, would they be easier to exploit for a would-be terrorist than one of the bigger sites?" Mac had a serious demeanor, but there was a wicked glint in his eyes when something amused him. He wasn't amused right now.

Daisy frowned. "It's hard to say. Most reactors, regardless of size, should have excellent security, but with anything that involves humans, well…"

"A cynic after my own heart."

She tried to imagine how a terrorist might view it. "We're told the safety features on large-scale, modern reactors make them unappealing for terrorist attacks."

"That's how we want to keep it."

Why was he talking to her? A lowly grad student. "Surely the FBI has experts on nuclear threats?"

"Yes, ma'am. Expecting one of the WMD guys from SIOC to join the task force once we *prove* a connection to Bocharov, but until then the director is reluctant to jump the gun so to speak. I appreciate you giving me a rundown on this so I don't look like a complete moron when he turns up."

"Somehow I doubt anyone thinks you're a moron."

"You haven't met my fiancée."

She laughed.

"Talk me through the safety features, one-by-one."

She pulled up another basic diagram from the internet.

"In broad terms, as all sites will vary in how they're set up, we have the three Cs. First, is control. We have to *control* the reaction. Under normal operations, we do this with control rods which absorb neutrons and slow down the reactions inside the reactor. They can be inserted deeper into the reactor core or removed, depending on if we want to increase or decrease the rate of the chain reaction.

"For emergency situations, we have systems that allow us to inject material into the core to poison and stop the chain reaction —Xenon-135 usually. These backup systems aren't reliant on the power grid and can be manually activated if necessary."

She took a sip of the coffee Jordan had brought over earlier. She was trying not to think too much about that kiss. Trying not to think too much about how his past had moved her.

"Next we have the second 'C.' The *cooling* element. In the most basic terms, nuclear fission produces heat, which produces steam that turns turbines and produces electricity for the grid. But if the core gets too hot, it's going to damage the integrity of the rods and housing, and that's bad. So we need to cool the reactor to prevent the core from overheating."

"Meltdown."

Daisy nodded. "Which would be bad."

The glint appeared. "Even I know that much."

Daisy grinned. "Generally, water is pumped from a lake or reservoir to cool down the fuel rods. Facilities rely on the main electrical grid for this, but most sites have at least two backup generators to keep water flowing in an emergency. This was the problem at Fukushima. The main electrical system was knocked out by the initial earthquake. Then, while they were trying to fix that issue, they were hit by the thirteen-meter-high tsunami, which took out the backup generators and killed the technicians who were trying to fix the problem. After that, they lost the ability to cool down the core, and the result was a meltdown in three of the six reactors."

"Could it have been avoided?"

"According to after-accident reports and 20-20 hindsight, sadly, yes. They should have prepared for the possibility of an earthquake and tsunami in that area. Unfortunately, the safety culture of the company at the time was reported to be an issue—a common denominator for all three major nuclear accidents: Chernobyl, Three Mile Island, and Fukushima Daiichi—which blows my mind when you're working with something as dangerous as radiation. People have to be able to challenge authority and safety practices without fear of losing their jobs. Otherwise, people keep their mouths shut. Japan had a very hierarchal system, as is their culture. Chernobyl was dealing with a bad design, bad safety protocols, and everyone being too scared to admit when someone fucked up because they feared the consequences." She leaned back in her chair. "They should have respected the science. Regulatory agencies need to be independent and do their jobs. They should inspect the shit out of places and not let safety regs be voluntary for commercial companies."

Mac grunted and pointed to a line on the screen. "So taking out the cooling abilities would trigger a meltdown?"

"Not *necessarily*," Daisy said cautiously. "Not if they can shut down the reactors safely first. Plus, there are additional systems in most places to make sure the flow of cool water over the rods continues, such as pressurized nitrogen and other methods to move water while repairs are made."

A frown crumpled his brow. "Why was Chernobyl so much worse than Fukushima?"

"The third 'C.' *Containment*. Containment of the radiation starts with ceramic pellets holding the radioactive material—typically in the form of enriched uranium oxide. These pellets are housed inside a rod commonly made of zircaloy that is resistant to heat and corrosion. The work I'm doing with my supervisor is on making pellets and rods even safer and more efficient. Rods are loaded into pressure tubes and those, in turn, are housed inside a metal framework that is situated inside a reinforced concrete vault. Then there should be a containment structure made of reinforced concrete and steel around the whole reactor. Chernobyl didn't have one. Fukushima did."

"So," Mac stated, "the three Cs for nuclear safety are control, cooling, containment."

"Exactly."

He picked things up fast. Most of the people she'd met who worked for the FBI did. Except for Blue Team. Blue Team were losers.

"And safety protocols exist so that if something goes wrong with one of the three Cs, the other safeguards come into play?"

Daisy nodded. "They're complex systems but surprisingly robust nowadays."

Mac's lips firmed. "But not infallible?"

"Not infallible, no." Daisy held his serious gaze. The first real whisper of fear skated across her shoulders. "If they took out any of the safety systems before the reactor could be shut down, then a power plant could be in serious trouble."

Could a Russian arms dealer really be planning to attack a nuclear facility? It was speculation, that was all. Even if they were planning an attack, it didn't have to be in the US. It could be anywhere.

"Why would someone, a terrorist for example, deliberately

target smaller reactors rather than the larger ones? Seems like the larger ones could potentially cause a lot more damage."

She frowned. "Some of the arguments against the SMRs are that people think the safety protocols may not be as robust, and that the reactors are less efficient and produce more waste than a typical reactor. And they don't know how they'll withstand natural disasters such as an earthquake or tsunami—like the one that hit Fukushima. Or how wildfires might destroy the surrounding buildings and infra-structure. And they don't know how they might be targeted by hostile nations."

"Which is essentially our concern too."

"Yup." Daisy covered a yawn. No matter the seriousness of the threat, it had been an exhausting 24 hours.

"Who'd be dumb enough or evil enough to target a nuclear facility though?" Mac's brows crunched. "They can't dictate which way the wind blows."

"And radiation is an all-inclusive killer."

Mac raised his head. "Is it possible someone was interested in Tremblay's research to target a specific facility?"

"I guess." She frowned. "But why kill him? Seems to me someone with bad intentions could find out how these things work better by leveraging someone who works at a specific facility or an engineer familiar with the project."

"Or attend a conference on nuclear engineering?" Mac's mouth smiled, but his eyes didn't.

She stared at her screen. "That level of information would be way over most people's heads and not specific to any one facility. I struggled with some of the talks that were heavy on theoretical physics."

"I'd be asleep in under a minute." Mac's jaw flexed under his fingers.

"François might have had blueprints or designs of systems on his laptop, but they didn't steal the laptop, right?"

"It was still in his room, although no telling if someone had gotten into it or not. I appreciate the overview, Daisy. I have to admit this stuff scares the shit out of me—this and biological and chemical warfare."

"That's what sparked my interest. How can I make it safer?"

"I admire your dedication." He took a sip of his own coffee. "So you and Jordan Krychek, huh?" His lips tweaked. "I can't wait to hear what your father thinks about that."

"Why are you all obsessed with what my father thinks about *my* sex life?"

"Revenge." He huffed out a deep laugh. "We've had to put up with him all these years. Don't worry, I'll leave it alone. I already have enough ammunition with him marrying a much younger woman." He grew serious. "I was damned glad to get him back in one piece."

Emotion clogged her throat. "Me too."

"But it doesn't mean I'm not gonna bust his balls at every opportunity."

"Whose balls?" Jordan came over with a wary expression on his face.

Mac's eyes glinted again, but he gave her a wink. "Anyone who doesn't help me figure out if this sonofabitch is who we think he is."

"I'm sure."

"Which is why we're all here, Krychek. Any sign of him on the Dark Web?"

The man called Alex Parker spoke up. "Not exactly."

"What does that mean?" Mac asked impatiently.

Jordan answered, "Too many potential arms dealers on the Dark Web to know for sure. We do know he didn't reuse any of the old bank accounts or IP addresses or usernames." Jordan lowered his voice and shot a quick glance over his shoulder at Detective Granger who was hunched over a laptop with Lucy Aston. "I don't like having Chicago PD involved."

"You genuinely think your old friend had something to do with it?" Mac's voice was soft.

Jordan shrugged. "Only a handful of people in the FBI knew

about my undercover role. I hadn't ever been into the Chicago Field Office before the night of the fire. More CPD officers knew though."

"They lost four of their own."

"Maybe the snitch didn't realize what would happen, maybe they didn't care. But whoever it was, knew they were signing my death warrant."

Daisy shivered.

"We never discovered how Bocharov found out." The lines around Jordan's eyes cut deep, and she ached for him. "But I wonder if you asked Parker to investigate now, if he might find something. Some payment. Someone living beyond their means? Otherwise, we might be sitting here with someone feeding Bocharov everything we discover."

Mac stared over at where Agent Crabtree sat talking to someone at the NSA on a secure line. "I can't ask Parker to investigate Chicago PD or the FBI agents involved without probable cause."

Jordan's expression fell.

"Maybe we'll get lucky and some willing civilian will approach him privately."

Mac's and Jordan's gazes both swung to her.

"Fine." Daisy gave a slow smile as she watched Alex Parker laugh at something Lucy said. "It's not exactly a hardship."

Jordan scowled, and Mac grinned.

Mac's phone dinged. His lips twisted to the side as he read the message. "The Mexican authorities are sending the results from the DNA analysis of the blood samples from Tremblay's room."

"What will that prove?" Daisy thought about everything she knew about the case so far. "You said it was possible someone tampered with the original sample and the FBI is using the wrong profile as a comparison. How can you trust the results?"

Jordan and Mac exchanged a look.

"I'll recognize the original sample material." Jordan headed for the door.

"Can I come with you?" Daisy asked.

Agent Crabtree looked up from his screen.

"Not this time." And, with that, Jordan was gone.

"Dammit." Look at how easily he left her behind.

"You go have a quiet word with Parker, and I'll see how Granger and Lucy are getting on with the conference attendees. We could use your help with that, if possible." He checked his watch. "We'll be working for a few more hours, but if you need to rest…"

Daisy stifled another yawn. "I'm good for now. Think you could organize some food?"

"Pizza?"

"Man after my own heart."

His eyes twinkled and made her smile even as anxiety started to rise inside her about what this all meant if Jordan was right.

18

Jordan dialed one of his HRT colleagues, Seth Hopper, as he jogged across campus toward the National Laboratory building.

"S'up?" Hopper answered sounding breathless.

"What's the name of Zoe's friend, the hot forensic scientist?"

"Coco Monserrat. Why? One woman not enough for you?"

Jordan caught the caustic edge to Hopper's tone and bristled. "You talking about Daisy?"

"I thought something was up between you two last month." Disapproval dripped from his friend's tongue.

Jesus. He couldn't explain the truth on a cell phone. And it was better if the guys believed the two of them were an item, for now. He went with flippant. "You can't help who you fall for—"

"There's a code, Jordan. You mess with family, you break the code."

Even though the words coming out of Hopper's mouth reflected Jordan's own values and beliefs, they sounded like old-fashioned bullshit coming from someone else. Daisy was rubbing off on him. "Maybe she messed with me."

"You couldn't fight her off?" Hopper huffed. It sounded like he was working out.

"The same way you fought Zoe off when you were her bodyguard?"

The silence on the other end of the line told him he'd struck a nerve. But Seth was the one standing in a glass house with a brick in each hand. Jordan wasn't afraid to shatter a few windows, but he'd rather find Bocharov and stop a potential terrorist threat than untangle the mixed feelings and emotions he had regarding Daisy.

"Ackers tell you what's going on?"

"Yeah. I called Zoe and told her to cancel her upcoming visit. The last thing I want is to put her in danger."

"Copy that." Jordan was at the lab now. The sun was starting to set, sending cool white rays through the thin gray clouds reflecting off the wall of windows. Urgency scraped along his nerves like fire ants on the hunt.

"You really think it's the guy who killed your family?" Hopper's voice was soft now. Ackers had obviously filled them in on everything.

"Yeah." Jordan braced himself for sympathy.

"Let us know when we can help bring this motherfucker down. You don't have to do this one alone, no matter what anyone tells you, *comprende*?"

Gratitude caught him at the back of the throat. They'd gone from bickering to willing to die for one another in the space of a minute. Because that's what family did.

"*Comprende*."

"Watch your back. And keep both eyes on Ms. Montana." Dark amusement laced Seth's voice. Less judgment, more acceptance. "She's a slippery one."

Seth was right about that. Jordan hung up and pressed the buzzer to be allowed entry to the laboratory building. At the desk, he asked for Dr. Monserrat and waited. Five minutes later, the elevator opened and a beautiful woman with light brown skin and curious deep brown eyes came over to meet him.

They shook hands as he introduced himself. "I need to find

evidence from an old case and have it re-examined for DNA. Tonight. It's urgent."

Curiosity turned to disappointment. "I'm afraid that's not how it works. You can't just walk in here—"

"Wait"—he thrust his cell at her—"talk to the director."

Coco took the phone in surprise and stared at the screen.

Jordan stood behind her shoulder. "Director Rhodes, I need you to authorize Dr. Monserrat to rerun the DNA from the original sample for the case we're working."

The director tilted her head to one side.

"I want to examine the material and make sure it's what I actually submitted then compare it to the other samples."

The director squinted and then nodded slowly. "Get to work. I'll send the order through in the next five minutes, but don't wait."

"I'm a *forensic anthropologist*." Coco didn't look impressed with either of them.

"Do you know how to run the DNA samples?" the Director demanded.

"Yes," the skin between her brows puckered, "but far better for me to find one of the scientists who are experts in their field and intimately familiar with the equipment we have here if you want it fast and accurate."

"Then find one," the director ordered and hung up.

Jordan winced. "Sorry for the dramatics."

Reluctant amusement danced in her eyes. "No, you're not. Come on. We'll pull the evidence and see who's still in the lab. What's the case number?"

Jordan reeled it off from memory.

They headed down in the elevator to a temperature-controlled room. Coco sauntered—the movement was too sinuous to describe as simply walking—over to the woman who sat at the counter.

"Hey, girl. What can I do for ya?"

"We'd like the evidence boxes for…" She turned and looked at him expectantly, and he repeated the case number.

The woman punched it in and then disappeared through a glass door and came back with a paper envelope with a sign-out sheet printed on the back. The tech made Coco sign for it.

They turned to leave when he checked the back of the envelope and then asked, "When was the last time this was checked out according to your records?"

The woman went back to her computer. Peered at the screen. "It was only ever checked out once by Dr. Nygen who retired a couple of years ago now. Lovely man. He had it for a week to run DNA." She peered over her reading glasses. "He had a tendency to bring everything back at the end of the week in one go, rather than go back and forth."

"Thank you."

He followed Coco up to her office, where she offered him a clean lab coat, and they both donned surgical gloves, hair covers, and face masks. Sexy, it wasn't. Then he followed her into a pristine DNA laboratory packed with machines and fume hoods. Two other scientists worked in the far corner of the room. Coco walked over, as they eyed him with curiosity.

"Either of you two have time to help me out? I've been ordered by the director herself to get this DNA sample run ASAP. I did explain I was a forensic anthropologist and should ask an actual expert."

They shared a joint eye roll.

One woman checked her watch. "Sorry, I have to go straight from here to pick up my kids from soccer practice."

The bigger woman crossed her arms over her ample chest. "The director, huh?"

Jordan pressed his lips together. "It's important."

"Most of the cases we examine are from murder cases or sexual assaults. What's more important than that?"

"This is." Jordan held her flat, brown gaze.

She relented and huffed out a sigh. "Fine, I'm Dr. Espuna. Let's have a look at what we've got, shall we?" She donned fresh gloves, sprayed down the surface inside a fume hood with alcohol solution, dried it off, and then laid down a sterile plastic tray. She carefully shook the envelope until a piece of bloodied material fell out. It was a hand-sewn, white linen handkerchief that had yellowed around the edges with age. An elaborate J and K were embroidered into one corner. White on white. Each stitch sown with love. A small hole showed where a portion of the material had been cut out.

"Excellent. Snot *and* blood." Espuna smiled.

"You collected this?" Coco watched him carefully.

He fought the unexpected reaction at seeing that old hanky. Cleared his throat. "Yeah. A fight started in a club, one of many, and some guy clocked Bocharov." Konrad's last name was on the envelope beneath the file number, so it wasn't as if he were revealing information the scientists didn't already know. "I thought the bouncer was going to crap his pants, but luckily for me—I was the bouncer—it turns out Bocharov enjoyed a good fight. Bocharov punched the other guy, but the offender was smart enough not only to bolt, but to get the hell out of town. I offered Bocharov the clean handkerchief I had in my pocket."

"Did you arrange the fight?" Coco asked, amusement in her tone.

He smiled. "Lucky for me, I didn't need to that time."

"Your DNA is possibly still on here, as is potentially the other man involved in the fight."

"Yeah, his DNA is in the system as he ended up doing time for assault with a deadly weapon in Minnesota. My grandmother's DNA is probably on there too. She sewed the handkerchief for me."

"Can we get an elimination sample from her?"

"No." Memories of strong, soft hands that had baked a thousand loaves of bread and eyes crinkled with a concertina of laughter lines surrounding them flowed over him with a mix of love and grief. "She's gone."

The loss hit him anew.

He had so few physical reminders left of any of them that, when he saw one, it snapped his head back like the perfect uppercut.

The fire had destroyed everything. All the seemingly inconsequential things from kitchen utensils to well-thumbed family recipe books. He had some photographs. A favorite mug. A blanket his mother had knitted him. A medallion his sister had gifted him one birthday. A few letters they'd written to him while he'd been deployed overseas. That was it. That was the sum of all the generations of his family's history. The rest had been reduced to ash.

The knowledge that his grandmother's DNA mingled with that of the man who'd ordered her death repulsed him, but he pushed the emotion away. She'd been a practical woman, his *baba*. She'd have understood. "I assume you'll be able to compare her DNA to my DNA profile which is on file."

Lines gathered between Dr. Espuna's brows as Coco pulled up the online profile. "I don't really understand why I need to run it again. Dr. Nygen already got the FBI a sample that is in the system, and the case is closed, correct?"

"Whether the case is closed or not depends very much on your results. I need to know if whatever's in the FBI's system is the same as what's on that handkerchief."

Espuna turned sharply to face him. "You think the samples might have gotten mixed up?"

Did he lie?

"Or someone got inside your system and switched them out."

She shook her head. "Impossible."

"Nothing is impossible." He held her gaze.

Coco's expression turned worried. "That would throw every piece of evidence we've ever processed into doubt."

Jordan understood the stakes.

"People lose their liberty based on evidence processed in this lab. Their *lives*..." The rich cherry gloss on Coco's lips shone in the lab's lights. She inhaled deeply. "It can't be compromised."

"Dr Nygen didn't make mistakes," Espuna insisted.

"I need you to compare it to what we have in the system and then samples that were supposedly taken from a dead Russian arms dealer a decade ago and then to another profile that the Mexican authorities sent us today. See if there are any matches with the blood on that hanky."

"When do you need it by?" Espuna asked.

"How fast can you run it?" Jordan countered.

Espuna pressed her lips together thoughtfully. "I can run a rapid sample which will give us results in a couple of hours and also run one on the PCR machine overnight. I also want to process this DNA for long-term storage at -80C to help preserve it for future reference."

He nodded.

"If you want to come back in the morn—"

"No. I'm not going anywhere until we have results from that first sample. I want to make one hundred percent sure, so I can swear it in a court of law," on the souls of his dead family, "that no one tampered with the results."

"I should probably be insulted, but I want answers too," Espuna admitted.

"Can I be of use?" Coco asked.

Espuna shook her head.

"Then I'll head back to my office until the rapid DNA is complete and uploaded into the system before escorting our friend back to the atrium." Cocoa walked away, hips swaying. "And, for everyone's sake, Operator Krychek, I hope you're wrong about our system being compromised."

Daisy sat at the table where the six of them were going through background information on the other delegates who'd attended the conference in Mexico. It was weird knowing details about her boss and colleagues at Richmond, not to mention renowned experts throughout the world. Details they wouldn't want her to know.

"This is going to make great blackmail material when I need a reference or new job."

Mac, Regan, and Detective Granger gave her the side-eye. Lucy grinned. Alex Parker hid a smile. Thankfully, Agent Crabtree had headed back to DC, presumably to report in to his master, but promised to be back first thing in the morning. *Yippee*. Cisco had headed back to the TacOps building—apparently known as "The Center," which wasn't creepy at all—to run facial recognition programs using more powerful machines.

Where the hell had Jordan gotten to?

She guessed she wasn't really surprised. More disappointed at herself that she'd believed he'd be different.

She licked her fingers as she finished off another slice of mushroom pizza and figured she better hit the gym soon or she wouldn't fit into her jeans.

She grabbed another slice. Sometimes life threw enough shit at you that you shouldn't have to worry about fitting into your damned jeans.

"So far, we haven't found any red flags about scientists working with Russia, except for the obvious contenders from Russia and Belarus." Alex's fingers raced over the keyboard like he was playing a piano concerto. "We need to let the deeper background checks run overnight—that will include financials. We can parse the data tomorrow."

It was nearly 9 p.m. They were all flagging.

"Let's quickly work on reconstructing the timeline before we call it a night." Mac pushed aside his plate, wiped his mouth on a napkin, then picked up a marker for the whiteboard. "What time did Tremblay head to his room from the beach?"

"It was about quarter to ten, I think," said Daisy.

"Jordan and you were in the stairwell shortly afterward?"

"Probably a minute or two behind him in leaving the beach." Daisy wished she didn't have to lie to these people who she was starting to trust. Although, technically, it wasn't a lie. She just hadn't known Jordan was following her... assuming he wasn't lying to her about him not being the person to throw François off his balcony. But that didn't fit with the man she knew.

"Police reports say Tremblay hit the ground at nine-fifty-five p.m." Mac noted the times. "Not much time for a meet."

She shivered. Plus, François had wanted her to go to his room. He hadn't mentioned meeting anyone. Not that she could tell them that.

"Perhaps he interrupted someone searching his room?" Lucy ran her hand through her short hair, making the ends stand up. She wore a cute multicolor sweater and jeans and looked about as unspook-like as a kindergarten teacher. Although, now Daisy thought about it, people like that surely made the best intelligence agents.

"Or he witnessed something someone didn't want him to see on his way to his room." Jon Regan tapped his pen on the desk. He'd done a sweep of this room for listening devices after Agent Crabtree had left. The other agent's affiliation seemed to lie more with the seventh floor than with the task force, and no one really trusted the other agent.

"We know the cameras went off at nine-ten p.m. and back on at ten-ten p.m." Mac added the times and pressed his lips together.

Daisy had overheard Parker say they were still searching for the source of the interference, which had been cleverly cloaked. She hoped Cisco wasn't going to get into trouble for hacking into the system for Jordan. "If the cameras went off to cover a meeting with Tremblay, why was Tremblay on the beach with a bottle of red wine?"

"Maybe he changed his mind," Parker suggested.

"Not an option when you get into bed with the Russians," Lucy said quietly.

"Well, he did end up pancaked on the patio," Regan pointed out.

"Do we know if Tremblay had anything in his room that might be worth stealing?" asked Lucy.

Detective Granger pulled up the Mexican police report along with the list of items retrieved. "Nothing that is obviously suspect, but we don't know what's on his laptop."

"And whoever was in his room—whoever killed him—could have taken it," Regan pointed out the obvious.

"Krychek didn't notice him carrying anything so it would have to be small enough to put in his pocket," Mac noted.

"You can store a hell of a lot of secrets on a thumb drive and a hell of a lot of diamonds in your pocket." Regan seemed more subdued than usual. Tiredness or worry, Daisy wasn't certain which.

"I'm going to see if I can set up some protocols to figure out if Tremblay had some sort of cloud backup or if I can get into his email or download his cell records," Alex muttered.

Mac stuck his fingers in his ears. "I didn't hear that and make sure it's not done using FBI servers. I don't want the French or Mexicans accusing the US of interference when we're simply looking for answers. Nor the FBI Director for that matter."

Alex smiled. "They'd never know, but anything I don't do, I'll make sure not to do it from somewhere else. You should request subpoenas in case it's worth the FBI's time."

Mac nodded and added it to a list he had on his tablet.

"What if Regan is right? What if François simply witnessed something on the way to his room?" Daisy mulled over the idea. "The hotel cameras being off had to be a smokescreen for the Russian meeting *someone*. Maybe it wasn't François? Can we plot out who was in each room on that floor?" She knew her boss and several lab mates were on five. "Can we use any other cameras in the area, or people taking photos on their phones to place them somewhere other than the fifth floor? People are bound to have started videoing when Tremblay died." Pizza curdled in her stomach at the thought of his tragic death, and she put the last piece, uneaten, back on her paper plate.

Mac pointed his finger at her. "Good idea." He looked at Regan.

Regan shrugged. "We can do it at TacOps, but we should utilize SIOC's capabilities to do it faster."

Alex opened his mouth to speak, but Regan spoke over him. "Let the FBI do some of the hard work, or the director might think she doesn't need us anymore and privatize the whole freaking lot of us."

Mac stared at the other man thoughtfully. Nodded. "Regan's right. The less we share the more suspicious the director might get. And she's going to want to know how we obtain all our information so let's keep as much of it above board as possible. But we keep the Bocharov name locked down tight to need-to-know only." He held Granger's gaze as he said it, and the Chicago detective looked away, clearly pissed. "I'll call SIOC. The issue arises, however, in that we have no proof that this is anything more than a man falling off his balcony to his death and Krychek following a man with a Russian accent out of the hotel."

"Well, we have the fact someone chased us, shot at us, and the black limo being torched," Daisy countered.

Mac shot her a look. "I'm not arguing, but I know how the lawyers look at these things, and it's not like normal human beings."

Jordan burst into the room and slapped a piece of paper on the table.

Despite her fatigue, her heart skipped.

"Rapid DNA confirms there's a one hundred percent match between some of the DNA found in Tremblay's room and that of the sample I took from Bocharov ten years ago." He looked directly at her as he spoke. "Konrad Bocharov is alive."

19

Daisy insisted on dragging her suitcase up the academy steps. She looked small and delicate and vulnerable, her usual sass buried under a sixteen-hour day filled with danger, stress, and uncertainty.

Jordan had tried to take the bag for her, but she'd refused his help. Mac had ordered them all to get some sleep. Feelers had been sent out to all the other agencies and the Five Eyes intelligence agencies, and if anything urgent broke, they'd get called back in. Better to catch some sleep while they could.

The other task force members had still been packing up when they'd left, many living close enough to go home and sleep in their own beds for the night. Mac had been on the phone updating the director with today's progress.

Jordan resented not being allowed to go home and getting this thing over with sooner rather than later. He knew Bocharov would come for him, and he'd be ready. HRT would be ready. They'd examined his place from chimney pots to pilings, reactivated the cameras and alarms. Some of the guys had volunteered to hole up at his neighbor's place, in case Bocharov or one of his goons decided to pay a visit tonight.

"That's good news though, right?" Daisy paused to catch her breath at the top of the steps. "That the database wasn't altered."

"It's great news, but it means the asset who supposedly gave us Bocharov's DNA from the bomb site is compromised, because aside from the new face, Konrad didn't look like something that had been scraped into a plastic bag. Bocharov must have given him a blood and tissue sample, possibly even from his facial reconstruction operations."

Daisy shuddered.

Jordan winced. Sometimes he forgot she wasn't trained for this.

"What happens now? Will they be arrested?"

Jordan shook his head. "Not immediately. CIA and counterintelligence will be coordinating to see what he's fed them over the years and flag it. They'll do a deep dive into everything he's done. Everywhere he goes. Everyone he speaks to. Every email, internet site, text he sends. Figure out who his friends are and watch them too. It's a potentially rich vein of information as long as he doesn't know he's been blown."

She shuddered again, and he realized she was cold, not frightened. The temperatures were somewhere in the low forties, and she wasn't dressed for a Virginia winter. It reminded him of Tremblay lending her his jacket on the beach last night—more of a gentleman than Jordan apparently. He held the door wide. Compensating? Competing with a dead guy?

They were already inside now and almost at their rooms.

He leaned closer so he could whisper in her ear. "Let me check your room for listening devices when we get there, okay?"

Her eyes went wide. "They wouldn't."

He gave a wry tilt of his head. "They might." And he was heartily sick and tired of being spied on.

They walked past the cafeteria and headed for the dorms they'd been assigned. A woman at the desk handed him a single key.

Shit.

He knew what that meant. They were sharing a room, which made sense given they were supposed to be a couple. At least there should be twin beds.

Yeah, Jordan, another *lucky escape.*

He rolled his eyes at himself.

Even if her father hadn't been his best friend, she deserved someone she could have a future with. Not some cursed, damaged excuse for a human being like himself.

He knew that. Believed it down to his marrow. But it didn't mean that somewhere deep inside, a kernel of resentment and regret hadn't started to unfurl.

They were both mature adults who knew this wasn't going anywhere, so why shouldn't they make their own decisions about what they did when they were alone?

The fact it was temporary would only make it worse in the eyes of Kurt and his teammates. If you were going to break the code, it better be for something meaningful, not just a one-night stand or a short-term fling.

Not that he didn't care for Daisy. He *did.* And not simply because she was Kurt's daughter. He cared because she challenged him and looked incredible while doing it. That gossamer hair and pale complexion juxtaposed against those deep, navy eyes and red lips, and a tongue that could peel the skin off your back.

Yup.

He found everything about her hot. Worse, she was smart and didn't take any bullshit. And the fact she'd tossed him over her shoulder earlier should not have been a turn-on, and yet, it absolutely was.

But Jordan wasn't built for relationships. Never had been. Aside from his commitment to his team, he was a loner. Built for hookups and no-strings sex. His mouth went dry with sudden realization—that was exactly what Daisy had proposed.

"We're in here." His voice sounded a little strained as he pushed opened the dorm room door.

"Reminds me of college." From her expression she was clearly not happy with the reminder.

"It's basic," he admitted, "but should be okay for a couple of nights."

She sent him a funny look. "It's fine, really."

There were two twin beds in the room, and he let go of a breath. To cover his ridiculous disappointment, he tossed his bag on the nearest bed. Rubbed the back of his neck. "You want to take the first shower?"

Their quarters had a small ensuite, and he needed to search the place before he could even think about relaxing.

Daisy turned to face him. Even though the drapes were wide open to anyone who might be snooping, she stripped her T-shirt over her head and then shucked her jeans. She grabbed a towel wearing nothing but emerald-green lingerie and walked to the drapes, which she very deliberately closed.

She walked toward him, and he froze, but she didn't touch him, and he wished she would.

"See you in there?" She raised a brow again and gave him a come-hither look over her shoulder.

"Sure, *babe*." He forced the words past strangled vocal cords. "Two minutes."

She disappeared inside the bathroom, and he shook himself out of his stupor to begin an inch-by-inch search of the room.

There was no real reason for the director to doubt their story now that his theory about Bocharov had been proven correct, but he wasn't willing to entrust Daisy's freedom to his naïve belief in the justice system. He knew it could be bent and twisted to fit someone's agenda, and he knew very little about the new director's loyalties.

He huffed out a laugh at himself and his increasing paranoia.

The fact he was a small cog in the wheel should be reassuring, but he was jaded enough to know he and his teammates—and Daisy—were all expendable under the right circumstances. He had no intention of walking blindly into a trap or dragging others with him.

He quickly went through their luggage and, sure enough, there was a small electronic listening device in Daisy's case lining and another deep inside his pack.

He sat back on his heels.

What the actual fuck?

He exhaled and stared at the devices. He needed to ask Regan to look at them in case they were planted by hostile players, rather than at the director's bidding, but it wasn't likely given the timelines. They'd probably been placed before Daisy had been interviewed and certainly before the DNA results had come back.

Crabtree?

Most likely. He'd had access and was Rhodes's lackey.

He hadn't had the opportunity to retrieve them because he'd left early and probably assumed no one would find them. Jordan carried both devices into the bathroom and held them up as Daisy drew back the shower curtain. Her eyes widened in surprise, and he tried not to look below her chin.

The woman didn't have a bashful bone in her body. Or maybe this was her revenge for him dragging her naked out of the bathtub a couple of weeks ago. Tempting him until he forgot his promises. As if the image of her naked wasn't already imprinted on his brain on replay and living in his dreams in a better, happier alternative reality.

He dragged his eyes back to her mouth, her lips forming a perfect circle of outrage.

Didn't help.

He was definitely a sex addict because his thoughts were way too dirty for a nice girl like Daisy, even if the nice girl in question was completely happy in her own skin.

He pressed his pointer finger to his lips, so she didn't say anything to let the listeners know they'd been found out and then turned around and headed out of their room. He bumped into Mac in the corridor and held the two devices aloft.

Mac's brows clashed together in annoyance.

Jordan headed down to the kitchenette each floor had and found some tinfoil and a plastic bag, wrapped them up, and then popped them at the back of the freezer. He and Mac headed back through the fire door to the corridor outside their rooms.

Mac's expression was thunderous. "I'm going to demand answers first thing tomorrow."

"Maybe we'd be smarter not to say anything." Jordan held the man's furious gaze. "Perhaps see if Regan or Parker could trace it back to its source? It is illegal to record a federal agent without his knowledge, and I can't believe they got a warrant given I haven't done anything wrong."

Mac narrowed his gaze. "The director seems to have some kind of beef with HRT. Any idea why?"

"Nope. But it sure makes it hard to know whom to trust when your own bosses believe the worst." Jordan frowned. "You don't think they might actually believe I'm working for the Russians, do you?"

Mac shrugged. "From my interactions with her, I suspect it's more she's worried about making a mistake and looking foolish to her boss."

"If she can't trust us then we can't trust her to have our backs. And she should be more worried about why a supposedly dead Russian arms dealer killed a nuclear scientist."

Mac inhaled and then released the breath. "When I spoke to her a few minutes ago, I impressed the seriousness of the situation. I think that now we have proof Bocharov is alive she's fully onboard." He checked his watch. "I'm gonna call my fiancée and then get a few hours' sleep. I'll text Parker about the bugs on my personal cell. I want to confirm it is an FBI tap. You think Regan knew about it?"

The idea stunned Jordan.

He shook his head. "I don't know, but I always figured we had a good relationship. Regan doesn't like bullshit."

"Not even Jon Regan could refuse a direct order from the

director without the risk of being fired," Mac reminded him. "None of us can."

"I assumed it was a sheer fluke the luggage stayed in the hallway. Now I'm not so sure." His insides felt jumpy. He wasn't sure whom to trust anymore.

Mac squeezed his shoulder. "Get a few hours rest. You've got nothing to worry about. Without your eye-witness account, we'd have no reason to suspect Tremblay's death was anything except a tragic accident and wouldn't know Bocharov was alive and well and possibly planning something."

"It's only by chance that I was there."

"Unless they were deliberately targeting Daisy because of her father?"

"In which case, why didn't they attempt to grab her?" Jordan shook his head. "Luck or fate had me in that stairwell, and I'm pissed I didn't stop the sonofabitch while I had the opportunity."

Mac patted his back in sympathy, then Jordan headed back into the bedroom, grateful and a little disappointed to see Daisy already in bed. Her hair was damp, and she wore dusky pink, satiny, short-sleeved pajamas with white polka dots all over them.

What was wrong with sleeping in a grungy T-shirt like a normal person?

"We should be okay now." He grabbed his pack and some sleep pants before escaping into the bathroom.

When he came out ten minutes later, he was relieved to see she'd turned the light off.

"What if they use lidar to look through the walls?" Her voice dripped with rich amusement despite the sleepiness. "If you're concerned that could be an issue, you are more than welcome to climb in beside me if you want."

He stopped short, then carried on and stacked his belongings on a desk chair. "They'll see two exhausted humans getting a good night's sleep."

"You don't want a quick blow job to keep up the façade?" Her words held a teasing edge, but the imagery they evoked had him as hard as stone in two seconds flat.

Great.

He forced the reaction away. He was capable of doing hard things. Navigating across the Arctic at minus forty. Swimming ten miles in the open ocean. Flying a goddamned jet. "I think that might cross the line from façade into actuality."

He heard her roll over to face him as he crawled under the thin blankets. "Like this morning, you mean?"

He'd almost convinced himself this morning on the jet had been another of his dreams. The feel of her, the scent of her, the sounds she made when she came.

Sexual arousal made him clench his fists in frustration. He couldn't allow it to happen again, no matter how tempted. "Sleep well, Daisy."

It was dark when she woke, and for a few long moments, she didn't know where she was. Her fingers tightened around the bedclothes as she fought for knowledge inside her fuzzy brain, but facts were sluggish from the residue of deep sleep.

Her heart raced.

What had woken her?

Dark shadows rippled over the ceiling as the wind blew the trees outside. She held her breath and searched the shadows for clues.

A tortured cry rang out.

Krychek.

Quantico.

"No. No. *No!*" His head rolled restlessly back and forth on the pillow.

He was dreaming. A nightmare this time.

She sat up, slid her legs out from the covers, and hurried across the narrow space.

"Jordan," she whispered. She could make out his contorted expression in the dim light and hear his ragged breathing. Sweat glistened on his forehead.

"Jordan?" No response.

She touched his shoulder softly, but he grabbed her hand, still in the throes of this nightmare, and twisted her arm until she fell to her knees, then backwards onto the floor. She held back a squeak of surprise as he rolled on top of her, holding both hands over her head and crushing her with his weight into the thin, scratchy carpet.

"Jordan. Wake up. *Jordan*." She stared into wide-open eyes and watched him blink from the depths of sleep to fully awake, fear and embarrassment warring on his features.

He let go of her wrists and reared up on his hands.

She ran gentle fingers over his anguished features. "Hush. You're okay. You're okay now."

"Did I hurt you? Did I?"

"No, no. You didn't hurt me. I tried to wake you up that's all. You were having a nightmare."

"Shit." He went to roll off of her, but she wrapped her arms around him, stopped him.

"Let me hold you a minute." She thought he was going to argue, but the fight drained out of him, and he collapsed down to the floor, rolling her so she lay on top of him, the race of his heart thrumming through her thin pajamas.

They lay there in silence as he stared up at the ceiling, and she stroked him, trying to calm him, soothe him. Gradually, his breathing settled. She pressed against his side, unable to resist the lure of this man's body, even though now was not the time. But what better way to forget a nightmare than to replace it with something fun?

"I think I prefer the sex dream," she whispered in his ear as she drew her thigh over his.

His arm tightened around her as he stiffened.

She thought he was going to pull away. She wanted to kiss him but couldn't cross that line without *some* encouragement.

"So do I." His breath ruffled her hair, and she raised her head to meet his heated gaze.

Those eyes looked like an invitation, but she didn't want to be the one to make the first move. She wanted him to finally admit he wanted *her* too.

Didn't mean she couldn't tempt him though.

She placed her splayed hand over his heart. "You feel cold." That was a lie. "I've heard the best way to warm someone up is through skin-on-skin contact." Her hands went to the bottom of her PJ top, and his eyes followed. "Would you like that?"

She heard him swallow. Saw him nod woodenly.

She pulled off her top and tossed it up onto his bed. Watched his expression battle between lust and denial, saw the moment lust won.

He cradled the back of her head and rolled her onto her back in one sure motion. His mouth latched onto her nipple as he spanned his hands under each side of her ribcage to raise her up to feast upon.

Pleasure streaked along her nerves, and she was instantly, achingly aroused. She wanted him inside her. She didn't want him to think or remember all the stupid reasons he'd invented so they couldn't do this.

It was just sex. Nothing wrong with good, healthy sex, despite how the puritanical prudes tried to convince people otherwise. The more those people tried to impose their own beliefs on others, the more she figured they had something to hide. But Jordan's issues were due to the fact he'd placed her off limits because of who her father was, and he needed to get over that.

His lips moved to her other breast while his fingers rolled the first delicate peak and made her squirm.

Thankfully, he knew what he was doing, and this was going to live up to her own hopes and expectations.

She bowed up off the floor and heard him groan in appreciation. She shimmied out of her shorts and kicked them off.

Heat built as desire climbed. She ran her hands over the rippling muscles of his shoulders as his magic tongue teased the delicate tissue of her nipples. She tugged on his short hair, but he wasn't to be rushed, no matter how much she wanted him to get to the main event. He moved downward instead of up, pressing her thighs wide apart as his clever mouth licked the seams where her thighs met her torso.

His breath on her skin, the scrape of his day-old beard, combined to make her shudder with want. He knew exactly the right amount of pressure to apply when he found her clit, swollen and pulsing. He pinched her nipples and pressed the flat of his tongue against her as she found herself balancing on that ledge and then careening right over.

Sweat broke out on her skin as she landed in a damp heap.

"Christ, you are beautiful when you come."

She laughed, then pushed at his shoulders. "My turn."

For a moment, he looked like he wanted to argue but after a brief pause he shifted to the side.

She darted into the bathroom and ran back with a strip of condoms from her toiletries bag, quickly, before he could retreat into his defensive shell and change his mind.

She knelt beside him. "Roll onto your back."

She smiled as he did as she asked and eyed the erection tenting his pajama pants.

It had been a long time since she'd been with anyone. When her ex had cheated on her with her best friend, she'd also retreated into a defensive shell, but with Krychek, she could have this without the emotional baggage of wondering what it meant and if it would go anywhere.

It wouldn't.

Jordan would rather face an armed hostage taker than start dating. She'd gotten that vibe loud and clear over the past few weeks. And she knew better than to invest her own happiness in another human being.

They were perfect for one another.

She straddled him, then grabbed his hands to press them into the carpet above his head. She kissed his cheek, his jaw, the edge of his mouth, testing his control. She moved to his neck as he tried to capture her lips. The pulse in his throat leaped under her tongue as she let go of his hands and kissed the smooth, elegant lines of his collarbones, down those heavy pecs to tease his flat nipples. Her fingers skimmed the bumps of his abs, and her tongue played with his bellybutton, even as her hands hooked into the waistband on his pants and drew the plaid material over the impressive length of his penis.

He opened his mouth, but no words emerged, clearly at war with himself, obviously losing the battle.

She met his hot gaze as she took him deep into her mouth, felt his thighs bunch as she made love to him, finally felt him cede control as she pleasured him.

She could feel his reaction, feel how close he was, right on the edge. She grabbed one of the condoms and ripped it open and slid the slippery material over his silky length.

She straddled his thighs and placed the tip of him against her opening, just the tip. She needed to know this was an experience they were sharing as equals. "Are you awake this time, Jordan?"

His eyes gleamed with something almost feral as he gripped her hips and surged inside her. She clamped around him, and instantly her inner muscles shimmered in a cascade reaction, but she wasn't done with him, and he wasn't done with her.

She leaned over and finally took his mouth before sinking down and taking him inside her again, slowly, even though she knew instinctively that he wanted rough. This was her show. She traced those lips, memorized that tongue, that mouth. The taste of him mingling with the taste of her. She set the tempo, took the sensation up another notch as she moved her hips sinuously over him.

But her own orgasm overtook her again and she shattered, crying out as the pleasure hit her in waves.

He didn't let her land this time. He flipped her onto her back and drove inside her, keeping her on that endless wave that didn't crest, but instead grew as he slid over her clit, again and again.

She dug her nails into his back and held on. Wrapped her legs around his hips, taking him even deeper, until it felt as if they were one, striving for the ultimate completion.

She came again in another rush of sensation that made her sob out his name in a strangled cry. He jerked against her, once, twice, three times, then collapsed on top of her.

She lay there hardly able to breathe, unsure if it was because of the force of her release or because of his solid weight.

She squeezed her muscles around him and felt him grunt.

He withdrew, careful of the condom, and headed to the bathroom.

The floor was cold without him beside her, so she crawled up into the bed and dragged the sheet over her.

Jordan came back into the room and hesitated.

"I'm cold," she murmured sleepily.

He didn't say anything, but she felt the mattress dip and then his bare skin pressed against hers in the narrow confines of the twin bed.

"That wasn't bad, considering," Daisy muttered into the pillow, hiding a smile.

He bit where her shoulder joined her neck, hard enough to make her toes curl. Then he covered them both with the thin blanket and wrapped his arm around her.

"Go to sleep."

20

Jordan was dreaming again. He let his hands roam across the smooth skin and inhaled that scent that was all Daisy. His dick was hard again, pressed between her ass cheeks. If she knew what she did to him…

She pushed back against him, and he cupped her small breasts, pinching the nipple hard and enjoying the way she cried out and moved more urgently into his hand.

She shifted away in his dreams, and he woke, startled to find a very real Daisy kneeling, hands against the wall with her thighs spread as she looked over her shoulder in clear invitation.

His dreams had never looked this good.

Jordan didn't consider himself a weak man, but right now he could no more stop from taking what Daisy offered than he could gnaw off his own arm.

He snatched up a fresh condom from the floor beside the bed, tore open the wrapper, and quickly slipped it over his aching length.

He moved behind her and, in the gray, filtered, pre-dawn light saw the mark he'd made on her neck last night. It shouldn't send a dark thrill of possession through him, but God help him, it did.

He forced her thighs a little wider to accommodate his own.

Then held up her fine blonde hair with one fisted hand as he trailed a finger gently down her perfect silhouette. She shivered and then giggled.

"Ticklish?" he murmured as he nuzzled the back of her ear. He didn't like hearing his own voice. It reminded him this was not a dream. This was him fucking his boss's daughter against a wall on FBI property, even though he knew it was wrong, even though it could ruin a lot of important relationships when whatever this was between them ended.

He was going to burn in Hell, but he'd known that ever since he'd watched those flames destroy his family a decade earlier.

"Unfortunately," she admitted.

He ran his fingers gently down her side again, and she quivered against him. He whispered the callouses on his fingers over her breasts, cupping them, feeling their soft weight in his palms, brushing his thumbs over the sensitive tips. She pressed back against him, and the lump in his throat grew so large he couldn't swallow.

Everything about her was so perfect it made him ache.

She reached down and tried to touch him. He took her hand and pressed it against the wall, then dipped his fingers into her damp heat to make sure she was ready for him. He pressed forward, working his way inside her tight folds and nearly losing his mind as she ground herself back against him.

He found a rhythm that matched hers and thrust deep, fingers roving over her body and finding all the pleasure points. Her head leaned back on his shoulders, and her soft hair brushed his warm skin as he found her clit. He stroked it, gently at first but increasing the pressure and the timing to match his thrusts.

He moved forward, until she was pressed flat against the coolness of the wall, sandwiched by his body, unable to move, unable to do anything except take whatever he decided to give her. She moaned.

He slowed it down, not wanting it to end too soon, moved her hair aside so he could graze on her neck. Felt the wild beat of her pulse beneath his lips.

He pulled out, and she wriggled, as if seeking him.

He drew her back against him, letting her take whatever she wanted, use him however she wanted.

Daisy didn't need to be told what to do. She was his equal in this realm. Maybe more than his equal. She knew what she wanted and wasn't afraid to take it. He watched the bones of her spine press against her skin as she rode him, hands against the wall, moving in such a way he almost lost it.

Knowing he wouldn't last much longer, he found her nipple with one hand and clit with the other. Squeezed both with just enough pressure for her to shudder against him and cry out in pleasure.

He held her as he surged upward, again and again, pistoning into her. She moved her legs farther apart, and he sank even deeper, and it was all over for him.

A harsh, guttural cry erupted from his throat as he pressed her hard against the wall and catapulted over that chasm from the dark into the light as sunbursts exploded through his brain.

His heart pounded as he held them there while his brain realigned and her legs regained their strength.

His cell rang.

Reluctantly, he pulled carefully away and grabbed the phone off the bedside table.

Kurt's name flashed on the screen of his personal cell.

He looked at Daisy as she flopped naked back onto the blankets and grinned at him. Something twisted inside his chest because despite how much he loved and respected his friend and boss, he'd do it all again in a heartbeat if she offered.

Self-disgust crawled over him. He couldn't last a couple of weeks without sex? What the hell was wrong with him?

He headed into the bathroom, getting rid of the condom even as he answered.

"Hey, Jordan. I know it's early, but I figured you'd be up."

"Yeah." His voice rumbled through his chest. Jordan closed his eyes. "Everything all right?"

"Row finished with the insurance people yesterday, and they've agreed to pay her what's owed. Didn't hurt the UK media have made her a deity here for what she went through."

"What you both went through."

"Yeah, but I'm trained for that shit. We're going out to dinner tonight with some of her friends and head to London tomorrow. She has a temporary visa we need to pick up from the US Embassy sometime next week. Plus, she wants to drag me around the National Portrait Gallery and some museums she likes before we get our flight home."

The man sounded happy. Really happy. Now was not the time to spoil that with a sordid confession of how Jordan had just violated his daughter—again. No, he needed to keep that confession until they were face to face. Man to man.

Then Kurt could beat the fuck out of him, and Jordan would let him.

"I wanted to thank you for taking care of Daisy. Ackers told me what happened."

Ackers had probably told him they'd faked a relationship to give Daisy an alibi. Ackers and Kurt would both be disgusted with him when they learned the truth.

"She's safe." He forced the words past a closed throat.

"Thank you. I know she's a handful, but keep her close, yeah?"

Oh, he was keeping her close, all right. Too close.

Jordan stared at himself in the mirror, loathing what he saw there. "I'll keep her safe. You have my word." He just couldn't promise he wouldn't fuck her every opportunity he got in the meantime.

21

"Word just in. Anton Levi was found dead in his Berlin apartment last night." Mac's expression was pissed as he paced impatiently.

Jon Regan, Alex Parker, Detective Granger, Agent Crabtree, and Jordan stared at one another with varying degrees of dismay. A new guy from WMD named Harry Marcus sat beside Lucy Aston. Daisy couldn't read either of their expressions.

"German authorities are leaning toward erotic auto-asphyxiation as method of death. I think we might be able to suggest they take a closer look."

"What was wrong with the window?" Jordan asked sarcastically.

"First floor apartment."

"Figures."

Daisy frowned. "Who is Anton Levi? Can you say?"

Mac shot her a look as if weighing the information versus her trustworthiness.

She'd be pissed except she knew how seriously these people took their rules.

"That's the asset who collected the DNA sample that supposedly came from Bocharov. He swore he'd personally witnessed Bocharov's death."

"How did the Russians discover he was blown when we only figured it out last night?" asked Detective Granger.

"Good question." Jordan stared hard at the guy. He'd been pissy ever since he'd gotten that phone call this morning. Or maybe it was how he acted post coitus. Like a jackass.

Granger glared back. "It wasn't me—I didn't even know the guy's name."

"You didn't need to know his name. Just that the FBI had figured out Bocharov wasn't dead."

"I'm not on that bastard's payroll"—the detective's chair screeched across the floor as he surged to his feet—"and I'm sick of you suggesting otherwise."

Jordan stared him down, all coiled muscle and deadly intent. She wanted to reach out to soothe him, but Krychek had retreated from the thorough, considerate lover, back to the ice-cold operator she'd first met.

"Levi's death warrant was signed the moment you spotted Bocharov in Mexico," Lucy cut in. "They'd know you'd chase down the lead. You said Bocharov was bleeding, so he knew he'd probably left DNA in Tremblay's room. Levi would have either been called to Moscow or, if he wasn't deemed valuable enough, or if the Kremlin simply wanted to send us a message, they'd have ordered the hit."

"Levi knew what he was getting into when he started playing us against one another," Jordan bit out.

"High-stakes poker with power-hungry murderers. Yup. He knew the risks." Mac crossed his arms over his chest.

How matter-of-factly they all talked about death…

"I should inform the Director." Crabtree started to rise.

Mac took a plastic bag out of his suit jacket pocket, full of the smashed component parts of small electronic devices. Tossed it across the table. "Here, you might want to give her those while you're at it."

Crabtree flushed scarlet and then swallowed tightly.

Daisy forced a grin. "If she wanted to hear Jordan and me fuck, she should have just asked. We might have let her watch."

Jordan's skin was ashen even though they were supposed to be pretending to be an item regardless of whatever was really happening between them. The fact he was so ashamed of what to her had been a perfect synchrony of physical needs being met made something inside her shrivel up.

"The director should be careful where she gets her tech. Any idiot could be listening in on that pile of shit." Regan sounded quietly furious. "God knows where that came from. State probably. Tell her my interns build better bugs on day one of the program."

"The Director denies any and all accusations of misconduct—"

"Can it." Mac raised his voice over Crabtree's denials. "If I find any more reason to suspect I can't trust you to be a team player, you will be sidelined so hard you won't even see the playing field. Understood?"

Crabtree nodded and sat. "Sir."

"And the Director knows about Levi. Who the hell do you think told me?" Mac moved on. "Any progress on motive for killing Tremblay?"

Alex Parker scrubbed his hand through his short, light-brown hair. He looked tired. Like he hadn't slept. "Funny thing. This morning, I uncovered stories and media posts dating back six months of people accusing Tremblay of inappropriate relationships with students. And comments suggesting he threw himself off the balcony because a group of young women were about to go public with evidence that he used his position to obtain sexual favors."

Shock and disappointment rushed through her. "Wow, I didn't know him well, but I expected better of the man."

"Yeah, well, these posts and comments didn't exist yesterday."

She caught her breath. *What?*

Those silver-gray eyes of Alex's were intense as they met hers.

"Someone planted them overnight. It took that someone a little time to create the fake online identities of the *women* involved." He used air quotes around the word "women." "But they were sloppy. Minimal background and a lack of other social profiles and certainly no government ID. A lot of the comments coming from known Russian bots. You can bet your ass willing idiots will amplify the signals even more, believing the victims are genuine, and make the accusations appear legit enough to pass the initial round of public scrutiny."

She shivered at the scale of the deception.

"Why bother?" Jordan demanded.

"To give the authorities reason to stop investigating Tremblay's death as suspicious? To make suicide more of a possibility." Alex leaned back in his chair.

"But we now know for certain Bocharov was there, so it won't matter in terms of our investigation," Jordan pointed out.

Agent Crabtree looked startled. "You proved it? Unequivocally?"

Mac frowned. "Yeah, after you left last night. Your boss didn't tell you?"

Crabtree sipped coffee and then carefully wiped his mouth and shook his head. "If I can be frank, the director asked me to assess Operator Krychek and Miss Montana's interactions to ascertain whether or not they are genuinely in a relationship. Considering the tension between them this morning, I now have no doubts."

Jordan gave her the side-eye as if it were her fault.

She crossed her arms and stared at the ceiling tiles.

"What else?" Mac demanded.

Crabtree shrugged. "To keep her informed of anything important that doesn't appear in your reports, but as I seem to be the last to know anything important, that seems irrelevant. I am simply following orders, ASAC McKenzie. If you want me off this task force, you'll have to take it up with the director. Trust me," he sounded bored, "I'd rather be in DC."

"We could lock him in a cage somewhere until this is all over," Jordan suggested.

Daisy wasn't sure he was joking.

Crabtree's phone chirped and he swore softly as he checked the screen. "The director wants me at HQ for a meeting ASAP."

"Saved by the bell," Alex said dryly.

Crabtree shot him a look as he gathered his things, including the plastic bag of electronics, which he stuffed into his pocket. Crimson stained his cheeks. He left without another word.

"But *why* are the Russians chumming the water with Tremblay? Why do they care whether we think it's suicide or murder?" Lucy asked. "Bocharov is presumably long gone from the reach of the Mexican authorities, and based on Krychek's sighting and Levi's murder, the Russians have to assume we know Bocharov is alive. Why go to the extra trouble of disgracing Tremblay's legacy?"

"Cleaning up loose ends," Alex suggested.

"But why?" Lucy insisted.

"To muddy the waters." Alex leaned forward, his forehead creased in thought.

"Always," Lucy agreed, narrowed her gaze. "But once they're safe from apprehension or consequences, they rarely bother to cover their trail, especially when they have plausible deniability."

"Because they're not done yet." Daisy said what everyone was thinking. "Whatever their mission is, it's not over, so they want to deflect attention away from the fact François might have been murdered."

"As of yesterday, there was nothing in Tremblay's background to suggest he was working with any bad guys or taking payments from anyone except the institution where he works. The guy was definitely a womanizer, given the amount of sexting he did with various individuals." Alex grimaced. "If I ever see another dick pic, it'll be too soon."

"Amen," Daisy and Lucy said together.

"Everything I saw was legit if not necessarily ethical." Alex's lip curved wryly. "But what are the odds we find some money tucked away in some bank account soon. Maybe in Malta?"

Lucy huffed out a laugh. "I would not take that bet. The Russians are clearly trying to lead us in the direction that Tremblay was compromised in some way. They want him to be the focus of our investigation."

Mac jerked his tie from his shirt collar and stuffed it in his jacket pocket. "Assuming Tremblay was simply an innocent bystander who got caught up in this, we're back to looking at who else the Russian might have been meeting on the fifth floor. And who else might not want to be seen with Bocharov. Cameras went down when most people were at the banquet. Do you remember anyone leaving the dinner, Daisy?"

She shook her head. "I wasn't paying attention. The conference didn't officially end until six-thirty p.m. and the dinner ran late. Everyone was hungry."

"Analysts at SIOC worked through the night and got back to us with a pretty comprehensive list of people in the lobby between nine-fifty p.m. and ten-oh-six p.m., who we can assume weren't meeting with the Russian on the fifth floor at the time of Tremblay's death. Which whittles the list down to only nineteen delegates who are unaccounted for, not including Daisy and Jordan."

"There was a free bar," Daisy joked weakly.

"Explains it." Regan grinned, bared his teeth.

"What about other hotel guests?" Daisy found it hard to believe any of her colleagues would willingly be in league with an arms dealer when they knew the dangers involved with radiation.

"We can't rule them out, and SIOC are running background checks." Alex opened his laptop and projected the screen onto the whiteboard. "This shows a floorplan and the guest names for each of the rooms between the elevator and Tremblay's room, all the way up to the end of his corridor."

Daisy peered closer and her heart sank.

"The ones highlighted in red are the people who had rooms on

Tremblay's floor but were not seen on the video downstairs in the immediate aftermath of his death."

A ball of numbness expanded in her chest making it difficult to breathe. "Five of those eight are from my lab."

"Correct. Wilson Williams, Roger Thompson, Mira Jahood, Amed Hussein, and Emilia Osbourne."

"Amed and Roger shared a room as did Mira and Emilia. Les Poplar had a room on the sixth floor. He didn't make the banquet. Said he felt sick—probably still hungover from the night before."

Mac rested his hip on the desk. "You and Les were the only ones in your group not to be situated on the fifth floor. Was that intentional on your part?"

She shook her head. "A lot of the others arrived a day earlier than I did, and I didn't want to share a room with Les." She glanced at Jordan. Remembered their cover story. "For obvious reasons. Plus, I got a nice view of the ocean."

"The cynic in me wonders if someone made sure the daughter of a senior member of the FBI was not on the same floor as they were," Mac mused.

Daisy made a fist with her right hand. "That, I couldn't tell you, but everyone knew who my dad was after that plane went down in Zimbabwe."

Mac's shiny leather shoes creaked. "How well do you know your colleagues?"

"No." Jordan glared at Mac, but she didn't know why.

She shot him a look. "I've been there since September, but busy with a literature review most of this term." She bit her lip. "I've deferred a lot of course work with everything that happened with Dad. My supervisor has been very accommodating."

"In addition to the work Granger and Lucy did yesterday, we have agents digging into the background of everyone on the shortlist, looking for something, anything...and we'll begin actively monitoring them and their communications as soon as the subpoena comes through." Mac looked down at his hands.

The reality was gradually seeping in that the Russians might be planning some sort of attack, probably under the guise of a terrorist organization. And the fact he'd shown up at a nuclear engineering conference led to the inevitable conclusion that any attack would involve either a nuclear device, a dirty bomb, or the deliberate sabotage of a reactor.

It was a horrifying thought, exactly what she'd dedicated her life to preventing.

"We'd like your help."

Her heart sank. "You want me to spy on my lab mates?"

"No way." Jordan's jaw was clenched so tight it looked like it might break.

She wished he was worried about her as much as he was worried about the promise he'd made to her dad. And the fact she wished that meant she was getting more entangled than she'd intended. Time to make it stop. The sex was great but not worth the heartbreak that would surely follow if she allowed herself to care for him.

"It makes sense." She shrugged. "I have to go back at some point anyway. This way I can search offices or plant bugs or whatever it is you want me to do to enable better access."

"It's too dangerous." Jordan's voice was flat.

She understood his concern. "It's not the same as what you did in Chicago. I'm not pretending to be on their side. I'm going about my studies the way I should be anyway. There's nothing suspicious about that. It's only a matter of time. You know that."

"And what if one of them is the bad guy and working with Bocharov and suspects you're working with the feds?" Jordan challenged.

"Then we'll know who the hell the bad guy is, won't we?" Better than never knowing whom she could trust.

"This is a foolish plan. She's an untrained civilian." Jordan sounded quietly furious.

She bristled. "*She* can take care of herself, especially when armed—which I will be, when not on campus."

"You think those Chicago Police Officers who were slaughtered weren't armed?" Jordan stood as if unable to contain the energy inside him while seated. "You think they felt the bullets that pierced the back of their skulls?"

Granger flinched.

Tears pricked Daisy's eyes because she knew where his anger came from. From guilt and grief. "What I know is that *if* one of my co-workers is planning to sabotage a nuclear plant then we need to figure out who, fast, before we are all scheduled to help insert a new type of fuel rod at Moses Lake Nuclear Power Facility this week. If I'm in a position to help stop them, then I damned well will, whether I'm an untrained civilian or not."

Silence fell like an axe.

"We could shut the site down," Jordan insisted.

Harry Marcus spoke for the first time. "If we shut down the facility too early, they'll go underground. We might not discover the next plot until it's too late. And we need to remember, Daisy's coworkers are not the only potential suspects. We can't shut every facility indefinitely. That's a win for the terrorists. Next thing we know, we'll be fielding threats across the US on a continuous basis. We need to figure out who is involved and shut *them* down. But we can delay whatever is supposed to happen this week if we don't ferret them out beforehand. And we can pull in other experts to make sure everything is legit."

"Then I'll go with you," Jordan stated.

"No one will speak to me if they think I'm still seeing an FBI agent." She shook her head. "We need to break up."

"Daisy," Jordan implored.

"We can make this work," Mac insisted.

"Would you put Tess in this position?" Jordan snapped.

Mac's mouth hardened. "She's been in worse." He shook away whatever he was going to say. "Whether we like it or not, Tess and Daisy are both in potential danger regardless of whether or not Daisy goes back to school. If there's a nuclear incident who knows how many it might kill? Not to mention it could poison the entire eastern seaboard with gamma radiation for the next hundred years. It would destroy the United States as we know it and reshape world order."

"Property devaluation would be a bitch." Regan smiled, but it didn't reach his eyes.

"No pressure." Alex sent her a wink.

"It's not fucking funny," Jordan snarled.

Alex held Jordan's stare. "I have a wife and child that I would die for a thousand times a day who live not fifty miles from Moses Lake. If you think I find this funny, you are not the man I thought you were."

Jordan closed his eyes. "There has to be a better way."

Daisy stared at him. "I don't see what harm it could do. I'll play the weepy blonde whose asshole boyfriend cheated and dumped her. Regan can give me one of those invisible earpieces and maybe a camera and tell me what he wants me to do. The least I can do is see how everyone reacts to me being back."

"We can be right outside in the van," Regan suggested. "We can have agents inside posing as maintenance workers planting monitoring devices. She won't be unprotected."

"It's a Saturday. It will be a lot quieter to go in there today. We should be able to get some serious snooping done, especially if we can maybe get into some of the offices that are usually locked."

"We can do that," Regan confirmed. "Get us the warrants, and we can do any damned thing we need."

"In the meantime, we can maybe bait a trap for a bear elsewhere," Alex suggested.

Daisy glanced sharply at Jordan.

The thought of him being in danger made her want to throw up and that was another reason to get out now. She had enough to worry about with her dad constantly doing things he wasn't allowed to talk about.

"I still don't like Daisy being involved." The ghosts were back in Jordan's eyes, wreaking havoc as he held her gaze. "I promised your father I'd protect you."

The pain was unexpected, like an icepick to the heart. The fact she wanted him to care about her for her own sake was ridiculous. She knew who he was. A man of unbendable honor, dedicated to his career—one who didn't want any complicated relationships.

She'd used him for sex.

No strings. No emotional hangups. The perfect setup.

Until it wasn't.

Somehow, along the way, she'd misjudged the situation.

It made her next words easier rather than more difficult. "I'm sorry, Jordan. This thing between us isn't working any longer. It's not you, it's me." With that she stood and walked out to the washroom so the rest of them could fight about the details, and she could deal with the fact she'd begun to develop feelings for the idiot.

She looked in the mirror and hated the grief she saw reflected in her own eyes. There was no way she was going through heartbreak again. Been there, got the T-shirt. It was time to move on and put Jordan Krychek firmly in her rearview, where he truly belonged.

22

Jordan watched Daisy leave Building 64 with half the task force in tow and had to force himself not to chase after her and insist on being her bodyguard. She was better off without him. His presence put her in more jeopardy.

So why did he feel like his arm was being ripped off?

He texted Ackers. A small team of operators were ready to shadow her 24/7 whether she knew it or not—until they got another call out. More of Gold Team were taking turns staking out his neighbor's property as TacOps surveilled his cabin in the woods.

Mac's phone pinged. "TacOps sent through a facial recognition hit for Bocharov entering Mexico from Guatemala day before you saw him in Veracruz. Used the name Lars Thorwald. Swedish national."

Lucy narrowed her eyes. "That name sounds familiar." She typed it into her laptop. "Oh, no, just a character out of 'Rear Window.'"

"That makes sense actually. He was a big Hitchcock fan. Any record of him leaving Mexico?" Jordan needed to concentrate on the hunt. That was the only way to truly ensure Daisy's safety. Eliminate the threat.

He was no good distracted, and Daisy was every type of distraction.

"Not yet. TacOps are working with analysts at SIOC to try to backtrack his movements prior to that."

"It's more important to put resources into finding where he is now, not where he was yesterday," Jordan argued.

"Our systems can do both and hopefully point to any of his contacts which might lead us to alternate forms of transportation." Mac put his hand on his shoulder, lowered his voice. "You okay?"

"I'll be fine when Bocharov is no longer able to hurt anyone."

Mac's lips pinched. "By which I know you mean arrested and put in a SuperMax facility for the rest of his miserable life."

"Yeah. That's what I mean."

Alex Parker came over to speak quietly. "I ran analysis on the people involved in your undercover op back in Chicago. Your FBI handler was a woman called Jenna Stork, correct?"

Jordan felt himself grow still on every level. "Correct."

"I tracked some payments from some of Bocharov's accounts to an offshore bank account in the Caymans before he disappeared. I also found records of unreported trips made by Agent Stork to the Caymans around the same time as several large withdrawals."

Jordan felt a buzz in his blood. A woman he'd trusted. A colleague who should have had his back.

"Turns out she retired early."

Something rumbled inside him. A vault opening. "Where is she now?"

Alex opened his laptop and showed him a small dot on the map. "Flew into DC this morning from the US Virgin Islands, where she has a nice house with a pool."

"You're tracking her cell phone?" Mac hissed.

Alex shrugged. "Want me to wait for a subpoena?"

"Let's keep this very quiet," Mac murmured.

"Call me cynical, but she's either heard about Anton Levi and is worried the Russians will eliminate another loose end, or she has been coerced into the investigation under threat of exposure to find out what we know."

"Leveraging her old contacts." Jordan felt hollowed out. "Sonofabitch." The sense of betrayal was almost overwhelming. Or maybe that feeling was from Daisy leaving him behind without a second glance.

So long and thanks for all the fucks.

His tongue felt like sandpaper.

It was probably for the best. She'd told him no emotional entanglements, but he was dangerously close to falling for her, and neither of them needed that kind of idiocy.

He nodded toward his old friend Granger. "What about him?"

"No money trails that I've found yet. Doesn't mean he couldn't have been paid in some other way, or coerced in some other fashion—threats to his wife, his kid—but there's no proof that he's anything except a solid cop."

Shit.

All these years he'd blamed Granger.

Really, he should have let the blame fall squarely where it belonged. On his own shoulders for being arrogant enough to take on a job that he knew was dangerous to his family's welfare. He'd never imagined Bocharov would do what he'd done, that he'd have that capacity for such ruthless violence against the innocent. But Jordan should have known. It was his fault they'd been murdered.

He took a step toward Granger, but Alex stopped him with a hand on his arm. "As difficult as this must be, I suggest we wait until after we pick up Stork before we say anything to anyone else."

"We don't have a warrant," Mac argued between clenched teeth.

"Don't need a warrant to have a conversation," Jordan pointed out.

Mac looked torn. "We could have agents from the Washington Field Office there in twenty minutes."

"She won't talk to them. She'll talk to me," Jordan insisted.

"Fine. Bump into her. Take her somewhere nice for lunch. Parker has your back. I need to stay here and coordinate all the different threads, including what's happening at the University of Richmond physics department. But I want ears on the meet when you get there. We play this by the book, Jordan, or you won't get to play at all."

Jenna Stork sat at a high table in a diner opposite the Ford Theater when Jordan sank into a seat beside her.

"Agent Stork?"

She startled and blinked rapidly. "Jordan, what a surprise!"

She sounded genuinely happy to see him, but then she'd seemed genuinely upset the night his family burned alive.

He gave her a puzzled smile. "What are you doing in DC? Based at JEH now?"

"What? Oh no." She shook her head, and her long dark hair fluttered over her grass-green sweater that she'd paired with a dark gray, tweed skirt and black leather boots. She had that prim and proper middle-school-teacher vibe going on. "I retired a couple of years ago."

"Retired? How come? Or is that a personal question?"

She took a sip of coffee while the server came over and he ordered pancakes. He hadn't eaten yet today. Too torn up with remorse and guilt over making love to Daisy, and then the goddamned anger over her ditching him without a backward glance.

Apparently, when she'd said no strings and no emotional entanglement, she'd meant it.

Finally, Jenna Stork spoke. "It's a little personal, but I think we went through enough together that I can share."

Drawing him into her confidence with their shared experience, building that connection. It took everything in him not to wrap his hands around her throat and squeeze.

"After you moved on to HRT, I met someone. A really sweet and interesting someone." She smiled and wiped at her lips with a napkin. It came back stained red with lipstick. "As much as I loved the job, and I did love it." She swallowed and stared at the thin gold band on her ring finger. "I realized I loved Charlie more, and when Charlie was forced to move to the US Virgin Islands by his firm...I knew I had to go with him."

"That's great."

She looked at him with sad eyes. "It was until Charlie died, two years ago. Massive heart attack, and he was just gone." Emotion shook her voice. "Between losing him and working the Bocharov case, it brought home that we don't live forever and shouldn't take happiness for granted."

He rubbed his thumb down his coffee mug. "I'm sorry about your husband. That has to be tough."

Sadness settled over her features. "Thank you. I guess we've both experienced tragedy in our time."

"Steady." The voice in his ear was Parker's.

Jordan felt as if his jaws were wired shut but somehow forced a smile. "Oddly enough, I met a spook recently who told me I'm a 'cautionary tale' at Langley."

"Ouch. Why were you talking to a spook?"

"I can't say, sorry."

"Classified." She nodded sagely. "Of course. Sometimes I forget I'm no longer part of the Bureau."

His pancakes arrived, and he drowned them in maple syrup and dug in. "So what drags you from paradise?"

She sighed dramatically. "A friend of mine called in crisis."

I bet they did.

The salt of the bacon, combined with the sweetness of the syrup and pancakes, made him want to groan with pleasure. He had to stop himself taking a photo and sending it to Daisy because he knew she appreciated her food.

You and Daisy are done, motherfucker.

"Your friend lives in DC?"

"Maryland. I figured I'd visit a couple of my favorite DC hangouts"—the Russian Embassy perhaps?—"and maybe find a decent shopping mall before heading that way. As much as I love USVI, the shopping sucks."

"Then you must have saved a fortune living there."

"Ha. Funny. I wish." She took a big gulp of coffee. "Charlie left me financially secure which isn't the same as having him around, but at least I don't have to go back to the grindstone."

"I always thought you were a good agent."

She shot him a nervous look. "Thanks. I tried, but sometimes it was a little too dangerous for my liking. Why are you in DC? I thought you were still in Quantico with HRT?"

Her brown eyes were completely guileless. Maybe they were wrong about her. Maybe she'd been set up to take the fall?

"Chasing a lead. You'd be interested actually, kind of serendipitous to run into you, but I can't really talk about it."

"Classified." She blinked rapidly and nodded. "I didn't think HRT did that. I thought it was all macho chest-thumping and fast-roping out of helicopters. I was sorry about the operator who died on New Year's Day. Was he a friend of yours?"

The woman poked the raw wound.

"Yeah," he cleared his throat. "One of the best men I ever knew."

"Sorry to hear that." She placed her hand over his and he froze. Then she let go and ate a little more of her sausage. "That must have been difficult, but it's kind of why the decision to leave wasn't that difficult for me in the end. The idea of bullets flying or hunting down evil monsters seemed a lot more exciting when you weren't the one doing the chasing."

Being in the middle of it, stopping the bad guys, that was the whole point.

"I was lucky. I had Charlie for a few years. Did *you* ever meet anyone special?"

Was she hitting on him?

Or trawling for information?

Or both?

He cut more pancake and stuffed it in his mouth. Then spoke around his food because he was sophisticated that way. "I thought I had, but it turns out she was just after my body." And damn if that didn't sting a little.

She leaned back and laughed. "Well, I'm not surprised."

"She dumped me this morning."

"I'm sorry about that. She's a fool."

He let his gaze warm up as if he wasn't full of revulsion. "You think so?"

Her gaze lingered on his mouth. "I do. I mean it's a great body, but I know the heart and soul of the man is even better."

Laying it on a little thick, but he figured she was on a deadline.

"Maybe we could meet up a little later?" She touched a finger to the back of his hand, the one without the wedding ring. "You know. Catch up properly."

"My ego *is* a little dented. I don't remember the last time I was dumped." He shot her a heated look and a flirtatious smile. "Her loss. I'll get over it." He let his eyes wander over her pretty features. "I think I already have."

If this woman was in league with Bocharov, he wanted them both to know he'd been jettisoned like a piece of space junk and that he didn't give a shit. He wanted them to believe Daisy was nothing but a convenient hookup he'd taken advantage of.

Jenna stared down into her lap and frowned. "You know, I've often thought about you over the years, Jordan, and about what happened. It was so terrible. I'd do anything to make it up to you. To take away that pain."

Whoa. Was she genuinely making a pass at him? Did she think spreading her legs would make up for his family dying in an inferno?

Was she out of her damned mind?

He kept the atmosphere light rather than let the darkness overwhelm him. "Hey, it wasn't your fault."

"I know, but something went wrong that shouldn't have. CPD…"

"Fucking CPD." He pushed his plate away abruptly.

"Agreed. Incompetent at the best of times." She looked up at him through dark lashes. "Anyway, perhaps I could bolster that ego of yours by telling you I've always found you very attractive. Of course, there was no way I could admit that when I was technically your superior. But as a civilian, and a recent widow who is only in town for a few days, I hope I can be honest. Perhaps, we could help comfort each other in some small way. We could meet after you finish work?"

"What about your friend in crisis?"

She gave a little shake of her head. "I told them I was arriving tomorrow because I wanted to take a full day for myself." Her dark eyes shone when they met his. "We could grab dinner, say about seven? For old time's sake and take it from there?"

"I don't want to take advantage of a grieving woman."

She smiled sadly enough that maybe Charlie had been real. "Life is for the living. Charlie would understand."

"Where are you staying?"

She named an expensive downtown hotel and gave him her number.

"Okay, I'd like that. I'll meet you there."

"I better go." Her eyes danced. "I want to hit the mall and buy something nice to wear."

"Doesn't matter what you wear. You always look good."

She smiled and then hurried out the door.

Alex Parker slid in beside him with his own stack of pancakes. He surreptitiously felt beneath the counter and along the far edge obviously searching for listening devices.

Neither looked at the other.

"You manage to place the bug?" asked Alex.

"Slipped it into her purse."

"We'll track both the bug and her cell, see if she spots it and tries to ditch us. I have one of my people following her to the mall —if that's where she goes."

"She'll go straight to meet her handler," Jordan scoffed.

"Let's hope so."

"How good is the person you have following her?"

"Surprisingly good for a teenager."

Jordan tried to hide his shock. "You're kidding."

Alex shook his head. "I caught her when she tried to pick my pocket once. When she was twelve. She was living on the streets. I offered to find her a decent foster home and a scholarship to college if she could get the grades required to get in. Now she attends American University here in the city. Got good enough grades for a full ride and the foster placement worked out so well they adopted her."

That was pretty impressive. "Why isn't she in class?"

Alex gave him an odd look. "It's a Saturday."

Jordan blinked at him. "Shit."

"You okay?" Alex's voice held compassion.

"Worried about Daisy," he admitted.

"Understandable, but she's protected. You don't have to do it alone anymore." Alex cocked a brow. "Although, I guess you had someone in TacOps giving you a hand."

"Regan told you."

"I found a faint trail that led me to Florence Cisco, but that was access only. Regan confirmed it. She didn't have anything to do with taking the cameras offline."

"I shouldn't have asked for her help."

"No one expected what happened to go down, but after HRT's recent run-in with Lorenzo Santiago, the potential for danger is high for active duty Federal Agents, which is why Kurt asked you to watch Daisy in the first place. Don't bother to deny it." Alex shot him an amused glance when Jordan opened his mouth to do just that. "And don't bother to deny something real happened between the two of you, either."

"Kurt is going to despise me."

"He's an adult. He'll deal with it." Alex shrugged. "You're really worried about her."

"Wouldn't you be?"

"Yeah, but you know what I meant. She means something to you."

"Of course, I care about her." Jordan stared down at his hands. "She's Kurt's daughter."

Alex chewed another mouthful of pancakes, but the look he shot Jordan was full of wisdom and pity.

"Fine, it's more than that, but she's strictly no strings. And I don't do relationships. We're completely incompatible."

"On the contrary, it sounds like you're perfect for one another."

Jordan tried to force the image of those deep blue eyes and pretty mouth out of his mind. "Last woman I was in a relationship with tried to kill me."

"Rude."

"Daisy is completely unreasonable and won't listen to reason."

"Women." Alex shook his head in agreement.

"Bullheaded and stubborn."

"I plead the fifth."

"Funny." Jordan drew in a long breath. "And smart. I can't even think about becoming involved with anyone right now. That fucker murdered a stripper because we had sex once." He squeezed his eyes shut as he thought of Ana. "Shit, I should never have touched either of them..."

"You created the alibi to protect her in the moment. The rest followed on from that." Alex popped a crispy piece of bacon into his mouth. "You're right to be concerned about her, but you being there was the biggest break of luck the FBI could have had under any circumstances. Bocharov doesn't mess around, and I have my entire team on high alert." Alex checked his phone and placed it between them. "Looks like Stork is headed to CityCenterDC like she said."

"What's the plan?" Jordan was itchy with the need to do something, and the fact he didn't know what Daisy was up to was driving him slowly nuts. Was she flirting with one of the guys?

What would she say if she found out he'd arranged to go on a date tonight?

Not that it was a real date.

Would she care? Even a little?

"We'll head back to my apartment and monitor what she does." Alex checked his watch. "See if we can find you something suitable to wear."

Jordan looked down at his black tactical pants and black shirt. At some point he needed to grab clothes from his home. "You don't need to get back to the family?"

"We have a possible lead I don't want to waste. I told Mal about the threat. She understands the stakes, and she's busy on a case." Alex downed his water and ate the last of his pancake. "I wonder if Stork realizes the prevailing winds might carry danger all the way to her precious slice of paradise?"

"She's a hell of an actress."

"Yeah, Charlie never existed, not as a husband anyway. I ran her background earlier."

"Figured. Never took her for a liar. How'd she beat the polygraph?"

"Vodka?"

Jordan laughed and pulled a face. "I fucking hate vodka."

He paid the bill then pushed outside to follow Alex discretely down the street, all the time wondering what Daisy was doing and if she was safe.

23

Daisy rode to Richmond with Jon Regan, Florence Cisco, and Harry Marcus in an old panel van that sported ladders and advertisement banners for painters out of the historic city. Harry sat on the floor, showing her the basics of what to look for in a detonator or explosives.

"Looks like blocks of putty."

"Exactly."

"So you can shape it however you want?"

"Within reason." Harry wiped his hands on a rag.

She leaned closer and wrinkled her nose. "It smells kind of nice. Like ether or nail polish remover, but more flowery." She laughed at herself. "Eau d'C4."

"That's right." Harry nodded approvingly then pulled out a few detonators to show her. He explained how they worked.

She grimaced as she handed them back. "And people say my work is dangerous."

Harry laughed at that. "In my opinion, this kind of thing isn't that dangerous if you know what you're doing, but—" he tapped his nose, "—never assume you know everything."

"Knowledge is power, but don't get cocky."

"Exactly."

The drive wasn't that long but they stopped at a fast-food joint on the way because apparently nerves made her hungry, and she had to admit to being nervous. And a little bit glum.

You'd think worrying about a potential attack on a nuclear facility would be enough to occupy her brain but no. Her mind kept drifting back to Jordan's expression when she'd left. Those damned eyes of his.

What she'd seen there had churned up her insides, and she didn't want churn. She wanted cool and unruffled waters and *sayonara, baby.*

She did not want hurt.

She did not want the emotional vulnerability.

Perhaps it was simply how she was built, in which case it was best she avoid relationships altogether. She could live without sex if that was the price. The sex she and Jordan had shared had been better and more intense than anything she'd experienced before—but the pain seemed commensurate with the pleasure, and that wasn't what she'd signed up for.

She'd started to really fall for the guy.

Her mouth went dry.

He could never know.

She was wrong to have seduced him. Wrong to have used sex as a weapon of payback, especially one that might drive a wedge between Jordan and her father because of their old-fashioned notions.

As much as she wanted to assert her independence, she should have used words, not actions to articulate how she felt—no matter how attractive she found the guy.

Note to self: Avoid attractive men in the future and definitely do not have sex with any of them.

How would Jordan react knowing her cavalier words had backfired on her after only a few days?

He'd probably pity her and gently disengage while sacrificing himself to her father's wrath for sullying her honor.

The thought made her roll her eyes and then push all the feelings pin-balling through her mind like a cascading chain reaction firmly into their own lead-lined box. She didn't need him, and she certainly didn't need her father's input on who she had sex with. Which was going to be no-one from now on.

"Daisy?"

She jolted out of her self-absorbed thoughts as Regan said her name and obviously not for the first time. "Yes?"

"You ready?"

She put her head firmly back in the game. "Absolutely."

If one of these people meant to cause harm, she was more than ready to weed them out. The last place they should be working was in the realm of nuclear safety.

They stopped at her car, dropped her suitcase in the trunk, then grabbed her parking pass and drove past the Country Club and onto the beautiful campus of University of Richmond. They headed to the Science Center, where she did most of her work in her advisor's lab. They didn't store hazardous materials here. This was where they designed prototypes to test new materials and designs. They then tested the prototypes in a test reactor on a larger scale and analyzed the performance of their designs at various government facilities, including at Oak Ridge National Laboratory, which had been built specifically for the Manhattan Project. Successful prototypes were then scaled up and installed in actual working nuclear reactors. This was what they were scheduled to do this week. Insert the new rod technology into a reactor and monitor performance. Roger and Amed would virtually live at Moses Lake for the next month, keeping an eye on readings, and then cut back to weekly visits with remote monitoring done in conjunction with the on-site staff who ran the facility and managed each reactor.

They parked out front of the pretty red brick building with its unusual Gothic buttresses. Leaves had started to bud on the maples, and pockets of purple and yellow spring crocuses provided a defiant pop of color beneath.

Cisco and Regan immediately began climbing into white coveralls.

"What would you like me to do?" asked Harry.

"Stay with the vehicle." Regan zipped up the front of the paint-smeared cotton. "Last thing we need is the wrong person finding this lot." He swept his hand to indicate all the high-tech equipment. "If we discover anything suspicious, we'll call you in, okay?" They'd brought monitors that sniffed out any chemicals involved in bomb making.

Harry nodded. He'd had a supply of a non-explosive substitute for C4. Should they discover the worst, and if circumstances allowed, he would swap out the explosives for the benign putty. That was the main reason Harry was here.

Regan handed her an earpiece. "This connects us all to one another. Just don't do anything dumb like they do in the movies and touch it every time someone speaks."

Daisy slipped the tiny, transparent device into position, fluffed her hair, and then put two fingers against her ear. "Gotcha. Over and out."

Regan grinned and shook his head. "Smartass." He handed her something that looked a lot like a watch battery. "Put this in your pocket. It serves as a tracker and a bug."

"What happens when I need to use the washroom?"

Regan pulled a face. "You ever seen *Casablanca*?"

She shook her head.

"Just whistle."

The parking lot was empty except for one car that she didn't recognize. "No guarantee there's no one here though. A lot of us bike or walk to campus." Her apartment—the top floor of a beautiful old Victorian—was only a five-minute bike ride away.

Regan slipped a rubber wedge into her palm. "You head inside but leave the door ajar with this. We'll get the ladder and paint pots before we head inside to…?"

"Labs are on the second floor as is Williams' office. Student space third floor. I want to start there if it's empty."

"Okay. We're gonna set up outside the labs in any space that looks paintable."

"All clear outside." Cisco scanned the monitors.

Daisy nodded and climbed out the side of the van that couldn't be seen from the windows of the massive building.

She strode across the arch-shaped lot and jogged up the steps. Used her keycard to buzz in, checked for anyone around—there was no one—and quickly bent and placed the wedge in position to leave the door open for Regan and Cisco.

She checked her snail mail slot on the way past, habit more than anything. She rarely got mail. Emilia had a small package, and Daisy desperately wanted to know what was inside.

It was difficult not to imagine something nefarious when in reality, it was probably a small gift from home—her mom lived in California—or a retail sample or something completely innocent and mundane. Perhaps she'd swipe it on the way out or ask Regan to take a peek.

She headed for the stairs and jogged her way up to the third floor and the area where all the grad students had their cubicles.

She set her bag on her seat and took a good look around to make sure no one was sleeping under a cubby, which had been known to happen.

"See anyone around?" She had to resist the natural urge to touch her ear.

"Not a soul," Regan assured her.

Daisy started at Mira Jahood's desk, checking her lab book for anything suspicious. Rifling through the pile of books on the desk, she recognized one she had requested from the library that she needed for her lit review. She'd ask Mira on Monday if she could borrow it.

Next was Amed Hussein. Both he and Mira were second year PhD students from Pakistan. There was a photo of his wife and child tacked to the side of the cubby and a prayer mat under his desk.

Nothing suspicious.

Then she noticed a thick, white envelope hidden between two textbooks. Her heart thumped as if she'd been running, and she checked over her shoulder. "I've found an envelope on Amed's desk. What should I do?"

"Opened?"

"No."

"Shit. You have any gloves up there?"

There was a random box on the table from Halloween last year when they'd made stupid balloon decorations. It seemed like a thousand years ago now. A lifetime ago.

"Yep."

"Suit up. Find a plastic bag and put it inside. We'll open it later and then seal it again. You'll need to put it back exactly as you found it, so pay attention to detail. Be careful."

The warning filled her with dread and pushed away her qualms about invading Amed's privacy. The letter was probably something completely innocent, but she certainly wouldn't reveal any secrets.

Where did the buck stop though?

Did the price of liberty justify poking, not just her nose, but the federal government's nose, into personal matters?

If the consequences of ignoring the letter wasn't the potential destruction of a swathe of the East Coast and the people living there, she'd have refused. But it was.

She hated doing this to someone she liked and admired. She forced herself to pull on gloves and then found a fresh unused garbage bag in the base of the trash can. She put the letter inside it, then inside her bag.

Hurrying to Les Poplar's desk, a third year PhD student from Ohio, she searched it. She found some dirty doodles in the back of his lab book and realized this was what he was scribbling during lab meetings. There was a short, stacked woman with curly blonde hair wearing a cowboy hat and high heels.

Her?

She was pretty sure it was supposed to be her.

Ew.

Apparently, the guy didn't know how to sketch clothes.

That was great. Just great. She snapped the book closed and put it back.

Asshole.

Next, she hit Roger Thompson. The post-doc originally from Yorkshire with a delightful accent and roguish charm. His desk was messy to the point of overwhelm, but no bomb-making manuals or weapons of mass destruction instructions in sight.

She whizzed through the desks of the remaining master's students, then got to Emilia's cubby next to hers.

"Incoming," Regan warned.

She'd just crouched down beside Emilia's desk when the squeak of the door had her bolting upright and tripping into Emilia's chair.

"Hey, I wasn't expecting you back." Emilia frowned. "What are you doing?"

Daisy steadied herself, then shot her hand to her ear. "I dropped my earring, but I found it again. You startled me. What do you mean you weren't expecting me back? Like, ever?"

Emilia shrugged. "Well, you know, after all the outcry suggesting you had something to do with Professor Tremblay's death."

Daisy wrapped her arms around herself. "You don't believe any of that, do you?"

Emilia pulled a face. "Well, I didn't know what to believe at first, and then it turns out you're hiding a secret FBI boyfriend." Her glance turned sly. "How come you didn't mention him?"

They weren't close, but they spent a lot of time together.

"He's a close friend and work colleague of my dad's. He wanted to keep us a secret."

"Oh, dating the dad's best friend. *Hmm.*"

"Don't say it like that," Daisy snapped. She wasn't a cliché. Except, of course, ever since her ex had started screwing around with her best friend she was. "Anyway, it's over now."

"Over?" Emilia didn't look convinced.

"When I was with him over the past couple of days, I found out the bastard had been seeing another woman behind my back." Tears burned in her eyes at remembered heartbreak that had nothing to do with Jordan, but she used it. "I broke it off. Came back to work. I was hoping the scandal had died down."

Emilia placed a hand on Daisy's arm. "Ridiculous really. Everyone knew what Tremblay was like. No one would blame you if you had—"

Daisy jerked away. "I didn't throw François off his balcony."

Emilia raised her hands dramatically. "Okay. Calm down."

Calm fucking *down*?

"I am *calm*." Inside Daisy raged. "I have an alibi for the professor's death because I was *with* someone, and I would never murder François. For all I know, you killed him. It's obvious you didn't like him very much."

"Easy." Regan murmured in her ear.

Emilia shrugged, unconcerned. "He was a creepy old man who was always trying to get into someone's panties. Why would I like him?" Emilia tossed a heavy textbook onto her desk where it landed with a thud. "I was surprised you spent so much time with him, but then I hear your FBI boyfriend is old too."

"He's *thirty-four*. But, like I said, he's not my boyfriend now."

"When you were eleven, he was twenty-two. How can you say that's not creepy?"

"When I'm fifty-three, he'll be sixty-four, which sounds perfectly acceptable. It's all relative."

Emilia gave one of those shrugs that said she still believed she was right. "You're so naïve, so innocent."

"Listen, sister, I haven't been naïve or innocent since I was thirteen years old and my tennis coach put his hand under my skirt in the equipment room."

Emilia blinked.

"I was wearing very sexy and provocatively short tennis

whites, so it was probably my fault, right?" Daisy took a big swallow as if affected by the memory.

"Motherfucker." Regan.

"What happened to him?"

"Nothing that day." She crossed her arms over her chest. "I froze."

Emilia looked both sympathetic and condescending.

"Next time he tried it, I smashed him in the face with a racquet so hard I broke his nose, and I told him if he ever tried to touch me or anyone else again, I would report him to the school and the FBI. That seemed to get his attention."

"Did he behave after that?"

"As far as I know."

"But you don't know for sure." Emilia crossed her arms over her chest, mirroring Daisy. "You should have reported him."

"I was thirteen and scared half to death. He made me think it was my fault."

"You do seem to send the wrong signals sometimes."

Daisy's blood pressure surged to the point it felt as if the top of her head might blow. "I do *not* send the wrong signals. I'm just not a bitch to everyone."

"Remember the mission," Regan whispered urgently in her ear.

Emilia waved her rebuttal aside. "Anyway, there are so many stories like that which is why I didn't like Tremblay, and neither should you have. Did you see the posts all over the internet?"

"Posts?" Daisy shook her head. "I avoided the internet after the thirtieth death threat."

"Well, let's say his death was probably more painless than he deserved."

"What a terrible thing to say." Daisy didn't mind a little justified violence, but she also believed in the justice system. A byproduct of growing up with an FBI agent for a dad, she supposed.

"It's all coming out now how he abused young women."

"What? Oh, my God. That's terrible."

"Yes, you had a lucky escape." Emilia's brown eyes flashed amusement. "I bet Tremblay was surprised when your boyfriend turned up and ruined his plans. Maybe that was the final straw. Or maybe your FBI guy threatened him…"

"My FBI guy—*ex guy*—is not the jealous type."

Emilia's lip curled. "Probably because he was busy screwing someone else on the side."

Pain sliced through her. "Did someone hurt you, Emilia? Is that why you're so mean?"

The other woman's chin snapped up. "I'm sorry if I hurt your feelings, but you said yourself he was cheating on you."

"Yeah." Daisy's eyes smarted. "But you don't have to enjoy it so much."

Emilia looked uncertain for a moment, but she quickly recovered. "I'm upset about Tremblay abusing students, that's all." She visibly shuddered. "It could have been either one of us."

"I guess." Daisy forced a tremulous smile because people were buying the disinformation being put out there, hook, line, and sinker. "I'm going down to the lab to set up some stuff for next week."

Emilia eyed her again. "Professor Williams said you wouldn't be back until Wednesday."

"Like I said, I changed my mind." Daisy shrugged again. "When I found out about the other woman, I decided not to stick around. I don't think he's even noticed I left yet and doubt he'll care when he does." She gave a bitter smile. "I'm done with men. They all suck."

"Aw, shucks." Regan drew out the last word.

"Williams had Amed sorting out some of the things you'll need for your test array so you might want to check in with him before you touch anything." Emilia bent to retrieve her lab book from her desk and slid it into her laptop bag.

Rats. Daisy had missed her opportunity to examine it.

"I'm heading home." The other woman slung the bag over her shoulder. "See you Monday?"

"Yeah, see you Monday."

She waited for a few minutes until she spotted Emilia through the window, walking swiftly across the forum, north toward the commons and the lake.

"She's gone. I'm going to check her desk quickly and then meet you down at the lab, although it seems a bit pointless. What sort of terrorist leaves evidence in a semi-public place?"

"The sort who doesn't want it found in their private space. Wait up, Crisco is coming to you first. Haven't seen anyone else around yet, but they might be inside the labs."

Crisco was Regan's nickname for *Cisco*. Why, Daisy didn't know.

"We have been conducting a few searches and," he coughed, "perhaps Crisco went a bit wild with electronic spookery, but this trip has been very useful. Very useful indeed. Thanks for helping us out."

"No problem." But she hated it.

"Were you really abused by your tennis coach?"

"Hell no. My tennis coach was a lovely woman called Elizabeth Boyle. My favorite teacher."

"You're a scary good liar."

"When you have parents like mine you have to be."

She quickly searched Emilia's desk and found only research papers, which the FBI might deem suspicious but were basic reading in their field, and a copy of *War and Peace*, which was more impressive than suggestive.

Wasn't it?

Dammit. Was she going to be unsure of everyone now?

She placed the tablet she'd used at the conference on her desk and left it there. She assumed the FBI had poked through it but there was nothing to see. It was heavy, and she was happy to lighten the load for her walk home.

Cisco came inside and gave her a shy smile. Then she undid

the casing around the light switch and attached something to the wires. Less than 30 seconds later, she had the whole thing reassembled.

Daisy gave Cisco a head start back down the stairs as she didn't want anyone spotting them together.

She popped her head into her lab and saw Amed had indeed placed a bunch of empty Zirconium alloy fuel rods, as well as some new silicon carbide ones, which she was planning to test next month.

She checked them over, looking for anything unusual, but they appeared normal. It wasn't as if these would be going into a commercial reactor anyway.

She walked around the large lab space and began opening the cupboards under the benches, one by one, but she saw nothing that resembled explosives or detonators.

"Where do they keep the fuel rods they intend to use in this upcoming experiment?" Regan asked in her ear, making her jump.

"They're being manufactured at a fuel fabrication plant in North Carolina. Get shipped on Tuesday, and we are all helping and observing the replacement process on Wednesday."

"We need to make sure that factory and shipment are secure."

"Good idea, but I know they have good security from when I visited last Fall. We had to be vetted before we were allowed inside, and we were supervised the entire time."

"Anyone fail the vetting process?"

"Not during that visit. It was Wilson, me, Amed, Mira, oh, and Les."

"I'll doublecheck and make sure. And tell WMD to get involved there."

She climbed to her feet and closed the last cupboard door. "I didn't find anything." It would have been too easy if she had. "I'm going to head back to my place now on foot. I don't want to be seen with you guys—"

"Now you're hurting my feelings."

She smiled the way he'd meant her to.

"Give us five minutes, and Crisco will follow you home. She's the only one who could pass for a student."

"I don't need a babysitter."

"Krychek thinks otherwise."

"Krychek is paranoid."

"He's got good reason."

Daisy exhaled. "Fine, but I don't want anyone in my place."

"Don't worry. We'll find somewhere to sleep. A park bench maybe—"

"God." She gritted her teeth and looked up at the ceiling as she counted to five. When she looked back down, she noticed Emilia's package was gone. She blew out a deep breath. "Fine. You can stay with me, but you're all on the floor or couch. I get the bed to myself."

"I thought you liked older men?" Regan said slyly.

Daisy pushed out of the main door as she raised her face to the fresh breeze that was starting to smell like spring.

"Too soon?" He spoke almost gently.

"Too soon," she agreed.

Daisy had forgotten she had a half-finished puzzle on her small dining room table. Instead of allowing her to tidy it away, Regan and Cisco had both immediately started work, placing their laptops open beside them so they could monitor all the different feeds while piecing together a picture of old candy bar wrappers.

Harry Marcus had gone to a hotel. The FBI wanted him to stay local, but as a top guy for WMD he also had other work to catch up on, including making sure the fuel rod fabrication factory was on high alert and the upcoming shipment protected. And she wasn't lying when she said her apartment was small. She had a couch and a small blow-up mattress that she'd slept on before the new queen-size bed she'd treated herself to had arrived.

The need to sleep in her own bed tonight, to go to sleep and pretend everything was normal, was almost overwhelming.

Daisy unpacked from her extended trip to Mexico and headed down to the laundry with her mountain of washing, surprised but grateful they let her go alone.

When she got back, she decided to push it further. "I could really do with a grocery run. I'm out of coffee. What do you guys want to eat later?"

"Write a list. Crisco can go grab stuff."

Obviously, it had been too much to hope for. She dipped into her laptop bag for a pen and her wallet and touched slippery plastic. "Oh, crap. I forgot about the letter I found."

"Shit." Regan climbed to his feet. "So did I." He rubbed the bridge of his nose. "I need sleep. Crisco, head to the store and grab coffee, lots of coffee, milk, food for tonight, breakfast, and enough for a day in the van should it come to that. Pick up a glue stick too."

Florence immediately headed out.

"Will she be okay alone?" Daisy asked as she listened to her footfalls receding on the stairs.

"Don't let appearances deceive you. She's a trained FBI agent who is damned good with a weapon. She should be fine in a grocery store." He looked like he was about to say something else but stopped himself. He pulled surgical gloves out of a side pocket of his bag and pulled them on. "You got a tea kettle?"

"Sure. Not an electric one." Daisy went and dug it out from under the counter, filled it with water and stuck it on the burner. "My mom's a tea addict. Oddly enough, I think Rowena is too. Obviously, my dad has a type."

Regan barked out a laugh. "Your dad is a hell of a lucky guy."

"I should call him."

"Don't let me stop you."

Daisy looked at Regan's twinkling eyes and decided she didn't have the energy to deal with the mischief he might create. "Hmm. Tomorrow might be better, it's nighttime there now."

After a couple of minutes, the kettle began to shrill.

Regan carefully unwrapped the envelope out of the plastic bag. He laid the envelope on her beaten up counter and photographed it front and back. There was no address on it. "Got a butter knife?"

She passed him one out of the drawer.

"Does that really work?" She nodded to the steaming kettle.

"Yeah." He looked up. "The issue is you don't want to get the paper so wet it warps because then it's pretty damned obvious what's been going on, especially if you're a terrorist with something to hide. It's good quality paper which helps."

He held the seal above the flipped spout, and moved it slowly back and forth, nudging the blunt edge of the knife into the gap and slowly easing the gum apart. Then he moved it away, and Daisy turned off the heat under the kettle.

Regan unfolded the letter.

Daisy stared at the beautifully scripted words that meant nothing to her. "What language is that?"

"No idea. Where's Amed from?"

"Pakistan. I don't know exactly where, but I know he has a wife and child there who he hopes can move here next year."

Regan took photos and turned it over, then photographed the other side.

"Signed 'Amed Hussein.'" She pointed to his signature at the bottom. A letter he's written but hasn't mailed yet?"

Regan didn't answer. "I'm going to send it to a translation expert at the National Laboratory."

Daisy snapped a photo and opened Google Lens. As she read, she reached out and gripped Regan's forearm. "I can't make out all the words, but does that say 'jihad'?"

Regan looked at the screen. Swore. "Handwriting is too messy to be sure." He picked up his cell and dialed a number. "Lisa, I just sent you a photo of a handwritten note. You got it? I need a translation ASAP. Nope, not first thing in the morning. Now."

Daisy couldn't make out what this person was saying, but she sounded pissed to be disturbed on a Saturday evening.

"Would I ask if it wasn't vitally important?" Regan raised his face to the ceiling as if imploring some unseen force.

"That was one time!" His voice rose with frustration. "Okay. Good. Thanks. I owe you. It's what?" He looked at Daisy in frustration. "Where can you find someone who speaks endangered languages of Pakistan in the next twenty minutes?"

Daisy sucked in her lips. Could Amed really be involved in something dangerous?

"I don't care. Wake them up. Wake them the fuck up like it's the eve of 9/11 and you're the only one who can stop those goddamned planes from taking off."

He disconnected the call. There was something in his eyes she hadn't seen before. Worry.

"I need to call the director."

"Use my bedroom." She found herself shaking. "Amed's a nice guy. Kind. Helpful. I can't believe he would be involved in hurting anyone."

"And serial killers are always those polite fellas who keep to themselves and never cause any trouble." Regan went into her bedroom and closed the door.

For the first time in what felt like weeks, she was alone the way she usually liked. Except this time, it didn't feel good.

She couldn't believe Amed would be involved in anything that hurt people. He was a nature lover and always respectful of others. She sat on the couch and hugged her knees. This had to be a mistake. She wanted to call Jordan. Get his opinion. Hear his damned voice.

Her finger hovered over his name. The temptation to press the call button almost overwhelming.

That's what happened when you started to rely on people. And when he didn't pick up, when he was too busy or doing Top Secret things in Top Secret places—who'd comfort her then? Herself, that's who. The only person she could genuinely rely on.

She tossed her cell onto the coffee table, then heard heavy footsteps on the stairs.

Shit.

Was that Florence back so quickly? Or the owners from downstairs coming to check on her? Or some bad guy. She dashed over to where she kept her Glock in a gun safe with a fingerprint lock. She quickly pulled it out and went to stand around the corner in the kitchen.

The door banged open, and her heart jolted.

"Can someone give me a hand?" Florence yelled.

Feeling ridiculous to be so freaked out, Daisy called back. "Coming."

She slid her weapon into her oversized hobo purse and followed the other woman down the stairs to help unload groceries and quietly update her on the situation.

She and Florence were putting the food away when Regan strode out of the bedroom. "You told Crisco about the developments?"

Daisy nodded.

Regan pointed at the letter then grabbed the glue stick. Took everything to the dining table. "We need to get this back into place *exactly as you found it*. ASAP."

The smell of roasted chicken wafted through the small kitchen, but rather than making her feel hungry, it made her feel sick.

"Let me grab a sweater." She went into her bedroom and pulled on a crimson turtleneck then tried to calm herself for a moment. It wasn't easy.

It had to be done.

She found some black ankle boots and tugged them on. Headed back into the kitchen.

Regan put the envelope in the plastic bag and handed it to her. She grabbed her bag and tucked it inside.

"I should bike there."

"No."

"Then at least let me drive my own car. Otherwise, someone is going to spot me getting out of your van, and the gig's over."

The muscles in Regan's jaw worked.

"I need to go in alone. I'm usually alone."

He inhaled a deep breath. "Fine. Let me get you a camera to wear. Wear the earpiece I gave you earlier. Crisco, arrange a parking pass for the van to be on campus tomorrow, something no one will question."

Florence nodded and got straight to work on her laptop.

Regan rooted in his bag and then turned around and hung a pendant around her neck. It was chunky and Victorian, and she kind of liked it.

"Whatever happens don't take it off."

She fingered it and nodded.

"I'm gonna called Harry for backup. We'll be outside the building in an unmarked car."

She nodded.

"Don't freak out and shoot anyone with that Glock you have in your purse unless you know for sure it's not one of my guys. Understand?"

She frowned as she pushed the Glock deeper into the confines of her bag. "You just happen to have 'guys' available here at the snap of your fingers?"

Regan's smile didn't reach his eyes. "I got guys everywhere."

"*Hmm.*" She decided against a coat. "I left my tablet on my desk so that's my excuse should I need one. I'll say I forgot it."

Regan crossed his arms over his chest and stared down at her. "If you run into anyone, act normal. If you run into Amed Hussein, act *really* fucking normal, and then get the fuck out of there. Start crying or something."

"Crying is normal?"

"After all that online shit people have been throwing at you? I'd say crying would be pretty normal."

"For you, maybe." Daisy pulled her shoulders back and nodded. "Okay." Picked up her car key from the rack near the door. She hesitated. Cleared her throat. "You know, Jordan got me pretty paranoid about bombs and stuff." She swallowed. "I don't suppose someone can take a quick look under my car?"

Regan's blue eyes pierced her. "Already taken care of."

"Oh. Good." She took another deep breath to fortify herself. "I'm ready."

"Put it back *exactly* as you found it. *Capisce*?"

"Now you're the Godfather?"

"Now I'm God when it comes to this op."

"*Capisce.*"

24

Jordan had borrowed a brand-new, still-in-the-wrapper shirt from Alex. It was a pastel pink, and the other man said it had been a gift from his mother-in-law, but that pink wasn't really his color. Jordan wasn't sure it was his either, but clothes were the last thing he gave a damn about. The black suit, the dress shoes, and leather belt were borrowed from Steve McKenzie by way of his fiancée, Tess, who'd dropped them off at Alex's apartment building.

Jordan walked into the elegant black and white marble lobby with its gaudy gold accents with a couple of minutes to spare. The place reeked of Chanel No. 5 and the ripe odor of old money.

Jenna Stork popped to her feet from one of the plush emerald sofas in the lobby, wearing a strapless plum-colored sheath dress that stopped just above her knees. "Hey."

He stood back and let his basic appreciation for a beautiful woman take the lead. She had great legs, something he'd never noticed when they'd worked together.

"You look amazing." He looked down at himself. "Now I feel underdressed."

"Oh, you look great. I splurged a little." She took his hand and leaned forward to press a kiss to his cheek. Then spent a moment wiping her lipstick from his face while he concentrated on not letting his skin crawl.

"You have fun shopping?"

Her eyes sparkled. "Absolutely." She lifted one foot to show him mile-high stilettos. "Christian Louboutin says 'Hi.'"

He pulled a face. "I have no idea who that is."

She raised her face to the ceiling and gave a tinkling laugh as if he was just *too* amusing. "Doesn't matter."

The heels put them at eye-level. For some reason it made him think about Daisy who only reached his chin, even in heels.

"Where would you like to eat?" He stared into Jenna's hazel-brown eyes and wondered if there was room for a gun or some other weapon in her tiny purse. "I have a friend who can get us into The Dabney if you'd like?" Alex had connections everywhere. He looked down at her heels with a frown. "We can grab a cab if you don't want to walk."

"Oh, The Dabney sounds lovely, but," she pouted, "I took a chance and made a reservation here. I hear the chef is excellent." She ran her hand slowly down his chest, and he wondered how far she'd go to get what she wanted. "Afterwards, we could have dessert in my room."

All the way.

All the damned way.

Alex searched her room as they spoke. Jenna hadn't met with anyone after they'd talked earlier, but it didn't mean she hadn't communicated with someone.

He didn't drop her gaze even though he'd rather make kissy faces with a venomous snake. "That sounds like fun. I'm starving. Let's eat."

He cupped her elbow and escorted her into the restaurant, settled her into her chair before sitting opposite.

The server bought them water and menus, and they ordered a bottle of Grenache from Côtes du Rhône to share.

"How was work this afternoon?"

"I was in meetings for most of the day, so...frustrating."

"You said it was a case I might be interested in—"

"Yeah," he grimaced apologetically. "Sorry. I shouldn't have said anything. Don't want to get in trouble with the new director."

"Now you have me intrigued." She swirled ruby red wine in the glass before taking a large swallow.

"You know how it is."

The slight tightening of her lips gave away her annoyance. "What's she like? The new director?"

Information was always king in espionage, but he didn't want to give anyone anything they didn't already know. "I only met her once, and she was suitably unimpressed."

"You didn't charm her? That's not like you."

He pressed his lips into a wry line. "I don't remember being particularly charming when I worked with you."

"Oh, trust me, your undercover *bratva* persona was preferable to the Chicago SAC who reveled in belittling me for every mistake I ever made. You met him. You know what he was like."

"Yeah, but by the time I met him, I didn't give a shit about his opinions."

"Lucky you. I was hoping the first female FBI director would be better than he was."

"She's okay. I don't think my charm or lack of it factored into any judgment." Only his actions, which on the surface might appear suspect. "Enough about me. Tell me what life is like living in a Caribbean paradise."

Her long fingers played with the fine stem of her glass. She'd removed her wedding band. Maybe she knew him well enough to know that he wouldn't find it appealing to sleep with another man's wife, even if the husband was supposed to be dead.

"It was lovely for the first few years, but I confess that since Charlie died, I've been thinking about moving back to the mainland."

"Getting back into law enforcement?"

Her lips pinched. "I was thinking more about the Diplomatic Service."

"Oh, wow, yeah, you'd be good at that." And it would serve her masters' purpose—assuming the Russians were running Bocharov, which he was pretty certain they were.

A dimple appeared in her cheek when she smiled. "I'm glad you think so. What about you? You can't jump out of helicopters forever. What's next when you retire?"

"I haven't thought about it."

"Liar."

"No, I figure as soon as I start to think about what's next, it's time to hang up my boots, and I'm not ready yet. Still have a few bad guys to put in cages."

"Still the raging idealist, I see."

"Hardly." He grunted. "But still ready to defend the Constitution and Protect and Serve, as required."

"I've always found patriotic fervor a huge turn-on." Her lips formed a very seductive smile. "Do you want to skip the main course and go straight to dessert?"

"I need more time." Alex insisted quietly in his ear.

The server approached.

"Let me at least buy you dinner." And figure out how he was going to not strangle her once he got her alone.

His work cell phone rang. He swore. "Sorry, I need to take this."

She pulled a wry face. "That's something I don't miss, being at the Bureau's beck and call."

He acknowledged that with a nod, got up, and walked to the front of the restaurant.

"What's up?"

It was Mac. "We finally got into the records from the limo company Bocharov used in Veracruz—"

"I'm in the middle of—"

"Dinner with former Special Agent Stork, I know, but I thought you'd want to know that the company we discovered that rented the vehicle also owns a private jet that just landed in a small airfield near Jackson, Virginia, twenty miles northwest of

Richmond. Flight reports indicate nine individuals, eight men, one woman got off that plane, which is still at the airfield. They rented two big SUVs. We tracked down rented accommodation for them near Montpelier. Secluded fancy house in the woods. About ten miles south of Moses Lake."

Fear clutched his throat. "Daisy?"

"She's fine. Regan and Cisco are with her. We have HRT en route to stake out the house in the woods. Description fits Bocharov, but he used a different name this time, Perkin Bates."

Emotion soaked Jordan like rain. It was him. It was Bocharov. "Another Hitchcock reference."

"Figured. I wanted to know whether or not you wanted in on the arrest."

"Fuck, yes. But what about Stork…" He turned around but the table was empty. "Shit. She's gone. Head's up, Alex."

"Roger that."

"Do you have enough to arrest her?" Mac asked.

"She lied to me about being married knowing I'm a federal agent. Everything else is circumstantial, but we can't risk her skipping out. She's here for a reason."

"Agreed. You and Alex apprehend her and then have WFO take over so you can join Gold Team for the takedown. I'll contact Ridley Branson to give him the head's up."

"I'll call you back." Jordan ignored the confused-looking server, noted both elevators were occupied so sprinted to take the stairs.

"Any sign?" he asked Alex.

"Not yet, but she has a weapon in her main purse. A now unloaded weapon. I'm going to step into the bathroom, see if she calls anyone when she arrives. We might get a name or a number. The room itself was clean of listening devices, but the Russians would want to know what she'd been up to. If it was me, I'd intercept her cell. See if you can get her to admit her involvement and offer her a deal for what she knows."

Jordan knew what Alex meant. See if he could get her to turn

State's Evidence. Let her avoid the consequences of getting his beloved sister, mother, grandmother and grandfather murdered in the most painful and obscene fashion. He wasn't sure he could do it.

When the alternative was terrorism involving nuclear material and radioactive fallout, he didn't have a choice.

Her room was on the third floor and Jordan raced around the corner just as she reached her door. "Oh, Jordan, I was coming back down. I had to grab something from my room."

He strode towards her with a cocky smile. "Couldn't wait for dessert, huh?"

She opened her door and gave him time to catch it before she hurried inside.

"Nice room." He followed her in. The balcony doors were wide open, the curtains gently billowing. "You wanna get naked?"

Her lip twisted into an ugly snarl as she pulled a Ruger LCP II from the leather purse sitting on a chair near the window. "Let's stop pretending, shall we?"

"But you're so good at it."

"There was no way you happened to bump into me today. I'm not stupid."

He let the door click shut behind him and hoped to hell Alex had removed *all* the bullets from her gun. "How far were you willing to go, Jenna? I mean, I know death isn't an obstacle but were you going to try to fuck me into telling you everything you so desperately wanted to know? Or were you planning to kill me as soon as you got me naked?"

"I know you'll find it hard to believe, but I'd rather fuck a cockroach than you."

"Hard same, Jenna, hard same. I'd need intravenous Viagra to get it up for you. No offense."

"Bullshit." Her expression twisted. "Bull. *Shit*. You'll screw anything with a pulse. That's why that stripper had to die."

Anger surged through him. "That stripper had a name—Ana

Orlova. And she had a razor-sharp mind and a soft heart, and she didn't deserve to die."

For years, Jordan had blamed himself for Ana's death, shame grafting onto his soul like a succubus, and, by association, tainting the act of sex, twisting it into something sinful. Now, he realized, the revulsion he felt after having sex, no matter how amazing, stemmed from Ana's needless death.

But Ana hadn't died because she slept with him. She'd died because this bitch had ratted on him, and Bocharov was a vindictive bastard.

He thought about Daisy and her non-judgmental attitude toward sex and hoped, maybe, he could learn from her. Learn to forgive himself.

He took a careful step forward, feeling the weight of his weapon in a pancake holster at his back. The bathroom door was ajar, and he had to assume Alex was there to back him up. He needed to get Jenna to talk. He spotted her fake wedding band on the dresser. Put it on the tip of his finger.

"Put that down." She vibrated with rage.

Huh.

"Charlie is a figment of your imagination, sweetheart."

"You don't know anything about Charlie!" Her finger tightened on the trigger.

Would she pull it?

He calmly held her gaze as he replaced the ring on the sideboard. "No records exist of you marrying anyone called Charlie."

She waved that away. "Charlie is very real. She comes and goes as she pleases. She eschews traditional institutions like marriage, but it doesn't mean we love each other any less."

So Charlie was real, and Jenna cared about her. Or Jenna was a delusional, compulsive liar. Jordan wasn't willing to rule out either scenario.

"If you love Charlie so much, why are you here trying to seduce me?"

Her expression crumpled for a moment. "I didn't want to. I had to."

"The way you *had* to betray me, betray my family so that they were burned alive?"

"I didn't have a choice—"

"Oh, you had a fucking choice, Jenna." His eyes smarted with tears he would not shed in front of this bitch. "You chose to betray your oath and sacrifice me and my family to the wolves."

Jenna's mouth went white. "It wasn't my fault."

"What do you mean it wasn't your fault? Are you saying you didn't tell Bocharov I was the FBI's inside man? Did the money matter to you so much more than basic decency?" A knot of emotion wedged itself high in his throat. "To this day, I can still smell the burning stench of their bodies."

She took a step backward toward the window. She shook her head, and her hair flew around her bare shoulders. "That wasn't my fault. It wasn't my fault."

"Tell me what happened, dammit." Jordan edged closer. "If you're going to shoot me at least have the decency to first tell me why you sacrificed my family to that monster."

Her eyes widened. "I didn't know he'd hurt them. I swear I didn't know."

He raised his chin. "You assumed he was going to kill me, right?"

Tears formed for a moment, but she blinked them away. "I told myself it didn't matter. That you'd known the risks when you'd agreed to go undercover."

"That I'd signed up for it."

She nodded.

He had known the danger, but he hadn't signed up to be betrayed by his own.

"What happened? Tell me what happened. I need to know, before…" Before she figured out the gun wasn't loaded. Before the other Feds got a hold of her. Before he threw her out of that fucking window.

He clenched his hands into fists and held them against his sides.

Her hazel eyes were wide and uncertain, like a little girl's. "It wasn't about the money. It was *never* about the money. Two men were waiting for me inside my home the night before the fire. Somehow, the Russians figured out the FBI had an undercover agent in Bocharov's organization. I don't know how—maybe that spy they had at the Washington Field Office told them. Our reports used your code name, but my real name was on the file." The gun barrel wobbled in her grip. "They threatened me. Hurt me." Her voice cracked.

"Broke you."

Her eyes flashed before she admitted defeat. "I know I should have gone to my boss. Warned you. But they threatened my mother, who lived in assisted living at the time. As soon as she passed, I left the Bureau." She shook her head. Firmer now. "I never had a choice. You'd have done the same thing to protect your family."

"No, I wouldn't."

She looked annoyed at that.

"I can help you. Cut a deal."

"There is no-one and nowhere these people can't get to."

"Bullshit." Before she decided to shoot him, he added quickly. "Why are you here now? More money?"

"It was never about the money."

"But the money didn't hurt. Am I right?"

"I'm here for Charlie!"

"Charlie's a Russian spy?"

"What? No. They *took* her. Told me they'll release her after I find out everything you know and lure you to a specific location."

Jordan cocked his head. "So they can kill me."

"Probably."

Zero remorse.

"Your girlfriend know what you did?"

"She didn't know anything about what happened." Her hand

shook. "I never told her. It wasn't my fault. They have her. I have to save her…"

"Who has her, Jenna?"

"Bocharov. Bocharov has her. I don't know where. I have to find out what you know and then take you to the place they'll communicate to me, and they'll let her go."

"Communicate how?"

"They always find a way."

"Did you see them take her? Can you ID them?"

She shook her head. "She was supposed to come home yesterday from a trip, but she didn't arrive at the airport and wasn't answering her cell. When I got to the house, I found a note on the dining table."

"The FBI can help rescue her—"

"Don't tell me the FBI can help! I was an FBI agent, and it didn't help me!"

Because you were weak, and they knew it.

"I promise I will help get Charlie back. HRT, the Crisis Negotiation Unit—this is what we do. With your cooperation, we can find her. You don't have to be their whipping boy any longer. Turn the tables on them. They won't expect it." He took another step. "Show me a photograph of Charlie. We can find her. Otherwise, they'll play you like a marionette until they have what they want, and they'll probably kill her anyway, if they haven't already."

Her face lost all color. "Don't say that. I have proof of life." She groped in her clutch then pulled out her phone. She tossed the bag aside without dropping the nose of the gun away from his chest as she scrolled through her photos. "Here—"

The glass in the window exploded in all directions. Jenna toppled like a crumbling statue, half her face gone. Jordan threw himself beside the window as another bullet lodged itself in the door behind him.

"Alex!"

The other man yelled back. "Shooter was on the roof across the street."

Jordan risked a peek out of the window, pulled out his phone and put in a call to the Capitol Police and told them there was an active shooter on the roof and an FBI agent in the hotel opposite being targeted. One victim. Deceased.

Alex came and crouched beside him and then motioned to the connecting door on their right. "I'm going to see if I can catch the bastard. Wait here."

Jordan grabbed his arm. "Don't bother. He's long gone."

This was a professional hit. Chances of spotting anyone was minimal. If Bocharov had wanted him dead, he'd have been the first target. No, Bocharov had other plans for him, he was sure of it. The assassin wouldn't be hanging around waiting for a second chance. They'd have enacted their escape plan already. "Cops are gonna lock this whole area down. You'll end up detained with a weapon and no badge."

"I have a permit."

Jordan huffed out a breath. "Killer is in the wind."

He glanced at where Jenna Stork's bloody remains lay on the hotel carpet. He noticed her cell.

"Fuck." He stretched out his leg and hooked the device with his foot and brought it to them.

"Careful what you say. Her phone could be bugged." Alex took a piece of tissue paper from inside a shopping bag from a boutique and used it to touch the cell.

"Don't let that motherfucking thing shut down. We need to access everything on that cell, and there's sure as hell no way we can unlock it with facial recognition now."

Alex pulled out a keyring, like the one Jordan had and pressed a red button. "Signal blocker."

Jordan nodded.

Alex quickly went into the cell's settings and then pulled something out of his pocket. Inserted it into the charger portal. "Cloning device so we can leave this for the crime scene techs if you want. We'll have all the information. They can run DNA and prints."

Jordan stared at the background image on Jenna's cell, the face of the woman in a loving embrace with Jenna Stork.

"Is that Charlie, do you think?" asked Alex

"I believe so." Jordan nodded as a large stone settled in his gut. "She's also the woman who sat beside me at the bar in Mexico the same night Tremblay fell out of the window." He frowned at the image. "I don't think she knew who I was. If she did, surely, she'd have told Bocharov?"

The sound of sirens filled the air.

"Think she was there under duress? Forced to meet someone?"

Jordan shrugged. "Maybe? They could have threatened to shoot her girlfriend if she didn't do as they told her." He frowned, remembering. "She seemed more sad than stressed."

"Or she's part of the whole thing. Spent the past few years keeping Jenna on a string, keeping an eye on her, manipulating her. The willing idiot."

The bullet had come moments after he'd asked to see a photo of Charlie. "We need to figure out exactly who this person is."

Alex pocketed the cloning device and tossed the cell back toward Jenna's corpse.

Jordan climbed to his feet. Tried the door to the connecting room and found it locked. He kicked it open, thankful the room was empty as he strode through the darkness to the door. Alex followed.

Jordan called Mac from the stairwell. "Tell WFO that instead of questioning a suspect, they have a murder scene to process. Jenna Stork is dead, and someone tried to kill me."

25

It felt weird for Daisy to get behind the wheel of her car and drive, as if the world had fundamentally shifted since the last time she'd done it. She pulled away from the curb, feeling the weight of eyes on her as she drove past familiar trees and buildings.

The moon played peek-a-boo with the fast-moving clouds. The air felt heavy, the wind gusting, spitting rain. She parked out front of the physics building in an empty lot. The only light was the one above the main door. She shivered when she turned off the engine and felt the wind shake her car. She released a heavy breath and shouldered her bag. Tried not to slam her door before she hurried up the steps to swipe her card and push inside.

She headed straight for the stairs, jogged up them all the way to the top floor, and flipped the light switch.

The room looked like it always did. Full of books and computers, slightly cluttered, a little bit dusty. Einstein and Marie Curie bobbleheads sat on the window ledge, wisely nodding away.

How could evil inhabit this space?

She expelled another short, sharp breath, grateful there was no one around. She pulled out the letter and used the plastic bag to maneuver the envelope into the exact same spot as she'd found it.

She stood back and assessed it critically, moved a book over by a millimeter.

Satisfied, she grabbed the tablet from her desk and then strode to the door.

She froze as the door opened. Amed stood there, looking tired and pale, holding a baseball bat.

She pressed one hand to her heart and slipped the other into her bag, finding the cold metal of her pistol. "Oh my goodness, you *scared* me!"

"Daisy. It's you. Sorry." He rubbed his deep-set eyes and lowered the bat. "I didn't know you were back. I saw the light and figured I should check for an intruder." He shrugged his thin shoulders. "I'm sorry. I feel very paranoid lately. Like I'm being watched." He hunched his shoulders, and she swallowed tightly and tried to ignore the camera she wore around her neck and the guilt that weighed about a thousand pounds.

"Have you been here all day? I popped in earlier and saw Emilia but didn't see you."

He shook his head. "I was at home. It's my son's birthday. I spent most of the afternoon on a video call, watching him open and play with gifts with my wife and parents." His mouth turned down with unhappiness.

"I don't know how you can live so far away from him."

He frowned and for the first time ever she saw anger on his face. "You think I have a choice? You think I don't miss him every single day and wish they were here with me? I'm doing it for them."

Unease moved through her, and she let her fingers grip the Glock. "Doing what for them?"

"Learning. Bettering myself."

She relaxed.

"Finding a way to lift my family out of poverty." He rubbed his eyes again. "Apologies for raising my voice. Sometimes I miss them so much I can barely stand it. Now I have work to do."

"Can't it wait until tomorrow?"

"The sooner I finish, the sooner I can get to somewhere they can be with me."

Fear struck again. "What do you mean?"

"I applied for a visa for them to join me here, but it was denied." He stared at her with blank, unsmiling eyes, and a shiver of something cold snaked down her spine.

"Thank you for putting those rods on my bench." She forced out lightly. "Perhaps I could talk to you about it on Monday, if you have time? I know you have a lot going on with your big project this week."

He looked agitated and tapped the bat against his leg. "Maybe. But I need to make sure everything is perfect. I don't have much time…"

"That's okay," she soothed. "I'll talk to Wilson. I have a couple of basic questions about the best way to go about the initial steps anyway. I don't want to mess up."

He nodded at her, shadows under his eyes making him look as if he hadn't slept in days.

She moved toward him, and he stepped aside to let her pass. She kept her hand inside her bag. If he wanted to, he'd probably get a hit in before she could shoot, so she had to be prepared for that. "Goodnight then. Happy birthday to your son."

"Daisy," he said when she came abreast of him.

She stopped even though what she really wanted to do was run. She swallowed. "Yes?"

His dark eyes pierced her. "Be careful. It's dangerous for a woman alone."

She shivered and hurried past him, jogged quickly down the stairs and slammed out the front door, her heart pounding as she raced for her car. She sat there, lights glaring into the darkness even as the night pressed in on her.

Starting the engine, she reversed and drove faster than she usually did all the way home.

And she realized suddenly, the one thing Amed hadn't asked her during their tense interaction, was whether or not she'd had anything to do with François Tremblay's death—and she couldn't help wondering if that was because he already knew how Tremblay had died.

Jordan hitched a ride on Alex's company private jet and even got to practice his flying skills as co-pilot. They landed in the same airport where the Russian aircraft was still parked.

Alex was dressed completely in black. "I'm going to check out that other jet."

Jordan frowned. "You sure that's a good idea?"

Alex shrugged. "Won't know unless I try it."

"Better I don't know anything about it."

Alex smiled slightly. "I keep forgetting I'm surrounded by Feds."

He was married to one.

"Yeah, well, be careful, okay? This guy isn't an amateur." Jordan checked his watch. 2:07 a.m. He was torn between backing up Alex and getting to the muster point in time to join Gold Team for the raid.

Alex read his mind as he checked his weapons. "Don't worry about me. I work better alone. You texted Daisy yet?"

Jordan pulled a face. "She doesn't want to hear from me."

"Bullshit."

"What do you mean?"

"I was watching her expression yesterday morning. She only closed down and pushed you away after you told her you were worried about her because you'd promised to protect 'Kurt's daughter.'"

"I never said that." Jordan thought back while Alex silently watched him. "Fuck. I did say that."

Perversely, a strange kind of excitement moved through him. If his words had hurt her, maybe she wasn't as emotionally detached as she'd pretended to be. It didn't change the fact he had never been in a successful relationship. Given the snippets he'd overheard about the issues she'd had with her parents growing up, he suspected he'd need to fully commit to convince her he was worth taking a chance on. One hundred percent.

He didn't know if he was capable of that.

Doubt crowded out the short-lived optimism. Some people were better off alone. Plus, Bocharov was still out there, threatening everyone Jordan cared about.

"I'll call her in the morning, when Bocharov is in custody."

Alex pulled out a ski mask and dragged it over his face. He handed Jordan another, which Jordan reluctantly took. Better not to be seen exiting this aircraft. The pilot had instructions to fly on to Richmond as soon as they exited.

"You want coordinates for where I'm meeting HRT?"

Alex shook his head. "Mac sent them while you were being interviewed by WFO."

A process that had taken way too long as far as he was concerned. At least he'd been able to borrow a black T-shirt and tactical pants from one of the SWAT guys.

"Catch you later." Alex opened the door and disappeared into the night.

Jordan swiftly followed him and headed toward the main building where a black SUV waited.

He tapped on the window and pulled up his mask.

Grady Steel unlocked the door. "Thought it was Spiderman for a second there."

"You got my hopes up, for a moment. Tom Holland is hot. So are you, Krychek. Obvs." Meghan Donnelly, in the driver's seat, straightened and started the engine.

"What about me?" Grady grumbled.

"You're hot too, Grade."

"Feels like a pity compliment."

"You're my partner. I wasn't sure how comfortable you'd be with me calling you hot."

"As long as Brynn isn't in earshot you can call me hot."

Jordan caught her smile in the rearview.

Ryan Sullivan lounged in the back with a ball cap pulled low over his face and appeared to be sleeping. "What about me?"

"What about you?" Meghan was already speeding away from the airfield.

Jordan looked behind them, but there was no sign of Alex.

Ryan leaned forward. "You can't not say you don't find me hot if you find Tom Holland and Grady hot."

"That's a lot of double negatives in that sentence, and heat levels are subjective."

"For some people maybe," drawled Ryan.

"Oh, my God. Are you sure your ego can fit back there?"

"I don't have an ego."

Even Jordan laughed at that. It was good to be back with the team even as he worried about Daisy.

"I don't have an ego," Cowboy insisted again.

"But you get upset if I don't say I think you're hot," Meghan countered.

Cowboy sat up straighter and winked at Jordan. "That's because I know you're lying."

Meghan's hands gripped the steering wheel tightly, and Jordan could see the flexing of the muscles in her jaw while she silently strove for calm. "You know I'm armed, right?"

"And dangerous," Grady muttered out of the side of his mouth.

"You're hot, Krychek." Cowboy sent Jordan a grin. "All the girls think so. Even the boss's daughter."

Fuck.

"What about me?" Meghan asked with a quick look at Jordan in the rearview. She was trying to deflect the comments that were surely headed his way. He appreciated it. He just hoped they could get through this op before he had to deal with the flack.

"You?" Cowboy asked as if she'd spoken in Greek.

"Yeah, me, the person driving the vehicle. Do *you* think *I'm* hot?"

"On a scale of Tom Holland and Grady Steel, Donnelly, you're off the charts."

"Oh," she cocked her head, "but I'm not Ryan Sullivan hot."

"I never said that." Ryan's lips pinched.

Jordan added a little fuel to the fire. "You pretty much did."

"I think you're hot, in the most respectful and non-threatening, platonic manner possible," Grady said cautiously. "If you are cool with that and Brynn doesn't freak out when I tell her about this conversation later."

"You'd tell Brynn you think your co-worker is hot?" Ryan sounded aghast.

"Yes, I tell her everything that I'm allowed to." Grady sounded disgusted. "I fucking love her, man. I *want* to tell her everything. She lost a lot with everything that happened, and I'm trying to help her fit into her new life here, however I can."

Ryan scrubbed a hand over his face. "I'm happy to come by and tell Brynn she's hot any time she wants. I always did have a thing for redheads."

Jordan watched Donnelly stiffen but Grady laughed.

"She'd shoot you if you tried," Grady countered.

"I thought she'd forgiven me for our little misunderstanding?"

"Ha. It's not just one and done, man. You gotta earn forgiveness over the long term."

"Ain't that the God's honest truth." Ryan sighed. "Something tells me offering her sexual favors wouldn't be appropriate."

Grady turned around to glare at his colleague, and the car wobbled slightly.

"I'm kidding. *Jesus.*"

It struck Jordan that Ryan and Daisy had the same attitude toward sex, but both also used it as a deflection away from deeper issues. What was Ryan trying to hide? Jordan glanced from Ryan to Donnelly and back again.

"I think you're sizzling, Donnelly," Jordan said quietly.

He caught her smile and Ryan's frown. *Oh, yeah.*

She tilted her head to one side as if considering. "I'll take it. I could do with the morale boost."

"You need a morale boost? How come? Someone mess with you?" Grady queried with a frown.

She shrugged. "Some jackass."

Jordan stared hard at Ryan, but his teammate was staring out the window.

"In that case, you're ghost pepper hot." Grady told her. "And don't forget it. And that's from your partner who has impeccable taste in women, not one of the team Lotharios."

Jordan grimaced. That people were comparing him to Ryan Sullivan, the consummate ladies' man, was like a bullet to the chest.

Did Ryan feel as lonely as he did most nights?

Meghan pressed her lips together. "Appreciate it, Grade. Might have to get a tattoo of a ghost pepper on my ass now."

Ryan groaned.

Grady's teeth flashed. "Now give me the name of the fucker who hurt your feelings."

"Just some guy. Doesn't matter. His loss." She stared determinedly at the road ahead.

Jordan decided it was his turn to deflect attention now. "Now, if we are all confident of our sex appeal, can anyone give me a SitRep?"

Unusually, Ryan kept his brooding gaze directed out the window on the dark terrain.

Grady filled in the silence.

The world had flipped on its head.

"We have nine confirmed heat spots in a two-story mansion on a lake. Supposedly one woman, eight guys. Can't get a visual on any of them as they closed the blinds and as we didn't arrive until after two. They all appear to be in bed asleep except for a couple of bodyguards who are taking turns patrolling the grounds. Six bedrooms in the main house and a small servant's residence in the back, which also seems to be where the security is quartered."

"How many people do we have down here?"

"All of Gold Team. They pulled everyone off watching your place for now."

"What about Daisy's protection detail?"

He felt the weight of the interest of all three of the other people in the vehicle even though none of them so much as twitched an eyelid.

"Blue Team Echo Squad got pulled in to shadow her,"—she wouldn't like that—"but they've been diverted. We had a break in the case thanks to a letter Daisy found where she works that turned out to be a jihadist's suicide note in an almost extinct language from Pakistan. Blue Team are now assisting local SWAT to bring him in." Grady checked his watch. "They are all set to go the same time we move in on this house here."

Jordan's emotions swung between fear for Daisy's safety and the need to put Bocharov in a cage, or a grave, for good. "She's not alone though, right?"

"Two TacOps agents are with her."

That should be enough. Regan and Cisco might seem like nerds, but they were both fully fledged FBI agents, and Regan was no fool.

"One klick out from rendezvous point," Grady told him.

He couldn't resist any longer. He should be checking his weapon, but instead he pulled his cell and tapped out a quick message.

>When this is all over, we need to talk.

Even though it was the middle of the night, the answer came straight away.

>Nope. Not interested.

Disappointment filled him, and he thought about how to best play it. Begging wouldn't work with a woman like Daisy. He wasn't even sure what he wanted yet, just that he wanted more. Despite Kurt, despite the fact he should know better. He wanted more.

> Liar.

Then he turned off his cell, knowing that would infuriate her, and concentrated instead on the upcoming op, that might end the danger for good.

26

Daisy lay in bed looking up at the shadows dappling the ceiling and listening to the sound of traffic in the distance.

Didn't matter how tired she was, she couldn't sleep.

The FBI had finally deciphered the letter she'd taken from Amed's desk. It had been written in Gowro, a severely endangered language from the Kohistan region of Pakistan, that few people could read. According to it, Amed planned to carry out an attack in the name of *Allah*.

Nausea churned inside her. Daisy shifted restlessly on the pillow. It didn't make sense. He'd always told her how much he detested those who twisted the Koran to justify violence.

Had he been lying? Playing the long game to suck them into being blindly compliant or stupidly complicit? Was he working with Konrad Bocharov?

Her throat ached from holding back tears.

Amed would never see his family again. The pity of that competed with the awfulness of knowing he'd kill her and her lab mates and set off some kind of nuclear catastrophe that could do untold amounts of damage if he wasn't stopped. It was the antithesis of why she'd become a nuclear engineer. The antithesis of making the world a better place.

Had *he* killed Francois? Had the professor somehow uncovered his plan or seen him with Bocharov?

She didn't know. She assumed the FBI was trying to figure it out.

Cisco was on the couch while Regan had opted for the blowup mattress on the floor. She should have given him the bed considering she couldn't sleep anyway.

Where was Jordan?

Was he safe? Did he think about what she was doing, how she was feeling?

Her cell lit up on the bedside table, and she picked it up, staring at a message from the man himself, as if she'd conjured him with her thoughts.

> When this is all over, we need to talk.

God, no, not the dreaded "we have to talk" bullshit where he told her all the reasons they wouldn't work or how he just didn't suit her.

> Nope. Not interested.

Why would she be interested in hearing everything that was wrong with her? Or worse? Him suggesting they maybe see each other again, date for a little while, probably so he didn't feel so guilty regarding her father after he'd fucked her against the wall so earnestly that morning.

She blew out a short, sharp breath.

Oh, yeah, he hadn't been thinking about her daddy then.

The memory made her tingle.

Had it only been that morning? So much had happened since then, it felt like a month ago now.

She waited to see if he'd reply, maybe try to persuade her somehow.

But it already hurt and that was with all her barriers in place.

She wasn't about to pull them down and let him worm his way into her heart so he could shatter it later.

No way. Not this time.

Finally, he replied.

Liar.

Outraged, she sucked in a breath. WTF? The guy had some nerve. Her pulse buzzed as she contemplated how best to reply.

A sound snagged her attention. The creak of a floorboards and then her door opening. Sounded as if someone had left the apartment.

She swallowed. The FBI planned to arrest Amed sometime tonight. Maybe Regan had heard something. She thought about following him and asking him, but he wouldn't tell her until Amed was in custody and any co-conspirators were identified and locked up.

The knowledge made her heart hurt. She set her phone down and closed her eyes, determined to get some rest now she was home.

The Hostage Rescue Team positioned themselves in stacked formation, holding at the two main entrances, having decided not to go in via the roof because there was the distinct possibility that the occupants of the bedrooms would hear them below.

They'd captured the guy patrolling the grounds, quickly and quietly.

Jordan was last in line behind Ford Cadell and Hugo, the team's Belgian Malinois. The fact they'd let Jordan take part at all was a miracle and, no matter how tempted he was to put a bullet through Bocharov's front teeth, he would honor Ackers' trust in him and only shoot anyone who pointed a gun at him or his teammates.

"Target two down." Luke Romano confirmed they'd neutralized the second guard in the smaller house.

"On my count," Payne Novak instructed over the comms.

Shane Livingstone stepped up with the breacher.

"Five, four, three, two, one, go."

On "go," Shane hit the door hard, and it shot open and banged against the wall, but the guys were already inside and heading upstairs.

Jordan followed with his H&K 416 held to his shoulder. Echo Team had the other side of the house as Charlie Squad hit the stairs.

A man ran into the hallway buck naked. Raised his hands when he saw the approaching heavily-armed, black-clad figures. "What is the meaning of this? What is the meaning!"

"On the floor." Aaron Nash held the weapon on him as Malik Keeme slipped plastic zip ties around the man's wrists to tie his hands behind his back.

Despite his training, Jordan's pulse revved.

Livingstone and Will Griffin went into another room and had two more individuals out of bed and on the floor being restrained.

A woman started screaming.

Grady spoke over comms. "We have the target plus a female."

No shots had been fired, which was always a relief. In fact, aside from the guards, Jordan hadn't seen a single weapon. A feeling of foreboding began to fill him as he strode toward the master bedroom with Ryan Sullivan on his shoulder.

A bald, broad, chunky man was on his knees facing in the other direction to the bedroom door. Bocharov? The size and shape of his head and sound of his voice matched. "What is the meaning of this?"

"Quiet." Donnelly snapped.

But the man ignored her. "I demand to know what is going on. I demand to speak to your president, immediately."

President? Jordan frowned.

"I am the *Ambassador extraordinary and plenipotentiary of the*

Russian Federation to the United States of America, and I have diplomatic immunity as do my staff. I demand an explanation about what you are doing here, waving guns at us, threatening us. I will make sure every one of you loses your job. I will make sure you never sleep soundly again!"

"Is that a threat?" Grady bristled.

"No, young man, it is a promise."

Jordan lowered his weapon and strode around to stand in front of the bald guy. "Sonofabitch."

"Well?" Novak demanded in his ear. "Is it Bocharov trying to pull a fast one or not?"

Jordan swallowed the knot in his throat. "No, sir. I believe we just raided the Russian Ambassador."

It was the smirk that did it. The smirk that told him this had all been carefully choreographed and that the ambassador knew exactly who they were after and had deliberately tried to trick them.

It was a distraction, just like that night Bocharov had murdered his family.

His heart started hammering. He ignored the malevolent glitter in the other man's eyes, strode out of the room, and then hurried down the stairs.

He met Novak at the door and pulled the comms off and flung them away. "I need a chopper to get to Richmond ASAP."

"Why?" Novak's frown looked thunderous.

"Daisy—"

"Is fine. I just spoke to Regan and updated him. She's fine. She's in bed asleep." Novak clasped his hand on his arm.

Jordan shook him off. "Bocharov planned this. He planned all of it. I think he'll go after Daisy while we're all tied up in bureaucratic knots."

"Jordan, we just conducted an armed raid on the Russian Ambassador. There's going to be a fuck-load of paperwork and red tape to wade through. Frankly," Novak sounded worried and he was damn near unflappable, "we'll all be lucky to keep our jobs."

"He's part of the plan, goddamn it. The ambassador was in on it. This was staged deliberately to make us believe it was Bocharov."

Novak's expression was a cross between exasperation and pity. "Head back. I'll talk to you tomorrow, assuming the director doesn't arrest my ass for starting World War Three."

"It already started." Jordan strode toward the vehicles. He knew he sounded insane, but he also understood the enemy better than any of them. He had to get to Daisy.

He tried calling her, but she didn't pick up. He tried calling Regan, but it went straight to voicemail.

A shadow moved, and Krychek had his pistol out and pointed only to realize it was Alex Parker.

"Fuck. Alex."

"Sorry." The other man stepped out of the shadows. "What happened?"

"Motherfucker set us up along with help from the Russian Ambassador and his entourage. What did you find on their plane?"

Alex smiled. "Enough to know the ambassador is gonna have some tough questions to answer in the morning. The New York Times and Washington Post both got a hold of information proving he was in collusion with a Russian arms dealer previously believed to be dead and that he knew exactly what he was doing when he stayed here tonight."

They'd been set up. Just like he'd been set up all those years ago.

"I need to get to Daisy." Sweat formed on his back. "Novak thinks I'm paranoid, but why stage this kind of distraction only to humiliate us?" He shook his head. "It's what Konrad did the night he murdered my family, and I need to reassure myself he's not going to target Daisy."

"You care for her."

Jordan dragged both hands through his hair. "Of course, I *care* for her, but I'd be worried even if I didn't. He's a fucking monster, Alex. An evil fucking monster, and if he finds out you're helping me, everyone you care about is in danger too."

Alex held his gaze for a long moment, but this was not news to the other man.

Alex jerked his head toward one of the black Suburbans. "Think they'll miss one?"

Shit. They didn't have any transportation, and worry gnawed on his nerves like a mouse on a live wire.

Jordan looked back at the little bird helicopters set well back from where HRT had staged. Novak hadn't actually said no. "Let's see if the pilot will drop us off close to where Daisy lives. It's not as if he'll have anything else to do tonight."

27

Daisy woke with a start but for the life of her didn't know why. She was in her own bed this time, no Jordan Krychek nearby, having a nightmare because his demons were doing a jig on the family grave. Something inside her contracted in pain at the thought of how many years he'd been suffering. At how many nightmares he'd endured. She hated everything that had happened to him. She hated that she wanted to be the one to soothe him, to distract him, to make him forget his traumatic past.

As if *she* were special.

When, in reality, she was just last night.

She checked the time. 3:52 a.m.

Gave a gusty sigh.

She was not a morning person, not if she could help it. She snuggled back under the covers and started to drift off again.

Another muffled sound had her opening her eyes wide again.

Was that coming from the Pagets' apartment downstairs? Had one of her elderly neighbors fallen? Was there a break-in?

She swung her legs out of bed and slipped her feet into her sheepskin slippers.

She hesitated before picking up her Glock but decided better safe than sorry under the circumstances and then put her cell phone in the pocket of her red plaid PJs for the same reason. She snuck into the living room, spotted Florence fast asleep on the couch. Regan's bed was empty.

Maybe he'd decided to sleep in the back of the van? Maybe there was news about Amed's arrest and he hadn't wanted to wake anyone.

Was that what she'd heard?

Regan doing something Regan-esque?

She hoped Amed was okay. She didn't want him to get hurt. She wanted to understand how he could be so generous and helpful on one hand and plan their destruction on the other.

She headed to the apartment door and paused for a moment, listening.

There were sounds downstairs she couldn't identify. Someone moving around? Had there been a medical emergency? A burglary?

Gripping her Glock tightly, she started down and immediately the scent of something pungent assailed her nostrils. Gas? She wrinkled her nose. No. Shit. *Gasoline*. What the hell?

She hesitated on the stairs, and the next moment she heard a footfall on the landing outside the Pagets' apartment. The saliva in her mouth dried up, making it hard to swallow. She couldn't see due to the dividing wall, but there was definitely someone there. She held her breath and prayed they didn't come around the corner.

Regan?

It was probably Regan.

She almost called out but something stopped her. Would Regan be creeping around her neighbor's landing? Probably not. He'd be pacing somewhere, taking up space, using up oxygen.

Blood started to pound in her ears. She backed up a step, then another, trying to ease her weight down softly to avoid creaks. Then she hit a riser that groaned like a wailing cat.

She froze. Heart pounding.

Dammit.

A man appeared at the bottom of the stairs. Big. Bald head. Clean shaven. Small, beady, calculating, pale-blue eyes. He could have been handsome if not for the twisted sneer on his lips.

The man from Mexico. The Russian Jordan said burned his entire family alive.

Now the smell of gasoline struck fresh horror along every nerve.

She scrambled backwards as he pulled a large black revolver from the back of his waistband. She lunged for her door, then remembered the Glock in her hand, firing instinctively behind her, to give herself time to get inside her apartment and barricade the door.

She heard a cry of pain and looked over her shoulder to see him holding his left arm.

"I was going to gift you with a bullet as an act of mercy"—his accent was thick, his voice deep and guttural—"but now you deserve what you get, *you stupid little cunt*."

The door opened behind her.

Cisco fired at her assailant, and he leapt out of the way behind the partition but got a shot off. His bullet slammed into the wall beside Daisy, plaster spitting into her face with a sharp sting.

Cisco grabbed her arm, hauled her inside with surprising strength.

Daisy slammed the door behind them and locked it. Then jammed a nearby wooden chair under the handle. They ran into the kitchen, crouching behind the kitchen island as bullets rocked the door in its frame.

Cisco held a firing stance, waiting for Bocharov to burst inside. "Where's Regan?"

"No idea. I heard a noise downstairs and went to investigate."

"Without your bodyguard?" It was the first time she'd ever heard Florence sound anything but agreeable.

"You were asleep!" But with hindsight, Daisy felt stupid for not waking her first. "I thought it was Regan or my neighbors, who are elderly, having some kind of emergency. He has emphysema." It hit her then. "Oh God. Do you think Bocharov hurt them?"

"I don't know, but I doubt he dropped off a care package." Florence pulled her cell out of her pants pocket and dialed. She'd slept fully dressed, and Daisy wondered why she'd bothered to put on her PJs.

She'd been trying to pretend things were normal, but they weren't even close to being normal. She had a horrible feeling her life would never be normal again.

They both kept their weapons aimed at the door, but the shooting had stopped.

Florence's whisper was worried. "Regan's not answering his phone."

Daisy stared at her wide-eyed.

The idea of anything bad happening to Jon Regan was unthinkable.

He was larger than life and twice as sarcastic.

Cisco's mouth was tight as she made another call, this one to 911. Daisy checked her cell and even as she kept one eye on the door, she dialed Jordan.

"Hey." His background was really noisy, and it was hard to hear what he was saying. Daisy swallowed the lump in her throat that threatened to choke her.

She wanted to hear more of that voice.

"Hey back. Good news and bad news. Bocharov was here." Her voice was surprisingly steady as if she hadn't faced down a vicious killer. "I shot him in the arm, but we think he got away. Florence and I are safe in my apartment, but Regan's MIA," her voice rose in agitation. She couldn't hold it together anymore. "I'm worried about my neighbors downstairs and—" A sob choked off the flow of words.

"Okay. It's okay. We're calling local cops and putting out a description and roadblocks. Every cop in the city will be descending on that area ASAP. Stay put. He won't get away,

Daisy. Not this time. Just stay put and stay safe. ETA six minutes. I, er, I care about you."

He cared *about her?*

The admission floored her even though it wasn't a mad declaration of love. He wasn't a man who easily allowed himself to care about anyone outside his work. She knew that. Whereas she cared about people too easily but rarely allowed herself to admit it. Because it gave them too much power.

The power to hurt her.

The power to make her weak.

She noticed Florence's visible sniff of the air at the same moment she registered something that stopped her heart.

Smoke.

She'd expected it, having guessed Bocharov's plans after smelling the gasoline.

Terror nevertheless wound its way through nerves and flesh, twisted around sinew and burrowed deep into the marrow of her bones. Her hands shook. They were on the third floor of an old Victorian house with original, well-seasoned hardwood floors and original wooden siding. Every inch of this place—aside from the decoratively tiled cast-iron fireplaces—was a tinderbox of highly flammable material.

"I have to go, Jordan." She squeezed her eyes shut because she didn't want to tell him the rest, but she had to. "I-I think he set the house on fire."

He cursed and told someone to go faster and call the Fire Department.

"We're coming, Daisy. We're coming, and so is every First Responder within a ten-mile radius. Hang tight."

She remembered what he'd said about his sister and how Bocharov, or his goons, had shot her when she'd tried to escape via the window.

If they tried to leave, would they also be shot? Was her fate, after dedicating her studies to making things safer, to burn in an old house or be shot trying to escape the flames?

"I have to go. We have to find a way out of here, but whatever happens," her voice cracked, "this isn't your fault. None of it is your fault." And because she knew this might be the last time she ever spoke to him, she told him the truth. "I care about you too."

She swallowed the smoke already irritating the back of her throat and hung up before he could answer.

"We need to get out of here." Florence's brown eyes were wide, expression determined.

"Agreed." Daisy filled the sink with water and tossed in dish towels before grabbing a fire blanket she kept under the kitchen sink, ripping it out of its packaging. "When Bocharov did this last time, he shot Jordan's sister when she tried to climb out of a window. We need to get to the back door and then run for cover." Daisy wrapped a wet cloth around her nose and mouth and handed Florence the second. She turned off the taps although she had no clue why.

Old habits died hard.

"First, I need to check on my neighbors."

Florence tied the cloth bandana-like around her nose and mouth, eyes worried because she wasn't a fool. "Let's go."

They flung open her door and took cover behind the jamb, but there was no one there.

"They've gone."

Smoke formed a thick layer that rushed inside her apartment in a choking wave.

"Come on."

Cisco took the lead, but they both held their weapons. The idea that anyone remained behind when she could see the inferno at the bottom of the stairs was ludicrous unless this was a suicide mission.

The noise was incredible. The roar of the flames as they consumed fuel, deafening.

Daisy closed the door behind her and stumbled down the stairs. Cisco looked over the banister to the ground floor below. Her brown eyes held fear. "Can't get out that way."

Daisy ran to the back door of the Pagets' apartment which occupied the middle floor of the house. The ground floor was a fancy retail space they rented out to a realtor. Thankfully, the door was unlocked. She dashed inside, horrified to see their drapes already ablaze.

She'd fed their cat when Mr. Paget had needed to stay in the hospital overnight and Mrs. Paget had refused to leave him, so she knew the layout. She dashed to a door off the living room where they had their bedroom and burst inside.

What she saw made her stop cold. Despite the growing heat, ice invaded her veins.

The elderly couple both lay in bed, obviously dead. Strangled if the red marks around their necks were any indication.

Florence checked their pulses, took a photo, while Daisy stood frozen. What kind of monster would do such a thing?

The agent grabbed her arm. "They're gone. We have to leave."

The other woman began to drag her away. Then Daisy remembered Renfield.

"Wait." She jerked away and searched the room quickly, under the bed, under the chair, in the wardrobe. "They have a cat. A black cat."

Florence quickly searched the living room as Daisy ran into the kitchen. They were both coughing now. The smoke getting dangerously thick. She knew they had to get out of here fast. Oxygen deprivation was the biggest killer in house fires.

"Renfield." She grabbed and shook the bag of the cat's favorite treats, pieces scattering all over the counter and floor. Finally, a ragged meow sounded at her feet. She scooped him up and wrapped the fire blanket around him as he tried to escape, those sharp claws scratching at her skin until she was able to contain the furious beast.

"We have to get out of here," Florence yelled. She went to the window and threw it open. A bullet smashed the glass and made the FBI agent leap aside. "But not that way."

Florence jogged back to Daisy.

Daisy ran back onto the landing and looked down, but there was no escape that way. None at all. The flames were fierce now, like the inside of a forge. Heat blasted up the stairs.

"Back to my apartment," she yelled.

They thundered up the stairs and closed the door behind them. Florence put towels against the base of the door as they both panted.

Daisy coughed. Dammit. They were trapped. The flames were too intense to go down. They couldn't get out through the windows because of the shooter.

She thought she heard sirens.

Once the cops arrived, would Bocharov or his henchmen stick around? Maybe to pick them off while they were being rescued by some hot firefighter?

It was possible.

If she and Florence and Renfield didn't move, they were certainly going to die.

Goddamn it. She refused to stand here and burn. It wasn't her time. She wasn't ready. It would wreck her dad when he'd just found happiness.

A thought hit her.

Maybe...

No.

It was too dangerous. Might not work. They might get shot. They might burn or fall. All the options were awful.

But what the hell.

It was probably the only chance they had, a slim one at that. Better than sitting here and waiting for the inevitable.

She wouldn't give Bocharov that satisfaction. She'd rather die on her own terms than succumb to that fuckface's evil plans.

She grabbed a rucksack and wrangled the frightened feline inside. The look of betrayal in his yellow eyes made her want to weep, but she was going to need both hands to hold on, and she needed Renfield secure. She clipped the security feature on the zipper so he couldn't open it from the inside.

She grabbed her purse and stuffed her laptop inside. "This way."

Florence grabbed her laptop bag, slung it over her shoulder and ran after Daisy even though she looked confused. She stopped short in the bathroom.

Daisy turned on the shower and was shocked when water came out the nozzle. She stepped under the spray which was warm and made sure the outside of the rucksack was drenched.

"I don't understand…" But Florence followed suit, taking her glasses off before standing under the spray.

Daisy crouched at the hatch that led into the attic.

The board was nailed shut but not tightly. She sat on the floor and used both legs to kick it in.

Inside was small, dark, and hot as an oven. It was also full of cobwebs and spiders, but right now Daisy wasn't about to let her distaste for arachnids, nor her fear of enclosed spaces, paralyze her.

"This way."

She crawled through the narrow gap then dragged the pack behind her. Renfield was racing around inside the backpack like a Tasmanian Devil inside a dryer. She pulled the straps over her arms and onto her back and felt his claws strike flesh.

She gritted her teeth, edged cautiously along the center beam. It was so hot in here she felt as if her skin was starting to singe and the oxygen was evaporating.

"The skylight!" Cisco spotted the dirty glass up ahead.

Daisy moved faster, careful not to tread either side of the beam and fall through the ceiling. They reached the old skylight, and Daisy shuddered in horror at the big, fat spiders that sat there. Cisco had no such qualms. She batted them away, turned the handle, and shoved at the window. It was stuck, and Daisy's heart stuttered. It was getting difficult to breathe.

This time Daisy and Florence pushed together, and the window shot open.

Florence cupped her hands to hoist her up.

Daisy hesitated, but she was much shorter than Florence. Plus, the first one out got to test whether or not the shooter could spot them.

She hauled herself inelegantly through the opening and then wriggled onto her belly and turned back around, flattening herself against the slippery roof tile. Florence hauled herself up and out. Daisy grabbed the back of her pants to help drag her out onto the exposed roof.

They both lay there for a few seconds, panting hard. The skylight faced the back of the property, and they were sheltered from view by the apex of the roof.

Daisy crawled as far as she could to the right while Florence explored the left. She'd been hoping for some kind of multilevel roof or old-fashioned fire escape they could climb down.

There was nothing.

She and Florence stared at one another for a long moment. They'd made it outside, but there was no easy way off this roof. They were trapped.

28

Jordan had trained thousands of hours over the years so he could extend the gray zone during combat and operate without physiological stress responses screwing up his reflexes and fine motor skills. But, right now, panic had a stranglehold around his throat, and his lungs hurt as his heart thrashed wildly in his chest.

He couldn't lose Daisy.

No one could operate effectively in the black zone. He was useless to everyone, especially her. He started tactical breathing. Count of four inhale. Hold for four. Count of four exhale. Hold for four. Repeat.

He felt his heart rate begin to slow and his blood pressure ease.

"What's our ETA?" Alex demanded, checking his sidearm and watching him with concern.

"Three minutes out," the pilot told them, after contacting air traffic control over Richmond to clear the way.

Krychek got his finger out of his ass and called Mac to update the task force. He'd call Kurt when Daisy was safe. She was going to be safe.

"Bocharov attacked Daisy in her home, and he set fire to her building. She called me." Fuck, fuck, fuck. What if that was the last time he ever heard her voice? "She and Agent Cisco are looking for a way out. Jon Regan is missing." He feared the worse for the senior agent. Bocharov wasn't one to show mercy. "We notified emergency services. We need to make sure there aren't any snipers in the area preventing Daisy and Cisco from getting out." Like the bastard who'd killed his sister—and the one who'd killed former Special Agent Jenna Stork.

The same person?

Perhaps.

Bocharov sure didn't have the patience or the skill.

"We need Gold Team routed to Richmond, ASAP." He couldn't believe coherent words were coming out of his mouth. "You need to alert the airports. Put out BOLOs on Bocharov. Shut down all private flights. Alert the traffic cops and port authorities, and let's catch this sonofabitch. He'll be armed and dangerous, and he won't want to go to prison."

"I'll make the calls. You concentrate on getting Daisy and Agent Cisco out of that situation. Keep me updated." Mac hung up.

Jordan checked his weapon and then scanned the early dawn sky.

"There." He pointed. Black smoke was faint against the muted grays.

The pilot had already spotted it. He turned the aircraft slightly and increased the throttle.

They flew fast, but it seemed to take forever to reach the burning building, every second an eternity. They hovered over the street and Jordan was relieved to see firefighters rolling out hoses and beginning to pump water on the base of the structure.

The house had been a glorious mint green Queen Anne style Victorian with a turret at the front and decorative gingerbread trim that was singed with brown as the paint began to blister and ignite. He knew Daisy lived on the top floor in the converted attic, but that was all he knew. Even from here, Jordan could see the ferocity of the flames on the ground and middle levels—there was no way for a human to survive in those flames. The sight of it threatened to drag him back to that other time when he'd helplessly watched from the sidelines.

Not this time.

"The roof. Take me to the roof."

"Wait. What about snipers?" Alex asked.

"Doesn't matter." Jordan swallowed, needing to get to Daisy and Cisco.

"It matters if we get gunned down and can't rescue anyone."

Fuck, he was right.

Alex indicated a park at the end of the street. "Drop me there. I'll watch the buildings facing the fire, and if anyone appears with a rifle, I'll make sure they don't get the chance to aim for very long."

Even though every second counted in a fire, it was a good idea, especially when he remembered what Jenna Stork's face had looked like after that sniper's bullet found its mark.

"Hurry," he urged the pilot.

Alex jumped out before they'd even landed and sprinted away.

They swooped straight back up into the air, and the pilot swung to approach from the south. Flames were licking the eastern hip of the roof.

"Drop me there." He pointed. "Wait." Jordan couldn't believe his eyes. "You see what I see?"

Because of the shape of the roof, the women weren't visible from the front.

"Damn straight." The pilot grinned, bringing the bird in closer to the roof. Daisy knelt against the roof on all fours, whereas Cisco sat up and then, stood, waving.

"You're going to have to get real close."

"I know it."

Jordan climbed over the seats into the back and clipped into the safety harness.

The tall chimneys and the steep pitch of the roof made it incredibly dangerous for the pilot to get close without the main rotors or tail rotors touching something and killing them all.

The east end of the roof suddenly collapsed, sending up a wave of sparking embers. The turbulence sent the machine rocking wildly for a second. The women below cowered, trapped between burning timbers and deadly blades. Jordan leaned out of the machine, stretched out his hand and caught Florence by the forearm. She gripped tightly and he swung her onboard as the pilot struggled to steady the bird. She got her foot on the rail and boosted herself into the cabin.

He leaned out farther, and the pilot once again hovered closer to the roof. Daisy crouched away from the rotors but, when they got close enough, stretched out her arms to toss in her bag which he caught and threw on the seat. He didn't care about her belongings.

"Get in the fucking helicopter!"

"I'm trying." Her hair was damp and slicked back. Blood ran down the right side of her cheek. Dirt streaked her usually pale skin. He leaned farther out and Cisco grabbed his legs.

"I can't hold position for much longer," the pilot warned.

"Another inch closer."

"This whole roof is going to collapse."

"Jump, Daisy," he shouted. "Jump! For the love of God, you have to trust me to catch you. Jump!"

He watched her make up her mind and then take a determined leap off the tiles. As she did so, the roof beneath her started to collapse, and the pilot began to bank away from the inferno to avoid the heat wave.

Jordan caught her wrists, clung, refusing to let go. Her feet scrambled, and eventually her knees found the rail. He hauled her inside, gathering her close as she collapsed against him.

Cisco placed headphones over Daisy's ears. She'd already grabbed a pair for herself.

"I can't believe I almost lost you." Jordan could barely speak.

"I can't believe you got to us in time." Daisy's voice was gravelly. "Another few seconds, and we'd both have been dead."

He stared at the collapsing house which was way beyond saving. The idea of her dying in those flames ripped him apart. He closed his eyes, wrapped his arms around her, and squeezed tight. Then pulled away as something in her backpack bit him.

It didn't matter.

He pulled Cisco in for a hug too. She might be an FBI agent, but she was young and inexperienced, and she'd been through hell and survived. She was allowed to have a moment. They all were.

They landed back in the park, and the pilot began winding down. "Gold Team are rendezvousing here. ETA thirty minutes."

Alex appeared at the open doorway and grinned like a loon.

"Cut it a little fine, but good work. No visible threats on the street. My thinking is they booked it as soon as the cops showed up."

"There was a sniper earlier. They shot out the middle floor window when I attempted to open it." Cisco wiped the back of her hand across her forehead, smearing soot as Jordan and Alex exchanged a glance.

Jordan helped Daisy and Florence climb out of the bird, shielding them with his body and guiding them away from the deadly tail rotors. "Let's get you two somewhere safe so a medic can look at you."

"I'm fine," Daisy insisted, touching the cut on her cheek with a wince. "A few minor scrapes."

Cisco pulled away. "I have to find Regan. I'll check the van."

"Wait. The bomb squad needs to check that vehicle first," Jordan warned.

Cisco looked startled by that.

"Another of Bocharov's little tricks."

"You know how to check for explosives," Daisy insisted. "Let's go see if Regan is in there."

This fucking woman.

"You're a target."

"Jon Regan might be hurt or dying. I won't take away resources that could help him."

"Fine." He wanted to be angry, but he wasn't even surprised. He wanted to know what had happened to the head of TacOps even though he feared the worst.

"Hey, Harry Marcus is in town. They had him on the Hussein raid. We could call him in," Cisco suggested.

"I don't need Harry fucking Marcus to check for explosives." Jordan ground his teeth. "I'm as highly trained as Harry when it comes to IEDs."

Daisy raised her brow but thankfully didn't say anything.

Now who had the big ego?

Jordan and Alex and Cisco shielded Daisy on three sides, though she might not have realized it as they hurried toward the front of the street where the van was parked.

"My vehicle is parked behind the van," Daisy pointed out.

All three of them were scanning the row of houses in front. Many of the residents were on the sidewalk, huddled in small groups or talking in shocked whispers.

The four of them stopped about twenty feet away from the vehicles and did a slow 360, looking for shooters.

Mesmerized for a moment, Jordan stared at the flames as the old Victorian continued to burn. It reminded him of his nightmares and would add another layer of horror, only this one involving the woman at his side. He'd prefer a million sex dreams to the scorching reminder of death.

Daisy's fingers gripped his arm. "Hey, it's okay. Everything is okay."

The fact she was comforting him after she'd been through such a traumatic experience made his eyes water, just a little, but he blinked the moisture away. This was no time for weakness. Bocharov was in the wind, and he needed to catch the bastard before he harmed anyone else.

"I'm okay. It's you I'm worried about."

"I'm fine, considering. I need to talk to the fire chief about the Pagets, my neighbors..." Daisy's voice broke, and he wrapped his arm around her and pulled her tight, only to be bitten, again.

"What the hell is in that rucksack?" He winced as he looked at the teeth marks in his arm.

"Renfield." Daisy took off the pack, and he saw there were bloodstains on her clothes. "The Pagets' cat." Her eyes were huge, face filthy, hair almost gray and stinking of smoke. He didn't think he'd ever seen anyone more beautiful. "I won't dare let him out until we're somewhere he can't escape, but the poor thing has to be terrified."

He stroked a hand down her arm. "We'll get to a hotel shortly for a debrief. You can let him out there. He's lucky to be alive."

"Ron and Alma doted on him." Tears brimmed in her eyes and one spilled over making a track in the dirt. "They never hurt anyone, Jordan. They were kind. That bastard slaughtered them without a care just to get to me."

"To get to me." He squeezed her elbows. "None of this is your fault."

"It's not yours either. Don't you see that?"

Jordan shook his head. Maybe one day he'd be able to let go of the guilt, but he wasn't there yet, not when Bocharov had so nearly taken Daisy, and Cisco, and had murdered two more innocents.

His throat hurt. He desperately craved water and guessed they would too. But he needed to check out the TacOps van first. And Daisy's car. In case the danger wasn't over.

"You stand over there," he pointed to a house thirty feet away.

Daisy opened her mouth to argue.

He dragged his fingers through his hair in frustration. "Look, I can't concentrate on finding explosives if I'm worried you're in the blast zone."

She closed her mouth and nodded. "I'm not going to argue. I was just going to say, *be careful*." She lowered her voice. "And if you find Regan dead, don't let Florence see."

He nodded.

"Agent Cisco, watch Daisy," he instructed firmly.

Daisy took the other woman's arm and went to stand where he'd told her, which was a goddamned miracle. Alex was telling other people and first responders to clear space around the vehicles.

Jordan walked around the van and did a thorough visual inspection without touching anything. He wished he had Gold Team's tools, but if Regan was inside, he might be hurt. If there was a bomb, it could go off on a timer. Who knew how much time they had left?

Sweat dripped down his back, drenching his shirt.

It had already been quite the twenty-four hours, from the best sex of his life to rescuing a woman he cared about so much he'd have willingly thrown himself into that fire to save her.

That wasn't *care*.

That was *love*.

Whether he liked it or not, he loved the independent, scared-of-commitment hellcat who'd somehow stolen his heart.

Now wasn't the time to be distracted from what he was supposed to be doing. He couldn't think about the fact that the chance of winning her over was next to zero. He couldn't think that after all these years of pushing people away, he'd fallen for someone just like him. Isolated, focused on their career, unwilling to open up. Though their reasons were different, the results were the same.

He didn't miss the irony.

He had to focus. He had to focus and then track down and eliminate Bocharov once and for all. Putting him in a cage wouldn't keep Daisy safe. Only Bocharov's death would do that.

Then he could think about love and a new chapter of heartbreak if he couldn't persuade her to take a chance on him.

He circled the van again, saw nothing suspicious. There was nothing obvious inside the front of the van. He crawled onto the ground, wet from water running off the hoses. He inched his way beneath the vehicle, working section by section, knowing the clock could be ticking.

He found the improvised explosive device attached to the fuel tank. Wiped the sweat from his eyes as Alex crouched down and peered at him.

"Got any wire cutters?"

Alex handed him a multitool with the cutter extended.

"You might want to move farther away."

Alex shook his head. "I have faith."

Fuck. Shit.

How many people had he gotten killed in the past? "Fool."

"On the contrary, but don't make me regret it." The guy smiled.

Jordan nodded, wiped the sweat from his forehead again. He used his fingers to feel around the package and discover the simple mechanism connected to the cargo door.

You opened the door, the bomb went BOOM!

He closed his eyes and saw the device clearly in his mind, followed the circuit. Mapped out the whole system before isolating the wire he needed.

"Last chance," he warned Alex as the sharp blades caressed the plastic covering on the wire.

"Do it."

Jordan offered a silent prayer, and then cut the wire. When nothing happened, his heartbeat slowly returned to normal.

"Disarmed. Be careful in case they've boobytrapped inside." It was unlikely, but Bocharov enjoyed inflicting maximum pain.

Alex nodded as Jordan wriggled out from under the van. They stood at the back, and Jordan carefully eased open the cargo door, scanning for wires. Seeing none, he opened it wide.

Jon Regan slumped against a monitor. Blood covered half his face and most of his shirt. It didn't look as if he was breathing.

Grief hit Jordan unexpectedly hard.

Scanning the area for any tripwires and explosives, Jordan

climbed into the back to feel for the man's pulse, more as a formality than a necessity.

"Took you long enough." Regan's voice was a faint whisper from between cracked lips.

Shock and relief rushed him. "We've got you now, Regan. Any explosives I need to know about in the vehicle?"

"Don't think so, but I was out for a while."

Jordan quickly checked the area to make sure it was safe for others.

"Medic!" Jordan yelled.

EMTs pushed him aside as they quickly put a neck brace on Regan and carried him out. Cisco took her boss's hand and hurried with him to the ambulance.

Jordan stood there in the cold morning air, looked up to see his colleagues from Gold Team pouring out of the black Suburbans, throwing him worried looks. His gaze went to Daisy as she stood staring at him with huge, traumatized eyes.

An EMT had put an oxygen mask on her, and her color looked a little better than before, but her eyes told the real story.

Cisco jogged back to him, fury twisting her features. "They're taking him to VCU Medical Center. He said someone beat him with the butt of a gun."

She jumped into the TacOps van and, ignoring Regan's blood, pulled up some feeds on the monitors. She had blisters on her hands, but it didn't slow down her typing. They watched what had happened to Regan replay on the screen.

He glanced at Daisy to make sure she was still close by.

His cell rang. Mac. "They arrested Amed Hussein in his home fifteen minutes ago. He got a phone call warning him to get out shortly before, but Blue Team were already on site. They scooped him up and are busy searching his apartment building now."

"Regan's alive but injured. Bocharov left a bomb under the TacOps van for when we tried to rescue him."

"Sonofabitch. I want that entire street cleared. Every house searched from top to bottom. People don't want to cooperate, use lidar radar and see if anyone's inside. Get verification on all identities, just in case he stayed in the area to watch the show."

"If he was still in the area, he'd have detonated the bomb when I was under the van."

A sobering thought.

"Cover all the bases. I have a full-blown fucking diplomatic crisis on my hands with this Russian Ambassador fiasco, and Director Rhodes wants all of us fired."

"You should probably check the news."

"Why?"

"A little bird told me the Russians are going to be too busy covering their asses denying any involvement in the murder and attempted murder of American citizens on US soil to even attempt to leverage the raid how they'd originally planned."

Jordan heard the sound of the TV being turned on in the background.

"When can you get back here?" asked Mac.

Jordan stared at Daisy as she laughed up at the medic. Despite all her armor plating, happy was her default. How would she ever be satisfied with a miserable loner like him?

"Jordan? You there?"

Jordan jolted back to the conversation. "Might be better if the task force joined me here. I need to check in with Daisy and figure out the next steps to ensure her safety. And I need to talk to Regan. Talk to the local police. We rescued our own, but two innocent civilians died here tonight."

"I know it. And those Russian assholes are gonna have quite the conversation with State today by the looks of it. Relocating the task force to Richmond makes sense. I'll begin the process to set up at the Richmond FO, but I'm gonna be stuck in DC tomorrow in meetings."

"The joys of being the boss."

"Tell me about it. Oh, and by the way, tell Alex *thanks* and *good work.*"

"I don't know what you're talking about, but I hope to hell the

President expels the lot of them. They knew exactly what they were doing last night. They were a distraction while Bocharov was busy committing murder." The Russian's favorite way of doing business. "They knew his plans and were complicit."

"We haven't conclusively linked Konrad Bocharov to Amed Hussein yet."

"What about the phone call that warned him he was blown?"

"Burner phone. We haven't been able to trace it, nor find any digital correspondence."

"Maybe they did it with letters the old-fashioned way."

"Perhaps. Evidence techs are still going through his house, the university buildings where he worked, and the gym that he had access to." Mac paused. "We have every law enforcement official from here to Alaska on the lookout for Bocharov. He won't get away."

As Jordan stared at the smoke still pouring from the ruined house, he knew it was too late. He already had.

29

Daisy's teeth wouldn't stop chattering. The local police department's bomb squad, alongside Harry Marcus, were called in when Jordan found another device under her car. The thought of surviving that horrific fire only to be blown up when driving away was sickening. Whoever planned that was evil. Pure evil. She watched the cops clear everyone back and bomb techs approach wearing bulky blast suits, carrying shields.

Jordan hadn't had any protective gear when he'd disarmed the bomb under the van earlier, she realized—and she'd encouraged him to do it.

What the hell had she been thinking? That he was some superhero?

He could so easily have died.

They could all so easily have died tonight.

"Tell them to blow up my car," she insisted. "It's not worth anyone dying over."

"They'll want to retrieve the device intact if they can. Plus, the TacOps van could be damaged in the blast." Florence sat beside her on the back fender of one of the Suburbans HRT had roared in on. The cargo door was open. "We need to collect evidence. We need to build a case for when we catch these bastards."

The bomb tech in charge had refused for anyone to move the TacOps van farther away in case it inadvertently set off the car bomb, but considering fire trucks and ambulances and squad cars had rumbled up and down the street all morning, Daisy felt it was misplaced caution.

But who was she to argue with the professionals?

A crowd of people who lived close by had formed behind a police line at the end of the street. Another behind them. HRT were systematically searching each house, looking for the bad guys who might have holed up to avoid authorities.

It was a smart play.

Though the fire had largely been put out, timbers still smoldered, and the acrid smell of smoke saturated the air and made her stomach clench in reaction. A cough racked her lungs. The extra oxygen had helped. Didn't hurt that the medic had been gorgeous. She'd spent most of her time talking up Florence because the woman sure looked like she could do with a pick-me-up.

"Any word on Regan?"

Florence's expression was pure misery. "Last I heard, he was getting an MRI."

"Having his head examined. It was only a matter of time," Daisy joked.

Florence smiled weakly.

"Have you figured out what happened?"

"From what I was able to piece together, it looks like Regan went down to check something in the van. Not sure why. His cells are missing, and we're trying to track them and get the data off of them. Best guess is he heard something and came down to investigate, or he got a call. He was surprised from behind, beaten unconscious. Dragged into the van. They took his creds and his service weapon too."

"He's gonna be so mad."

Florence nodded. "He's going to blame himself for everything."

Daisy bumped her shoulder into Florence's. "Who does that sound like?"

The other woman hung her head even as she nodded. "Yeah, and it's bullshit. I almost slept through everything. If you hadn't woken me by confronting Bocharov, I'd probably never known there was a fire. I'd be dead right now and wouldn't even know it."

Daisy shuddered at the thought. "The smoke alarms would have woken us both."

"Maybe." Florence looked at her then, and the self-loathing in her gaze was hard to bear. "I'm going to quit. I'm obviously a shit FBI agent. I don't know why I ever thought I'd be good at this."

Daisy stared at the woman in shock. "Florence, you might not strut around swinging dick, but you returned fire on a Russian arms dealer who has evaded detection for more than a decade. You were shot at but continued to perform your duties, and you jumped off a burning roof onto a freaking helicopter. On top of that, you can do things with electronics and computers that make these guys look like kindergarteners."

Florence's lips tightened. "My superior is in the hospital."

"Your partner should have told you he was stepping outside."

Florence straightened her spine. "Damned right he should've."

"And I should have told you too. I'm sorry."

Florence held her gaze and nodded. "Forgiven." Then she grinned. "We did some bad-ass shit today, and it isn't even nine a.m."

"I need coffee."

Meow.

"Aw, poor baby is probably hungry." Florence glanced at Renfield who was now curled up inside a travel carrier one of the firefighters had pulled from a truck.

It had taken three people to get the cat safely in there, and they all sported fresh battle wounds.

"I need to see if the Pagets' daughter wants him. I spoke to

Mac, and he said FBI agents were going to inform her about the murder of her parents in person…" Daisy's voice trailed off. It could so easily have been her parents receiving that news today. Her loved ones being devastated. She didn't want to even think how badly it would have affected Jordan.

"I'll take him if the daughter doesn't want him," Florence volunteered.

"Really?" Daisy tilted her head. "I didn't think single FBI agents had pets."

"I live with my sister, so Renfield won't be lonely if I get involved in a case. She's a sucker for kitties and lost hers last year."

Daisy stared at poor Renfield, who watched her with accusing amber eyes. His owners had been such gentle people. "I think Ron and Alma would be pleased to know that whatever happens, Renfield will be cared for in a loving home, but"—she held up her hands and turned her wrists over to examine three long, thin scratches—"I don't envy your furniture."

The medic had treated the bites and scratches with salve, but they still stung.

In the distance, the bomb tech stood and signaled the all-clear. A tow truck was immediately waved through.

"Well, looks like my car survived the ordeal."

Florence nodded. "Hope you get it back before the holidays."

She huffed out a resigned breath. "I guess I'm going to get a lot of exercise in the meantime."

Jordan came out of a house and started walking toward them with a purposeful stride. Her mouth watered at the sight of him.

"He's been through a lot." Florence stared at him with her mouth turned down at the edges.

Daisy nodded.

Florence shot her a look. "Don't hurt him."

Her eyes welled with sudden tears. "To be honest, I think it's much more a question of him hurting me."

Florence touched her arm. "At least give him a chance."

The idea terrified Daisy, but she was worried about something else too. "Do you have feelings for him?"

Florence blinked at her in confusion. "Like *sexual* feelings?"

She nodded.

"Dude, I'm gay. I thought you knew that." There was a guardedness in her gaze now as if unsure of Daisy's reaction.

"Well, that's a relief." Daisy laughed. "I worried seeing us together might somehow be an issue for you."

"He's not my type." Florence cocked her head. "Neither are you, in case you're wondering."

"I wasn't." Daisy carefully took the other woman's hand and squeezed her palm, avoiding her blistered fingers. "I am hoping this might be the start of a beautiful friendship."

"I hope so too. I don't have many girlfriends—who even has time to socialize? *And* I'm going to make myself scarce." Florence gave her another quick hug and then headed over to talk to Payne Novak, Gold Team leader.

Jordan took Florence's place on the fender.

"All done?" she asked with forced brightness as if Jordan had been outside mowing the lawn or something equally mundane rather than hunting armed and dangerous killers.

"Street's clear." He dragged his hand through his hair, making it stick straight up on end. "Feds found more bomb-making instructions and material in Amed's apartment building, hidden in a basement storage cupboard. He's denying everything."

Her fingers went to her sore throat. "I can't believe it was him. He was so nice. He helped me so much."

"The best terrorists are those we don't suspect until it's too late."

Her eyes held his. The shadows were still there, but they held a gleam of hope now too.

"What about Bocharov?"

"We have every lawman in the country on the lookout, and he

was added as number one on our Most Wanted list. He won't get far." He spoke with confidence, but she knew it was a lie. He didn't want her to worry.

"When are you headed back to Quantico? Today?" She needed to remind them both he'd be gone soon.

He cleared his throat. "Task force is moving down here to make sure the terrorist plot is really foiled. I'll be here to make sure that Bocharov doesn't try for you again in the next couple of days."

After everything that had happened, she didn't mind the idea of a bodyguard, but it couldn't last forever. She knew how the federal government worked. Thankfully, she still had her gun in her purse for when she was on her own. "I'd say you could stay at my place, but it looks as if I'm going to need a new apartment." Tears bubbled up all of a sudden—for the Pagets, for the wanton destruction of their beautiful historic home, and for all the personal things she'd collected over the years—paintings from a friend, her beloved books, her most perfect mug. Her clothes.

"Crap. I'm crying about *things* when people lost their lives."

He wrapped his arm around her, and she let herself sink against him as hot tears streamed down her face.

"Sorry." She sniffed. "I'm not usually a crier."

"You earned a few tears."

She saw some of the guys from Gold Team out of the corner of her eye and tried to wipe her eyes and pull away, but he pressed her filthy face against his chest.

He smelled almost as bad as she did, so she took advantage of the moment and burrowed closer, as close as she could get.

"I know what it's like to lose all those connections to the past, Daze. I don't have many family photographs left except for a few I downloaded off their website before we shut it down and a couple I had on my phone. I was careless. I assumed they'd always be around. It's another wound. A hollow ache as memories of them gradually fade away."

She gripped his shirt. "At least I still have my family." Her fingers tightened. "You warned my mom and dad, right? You told Boulder Police to put someone on my mom because she won't listen to reason. I shot him, and then I survived his efforts to kill me. He's going to add me to his hate list."

Jordan's hand splayed over the back of her skull, and she found it frighteningly lovely.

"The local Field Office has been informed and will surveil both your parents whether they like it or not." His stomach gurgled audibly, and she pulled away, amused.

"Sorry." He laughed, sounding a little embarrassed. "I skipped dinner last night when my date tried to kill me."

She met his amused gaze. "There's a lot to unpack in that statement."

His lips twitched. "How about I tell you all about it over something to eat with the guys?"

She glanced over at the mob of Gold Team who all looked ridiculously handsome in their tactical gear and square-jawed seriousness.

She looked back at Jordan who was staring at her with an intensity that was hard to mistake. He wanted to take this thing public. Not just the lies told to get her out of Mexico, but the reality of *them*.

She gripped her hands together. "I don't know."

"Let's take it a day at a time, okay? You have to eat, right? Then we can go see Regan, get a proper statement, and kick his ass for breaking protocol. Head into your workplace and see if the evidence techs have finished up there."

She groaned and covered her face. "My colleagues are all going to blame me."

"They should be thanking you. Without you, someone would still be planning to kill them this week, and they wouldn't have found out until it was too late."

She sucked in a breath. "It does sound better when you phrase it that way. I still can't believe Amed would… I thought I was a better judge of character than that," she admitted. She didn't want to think about death anymore. She wanted to think about anything else.

"Let's go. I don't know if I can eat, but I do need coffee."

Jordan slid his arm over her shoulder and hugged her close, easing her into the melee of testosterone and madness.

30

Ten hours later, Daisy and Jordan arrived at a hotel, exhausted, feet dragging even though it was only 7:30 p.m. All she wanted to do was to close her eyes and sleep. Not think about Bocharov, or the Pagets, or people who tried to kill others for no good reason.

She knew she should be feeling relief. She was safe. The FBI had foiled Amed's terrible plan to slaughter them all before he hijacked the truck carrying the nuclear fuel rods, along with a shit-ton of explosives, and rammed it into the White House.

She wasn't sure how far he'd have gotten or how much damage he would have inflicted, but obviously none of this was good. The Russian Ambassador had been recalled to Moscow, and if she were him, she'd stick to the ground floor for the next decade or so.

So why did she feel as if she'd failed?

Because she'd been tricked? Fooled? Because two people were dead and another person she liked had turned out to be a lying and violent asshole who she'd never suspected.

Both her parents had called to reassure themselves she was fine, and she'd possibly glossed over the part when she'd been trapped on the roof with only seconds to live. They didn't need to know that.

She was surprised and grateful no one had captured the incident on video and weren't stitching Tik-Toks together of the rescue. Otherwise, her mom would be demanding she come home, as if she alone could beat Bocharov with facial expressions and angry-mom energy.

They'd visited Regan, who'd looked shockingly pale and fragile against white hospital sheets. He'd lost a lot of blood and had a minor skull fracture, but he was going to be okay thanks in no small part to his hard head. Florence planned to stay with him overnight. Renfield had been claimed by the Pagets' bereft daughter, who'd wept all over Daisy.

Wait until she discovered it was Daisy's fault her parents were dead. Saving the cat was the least she could have done.

She glanced around the hotel room dispassionately. She frowned as she eyed the single king-size bed. She wasn't sure how she felt about sharing that with Jordan now.

Everything had changed in the past twenty-four hours. She'd gone from ruthlessly trying to prove a point while maintaining her emotional distance to Jordan admitting he cared for her to teetering on the edge of falling head over heels for the guy because she was an idiot who never learned a simple lesson.

Sex? Not a problem. Sex she could easily handle, and it would even help take her mind off the events of the day. But holding, comforting, sleeping?

She wasn't sure she could handle that.

The air was chill, and shivers ran over her skin, making the scratches throb and the burns sting. Every injury was minor, but cumulatively they made her feel hurt and diminished, unsure how to deal with everything that had been thrown at her.

One day at a time was what Jordan suggested, but what happened the day he stopped caring? When he stopped calling? The day "one day at a time" became the occasional booty call and she was left with excuses and scraps and then dumped for someone prettier, more easy-going, with bigger boobs?

She didn't think she could bear the emotional fallout this time.

She hung her bag on a hook. It stank of smoke, but it was all that was left of her belongings except for the few items she had at work and in her car. She'd grabbed a shower and borrowed a set of clothes from an agent about her size at the Richmond Field Office earlier that day, but traces of soot, ash, tar, had embedded themselves into the grain of her skin, alongside memories of the Pagets lying dead in their bed and their beautiful house destroyed on the whim of a monster.

A monster she'd shot in the arm.

It was a pity her aim had been off. This nightmare would have been over by now if she'd shot the guy in the head.

"Let me run you a bath while I order something to eat."

Her throat ached at the care and attention Jordan had shown her all day. It couldn't last, and while she wanted to enjoy it, all she could think was that he'd be gone soon and she'd miss him.

Work.

Life.

She understood.

She really did.

She just didn't want to rely on him. Didn't want the lack of him to leave her destroyed. She was stronger than that. She had to be stronger than that.

"I can do it."

He was already in the bathroom turning the taps.

Federal agents had set up in various rooms around the hotel. They even had snipers strategically placed on the roof of this hotel and the one across the street. The Feds were taking no chances.

Knowing Bocharov was out there somewhere, probably raging that his plans had been thwarted by a female filled her with both satisfaction and unease.

She wasn't stupid, she knew she couldn't go about her life and simply pretend everything was okay. She also knew the FBI, Jordan in particular, wouldn't rest until the Russian was captured.

That could take *years*.

They couldn't protect her like this forever. It simply wasn't feasible. Nor did she want them to. She would need her life back sooner or later. Her solitary and busy life.

With no time for relationships.

She closed both blinds and drapes, immediately felt a sense of peace. She didn't want people watching her through windows, even if they were there to protect her.

Jordan came back into the room, taps running in the background.

"What do you want to eat?"

She shook her head. "I'm not hungry."

He squeezed her shoulders. "You have to eat. How about a glass of wine in the tub first?"

She turned, faking a smile. "You don't need to bother with the seduction routine, Krychek. You are definitely getting laid tonight."

Anger sparked in those blue-green eyes, the way she'd meant it to. "I'm going to ignore that as you've had a difficult day. I'll order you a steak sandwich and fries. I'll eat anything you don't want."

She watched him place the dinner order, and her stomach grumbled when he told her the kitchen was backed up and the food would be at least an hour.

He headed into the bathroom and turned off the taps. Came back into the bedroom and untucked her long-sleeved black tee from her waistband like she was a child who couldn't undress herself.

She didn't need to be taken care of. She didn't want to be taken care of. Not like that. Not as if she were special. She wanted the control back. She needed it.

"As we have an hour, we may as well make use of it." She

peeled up the shirt and tossed it away, then shimmied out of her pants, standing there naked.

He tilted his head to one side considering her in a way that made her nervous. She didn't like nervous, so she stepped toward him and reached for his belt buckle.

He stopped her. "Not so fast there, Montana."

She blinked at the use of her last name as he captured her wrists in one of his hands and backed her up against the bed. Her knees buckled.

He lifted her bodily and tossed her into the center of the duvet and then followed her down, fully dressed. He tugged her arms up over her head.

"What are you doing?" She sounded breathless, and that was even more humiliating after the way he'd manhandled her.

"I'm making good use of the next hour. I'm going to need you to hold on tight to the edge of the mattress. Don't let go."

She wasn't sure how to deal with this new dynamic. She was used to calling the shots, to shocking and seducing him, not the other way around. She frowned at him, feeling exposed and unsure. "I don't understand."

The blue-green of his eyes was vivid as he smiled, obviously amused. "I'm awake this time, sweetheart. We're going to do things my way for a change."

Her eyes widened, and she held her breath as a strange excitement filled her. But desire was tempered by fear. She was the one used to calling the shots in this arena. She didn't want to feel all the things he made her feel.

He didn't wait for permission. Not this time. Though she knew he'd stop if she asked him to, it was strangely intoxicating to be on the receiving end of this kind of male dominance.

He took her mouth, kissed her, softly at first, gently, making her relax, slowly, bit by bit, until her bones melted and she sank into the mattress and moaned.

She sank her fingers into his hair, and he stopped kissing her and removed her hand and gently placed it back above her head.

"My rules, remember?"

She blinked, but he was kissing her again, angling her chin to take the kiss deeper this time. Stoking the flames of her desire.

He nibbled her jaw, the vulnerable line of her neck. It took her a moment to figure out what he was doing as he toured various parts of her body. He was careful not to tickle her as his lips made their way across each scratch and burn, each bite and blister. Kissing each one better. Kissing her better.

A knot tangled in her throat. Emotion caught her off guard. "I can't…"

"You can." His tongue moved to her nipples, made the hard peaks beg for attention like ripe raspberries to be plucked into his mouth.

She gripped the edge of the mattress and closed her eyes, bowing up against that clever tongue.

He moved down her body, slowly. *So* very slowly.

"Please…"

"Please what?"

"Fuck me."

"I don't think so."

She opened her eyes to complain at the exact moment he put his hands on her thighs and sank his tongue inside her.

"Oh." It was all she was capable of saying as he feasted upon her until she was a quivering mess.

"Please, Jordan."

"Please what?"

"Fuck me." The words were spoken between gritted teeth. He was keeping her on the edge but never letting her go over, until every nerve sang with want.

"No." Instead he flipped her onto her front. She was more comfortable with this and understood what he wanted from her so she tried to get up onto her knees, but he wouldn't let her.

Instead, he started with a tender kiss on the cut on her cheek and the slight burn behind her right ear. Then her neck and the bites and scratches Renfield had etched into her flesh. Sweet tender kisses that she didn't know what to do with. Kisses that wanted to comfort her even as she fought against being comforted.

She brought her hand down to try to reach for him, but he paused and put her hand back up again.

"Do as you're told, Montana, and I might eventually let you come."

His words had her squeezing her legs together.

"Do it."

"Do what?"

She rolled over, and he let her as they stared at one another as if connected on some other level.

"Fuck me. Please."

"Are you begging?"

"Pretty please?"

The smile on his mouth was confident as he settled back between her legs and touched the tip of his tongue to her aching clit.

She opened her mouth in shocked surprise at how good that felt.

"God, yes. Pretty, pretty please."

He licked her. Lightly played with her clit, with her nipples, tweaking just enough to keep her in a constant state of arousal but not enough to tip her over the edge into orgasm.

"I want you inside me."

A funny light entered his gaze. "I want you to ask me properly."

"Don't you think I've suffered enough today?"

He stroked her G-spot, and she gasped.

"No, but I have." His lips were back on her breast now, fingers playing so gently in the slippery folds of her sex that she'd never come without more, but it felt so *good*.

"Please, Jordan, I'm begging you."

"Ask me to make love to you."

What? Her heart banged against her ribs. *What?* She swallowed. "Make love to me, Jordan. Please."

"I already am."

She gasped as he bit just hard enough to ignite sensation, just short of pain, and his fingers plunged deep and hard as the heel of his hand stroked against the quivering bud of her clit, and she was catapulted over that edge like a boulder against a battlement.

She shattered into a thousand pieces and lay destroyed as he climbed to his feet, completely dressed. The only thing letting her know he was not unaffected was the erection tenting his pants.

He slid his hands gently under her and lifted her and carried her through to the tub, placing her gently in the warm water.

"Enjoy your soak." He kissed her forehead and turned away.

"Don't you want to..."

He paused. "Not until I prove it's *you* I care about. Not the sex, not the fucking, not coming inside a willing body—*any* willing body. It's you. I think I love you, Daisy Montana. And you're going to have to figure out what to do about that because I'm not going anywhere."

She stared up at him, shocked. But she'd heard words of love before, and they'd still left her with her heart torn to tatters. Bitterness reared up inside her.

"Now who's the liar?"

―――

It wasn't easy having his words of love ignored, disbelieved even, but he also knew she was carrying a lifetime of baggage from abandonment issues thanks to a series of crappy boyfriends. His reputation and decidedly poor track record with women didn't help. And, as he had a time-consuming and demanding job—exactly the same job her father had when her parents had split—it was going to be an uphill battle to convince her he was serious about her.

But he'd never said those words before. Not even as a teen when he'd had more than his fair share of girlfriends from high school in the Ukrainian Village, and further afield within the great metropolis of Chicago. He'd come close to the feeling with a girl he'd met while posted in Texas once, but when he'd moved elsewhere the distance had proven it was only a fleeting attachment, a pale imitation of the emotions currently boiling inside him like a volcano about to erupt.

This didn't feel like a fleeting attachment. This felt like a concrete vault around his nuclear reactor heart.

He did something he should have done some time ago. He texted Kurt.

> I have something to tell you.

> Is Daisy all right?

> Yes, she's fine.

Better than fine.

> What do you want to tell me?

> I'm dating your daughter. Like, for real dating.

> Are you fucking with me???

> No.

> Pistols or swords?

Jordan almost laughed that Kurt would suggest a duel. Almost. He'd known the guy would be pissed.

> She's worth a bullet in the chest.

> How about getting your balls cut off?

Ouch.

I love her.

I'm still going to kill you.

Do me a favor and wait until they've caught Bocharov? Then have at it.

That silenced the other man. Jordan tossed his phone on the side table and scrubbed his hands over his face rather than wait for the litany of reasons why he had no right to touch Daisy.

As much as he loved Kurt, and he loved him dearly, it didn't matter what Kurt thought. Not anymore. It only mattered what Daisy thought.

Which wasn't looking great if the expression on her face a few minutes ago was any indication. But he had a plan. And he was smart and dedicated, and he didn't quit.

Not *ever*.

Maybe it would be enough.

There was no sign of Bocharov anywhere. He'd gone to ground. Amed Hussein was denying everything. The FBI had found the explosives and uncovered the plot outlined on a file on his computer and neutralized it as far as they could tell.

But until Bocharov was caught, Daisy was in danger. She either gave up her studies until they had the Russian in custody—dead would be preferable—and came to live in Quantico surrounded by people who'd protect her, or he gave up his job and spent the foreseeable future being her personal bodyguard.

He loved his job. Did not want to give it up. But he wouldn't leave her unprotected. Not from a monster he'd helped create.

He heard the water swoosh and then the knock on the door that told him room service had arrived. He checked the peephole, although there was security on every floor. Opened the door and checked the cart thoroughly before he tipped the guy and took the cart inside the room.

He set up on the small table between two small chairs but left the warming domes on the plates. He opened the wine and let it breathe while he fetched a bathrobe for Daisy. He knocked on the bathroom door before entering. "Food's here."

"Good. Because suddenly I'm starving." She rose to her feet and struck a pose. He let himself look his fill, tried to inoculate himself against the effect she had on him, naked or otherwise, but definitely naked. She stepped slowly out of the tub and he winced at all the marks of pain that littered her skin like flecks of paint.

She let him circle the robe over her shoulders as her hands roamed his chest and headed down. There was no doubt what his body wanted. She started to slide her hands down to cup his balls, and he bundled her up like a swaddled baby, carried her into the bedroom, and laid her on the bed.

Christ, she was gonna kill him, one way or another.

He flipped open the robe.

"Hands," he demanded.

At first, she looked confused and then amused as she reached up to grab the edge of the mattress. She lay spread beneath him like the perfect fantasy.

"How long do you plan to keep this up?" She glanced at his crotch suggestively.

"I told you."

She shook her head. "Until I believe you love me. Lover, there's no way you can last that long without sex."

He cocked his brow. A challenge. He thrived on challenge. "What do you care? You get your no-strings sex and can walk away whenever you want—assuming you can still walk that is—after a thousand amazing orgasms."

Delight flickered in her eyes. "A *thousand, amazing* orgasms?"

"As many as you want."

Her lips curved. Confident and wary all at once. "I like orgasms."

"Then hold on, *babe*. It's going to be a long night."

Jordan dreamt of heat and flame.

After devouring their food, he'd made love to Daisy—without breaking his vow—for the third time. Afterwards, Daisy had curled up naked on the far edge of the bed and fallen fast asleep.

He'd cleared away the food, showered, and then gone to bed in a black T-shirt and tactical pants that felt completely appropriate.

Sleep was no more his friend than Bocharov, and he watched the man laugh as he lined up every member of his family and set them alight, one by blessed one. And they stood there, human torches, staring at him with doleful accusing gazes, rather than fighting the evil sonofabitch.

And then Bocharov reached the last person in the row, and it was Daisy. She stood there with her arms crossed and looking pissed as if waiting for him to save her. Jordan fought against his bindings, unable to move, unable to save her as Bocharov smiled his evil smile and lit the next match.

"Jordan!"

He felt himself being shaken awake from a heavy sleep, and there was Daisy, safe, alive, and still pissed. His heart thudded and sweat glazed his skin.

"Are you okay?" She smoothed a lock of hair off his forehead.

Worried, not pissed.

And he realized in a way he hadn't fully grasped before, how much he projected his own feelings onto other people. How heavy the weight of his guilt was as it tried to drag him down, time after time.

"It's okay," she soothed gently, kissing his brow.

This woman who refused to love him.

He wrapped his arms around her and held on so tight it was a wonder she didn't protest. Instead, she gripped him right back.

They fell asleep, still tangled in each other's arms.

31

Her phone woke her at dawn, and she reached out blindly to answer it. "What?"

"Daisy, it's Wilson here. I wanted to check in."

She blinked at the time. She knew her supervisor was an early bird, but after everything that had happened, she'd hoped to sleep in—and get another chance to test Jordan's seemingly steely resolve. A glance around the room showed it was empty. He wasn't here.

A sharp pang was followed by the thought, "*Good.*"

All the better to get herself back under control.

Yesterday had been a shit show. No wonder her emotions had been up and down like a rollercoaster, making it impossible to think straight.

"I'm sorry for disturbing you so early, especially after all the terrible things that happened yesterday." Wilson sounded agitated. No wonder. "The thing is, I got a call earlier and spoke to the fuel rod manufacturers, the managers of Moses Lake, and the FBI Director. Director Rhodes was absolutely insistent that the new rods not be left sitting around. She's arranging an armed FBI escort to the reactor today, and the rods are to be inserted as soon as possible." He swallowed repeatedly. "With Amed gone, I was wondering if you'd like to take on part of his project? You won't need to stay at the reactor site, as Roger plans to pretty much camp out there, and he's more than capable. But if you could assist him with remote monitoring of the data and maybe give him the occasional break when he needs it, you'd be more than halfway to your PhD."

The work she was doing was supposed to follow directly from Amed's work, but she wasn't prepared, and it didn't feel right.

Her grip tightened on the phone. "Have you heard anything about Amed? Did he confess?"

"No. Nothing." Wilson sounded defeated. "I will never forgive myself for this."

It sounded as if he was crying, and she wasn't surprised. It had to be a massive blow when you dedicated your professional life to nuclear safety, only to be used as a conduit to cause harm. His legacy would forever be tainted by Amed's plans and his student's association with a Russian terrorist—and by the murder of François Tremblay.

At least it was a warning for everyone else conducting research. They were all potentially vulnerable and needed to be cognizant of bad actors.

"This will be the last full-scale test I ever conduct, Daisy."

"*What?*"

"My heart isn't in it anymore. I plan to move up my retirement date." His voice trembled. "I guess, what I'm trying to say is, if you want data for your PhD, you're going to have to step into Amed's shoes. There might not be another opportunity."

"But I don't know enough—"

"You're smart. Roger knows more than I do on the technical side. He's pissed, but he'll get over it. You can learn from him as we go. Once the rods are in place, there's not that much to do except monitor and collect data. The engineers onsite are in charge of all operational decisions. Whatever tests you plan to conduct have to be approved by them first. They are the chieftains of safety protocols and procedures."

He said it as if reminding himself that his inexperienced first year PhD student wouldn't be in charge of a nuclear reactor.

A relief for everyone involved.

She sucked in her lips. She wasn't sure that she was ready for this, but what choice did she have? At least Roger knew what he was doing.

"What time do you need me? I need to arrange transportation as the FBI has my car."

"The director said she'd send an agent to your location to accompany you and the others to the power plant."

Jordan wouldn't like that.

Her advisor read her mind.

"If your FBI boyfriend wants to come, he'll have to take it up with his boss. Moses Lake takes security very seriously and knows who to expect. As they should. Be sure to take ID, assuming you still have it?"

"I have my wallet. What time is this agent arriving exactly?"

"I don't know. Soon, I would imagine."

Crap. She didn't even have any clean clothes. "Who else is going to be involved today?"

"Les, Mira, Emilia, Roger. You and myself. The others are already on their way downtown. You'll have to text them where to pick you and this FBI agent up. Director Rhodes refused to say where you were staying."

"Shit." Daisy shot out of bed.

"My sentiments exactly. I have to consult with the Dean before I leave. I'll be late, but I'll see you there. In the meantime, I'll be praying nothing goes awry."

Daisy found a three-pack of new panties and a baby blue bralette draped over the pile of yesterday's clothes and wondered briefly who'd drawn the short straw and been sent to find women's underwear in the middle of the night. She quickly dressed and was pulling on her sneakers over socks that were way too big for her when the door opened and Jordan appeared, carrying two large coffees and a bag of something from a bakery.

Damn, he was good.

"Where are you going?" He put the cups down and tried to capture her in an embrace, but she ducked out of his arms and hit the bathroom. There was only one toothbrush, but she'd left fussy behind on that rooftop.

She spat and wished she had a hairbrush or moisturizer, but miracles stopped with underwear and toothpaste. She needed to go shopping. Resupply her life. But first she needed to rescue her fledgling science career out of the ashes.

She opened the door to find Jordan standing there wearing a heavy frown. She moved past him. Picked up the coffee he'd brought and took a large sip. She closed her eyes. It tasted divine and sent a signal to her brain to wake the fuck up. Now was not the time to be drowsy.

"My supervisor called. They've brought forward the installation of the new fuel rods by a couple of days, and if I want to finish my PhD, I need to be there."

"Has this been cleared?"

"Apparently, Director Rhodes is sending someone, an agent, to accompany the lab to the power plant. And," she said as he opened his mouth, "if you want to be included, my advisor said to contact the director and get permission because security at the reactor site is strict."

His cell rang. He picked up and frowned as he listened. "Roger that. Where? I'll be there in five minutes." He disconnected. "I have to go but I'll—"

"Ha. Big surprise." The bitterness in her tone shocked and disappointed her. This was what happened when emotions got involved. "Sorry. That's not fair. We both have jobs to do."

She hung her head, but he lifted her chin to meet his gaze. "I'm not going anywhere, Daisy. I need five minutes to check in with Novak before Gold Team heads out. They've had a sighting on traffic cams of Bocharov on Interstate 64, heading south toward Camp Peary and the Naval Bases there."

Her gaze flashed to his. "You have to go."

He shook his head. "No, I don't. I spoke to Ackers. I have another week's leave due, and I'm taking it to be with you."

She didn't miss the change in language, to *be with* her, not to *protect* her, even though that's what he'd be doing.

"And what happens after a week, Jordan? What if Gold Team loses Bocharov or the sighting was a mistake? What difference will a week make?"

He took her free hand. "I don't know, but if it comes down to your safety or my job, your safety is more important."

She huffed out a disbelieving breath. "What? You'd quit your job? Quit HRT?"

"Yes. Maybe I could get a transfer to the Richmond Field Office. Maybe I'll go private, or write a goddamned memoir, but you are my priority."

Tears smarted in her eyes, that he'd choose her over his career, that someone in this world might value her as much as their job, but she blinked the moisture away. "You can't do that. You love your job. Eventually you'd come to resent me—"

"No, I wouldn't. Not so long as you give whatever this is between us a real chance."

Her heart gave a crazy leap. The desire to believe him, to take a chance, was nearly overwhelming.

"I don't know." She dragged her hands through her hair and felt as if her brain might implode. "I can't think right now. There's too much going on. I need some space to think about whether or not I want to take a risk—"

"You think I'm not terrified of this thing between us?" He sounded angry. Not cold rage but molten fury. "Almost everyone I've ever loved has died because of me. I've been careful not to open myself, or others, up to that again. But there you were with your goddamned smart mouth and defiant eyes. Who would have thought that would have been such a fucking irresistible lure?"

She blinked at his vehemence.

"But guess what? There are no guarantees in life, Daisy. People fall in love, and they fall out of love again, and it isn't fair, and it hurts, but *that* isn't me. Once I commit to something, I commit one-hundred percent. You'll have to shoot me to get rid of me now."

She wanted to joke she had her gun in her bag, but she couldn't make a sound. The passion in his eyes and voice mesmerized her. She desperately wanted to believe him.

He stepped closer and held her by the shoulders. "Life is short, and even though Bocharov is still out there, still a threat, I've finally figured out it's too precious to waste."

His words brought her to her knees, and she didn't know how to deal with all the things he was telling her. All the things she was feeling. She wanted to believe him, she did, but her heart shrank away from the thought of being deceived.

Someone knocked on the door, and she jerked away from him to pick up her bag, slung it over her neck even as she recoiled from the smell of the smoke that still clung to it. He handed her the bag of pastries.

"Give me five minutes," he pleaded. "I'll get the clearance I need from the director."

"I need to go."

He stared at her, disappointment lighting those expressive eyes of his. "I thought you were braver than this. I was obviously wrong, but I'm not giving up on you, Daisy Montana. Not by a long stretch. One day, you'll realize I'm more than just a good fuck." He flung open the door, and there stood Special Agent Crabtree.

Jordan shouldered past him and then stopped, turned, and gave him a look.

Crabtree held up his hands in surrender. "I'm simply following orders."

Jordan pinned Crabtree to the wall with his finger. "Anything happens to her, you die, understood? Wait for me downstairs."

Crabtree found his spine. "I can't. The rods are due to arrive in less than an hour, and the director gave me strict instructions—"

"I bet she did. Send me your route. I'll be right behind you. And I will be contacting the director, so expect backup."

The other man nodded nervously. Jordan strode away to where Alex Parker and Payne Novak stood talking at the other end of the corridor.

Crabtree adjusted his tie. He looked pale and tired. The charcoal gray suit and cheery burgundy tie were decidedly at odds with what she was used to from the Feds she generally interacted with, but he was armed and supposedly well-trained.

"The others are downstairs and ready. They're waiting. Let's go."

She pulled the door closed even as she watched Jordan keep his back to her. She'd hurt his feelings. She'd disappointed him. Worse, she'd disappointed herself.

She'd jumped off a burning building, but couldn't risk the idea of opening herself up to a love affair?

Was she really that big of a coward?

Er, yes.

Should she go to him? Tell him she thought she was already in love with him, and it terrified her?

"Come on," Crabtree urged impatiently. "I'm sure Krychek will be along shortly."

Reluctantly, she turned away from Jordan. She needed time to clear her head and sort out her thoughts. To figure out how to navigate the future, even if it meant she might get her heart snapped in two again.

Crabtree headed straight for the elevator, and for once she didn't balk. Today, she was going to face her fears and start taking a few chances.

Jordan fumed in silence.

"What's going on?" Alex asked.

"Apparently, Director Rhodes wants Daisy's lab to complete the fuel rod install today."

"What the hell?" Novak scowled.

Jordan dialed Mac, but it went straight to voicemail. He tried Rhodes next, and the same thing.

"Do you have a vehicle I can use to shadow Daisy? I figure I can wait outside the facility if I can't get clearance. Not as if Bocharov is likely to be there if he's on I-64."

Novak shook his head. "Nothing we can spare, sorry. We're leaving in five minutes to the airfield. We plan to land ahead of him and have highway patrol set up roadblocks so we can contain him without too many civilians being in the area."

"How sure are you that this is him?"

Alex showed an image captured at a stoplight.

"Sure looks like him," Jordan agreed. He itched to go after the bastard, but Daisy was his priority now. He refused to be distracted, even by the man who'd killed his family and tried to kill her. He had faith in his teammates. They'd never let him down.

Florence Cisco appeared out of the stairwell. "Hey, what's happening?"

She had a set of car keys in her hand.

"You have a vehicle?"

She nodded. "Borrowed something from the Field Office here. I have to remove all the sensitive equipment from the van and drive it back to The Center then return the vehicle tomorrow."

She tossed the keys in her hand, once, twice. The third time he scooped them out of the air before she could catch them.

"Hey," Cisco complained as she reached for the keys, but he held them out of her reach.

"You know you'd rather spend the day watching Daisy's back than moving equipment."

Cisco grunted. "Only if you help me lug boxes later."

"Deal." He looked at Alex. "You coming with us or going with Novak?"

Alex pulled a face. "As exciting as sitting outside a nuclear power station all day sounds…"

"Yeah. I know. Boring as hell." He tried Mac again. "Fuck. Anyone spoken to Mac today? I can't get through to the guy."

Novak shook his head and muttered something that was possibly unflattering.

Jordan frowned. "Seems weird to fast-track the installation rather than delay it, under the circumstances."

"Nuclear fission waits for no man," Cisco joked in a deep voice.

"I guess. You see Regan today?"

She yawned, and he noticed the dark circles under her eyes. "He's being moved out of the ICU this morning."

"That's good."

"Still under armed guard."

Jordan nodded and frowned harder. "So why send *Crabtree* of all people to escort Daisy and the others to Moses Lake."

Alex frowned. "Crabtree?"

"Yeah, he was just here."

"Did you try calling Daisy's advisor?"

"Why would I?" Jordan asked.

Alex shrugged. "Not sure. Okay, I changed my mind." He addressed Novak just as the rest of Gold Team piled into the corridor. "I'm going to hang with these two. See if I can use the time to poach Cisco to come work in the private sector."

"Like you do." Jordan smirked as they all headed downstairs.

"Dude, I'm the boss. I get to spend my time however I want to."

"So you spend your time doing what Special Agents do, but without being paid?"

"When you put it that way…" They were heading out of the hotel's back door, following Cisco and the guys before they jumped into the Suburbans.

Novak tossed him three flak jackets and handed him a bunch of spare ammo. "Just in case."

"Appreciate it." Jordan wondered how he'd cope with leaving these guys who'd taken the place of his family. It wouldn't be easy, but he'd do it for Daisy. *If* she wanted him. *If* she was prepared to take a leap.

"Let's follow Crabtree out to the reactor site and hope the director sends approval by the time we get there."

"Better to ask forgiveness than get permission?" Alex joked as he slid into the driver's seat of the Ford Expedition SSV before either Jordan or Florence had the chance to do so. "My favorite idiom."

"Shotgun!" Cisco raced around the hood.

She missed the way all the operators of HRT braced and looked around for the danger.

Jordan shook his head and climbed into the back seat with the equipment. "I'm gonna keep trying Mac and the director. Cisco, you got a lock on Daisy's phone?"

She nodded and pulled it up on her laptop.

"She know you're tracking her?" Alex sped out onto the street and headed north.

"Hell, no." It would be another nail in his coffin.

"I warned her not to hurt you yesterday," Cisco confessed.

"What did she say?"

Cisco looked over her shoulder. "That you were more likely to be the one hurting her."

Jordan sank despondently into the leather seat. "Could have fooled me. She's like an armored tank. She won't trust me."

"Keep showing up. Keep showing her you'll stick," Alex advised.

"She'll come around," Cisco agreed.

"I hope so." Jordan blew out a ragged breath. "I really hope so."

But what if she didn't?

He swallowed his emotions and did his job.

32

Daisy got in the minivan to be greeted with a resentful silence from her colleagues, all except Emilia, who was watching her with a gleam in her eye. Agent Crabtree climbed into the front seat beside Roger, who was driving. He wasn't any help.

"Hey."

No response from the crew.

"Oh, hey, Daisy. How are you? I heard you almost died yesterday. Yeah, but that's okay. At least it was only my neighbors who were brutally murdered in a fire that destroyed everything I own." Emotion, barely beneath the surface, threatened to bubble up.

"What about Amed? You got him arrested for terrorism for fuck's sake." Roger's Yorkshire accent was deep and cutting. "You know he's not like that."

"I'm probably next," Mira declared with a sneer. "I'm Muslim after all."

"I didn't get him arrested." Although, thinking about the letter, maybe she had. *Dammit.* She hunched her shoulders. "I'm sick about what happened, but he made his own choices."

"And your FBI boyfriend was right there to clean up. I bet they give him a medal for catching the Islamic terrorist planning to blow up the White House." Mira directed a glare at Crabtree.

"That's not my boyfriend." Daisy almost laughed at the idea. "That's Special Agent Crabtree. Jordan is one of the good guys."

"You keep telling yourself that," Roger said bitterly.

She crossed her arms over her chest and stared miserably out of the window. Jordan *was* one of the good guys. So was her father. She knew there were dirty and shitty law enforcement officials in the world. She'd seen some in action and heard about many more, but she'd never heard or seen anyone in Gold Team do anything that made her doubt their commitment to saving lives, often at the risk of their own.

"At least now you can fast track your PhD on the back of Amed's hard work, even if he is an evil jihadist," muttered Mira.

"Leave her alone. They wouldn't have arrested Amed if they hadn't found evidence." This from Les, the guy who liked to draw doodles of her naked.

Great.

She opened her mouth to say that she'd never asked for any of this when Emilia plopped herself next to her.

"I thought you and the FBI guy had broken up?"

Daisy shrugged.

"You said he cheated on you, and you dumped him." The woman's black brows slashed together over her eyes. "Don't tell me you forgave him?"

She didn't want to paint Jordan as the bad guy. Not after he'd declared love for her knowing she might never say it back. Not knowing that, however impractical and terrifying to her heart, she actually wanted him to be a part of her future. She wanted to take that chance. Which meant it was likely he'd meet these people one day under circumstances not full of death and suspicion.

"I was mistaken about the other woman."

"Or so he told you," Emilia said silkily.

"What do you care?"

"I don't." Emilia popped up her shoulders in a jaunty shrug. "So, do the FBI believe Amed pushed Tremblay off his balcony?"

Daisy wearily shook her head. "I have no idea what they think. Believe it or not, they don't tell me anything." They probably told her a lot more than they should, but she wasn't going to admit that. "Why don't you ask Agent Crabtree there?"

Crabtree turned briefly and pushed his no-frame glasses up his long nose. "It's classified."

"Hmm." Emilia gave the back of his head a curious stare as he turned away. "Where is he? This sexy FBI lover of yours? Do you have a photo?"

"He's busy." She hunched closer to the window. "I don't have any photos." Which was a testament to the fact they hadn't spent a lot of time together under ordinary circumstances. Perhaps she was right to wait before telling him she had feelings for him. Everything had happened fast. Searching for her dad. The conference in Mexico. Tremblay's death. Being shot at. The private jet. Bocharov. The fire.

Maybe these feelings wouldn't last. Maybe they'd reduce to embers that stopped glowing even when you forced air on them. Like he said, there were no guarantees. Maybe she'd be the one to break his heart for a change.

Maybe she already had...

She hated that. She wanted to pull out her cell and text him but not with Emilia sitting right next to her with her nosy smile. Not with a hostile audience listening to every word.

"How did you escape the fire in your house?" asked Emilia.

"I climbed onto the roof and was rescued by helicopter."

"That's...wild." The girl laughed, her pretty eyes sparkling with amusement. "You're like a cat with nine lives—a black cat because people who cross your path often seem to end up dead."

Daisy flinched. Damn. "Then perhaps you should move away. Just in case you're next."

Emilia took the hint and went to sit next to Les, while Roger's and Mira's narrow-eyed resentment never wavered.

Man, she couldn't wait for this to be over.

———

Forty minutes later, Jordan, Alex, and Cisco were on Highway 33 and headed past fields and farmland northwest toward Moses Lake, backtracking the route of the flight they'd taken last night in the dark—the flight that was the only reason Daisy and Cisco were alive today.

Hell.

Every time he thought about it, he felt sick.

Cisco was hunched over her laptop. She cleared her throat. "Uh-hm. Mr. Parker, if you don't mind me saying, there's something off about that image the traffic cam captured."

"Call me Alex, and what's up with it?" Alex glanced over into her lap, and Jordan unclipped his belt to lean over the console.

"I went back and tracked the car in question an hour prior to where it was flagged, and I see the same car, same driver, same clothes, but not the same face. I mean he's a bald guy and the right build for Bocharov but no match with facial rec. It's possible they swapped drivers afterwards but—"

"You think Bocharov deep-faked his face onto that driver in the system somehow. Which should be impossible." Alex swore.

Jordan started dialing Novak and Mac on each of his two cells at the same time and put them both on speaker.

"What's up?" Mac asked.

"Novak."

"Listen up. Cisco suspects the image captured by the traffic cam might have been altered."

He watched the woman hunch her shoulders, but he was confident in her abilities even if she wasn't.

"How is that possible?" Mac yelled across the airwaves.

"Do we abort the mission?" asked Novak.

Jordan's heart screamed "yes" but his head said they needed to be more cautious. Bocharov was the master of manipulation and misdirection. What if Cisco's earlier image was the one that had been altered for just such an eventuality? "Can you get plainclothes cops to do a drive-by? Get visual confirmation on the driver?"

"Will do. We're still traveling south. Do we continue?" asked Novak.

"Have someone pick up the driver regardless of whether or not it's Bocharov," Mac instructed. "He's a bald guy, and he's driving toward several sensitive military installations at this exact moment in time—"

"Diverting our attention at the *exact moment* those fuel rods are being delivered to the nuclear facility." Jordan's blood turned to ice.

The g-force pressed him back against the seat as Alex accelerated.

"We need to lock down that facility before the fuel rods and scientists arrive," Mac ordered. "Split Gold Team. Half stay on the vehicle, the rest head to the reactor site. Mobilize SWAT teams for backup."

"You hear that, Novak?"

"Affirmative. Sending Echo and snipers to the facility ASAP. Charlie and SWAT take down the vehicle. I'm with Echo."

"I need to speak to the director," Jordan told Mac, "but I can't reach her."

"She's at the White House to discuss the Russia situation."

"According to Daisy, she authorized this and sent Crabtree as Daisy's protection detail."

"She seems to really like that little weasel. I'll contact her with an update. If I can't reach her, I'll talk to her boss."

"She won't like that."

"I don't care. I'm still in DC. If I have to go knock on the AG's door, I damned well will. If that fails, I'll have Dominic Sheridan call his godfather."

Dominic Sheridan was a negotiator at CNU. His godfather was the US President Joshua Hague.

"Keep me informed." Mac hung up, and so did Novak.

"It's too late to intercept the scientists." Cisco looked at another window on her laptop. The one tracking Daisy's cell phone. "They just arrived."

33

After they all showed their IDs to the armed security guards on the gate, Roger drove through and wound his way around various buildings. He seemed to know his way about the facility. He pulled up to a building with a large, black, stenciled "3" on the side of it.

Daisy reluctantly climbed out and felt the chilly March breeze ruffle her messy hair. She shivered without a coat.

Her bag was heavy, but she didn't want to leave it in the car. Thankfully, no one had searched them because she had her gun in her purse. A worrying lapse of security, but as she had no intention of using the weapon, one she'd report later. Much later. She didn't want to give anyone an excuse to cancel the test or hate her any more than they already did.

Les opened the cargo doors, and they all grabbed various tools and laptops then hiked up the steps to the control room, where they'd set up their monitoring equipment and where Roger would spend most of the next couple of months.

Thankfully, Agent Crabtree remained with the vehicle.

Upstairs, they introduced themselves to the plant manager, Lonnie Segall, who wore a blue tweed blazer with brown leather elbow patches over a black shirt and slacks, along with a pair of steel-toe boots. He had a smile and handshake that any car salesman would be proud of. Then they met the shift supervisor, Greg Sivik, who had deep grooves carved into his lived-in face. Greg wore a lab coat. Both had dosimeters attached to their chests.

The first thing Greg did was assign them each a dosimeter to make sure they were not inadvertently exposed to radiation and to monitor their exposure levels in the Contamination Area.

Roger took the lead. "I don't know where Professor Williams is, but he shouldn't be too long. I'd like to be ready to start as soon as the assemblies arrive. He'll tag in with me anyway." His mouth was downturned.

Amed was his friend. Daisy hated how awful and hopeless she felt about Amed even though the FBI had evidence he'd planned to hurt anyone who got in his way.

"If we could dress out, we can be ready to roll. I assume the spent rods have been removed and placed in the SFP?"

SFP was the Spent Fuel Pool where the old fuel assemblies were cooled after being removed from the reactor.

Lonnie pointed to a monitor showing a large pool of water that steamed eerily and glowed a chilling blue color—a result of the Cherenkov effect. "We did. Last week. The core was given a full safety inspection which it passed with flying colors." Obviously, Lonnie was the PR guy.

"Fuel rods ETA is five minutes." Greg checked his phone. "You can dress out now, either in pairs or all together. Wait in the balcony area and observe from behind the barriers. Be sure to take your clothes off on one side of the painted line and get dressed in coveralls and boots on the other side of the line. Anything that crosses that line stays on the other side until it can be decontaminated. We have respirators hanging up near the door, but given the radiation levels right now, they're not mandatory. Once in coveralls you do not pass back over the line. You forget something from the other side, you undress, shower, get it, and then get back into the coveralls on the other side of the line. Your naked body is the only thing allowed to pass back and forth between areas. Is that understood?"

They all nodded. She felt like saluting.

"Remove watches and all jewelry. If you don't want to go to the reactor floor you can stay here. We monitor all the systems and environmental conditions of the core and the reactor from this room." He switched on another large screen which showed the whole facility. "Time on the floor will be limited to fifteen minutes. You can rotate in and out. Most of the procedure is done remotely with cranes and other tools anyway. We're allowing you onsite as a training exercise so you understand how these facilities work in practice for when you head back to your labs."

"I'm happy to stay here," Emilia said. "Until the professor appears anyway."

Roger nodded. Shot Daisy a disgusted look. "You're up first with me. I want you to inspect and record the outside of the rod structure prior to it being inserted in the core. The camera system is available, yes?"

Greg nodded. "I'll show you where it is. I plan to escort you to and from the areas where you are allowed to go. I'll withdraw in-between. Stay out of the way of any workers and machinery, or I'll pull you immediately."

Daisy nodded. She could tell he knew what he was doing and that he took his job seriously.

She followed Mira into the female changing room, found a locker, and placed her bag inside. At least she wouldn't have to get naked with her supervisor—one advantage to being a woman in this case.

She stared at her cell phone for a long moment and then, because she couldn't not reach out to the man who'd put his heart on the line this morning, she texted Krychek.

> Sorry for being an ass earlier.

> U OK?

Ha. The fact he questioned her mental health because she apologized was not a good sign.

She gave him a thumbs up emoji and turned the device off before she got distracted and asked him about Bocharov. Now was not the time to be thinking about other things. This morning would form the basis for her entire PhD, and she needed to concentrate.

Even so, it was hard to feel motivated.

Amed had worked long and hard on these new designs. This was the fruition of his work, and she wasn't sure she should step into his shoes. She'd do the work that needed to be done today and figure out the rest later. Maybe the FBI would let her talk to Amed. She could ask him what he wanted her to do with his research.

She stripped off her clothes, earrings, watch, and placed them carefully inside her bag. She made sure the gun was well hidden under everything else. Then she stepped across the line and picked a pile of clothes on the other side. Some surgical gloves, lime green panties, and a T-shirt to go under the overalls. She shrugged them on, along with the lime green socks and steel cap boots that were a size too big for her. Then she followed Mira out the other door, each grabbing a respirator off the hook on the way.

Roger and Les were already there, dressed, and prepared. They stood on a wide viewing gallery that was sealed off from the reactor room itself. Greg stood beside them.

He examined Daisy and Mira top to bottom and nodded approval.

"The fuel rods arrived. The guys are unloading them from the truck now."

It was noisy on the floor as a few workers scurried about. An alarm sounded, and Daisy jolted. The platform began to vibrate slightly as the massive crane started up and swung slowly toward the doors that stood wide open. A massive rig was parked just inside with a pale plastic pod sitting on top.

Mira shot her a look of derision as she jolted, but then Mira hadn't been shot at yesterday.

Fluorescent lights cast shadows over the equipment and scaffolding. The scent was one of a mechanical room—warm oil, hot metal, ozone from the electronics.

"Okay. First two, put on your respirators and come with me. The others stay here."

She followed Roger and Greg down to the main floor, but the respirator was so big she couldn't see properly and almost tripped.

Greg went straight to a video recorder. "Here's the camera."

Daisy shoved the respirator back on the top of her head. Greg wasn't wearing one, and she'd never be able to get clean shots if she couldn't see. She took the video recorder and turned it on. Hung the respirator on a hook on a shelf and zoomed in and out on the reactor core that was empty and waiting for its new fuel supply. Then panned around the general area as the men set the crate down on the ground and removed the lid. Inside were classic square rod lattices of 17 x 17 and about four meters long and 20 cm across. Each fuel assembly weighed about half a ton, which was another reason to utilize machinery to move them into position.

She got in much closer to the shiny metal lattices and sniffed in surprise. She hadn't expected the faint scent of plastic. She sniffed again and frowned, then was forced to move back as the crane moved in to lift the first of the Zirconium alloy assemblies.

She filmed from a safe distance and was able to zoom closer as the crane lowered the metal lattice into its assigned slot.

She moved back to the new rod assemblies and leaned close again. And swore she could smell paint this time, too, mixed with the faint odor of something like nail polish remover. It was all very subtle, but she had a good nose.

Was it some kind of finishing agent coating everything? Something she wasn't aware of? This was her first time in an actual working reactor and the first time she'd seen brand-new assemblies up close.

Maybe they all smelled like this?

She wanted to ask Roger, but he was concentrating fiercely on the operation to the point that when Greg indicated their fifteen minutes were up, he scowled and shook his head.

Greg's expression turned thunderous, and Roger quickly nodded and strode toward the observation platform.

She scooped up the respirator and hurried to precede the Shift Supervisor. She knew that if they were exposed to too much radiation the safety board would investigate the plant. No one wanted that, but as the reactor was currently shut down, Sivik was being overcautious.

She paused on the metal steps behind the barrier. "Are the assemblies coated in something prior to shipping?"

He frowned in annoyance. "Coated?"

"I thought I smelled plastic or something."

Greg frowned. "They shouldn't smell of anything. It's a Zirconium alloy."

Daisy grimaced self-consciously. "Yes, I know." He obviously thought she was an idiot. "Sorry. I thought I smelled plastic or paint or something."

His eyes narrowed. "Perhaps it's your suit or the respirator?"

Daisy clenched her fists. "No. It wasn't that."

"You're holding up everything," Roger snapped.

Mira's upper lip pulled back on one side. "Ignore her. She's paranoid. Has an FBI boyfriend and now thinks she's some kind of super sleuth."

Daisy shrugged miserably. "I smelled plastic. Maybe it was from the shipping container."

Greg stared at her. "I'll check. In the meantime, you can send the video you took straight to your email then give the camera to one of these two. I'll be back in two minutes. Wait here."

"Jesus, Daisy. Are you deliberately trying to fuck this up for all of us?" Roger hissed.

Daisy blinked away the tears that threatened. They weren't sad tears. They were tears of rage, but she was professional enough not to lose it, here, in this space.

Later though, when the fuel rods had finished being installed, she was going to flay the Yorkshire man to the bone and tell the others exactly what she thought of them. Silently, she sent the footage to herself and handed the camera over to Les, who gave her a winning smile.

Ugh.

She pushed back inside the changing room to shower.

Roger stayed on the viewing platform.

She should probably stay and watch, too, but she was so angry she was physically shaking. Being unfairly attacked for asking a legitimate question was infuriating. You had to be able to question the process and understand all the details to be good at this stuff. Details mattered when lives were potentially at stake. And when it came to nuclear reactors, a lot of lives were potentially at stake.

A loud bang made her jump again nervously as she headed into the shower room. She hoped she wasn't getting some kind of PTSD from the fire. She should probably call her therapist as soon as she had time, but then she was going to have to talk about Jordan, and she wasn't ready.

She didn't want to parse down her weaknesses and fears for inspection, because when it came down to it, that's all it really was. Fear. Of being hurt, of being left behind. Fear of being defective and not lovable enough.

She liked to believe being self-reliant was her biggest strength...but perhaps, rather than making her strong, maybe being unable to rely on others was a flaw.

She didn't like that idea.

Didn't like it at all.

She unclipped the dosimeter, then began stripping out of her protective gear when she heard the door to the changing room open and then, without pause, someone headed straight through to the reactor building.

If that was Emilia, she was going to get her ass reamed by Greg when she arrived in street clothes which he'd probably make her burn.

Daisy couldn't help the little shimmer of satisfaction that moved through her at the thought of Emilia heading home in scrubs. She dumped the contaminated coveralls into the dirty laundry chute and quickly showered.

She stepped out on the other side of the line and grabbed a towel off the rack, scrubbing herself dry. She thought she heard noises, almost like gunfire, and wondered what was happening. Was there a mechanical issue? Maybe she should have stayed to watch, but she knew it was all being recorded. She'd watch from the control room where she didn't have to take constant abuse from people she'd thought were her friends.

34

Jordan's phone rang. The director. Thank fuck. He connected and was on the receiving end of a diatribe about not having permission to use her direct line whenever the hell he wanted. Like he was some asshole asking for a date rather than a professional dedicated to keeping people safe.

He tried to interrupt. "Director Rhodes."

She carried on yelling at him.

"Ursula!" He shouted loudly enough for the woman to shut up and listen for a moment. While she inhaled enough air to destroy him, he jumped in. "We believe Bocharov deepfaked his image onto the driver heading south. With you greenlighting the fuel rods to be inserted into the reactor today, we believe—"

"What are you talking about? I did no such thing."

Dread washed through Krychek. "Didn't you send Crabtree to escort the nuclear scientists to Moses Lake and get the fuel rods installed ASAP?"

"No. I did not. What the hell is going on, Operator Krychek?"

Fuck. He was starting to understand how big this was. "In that case, I believe someone spoofed your phone, and deepfaked your voice on a call with Professor Williams, the Moses Lake facility, and the fuel rod supplier to make sure that installation happened today. We have to assume we are under attack from terrorists and possibly a hostile foreign nation and to notify POTUS. The Commander in Chief needs to know what's going on."

"Where are you?" Her tone was urgent now.

"Three of us will be pulling up to the facility shortly. A good portion of Gold Team are en route in helicopters about fifteen minutes out, and the remainder of Gold Team is picking up whoever is in that vehicle, ma'am."

"Prioritize shutting down those reactors."

His mouth went dry. He needed to get Daisy to safety first.

"I understand your girlfriend might be in danger, but my order is to get those reactors shut down, otherwise South Carolina to New York City might become a radioactive hellhole in the near future. The political and economic hubs of our country, Jordan, are at stake. Not to mention if this is truly an attack and the terrorists are at the reactor building, it's possible you're already too late to save her. Now I need to update the president."

"Understood, ma'am." He hung up on the cold-hearted bitch. "She wants us to shut down the two operational reactors before rescuing Daisy."

"Makes sense." Alex kept his tone neutral.

Jordan glared at the back of the guy's head. "If it was Mallory?"

"Mal every time." In the rearview mirror Jordan watched Alex's lip pull back. "But in this case, it could be all our lives at risk if there's a meltdown, including Daisy's, Mal's, and Georgie's."

Jordan's mouth went dry at the thought of a nuclear meltdown happening in Virginia.

"Doesn't mean I'm willing to sacrifice Daisy," Alex continued. "But as awesome as the three of us undoubtedly are, we're going to need more equipment to stage a full-scale assault, especially when we don't know how many terrorists there are—or even if there *are* any terrorists. Maybe Bocharov's plan isn't a direct assault on the reactor but something more subtle. We can't simply roar up to the reactor building and tell them to stop. We don't want to tip them off we're onto them until we know exactly what we're dealing with."

Shit. Alex was right.

"So communicating with the people in charge and getting workers from the other reactors safely out as soon as they shut them down—that seems like something we can do in tandem as we figure out what the terrorists' plans are and where Daisy might be."

Jordan reached for his training and pushed aside all worries for the woman who'd come to mean so much to him over the past couple of months.

"We don't know for sure Bocharov is at the facility," Cisco added. "We're just assuming."

"He's there." Jordan texted Mac a quick update for the task force.

"What they really seemed to want is the fuel rods. Perhaps they're faulty in some way. Designed to fail? Maybe someone from the lab other than Amed Hussein is involved in the plot," Cisco suggested.

"My money is on Amed Hussein being the patsy in case the FBI got suspicious after Tremblay's death. This plot has likely been in the works for years." Jordan was pissed. "Possibly not the exact location or lab, but the rest of it. Crabtree has to be working for them."

"The question is, was he turned or did he deliberately infiltrate the Bureau to carry out this kind of attack?" Alex put in. "And I'm so fucking pissed they've managed to fool so much of our security features that I'll be happy to take him into a quiet corner to question him."

"It could be Bocharov wants Daisy to be associated with some sort of catastrophic failure aimed to destroy her career and reputation," Cisco offered without conviction.

Bocharov wouldn't be satisfied with a damaged reputation or

even making the FBI look like a bunch of fools. The man liked to inflict physical and emotional trauma.

He could have carried out this plan without dragging Daisy and Jordan into it, but instead he'd made a point of it.

Why?

Because Bocharov needed revenge. Jordan doubted the man's masters gave a damn about him, but Konrad had been waiting a long time to extract payback.

Bocharov knew he would come for Daisy, and that gave Jordan hope. If nothing else, Daisy was bait. Bocharov would keep her alive until he could lure Jordan to him and finish this thing between them once and for all.

Perhaps they weren't too late. Perhaps they'd caught wind of this before Konrad had even arrived and could get the drop on him?

"Get me the number of whoever the hell is in charge of Moses Lake, could you, Cisco? And then let's find a side entrance rather than go in the main gates. In case Bocharov has goons stationed there."

They'd get those reactors shut down, but his priority was always going to be the woman he'd foolishly gone and fallen in love with.

He tried Daisy's cell again, but she didn't answer, and his heart shriveled inside his chest. Where was she? Was Bocharov there? Had the terrorists already started killing people? His heart drummed, but he forced the fear out of his mind so he could operate.

Konrad Bocharov wasn't walking away this time.

It had to end.

Now.

Today.

Even if he had to sacrifice himself to get the job done.

35

Daisy opened the control room door and came to an abrupt halt. Her knees wobbled so hard she thought she might fall over.

Lonnie Segall lay slumped against the wall with a surprised look on his face and a bullet hole where his right eye should be.

She dashed forward to check his pulse even though she knew he was dead.

The saliva in her mouth dried up and her stomach clenched hard enough to make her gag. She glanced at the monitors and saw that there were other figures lying on the ground while other people, not wearing overalls, were wandering around and—was that Emilia?—trying to operate the crane.

Where were the others from her lab? Was Emilia being forced to help the terrorists?

Do this or we'll shoot you and your friends?

But that didn't make sense.

She'd been here in the control room.

With Lonnie.

Daisy stared at the man's ruined body and knew in that moment that Emilia Osbourne had been the one to kill him.

She tried to process what was happening on the screen. She spotted Agent Crabtree walking around unharmed and appeared to be consulting with—she peered closer to the screen as her heart hammered—oh, God, was that Bocharov? His features were disguised with a blond wig and a big, fat mustache, but it sure looked like him.

She fumbled for her phone and saw she'd missed eight calls from Jordan.

Shit.

She looked nervously around as she dialed him back. She went to the outside door and turned the latch, terrified to make a sound or draw attention to herself. She contemplated doing the same with the inner door, but what happened if one of the others from her lab had escaped and needed help?

She pulled her Glock from her purse and let the bag drop to the floor.

"Daisy?" Jordan's voice was cautious, as if expecting someone else to be on the line.

"It's me, but you have to listen carefully. I think the FBI made a mistake. Bocharov is here, in the Moses Lake reactor, not wherever you think he is. He's disguised with a blond wig. They've killed a bunch of the workers, including the plant manager who I'm in the control room with right now." Her stomach threatened to revolt.

"You need to get out of there."

Daisy watched the monitors with a growing sense of horror. "I can see everything that is going on from here. Agent Crabtree is working with that monster."

"How did you get away?"

"Sheer luck and being unable to deal with the general animosity of my colleagues."

He swore. "Do you know what their plan is?"

"No." She frowned thinking about what had happened on the floor. "I thought I smelled plastic and paint on the fuel rod assemblies which I wasn't expecting. I asked the shift supervisor"—whom she could now see lying on the floor in a pool of blood—"and he went to check them out. I headed into the shower room and heard someone I presumed was Emilia Osbourne walk out through the changing room. She didn't stop to put on PPE, which is a big no-no around here. I'm guessing she shot Lonnie Segall before she headed into the reactor building."

Her stomach wanted to rebel, but she wouldn't let it. She should be dead. If Emilia had seen her in the changing room, her fellow student would one hundred percent have put a bullet in her.

"Did you actually see any explosives or detonators?"

"No." Dread twisted in her gut like a tangled skein of wool. "The smell reminded me of the C4 Harry Marcus showed me the other day. Would it be possible to shape that into beads and maybe paint them the same color as the nuclear fuel pellets?"

"They'd still need a way to detonate the explosive. C4 won't explode without a detonator."

The idea of C4 being anywhere near a nuclear reactor almost made her bones liquify. "I have to stop them."

"No, you don't. We're here at the plant. Myself, Alex, and Cisco. Gold Team is on the way. You lock the door and stay away from the windows. Cisco has tapped into the video feeds so we have them online now and can monitor. We're shutting down the other reactors, and knowing you're safe means we can afford to wait for backup."

"What about the others?"

Jordan's silence made her want to weep.

Daisy stared at the scene and scrunched her brows in puzzlement. "It doesn't make sense."

"What doesn't?"

"Why go to all the trouble of disguising an explosive if you just go and kill everyone anyway? Oh, wait. Let me rewind the footage." She found an auxiliary screen that allowed her to view recorded footage independently. She rewound until she and Roger left the reactor floor. A minute later, she watched Greg Sivik start carefully examining the new rods. Suddenly, he was waving his hands and telling the crane operator to stop, to lift the assembly he'd just put in the reactor out again.

He'd spotted an issue.

Bile filled her throat as she watched with horrified resignation as Bocharov and Crabtree came inside the reactor doors. A dark-haired woman in a gray pant suit stood on the other side of the truck. She wore thick, dark sunglasses, her hands tucked under her jacket.

Then the shooting started, and that was the noise she'd heard. People being shot, dying, because of her.

Her mouth tasted like ashes. "I think I know what happened. After I asked if there was plastic on the fuel rods, the shift supervisor checked them out, and then it looks like he shut down the installation process." She looked at the hole in Lonnie Segall's face. "It's my fault they killed these people."

"No, it's Bocharov's and his co-conspirators. They killed them. You may have helped prevent a reactor meltdown."

She swallowed. She hadn't prevented it yet.

"Are you safe?"

She flipped the deadbolt into the reactor building. "Yes, but if they have a keycard or key, they'll be able to get inside. I have my gun. Security never checked our belongings for weapons." She tucked the weapon into the back of her borrowed pants and covered it with her T-shirt.

"Something they're gonna regret for the rest of their very short careers."

Her teeth chattered—shock, stress, the decided chill in the air all catching up to her at once. "What do I do, Jordan?"

"Hang tight. We're going to come in from the west side. Gold Team is almost here but don't want to be seen or heard, so they landed a mile back and are approaching on foot. We've had management shutting down the other two reactors and moving people out, but slowly. We don't want to warn Bocharov that we're here."

She watched on screen as Emilia figured out how to operate the crane and slid the next metal grid into the core.

Her mind whirled in fear. The idea there might be C4 in some of those rods was terrifying. "Is there any way you could detonate C4 in water without using some kind of det cord?"

"What about using sodium or potassium?" She recognized Alex Parker's voice in the background.

Both metals exploded in water. She blinked. Her brain flaring with ideas. "Coat it in some sort of soluble material that dissolves when the water heats up to a specific temperature as the chain reaction builds…" It was a clever idea. "The metal explodes and ignites the C4. Enough of both, and you'll compromise the structural integrity of the core, and it's doubtful the staff here would have the means to prevent a meltdown under those circumstances."

"Is that really possible?" Jordan asked.

Daisy swallowed the knot in her throat. "Theoretically, it could work. And no one would be any the wiser until it was too late. Except Greg Sivik took me seriously and realized something was up. He ruined their plans, so Bocharov and the others improvised instead."

"And now we're going to ruin their plans again. You stay exactly where you are and don't come out for anything."

She watched Emilia loading the metal lattices into the framework. "Please hurry. And Jordan?"

"Yeah?"

"I love you too. Even though it's a risk, and I don't want to feel this way. I do anyway."

"Don't you fucking die on me now, Daisy."

"I'll try not to, but you have to remember, if I do, it's not your fault." She hung up and then spotted a button that governed the power to the crane and other mechanical equipment. There was another button for the main water pump needed for cooling the reactor and producing power.

She watched Emilia grab yet another half-ton assembly in the automated jaws of the crane.

If Daisy killed the power, they'd know she was here and might come hunting for her. But they already knew she was alive, and she was sure they wouldn't leave until she was either dead or captured.

Jordan was nearby, as was Gold Team.

Surely, the more she could slow them down, the less radioactive material in the core, the better.

It was a risk, but with the stakes so high? It had to be worth it.

Her heart thumped madly.

And what was the alternative? Sit here safe in her secure castle until the bad guys were all gone, but in the meantime the core blew?

The reactor would take a few hours to heat up so the chain reactions could reach a level that then became impossible to slow down. Once the fission started, once the core itself was blown wide open, there would be no easy fix. It would be Fukushima all over again.

Bocharov was fixing something to the hinges of the outer doors. She leaned closer. Some kind of explosive device. Her jaw ached from gritting her teeth.

He was planning to blow the doors and destroy the last of the three Cs. Containment.

By blowing the reactor core, they'd eliminate any chance of *controlling* the reaction and probably damage any effective way of *cooling* the radioactive material, and, by blowing off the doors of the building, there went the chance of *containing* the radioactive fallout in the short term.

It would rival Chernobyl, creating a contaminated wasteland for hundreds of miles that would last for decades and decades to come.

She couldn't let it happen. She had to slow them down.

She slammed her hand on the power button for the crane. Watched as the machine jerked to a halt and the main lights flickered and dimmed.

Emilia glared up in the direction of the control room and began climbing down the steps. Even on the monitor, Daisy could see a gun tucked into the back of her jeans.

Bocharov shouted something to her and then dragged Les into the camera frame and pushed him onto his knees. Held an ugly black pistol to the student's head.

Daisy's heart lurched into her throat and lodged there making it impossible to breathe.

No.

Konrad Bocharov stared up at the camera and held up five fingers. Then four. Then three. Two.

No.

She slapped the button to restore power, and the room flared to brightness.

Bocharov smiled at her like she was a good little girl. Then he crooked his finger and then held up his five fingers again and slowly made it four.

Her heart thumped.

He wanted her.

No.

But Les...

She lunged for the lock and ran through the changing room without pausing, threw herself onto the top of the viewing platform in time for her to see Bocharov pull the trigger and for Les to fall in a broken heap at his feet.

Something hit her on the side of the head, and she went down to her knees.

Strong fingers gripped her arm and pulled her to her feet. She looked up as she cradled her head. "You fucker."

Agent Crabtree grinned at her. Tugged her toward the stairs. "Come. There's someone who wants to meet you."

"I don't want to meet him." She fought a wave of sickness as her head throbbed with pain.

"Well, unfortunately for you, you are not in charge."

"Why did you betray your country? How much did he pay you, you pig?"

He cuffed her around the head again and lights twirled above her.

"I never betrayed my country. Never." His eyes were bright with fervor. "I've spent years infiltrating your precious systems, years pinpointing your weak spots and sucking up to the assholes until I got myself exactly where I wanted to be."

She was going to have bruises on her arms and a concussion at this rate, but it was probably the least of her worries.

"I was planning on killing the FBI Director live on social media in her seventh-floor office"—his eyes danced with glee, then dimmed—"but we decided this humiliation would be so much worse. The first female FBI Director and she doesn't even know she has a traitor in her inner circle? Naïve and foolish." He smiled. "Weak. Having her order the fuel rod installation was the chef's kiss to the plan—not that she knew anything about it. Pity I can't kill the bitch anyway, but I'll be on my way to a better life. Somewhere I'll be hailed as a hero, and she'll be mocked as a fool."

"Is that all this is to you? An ego trip?"

He shoved her forward again.

She lifted her chin and stared him defiantly in the eye, twisting so he didn't get a good view of her back or the gun she had tucked into her pants. "Wherever you are, you will always be looking over your shoulder and waiting for the death that you know is coming your way, you little creep."

He went to strike her again, but Konrad Bocharov shoved him aside. "Check the perimeter. Tell Katya to get into position."

Crabtree stomped off.

Katya must be the other woman she'd seen, wearing the suit. Pretending to be an FBI Agent, Daisy realized suddenly.

Escorting the fuel rods?

Had the professor been involved? Crabtree said they'd faked Ursula Rhodes' voice to fool the other people involved. None of them were likely to question the veracity of the FBI Director when she ordered them to move up the install date of the fuel rods.

Bocharov's eyes raked over her, and even though she itched to draw her weapon she knew this wasn't the right time. She wouldn't be fast enough, and he would shoot her.

She held her tongue as he looked his fill, his expression twisted in distaste.

"My daughter told me you were pretty"—his cold blue eyes held contempt now—"I don't see it. But, then, I have never been attracted to blondes."

"I've never been attracted to evil, bald men, so we're even." She blinked as the rest of his words registered. "Your daughter?"

He held his hand out to indicate Emilia as she climbed back into the crane seat with a mocking bow. "My beautiful and brilliant daughter, Emilia."

Emilia Osbourne was Konrad Bocharov's daughter? Which meant they'd been setting this up for a very long time—probably since Jordan had infiltrated Bocharov's organization and sent him running ten years ago. It was pure bad luck Daisy was here too— or maybe it was fate. Maybe this had been her destiny all along— the Universe's cruel little joke of doomed love to complete its latest tragedy.

She realized something. "Amed Hussein had nothing to do with any of this, did he?" She and the FBI had fallen for the planted evidence, hook, line and sinker.

Bocharov gave a tight smile. "At least your racist profiling means he may survive today's events."

Suggesting they wouldn't. "He wasn't profiled. You set him up."

The backhand sent her reeling.

She wanted to berate him for killing Ron and Alma Paget, but knew he wouldn't care.

"Give me your phone."

She hesitated but when he raised his hand to strike her once more, she pulled it quickly out of her front pocket and handed it over. She didn't want him searching her. Her hand rested on her hip and inched toward her gun.

She froze when he held her cell to her face to unlock it and started reading her messages. She tried to remember the last thing she'd texted Jordan—when she'd apologized for being an ass and he'd asked if she was okay. There was nothing compromising on her cell, but the Russian was bound to find things he could use against her if he looked hard enough.

Her father would go scorched earth on this man, assuming Jordan didn't kill him first. She hated that. Hated knowing how her dad's newfound happiness might be destroyed because of her death and that Jordan would once again suffer.

Bocharov started texting, and she froze for a moment wondering what he'd write, presumably to Jordan. Something twisted and nasty that would hurt him. Then she remembered Jordan could see what was happening and would know it wasn't her. She glanced at the camera in a silent apology.

What choice had she had?

She looked at Les's crumpled body and felt regret she hadn't moved faster, but Bocharov would probably have pulled the trigger anyway. And he wouldn't have stopped there. He'd have pulled out each and every innocent and executed them until she'd unlocked that door.

Jordan would be so angry with her. Her eyes smarted with useless tears, and she sucked back the emotions that threatened.

"Get over there with the others."

"What's the plan? Blow up the reactor?"

He leaned so close she could feel his breath hit her cheek. "The plan is that you keep your mouth shut and do as you're told, or I'll put the bullet I saved for you on Saturday night into your ugly, weak skull today."

Her eyes shot to Les's body and back to Bocharov's, and she

stumbled backwards away from him until she sat off to one side of Mira and Roger on the hard concrete floor.

Mira was quietly weeping against Roger's chest.

Roger sent her a worried look. At least he didn't seem pissed with her anymore. For what that was worth.

Her heart tripped a beat as Emilia started the crane and began loading the next rod assembly.

Daisy stared around the building and realized that someone had removed all the control rods. If the terrorists managed to start the reactor, there would be no way to stop it.

36

When Jordan watched Daisy be dragged onto the reactor floor by that weasel Crabtree, everything inside him went calm.

Jordan knew that Echo Team and the snipers would be here any moment and moving into position.

"We can't under any circumstances let them get that reactor running."

"We have to get to the control room and shut it down," Alex agreed in a whisper. The three of them were crouched behind the Reactor No. 2's building. At least they'd been able to secure the doors into the other reactors and have the people in charge lower all the control rods to prevent potential meltdowns in those.

Reactor No. 3, however, was in enemy hands.

"If we do that, they're going to take the hostages one-by-one and shoot them until we do exactly what they want, the same way they manipulated Daisy. I'd throw everyone in the fire to save Mal."

"Gee, thanks," Cisco muttered.

"I'd save you next."

A dimple formed in her cheek. "I can live with that."

Jordan was too sick with worry to joke about this shit.

"There's a woman in the control room now." Cisco pointed.

He stared closer at the screen. Cisco had activated and accessed all the cameras inside the facility. She enlarged it.

"It's Charlie—Jenna Stork's lover. The same woman I met in Mexico." He frowned. "I really don't think she recognized me in Mexico. Maybe she was meeting with Bocharov or was acting as his lookout."

"That rifle she's carrying is a Dragonov sniper rifle. It may be the same one that killed Jenna Stork in DC last night."

"We're going to need a sniper up on that building over there." Alex nodded to a nearby structure. "In fact, we're going to need several snipers to take out as many terrorists as possible simultaneously."

Jordan called Novak with a SitRep. "We need snipers on the roof. How long until you can get everyone into position?"

The answer felt like forever.

"We need them sooner than that."

The camera angle meant he couldn't see Daisy anymore, and it drove him crazy. He could see Bocharov though, scrolling through Daisy's phone. "We can't be sure how many terrorists there are. I have four known, but maybe some of the others are dirty too...?"

Alex nodded. "Ah, fuck. There goes the last fuel rod into the core."

Jordan's stomach bottomed out, then his personal cell vibrated in his pocket. He saw that "Daisy" had texted him.

> The FBI Director said you are cleared to come into the facility. If you are close by, come to Reactor No. 3. Hurry. The others are being mean to me.

Jordan pulled a face as he climbed to his feet. It was the most un-Daisy-like message he'd ever read, but there was nothing for it.

> Be right there, babe. Don't take any shit from those losers.

They couldn't wait for Gold Team any longer. They'd run out of time. It was Jordan who Bocharov wanted anyway.

"You guys do whatever it takes to get inside that control room before they crank up the core."

"What are you gonna do?" Cisco asked.

"Do my best to slow them down. Save the woman I love and have a long overdue conversation with the sonofabitch who murdered my family."

———

Jordan strode toward the open door of the reactor as if he were some clueless prick. He'd seen Konrad set the charges on the doors but was careful not to look at them as Agent Crabtree stepped from behind the semi and indicated he stand and frisked him for weapons.

"What the fuck, Crabtree? This some sort of joke? Or have you lost your tiny mind?"

"You fucking guys. Always strutting around and thinking you're better than everyone else."

"We are better than everyone else."

"Hah. Doesn't look like it from where I'm standing." Crabtree relieved him of his favorite Springfield Custom Professional 1911-A1 and the Glock-23 he wore in his ankle holster. Jordan bit down on the desire to crush the man's skull under his boot.

It'd keep.

"What was that you said to me earlier, Krychek? You'd kill me if anything happened to Daisy?" The man sniggered, but the look in his eyes was pure contempt. "Well, something happened, but it looks like you missed your chance, chump."

Jordan needed to act surprised and outraged, and it wasn't hard. "What have you done to her, you sonofabitch?" He glared at the other man until Crabtree's smile faded. "What's going on? Where's Daisy?"

"Inside." Crabtree's eyes skittered around the grass and security fencing belatedly looking for backup. "We have a surprise for you."

Jordan headed inside and allowed his eyes to take a few seconds to adjust to the lights and shadows. His open mouth revealed his shock and horror at the people lying dead on the ground. Even though he knew Daisy was alive, relief hit him when he spotted her sitting near the base of the viewing platform looking relatively unharmed.

Then he saw Konrad Bocharov and let the fury take over. His hand went automatically for his weapon, but it wasn't there.

He roared like an animal as he rushed at Bocharov and allowed the Russian to hit him so that he fell dazed to the concrete floor. He was expecting the boot to the gut, but it didn't make it any less painful.

"Don't anyone interfere. This bastard is mine," the familiar guttural voice warned.

"Stop. Stop!" Daisy stood and Bocharov looked toward her and drew his gun and pointed it at her.

Hell, no.

Jordan swiped the asshole's legs from under him and watched Konrad land with the grace of a beached whale, the gun skittering out of his grip and across the floor.

Emilia Osbourne looked toward them with a frown before she started climbing down the ladder with a gun in her hand.

Jordan got to his feet and kicked Bocharov in the kidneys. "That's for my *baba*," He kicked him again, "and that's for my grandfather who could barely get out of his chair." He kicked him again, the tough guy sprawling across the floor, his wig falling askew. "That was for my mother and my beautiful sister."

Jordan let Konrad get to his feet and charge him. At the last moment, he darted aside and stuck out his foot, sending Bocharov crashing to the ground once more. "That was for the cops you slaughtered."

Konrad stood again and rushed at him in unseeing rage.

Jordan sucker punched him in the face. "That was for Ana, you sick sonofabitch."

A gunshot echoed through the space, and Jordan stilled as a bullet flew close enough to raise the hair on his arms.

"Enough! Get on the floor. Get on the floor!" Emilia screamed while Crabtree walked towards them looking uncertain.

Despite Bocharov's fearsome reputation, it hadn't been a fair fight. Jordan had spent the past decade training for this moment, and Bocharov was a lazy fucker who relied on his violent and ruthless reputation to intimidate those around him. The fact Jordan was surrounded by armed terrorists did make it a little more challenging.

If Daisy hadn't been caught in the crossfire with the fate of a nuclear reactor at stake, he would have enjoyed himself.

Jordan slowly got down on his knees as Konrad staggered to his feet, wiping at the blood pouring from his nose. The other man scooped down to pick up his pistol, clearly in pain.

Not enough pain.

"I should have killed you years ago with your pathetic family, but it was so much more fun knowing I'd broken you."

Jordan raised his chin. "You didn't break me, asshole. You murdered defenseless innocents and thought it made you a big man. And then you ran back to Moscow like the coward you really are."

The snipers hadn't had enough time to get into position yet. He needed to stall.

"I bet you had to beg your bosses to let you live. Did they beat the snot out of you, Konrad? Did they make you grovel and prove yourself all over again?"

Konrad's brows lowered over his beady eyes.

"Just kill him, Papa. He insults you."

This from Emilia Osbourne—and suddenly everything made more sense.

"Shit. She's your kid?" Jordan asked. *Come on, guys.* Where the hell were they? He raised his face to the roof and had to force himself not to react. "I should have known from the evil glint in her eyes. Where's the mother? Oh, wait. Was she the same woman you kept as a mistress or someone different?"

"What's he talking about, Papa?"

"There has only ever been one woman for me, Emilia. Your mother has my heart. But sometimes it was necessary to create the illusion of one thing to hide the reality of another."

"You banged her anyway, am I right? Just to keep up the illusion."

"*Do svidaniya*, motherfucker." Bocharov sneered down at him. "And know that your stupid little blonde cunt will die a slow and agonizing death, every second of which she'll blame you for her pain and suffering."

Jordan braced himself as Konrad drew back his foot as if he was about to play soccer with his head.

37

Daisy couldn't believe Jordan was baiting Bocharov this way. Her heart tumbled free-fall in her chest as the Russian went to kick Jordan in the face.

A blow that could kill.

Crabtree stood in front of her. She balanced on the balls of her feet and executed a roundhouse kick that sent the FBI agent flying forward toward Bocharov. Then she drew her weapon, everything feeling as if it were in slow motion. She aimed at Bocharov, the man who'd burned Jordan's family alive. Who'd strangled the Pagets in their own bed, who'd shot Les because she was one second too late, brutally slain the people who worked here today. The man who'd tried to shoot her, then burn her and Florence Cisco to death. The man who wanted to blow up a nuclear reactor.

Whatever qualms she might have about killing anyone were extinguished by the knowledge he was evil. Pure evil.

She fired four shots, one after the other until the Russian fell to the ground with a shocked expression on his face. Her dad had always told her to keep firing until you were sure the other person wasn't getting up.

She threw herself behind a concrete support pillar, yelping as something hit her left arm. Blinding pain flashed through her body, but she pushed it aside to return fire so Emilia and Crabtree didn't have the chance to shoot at Jordan or the others.

Suddenly, more gunfire rang out, and Daisy looked over to see Alex Parker above her on the stairs that led to the viewing platform. Black-clad tactical operators poured into the building from the roof and through the open reactor doors.

Her left arm was numb. Blood dripped down her arm from a ragged hole above her left elbow. No exit wound. She had the horrible feeling the bullet had hit and wedged in her humerus, which she didn't think was very funny. She placed her weapon on the ground and tried to raise her hands in the air, so she wasn't mistaken for one of the bad guys.

She slipped from behind the column, desperately searching for Jordan.

She couldn't see through the teeming bodies of law enforcement and couldn't get through.

"Jordan. Jordan!" she yelled.

"Here." He stood behind her, looking exactly as he had when she'd left the hotel earlier, with the addition of a reddened cheek where Bocharov had gotten in that first punch.

"You okay?" His alarmed gaze ran down her body spotting the blood she was trying to staunch. "Fuck." He stepped forward and took her arm. She tried not to wince. "You're shot."

"It's only my arm." It hurt like hell. "If I can get it bound up, I can help unload the rods."

"You need to sit down."

She shook her head. "We have to get those rods out of that core. If the water gets in there, we have no control rods in place and no way to stop a chain reaction." She swallowed repeatedly, knowing her voice was getting louder. "And if we're right about the explosives…"

"Here. Sit on the chair. Nash! Get over here."

She slumped ungracefully into a seat.

"Hey, Daisy." Aaron Nash, the epitome of tall, dark, and handsome, came to squat beside her.

"You need to check the injured—"

"We did." Aaron's mouth pinched. "Double taps don't leave many survivors, I'm afraid."

She spotted Emilia and Crabtree laying sprawled on the ground like rag dolls.

"There was a woman too. Pretending to be an FBI agent. I don't know where she went."

Alex Parker came over and squeezed her uninjured shoulder. "We got her. Cisco is guarding the control room. No one will be touching any buttons in that room until the safety board clears it first."

Tears pricked again, and she was so sick of feeling like she was about to start crying.

Aaron grimaced as he cleaned up the blood. "You know what I'm going to tell you, right?"

"The bullet's still in there."

He nodded, his pretty dark eyes full of sympathy. "Going to need surgery."

Dammit.

"I'm not going anywhere until those rods are removed from the core. Someone's going to have to remove them and then go through the ceramic pellets one by one to figure out which are uranium dioxide and which are something else. We could probably tell plastic explosives with texture, but I don't know about metals, if there are metals. Maybe weight?"

"And you think that someone should be you?" Jordan stared at her like she'd lost her mind.

She opened her mouth to say something and then closed it again.

Roger and Mira came to stand beside her.

"We can assist. I've handled the ceramic pellets before. If you tell me what else we're dealing with, I'm willing to get started." Roger's tone was conciliatory.

"I'm sorry we were mean to you earlier," Mira said quietly. "Emilia told us some stories about things you'd supposedly said about Amed." Her face crumpled. "We believed her until we watched her shoot the Shift Supervisor in the head."

Daisy nodded even though it was hard to forgive. Her tongue went dry, and she struggled to speak. "I'm sorry I didn't get here fast enough to save Les."

Roger shook his head and wrapped his arm around Mira again. "It was an impossible choice that bastard asked you to make, and we all know it. I'd have stayed where I was safe and covered my ears."

Still...

Ryan Sullivan came by and held out his palm to give her a low five with her good hand. "Crazy Daisy strikes again."

"What?"

"That's what I'm gonna call you from now on." His eyes danced with delicious merriment. "Not for gunning down the FBI's number one Most Wanted bad guy and saving our boy here while we all watched." He clapped Jordan on the back. Hard. "But for being crazy enough to date the guy."

She looked up at Jordan. "I love him."

Ryan shook his head and walked away. "Definitely Crazy Daisy."

"Time to get you to the hospital." Jordan bent down and gathered her into his arms. "Hey, Cowboy," he called the other man closer. "You never answered the question in the car last night."

The man's eyes immediately hooded. "What question?"

"Whether or not you think Donnelly is Ryan Sullivan hot."

Ryan's face went as still as a lake on a windless day. "Not appropriate."

"Yeah, I thought so," Jordan whispered. "You call my girl crazy again, I'll tell everyone on the team you've got the hots for one of our own."

Ryan's pretty mouth thinned. "I don't know what you're talking about."

Daisy touched his arm because he looked so angry and miserable. "It gets better."

Ryan shook his head and took a step back. "It really doesn't."

Jordan carried her through the throng of people. Some reactor workers had been allowed in, and Hunt Kincaid was handling the crane like a pro.

"He's a former engineer," Jordan told her. "He's got this."

Daisy felt herself sag against Jordan's chest as her head began to swim. "I guess I don't feel so great."

The next thing she knew everything went black.

38

Jordan paced the waiting room, ignoring Alex's offer of coffee. The other guy had driven like a maniac to the nearest ER, and Daisy had immediately gone into surgery. He'd been waiting with him ever since. More than an hour now.

Lucy Aston and Detective Tobias Granger pushed inside the door.

"Is she okay?" Lucy looked frantic.

"Still in surgery." Jordan was numb with dread, but he looked at his old friend from school and swallowed the knot in his throat. "I owe you an apology. You didn't betray my family."

Granger held out his hand, and Jordan shook it. "I didn't, but I'm as guilty as you are when it comes to their deaths, and I'll never forgive myself."

"Maybe it's time." Emotions rushed up through the numbness. "Maybe it's time we both forgave ourselves for doing our best to get a monster like Bocharov off the street—and failing."

"You got him today." Tears glistened in the other man's eyes. "You got him today."

"Daisy killed him, but let's keep that need to know."

Granger nodded. "No one will hear it from me. I'm gonna get some coffee. Lucy?"

The former spook nodded, and they went to hit the cafeteria for supplies.

After they left, Jordan pulled on his hair until it felt as if he might wrench it out of his head. "What is taking so long?"

The door opened again, and there stood Kurt Montana, looking as if he'd walked all the way from England.

"Where is she?"

Jordan shriveled inside. He'd promised to keep this man's daughter safe and ended up almost getting her killed, twice. "In surgery. Bullet hit her arm. She lost a lot of blood, and they suspect she has a concussion, but they didn't want to wait to operate in case the bullet had fragmented."

Kurt knew the dangers of a bullet wound. Jordan didn't know why he was explaining.

Row pushed through the door behind him and came over to grab his hand. He noticed the big sparkling diamond on her left ring finger. "Is she okay?"

"As far as I know. The doctor might tell Kurt more." He sank to the nearest seat, staring at nothing. Feeling hollowed out and numb.

Row sat beside him and squeezed his hand. "Can you tell us what happened?"

He shook his head.

Thankfully, Alex started talking them through the day's events.

Jordan zoned out. All he could think of was how pale she'd been when he'd last seen her. What if part of the bullet had entered her bloodstream and caused a clot? How could he have delayed so long before rushing her here?

She'd seemed fine.

He swallowed and then felt a hand grip his thigh. He looked down. Then Kurt took his hand and squeezed tight.

"You take good care of her, son. Promise me."

Jordan could barely speak. "If she'll let me."

Kurt snorted. "Got that right. She came out that way. Obstinate and scrappy."

"I wonder where she gets it from," Row said dryly.

"Wait until you meet her mother. Fuck." Kurt ran his hands through his hair. "You're gonna have your work cut out with your mother-in-law."

"Not with me though." Row squeezed his forearm.

"I forgot to say. Congratulations."

Kurt nodded.

Row smiled determinedly. "We'll celebrate when Daisy's better."

Yeah.

But a sinking feeling hit Jordan. Was this his fault? He'd always believed he was cursed. What if that was true? What if he was the reason Daisy…

He couldn't think it.

But he was so used to the people he loved dying.

Emotions pummeled him. He couldn't do this. He had to get out of here.

His stomach clenched, and he stood.

A doctor came into the room wearing scrubs and carrying a clipboard. "Daisy Montana's family?"

"Yes."

Kurt stood. Cleared his throat. Took Row's hand as he said, "I'm her father."

"Your daughter lost a lot of blood and suffered a mild concussion, but she's going to be fine."

Jordan collapsed down into the chair and held his face in his hands as the tears came. She was going to be fine, and he felt as if he'd run ten marathons in a row.

He swiped them from his face and went to stand next to Kurt. "Can we see her?"

"You are?" the surgeon asked.

Jordan straightened. "I'm her partner."

The surgeon glanced from Kurt to Jordan and nodded. "She's

being taken from recovery down to the surgical ward. In about half an hour, you can visit with her for a short period. Two people at a time."

Jordan wiped his eyes again and then swung around to face the door as the guys piled in. All of Gold Team, minus Hugo the Belgian Malinois, crowded inside.

"She's okay," Kurt said holding up his hands for quiet. "And I'm not going to kill him."

The whoops started, and the surgeon grinned and turned away. Suddenly, Jordan was lifted off his feet and passed from operator to operator. They finally put him down when the charge nurse came in and scolded them all for being noisy.

"You got a ring, pal?" Ryan Sullivan asked wryly.

Jordan's heart hammered. "Not yet. Shit. We've never even been on a date yet. Too busy saving the world."

The side of Ryan's mouth pulled back in a slow grin. "Reminds me of when my brother got hitched." Ryan's eyes held Jordan's with a look of all seriousness. "About that other thing."

Jordan looked over at Donnelly, who was laughing at something Grady said. "What other thing?"

Ryan clapped him on the back. "Exactly. Oh, looky here. Looks like the doc is calling you over. I'm gonna go chat up the pretty nurse at the front desk. Some of us have a reputation to uphold."

Jordan was already pushing through the crowd.

39

Daisy floated back to consciousness on a wave that felt a little like when she used to get drunk and stoned on weed in high school, but knew this wasn't that. She opened her eyes and saw her dad and smiled sleepily. "Hey, what are you doing here?"

Where was she even?

He scratched his forehead and gave a big sigh. He held her hand in his big rough one, and his shoulders slumped.

"Oh, I remember." She shrugged and felt the constraint of motion in her left arm. Looked down. "I was shot." She frowned. "Jordan." Her voice rose anxiously. "Where's Jordan..."

She swung her head around and found him standing on the other side of the room looking worse than she felt. His blue eyes were bloodshot with worry. Hair standing on end as if he'd run his hands through it a thousand times. Stress had carved deep grooves around his mouth.

She gave him a smile because he looked like he needed one. "I'd hold your hand too, but this one is out of commission." They'd put her left arm in a sling, but she was able to wiggle her fingers a little. It hurt, but not too much.

"What happened? Did I black out?"

"Fainted."

"Damn. That sounds girly."

"You lost a lot of blood." Jordan cleared his throat. "The bullet didn't break the bone which is a miracle and didn't fragment." He held up the slug. "It made a hole in the humerus, but the surgeon seems confident it'll heal."

"I'm going to wear that as a medallion around my neck if the FBI let me. Did you tell Dad we were sleeping together?"

Her dad growled, and she grinned. He deserved this.

"No." Jordan's cheeks turned deep red. "I told him I'm in love with you."

"Oh. Well, I was going to tell him it was punishment for him interfering with my life, but now you've gone and ruined it." It was her turn to blush. "Did you tell him I loved you back?"

Jordan sat on the bed so they were hip-to-hip. "I figured that was up to you."

Kurt scratched his head and climbed to his feet. "Okay. Now I'm convinced there's nothing seriously wrong with you, I'm going to grab Rowena then talk to Novak and Ackers and the goddamned FBI Director about the situation and our national response." He bent down to kiss her forehead, then straightened and sent Jordan a warning look. "I'll give you guys a few minutes alone if you can behave yourselves."

He headed out.

Daisy snorted. "What does he think we'll do in a hospital bed? Although, I'm sure we could manage." She glanced up with delight. "Look, there's even a headboard."

Whatever pain meds they'd given her were definitely working because she wanted to giggle at Jordan's slightly horrified expression.

"You're gonna get me killed."

She pulled a face. "Never."

He came around to the other side of the bed and sat down, finally took her hand. "I'm sorry you got hurt today. There's going to be a major investigation and a lot of diplomatic fallout."

"As long as that's the only kind of fallout." She grew serious because he looked so miserable, and her teasing wasn't helping the way she'd hoped. "So many people died, but it could have been a lot worse. A *lot* worse. I feel terrible for the facility workers and Les"—memories assaulted her in a cascade that made her want to weep—"but I'm not sorry about shooting Konrad Bocharov, and I'm not going to lie when they ask me about it."

"There were enough witnesses wearing body cams that you'll never have to justify yourself to anyone. Anyone questions you like a suspect, I'll shoot them myself." He kissed her knuckles, which was super sweet. His were scraped raw. "I am sorry you had to take a life though."

"He was a despicable human being, and he deserved to die." She sucked in her lips.

"You did me a favor by eliminating that scum from the world, but I'm sorry you have to carry that burden."

"It's not a burden." He looked unconvinced, but she wasn't lying. "I know it probably should be, but after everything he did, and what he tried to do at the reactor…" Talking about it brought it all back in vivid detail. "I thought you were about to die. There was no way I was letting that happen."

He squeezed her fingers. "I wasn't about to die. The guys had the situation in hand, but you definitely beat them to the punch with Bocharov. I failed in my promise to keep you safe."

"I'm here, aren't I?"

He laughed at her dry tone but still looked like he wanted to weep.

"Crabtree was some sort of deeply planted Russian agent. He bragged how he was going home to a hero's welcome."

His jaw flexed. "And I let you walk away with him."

"He was FBI. We both trusted him." She raised her hand and rubbed her fingers over the scruff on his cheek. "And here I am, alive and sassy, and those motherfuckers are dead."

Jordan swallowed tightly.

"You have to get over the hero complex, Krychek. You can't be everywhere."

"There's going to be a big shake up and a hell of a lot of digging into Crabtree's background. Alex Parker's firm has been called in to do deep dives on all FBI employees."

"Even you?" She raised a brow at him.

"The FBI knows every damned thing about me including that I'm in love with this incredibly smart, hot, brave physicist. I'm hoping we can figure out a way to make it work. Thankfully, Richmond and Quantico aren't that far apart. I can move so I'm even closer, and if that isn't enough, I'll look into positions in Richmond like I said."

"You don't have to move. I like your little cabin in the woods, minus all the surveillance tools."

"You're willing to give this thing between us a try?"

She stared at him, this handsome man who went up against armed assailants without fear, but who looked scared to death right now. She wasn't scared anymore. Jordan wasn't the kind of man to make promises and then break them. And he might argue he'd broken a promise to her father, but despite everything, he'd kept her safe—from climbing the outside of a hotel seven floors up, to pulling her into a helicopter off the roof of a burning building, to strolling into a nuclear reactor full of people who wanted to kill him. He'd put her first, protected and cared for her above all else.

And that made her melt.

It was a little humbling to realize that, deep down, despite all the years of pushing people away, what she'd really wanted, really craved, was someone to give enough of a damn to take care of her. To rein in the wild-child and nurture the vulnerable woman hidden deep within.

Didn't mean she was any less capable or independent. Didn't mean she wanted to settle down and bake cookies. It *did* mean she might let him boss her around in the bedroom occasionally—make that *often*. It did mean she'd let him take care of her the way she wanted to take care of him sometimes. With tenderness. With love. With steadfastness and loyalty.

"I'm more than willing to give this thing between us a chance. But I want us both to be happy, so no giving up careers just yet. Which doesn't mean it's going to be easy," she warned.

"Easy? Where is the fun in easy? We'll figure it out." He grinned and the weight of the world seemed to lift off his shoulders. Then he sobered. "I'm sorry you were hurt because of me."

"This wasn't because of you. You were the reason we found out about the plot and were able to foil it. Without you, I'd probably be lying in a pool of blood in a nuclear reactor headed for meltdown right about now."

"Fuck, Daisy. Don't say that." His eyes went wide. "I might be sick."

She smoothed a thumb over the back of his hand.

"I wish I could promise my job will never put you in jeopardy again."

She squeezed his fingers hard. "I know what your job means to you."

"I'll give it up for you." He spoke so fervently she knew he was telling the truth.

"I don't want you to." She shook her head. "It's because of Dad and his job I know how to take care of myself."

"Which you proved today."

"I did. Yes." She stared down at the white cotton sheets. "Proving I don't *need* you to protect me, but I really like having you around." She looked up and caught that blue-green gaze which brimmed with both fear and happiness. "I know there's a risk attached to your job. There's risk attached to mine too. We'll both be careful."

He swallowed. "I won't take you for granted, Daisy. If the job becomes a wedge between us, I'll find another one. I know what's most important—you."

He was going to make her cry. She forced back the emotion.

"What happens next? With the case?" She braced herself. "Or is it a secret?"

"A big-ass investigation and probably a zillion congressional hearings. Oh, one thing, the FBI wants to keep a lid on the fact that Charlie survived the takedown."

"Charlie?"

"Charlotte Sumner aka Katya Abramović. The other woman who was there," he explained. "Cisco called me after she observed her interview. Turns out Bocharov had a wife and child—Emilia Osbourne—who no one knew anything about. I mean there were rumors but never any proof, and we put it down to the myth of the Russian *bratva*. Charlie claims the Russian authorities made her stay in the US and maintain her cover, even seduce a female agent who Bocharov had threatened into working for him. I don't think I told you it was former FBI Agent Jenna Stork who betrayed me in Chicago. She's the person who got my family slaughtered, not anyone in the Chicago Police Department." He stared down at their clasped hands. "Pretty sure Charlie put a bullet in Jenna's brain in DC before heading down to meet her husband and daughter for the pièce de résistance—not that she's admitted any of that yet. Now that her daughter is dead, she wants revenge on the system that 'forced her to do all those terrible things'—her words apparently."

Remembering Emilia's vicious betrayal hurt. She'd seen the mad gleam in her eyes. Knew that the other woman would have happily slaughtered them all. "What's going to happen to Charlie?"

"I think she'll be held for a long, long time. And if she provides enough useable intel, maybe they'll let her go into the WitSec program." He shook his head and played with her fingers. "I don't think she'll be a problem for us."

"Did she say what happened to François Tremblay?"

"Apparently he spotted Bocharov coming out of Emilia's room and, having spent so much time covering his tracks, the Russian worried the Frenchman might become suspicious. The meet had been planned to discuss final steps for the op and set up Amed as the fall guy. Charlie was downstairs at the bar hoping to catch a glimpse of her daughter as they hadn't been allowed to communicate since Emilia started college. Ironically, if Bocharov hadn't fallen back on his baser instincts and murdered Tremblay, we would never have uncovered their plot before we could stop it."

It was all so awful. The capacity for causing death and destruction seemed unlimited as long as they got what they wanted.

"The reactor is definitely secure?"

"Shut down, safe and sound. Cops stopped your advisor on his way to the reactor." Jordan's eyes went soft. "He didn't have a clue as to what was going on and appeared to be devastated."

Her heart hurt. He was such a lovely man.

"I believe the FBI plan to release Amed Hussein as soon as they can one hundred percent verify his version of events. The State Department is bringing his wife and child and parents across for a visit."

"Trying to make up for a terrible experience."

Jordan shrugged. "It's more than they usually do."

Daisy nodded. She suddenly felt exhausted. "So many lives lost or irrevocably changed."

"I'm sorry."

She touched the cheek that was starting to darken with a bruise. "I've lost a house but gained a partner I love and trust, and the knowledge that I did something worthwhile. I actually helped prevent a nuclear disaster today, and that's exactly why I've studied all these years in the first place."

He captured her fingers and kissed them again. "You were incredible. We'll figure it all out, one step at a time."

She nodded and felt the first zing of pain streak along her arm. "Oh. Ouch."

"You okay?"

"The pain meds are wearing off."

"I'll call the nurse."

"Don't. Not yet." She squeezed her fingers tighter around his to prevent him from leaving.

Jordan sighed. "Hopefully Charlie can help us ferret out any other moles. Along with how and where they made the replica rods. The original truck driver was found dead in a factory north of Richmond, so that's the most likely spot for the switch. Emilia presumably gained access to the designs while working in the lab."

"This is going to turn the nuclear industry on its head." Daisy didn't know what would happen to their research now. Her advisor might really decide to retire early, and she wouldn't blame him.

"At least it can change before we have a massive accident. Safety and security protocols can be easily implemented to monitor for C4 or other explosive materials coming inside a reactor." Jordan was trying to make her feel better.

"I actually find it kind of fascinating…"

"What?"

"The explosive stuff. Maybe I'll ask Harry how he got onto the bomb squad."

Jordan went pale. "Great. Later. When you're better."

She smiled. "Did I tell you I love you, Jordan Krychek?"

He laughed. "I could hear it again."

"I love you. And I'm going to prove it to you as soon as I get out of this place."

"You won't be getting out of here until tomorrow at the very earliest." His voice firmed. "Proving anything can wait until you are completely healed."

"Is that an order?" She fluttered her lashes up at him, and he flushed again.

He leaned down and finally kissed her. "Damned right it is."

"I like it when you get all masterful with me."

"Really," he raised a superior brow. "I hadn't noticed."

Warmth spread through her chest. "I like how you make love to me."

His eyes changed, vulnerable again. "I do, too."

"And how you fucked me against the wall at the academy."

His eyes widened, then narrowed, irises no longer shadowed and tormented but deeply amused and slightly turned on. "You better behave with your dad around. It's only because you got shot that he hasn't beaten me to a pulp yet."

She skimmed her fingers over his jawline. "He loves you. You have a new family now."

He smiled, just a little. Kissed her knuckles. "Go to sleep, Montana."

This time she let herself drift. Let herself believe that he'd be there when she woke up.

Thank you for reading *Cold Heat*. I hope you enjoyed Daisy and Jordan's story. Are you ready for the next exciting installment of the Cold Justice® - Most Wanted series?

Order *Cold Rage*...the next Romantic Thriller from *New York Times and USA Today* bestselling author Toni Anderson.

If you enjoyed this book please consider leaving a review at your favorite vendor or on your socials. Reviews help readers find books that might be right for them. Thanks so much!

Love the Cold Justice® series?
Don't miss the gripping audiobooks—expertly narrated by Eric G. Dove—and explore the world of Cold Justice® through exclusive bundles, available on Toni's author store:
https://toniandersonshop.com

USEFUL ACRONYM DEFINITIONS FOR TONI'S BOOKS

ADA: Assistant District Attorney
AG: Attorney General
ASAC: Assistant Special-Agent-in-Charge
ASC: Assistant Section Chief
ATF: Alcohol, Tobacco, and Firearms
BAU: Behavioral Analysis Unit
BOLO: Be on the Lookout
BORTAC: US Border Patrol Tactical Unit
BUCAR: Bureau Car
CBP: US Customs and Border Patrol
CBT: Cognitive Behavioral Therapy
CD: Counterintelligence Division
CIRG: Critical Incident Response Group
CMU: Crisis Management Unit
CN: Crisis Negotiator
CNU: Crisis Negotiation Unit
CO: Commanding Officer
CODIS: Combined DNA Index System
CONUS: Contiguous United States

Useful Acronym Definitions For Toni's Books

CP: Command Post
CPD: Chicago Police Department
CQB: Close-Quarters Battle
CRISPR: Clustered Regularly Interspaced Short Palindromic Repeats
DA: District Attorney
DEA: Drug Enforcement Administration
DEVGRU: Naval Special Warfare Development Group
DIA: Defense Intelligence Agency
DHS: Department of Homeland Security
DOB: Date of Birth
DOD: Department of Defense
DOJ: Department of Justice
DS: Diplomatic Security
DSS: US Diplomatic Security Service
DVI: Disaster Victim Identification
EMDR: Eye Movement Desensitization & Reprocessing
EMT: Emergency Medical Technician
ERT: Evidence Response Team
EV: Electric Vehicle
FOA: First-Office Assignment
FBI: Federal Bureau of Investigation
FNG: Fucking New Guy
FO: Field Office
FWO: Federal Wildlife Officer
IB: Intelligence Branch
IC: Incident Commander
IC: Intelligence Community
ICE: US Immigration and Customs Enforcement
HAHO: High Altitude High Opening (parachute jump)
HK: Heckler & Koch (a German firearms manufacturer)
HRT: Hostage Rescue Team
HT: Hostage-Taker
JEH: J. Edgar Hoover Building (FBI Headquarters)
JTTF: Joint Terrorism Task Force

Useful Acronym Definitions For Toni's Books

K&R: Kidnap and Ransom
LAPD: Los Angeles Police Department
LEO: Law Enforcement Officer
LZ: Landing Zone
ME: Medical Examiner
MO: Modus Operandi
MVP: Most Valuable Player
NAT: New Agent Trainee
NATO: North Atlantic Treaty Organization
NCAVC: National Center for Analysis of Violent Crime
NCIC: National Crime Information Center
NCIS: Naval Criminal Investigative Service
NFT: Non-Fungible Token
NOTS: New Operator Training School
NPS: National Park Service
NTSB: National Transportation Safety Board
NYFO: New York Field Office
OC: Organized Crime
OCONUS: Outside of the Contiguous United States
OCU: Organized Crime Unit
OPR: Office of Professional Responsibility
POTUS: President of the United States
PT: Physiology Technician
PTSD: Post-Traumatic Stress Disorder
RA: Resident Agency
RCMP: Royal Canadian Mounted Police
RIB: Rigid Inflatable Boat
RPG: Rocket-Propelled Grenade
RSO: Senior Regional Security Officer from the US Diplomatic Service
SA: Special Agent
SAC: Special Agent-in-Charge
SANE: Sexual Assault Nurse Examiners
SAS: Special Air Squadron (British Special Forces unit)
SERE: Survival, Evasion, Resistance, and Escape

Useful Acronym Definitions For Toni's Books

SCIF: Sensitive Compartmented Information Facility
SD: Secure Digital
SIOC: Strategic Information & Operations
SF: Special Forces
SFP: Spent Fuel Pool
SMR: Small Modular Reactors
SSA: Supervisory Special Agent
SWAT: Special Weapons and Tactics
TC: Tactical Commander
TDY: Temporary Duty Yonder
TEDAC: Terrorist Explosive Device Analytical Center
TOD: Time of Death
UAF: University of Alaska, Fairbanks
UBC: Undocumented Border Crosser
UNSUB: Unknown Subject
UR: University Of Richmond
USSS: United States Secret Service
ViCAP: Violent Criminal Apprehension Program
VIN: Vehicle Identification Number
VSP: Virginia State Police
WFO: Washington Field Office
WMD: Weapons of Mass Destruction

ACKNOWLEDGMENTS

If I'd paid more attention to physics lessons at school this book would have been a lot easier to write! However, unlike high school physics, I thoroughly enjoyed the research I had to do for this book but hope I never need to use it in real life. Thanks to my brother, for mulling over my ideas about nuclear sabotage without calling the men in white coats. Massive thanks to "Dave" for brainstorming ideas that could get us both arrested if this was anything but a figment of my dastardly imagination.

A special mention to Cam Barth and his wife, Megan Cooley, who lost their beloved cat, Renfield, this year. I named the kitty in this book "Renfield" in his honor.

Thanks to Kathy Altman, who, as always, was the first person to read this and provide excellent feedback. Rachel Grant provided a beta read for the ages, which is just one of the reasons I love her. Jodie Griffin spotted errors that got through three rounds of editors and I appreciate her love of the characters more than I can say.

Quick note. Had my son been a girl I'd planned to name him Daisy. He is eternally grateful he was born male. But I finally have my Daisy and I love how fierce she is.

Credit to my fabulous editorial team, Lindsey Faber, Joan Turner at JRT Editing, and proofreader, Pamela Clare (yes, *that* Pamela Clare!). What an amazing group of people I have to support me.

Appreciation to my assistant, Jill Glass, who helps so much in running the day-to-day business of being an author. Thanks also to my wonderful cover designer, Regina Wamba, for her gorgeous artwork. Kudos to Eric G. Dove for being the voice of the Cold Justice® books and for being such a lovely human being to work with.

Smooches to my four-legged buddies, Archie and Fergus, and also to my two-legged husband who helps me in every way.

Oh—and despite my deep affection for em-dashes, I am 100% responsible for the creation of this story. Thank you for supporting this human in all her flawed glory.

ABOUT THE AUTHOR

Toni Anderson is a #1 Apple Books, #1 Nook, Amazon Top 10, *New York Times*, and *USA Today* bestselling author whose Romantic Thrillers have captivated millions of readers around the world. Best known for her critically acclaimed COLD JUSTICE® series, Toni's work seamlessly weaves together compelling characters, psychological suspense, and unforgettable love stories.

A two-time winner of the Daphne du Maurier Award and finalist in the RITA®, VIVIAN®, and double finalist for the Romantic Novel of the Year Award, Toni's books have been translated into multiple languages and praised for their emotional depth and unflinching realism.

Originally from a small town in England, she now lives in one of the coldest places on earth—Manitoba, Canada—where she writes full time, researches obsessively, and occasionally rescues her dogs from snowdrifts.

Check out Toni Anderson's shop with exclusive merch and offers:
https://toniandersonshop.com
Sign up for Toni Anderson's newsletter:
www.toniandersonauthor.com/newsletter-signup

facebook.com/toniandersonauthor
instagram.com/toni_anderson_author
tiktok.com/@toni_anderson_author
bsky.app/profile/toniandersonauthor.bsky.social

Made in United States
Cleveland, OH
24 January 2026